OXFORD WORLD'S CLASSICS

# LADY SUSAN, THE WATSONS, AND SANDITON

Jane Austen was born in 1775 in the village of Steventon, Hampshire, the daughter of an Anglican clergyman. The Austens were cultured but not at all rich, though one of Austen's brothers was adopted by a wealthy relative. Other brothers followed professional careers in the Church, the Navy, and banking. With the exception of two brief periods away at school, Austen and her elder sister Cassandra, her closest friend and confidante, were educated at home. Austen's earliest surviving work, written at Steventon whilst still in her teens, is dedicated to her family and close female friends. Between 1801 and 1809, Austen lived in Bath, where her father died in 1805, and in Southampton. In 1809, she moved with her mother, Cassandra, and their great friend Martha Lloyd to Chawton, Hampshire, her home until her death at Winchester in 1817. During this time, Austen published four of her major novels: *Sense and Sensibility* (1811), *Pride and Prejudice* (1813), *Mansfield Park* (1814), and *Emma* (1816), visiting London regularly to oversee their publication. *Persuasion* and *Northanger Abbey* were published posthumously in 1818. *Sanditon*, a new novel, was left unfinished at the time of her death.

KATHRYN SUTHERLAND is Professor of English Literature and Senior Research Fellow, St Anne's College, Oxford. Her recent publications include *Jane Austen's Textual Lives: From Aeschylus to Bollywood* (2005) and, with Marilyn Deegan, *Transferred Illusions: Digital Technology and the Forms of Print* (2009). She is editor of *Jane Austen's Fiction Manuscripts: A Digital Edition* (2010) and the expanded print edition, 5 vols (2018). In the Oxford World's Classics series she has also published editions of Walter Scott's *Redgauntlet* and *Waverley*, of Adam Smith's *An Inquiry into the Nature and Causes of the Wealth of Nations*, of James Edward Austen-Leigh's *A Memoir of Jane Austen and Other Family Recollections*, and Jane Austen's *Teenage Writings*.

# OXFORD WORLD'S CLASSICS

*For over 100 years Oxford World's Classics have brought readers closer to the world's great literature. Now with over 700 titles—from the 4,000-year-old myths of Mesopotamia to the twentieth century's greatest novels—the series makes available lesser-known as well as celebrated writing.*

*The pocket-sized hardbacks of the early years contained introductions by Virginia Woolf, T. S. Eliot, Graham Greene, and other literary figures which enriched the experience of reading. Today the series is recognized for its fine scholarship and reliability in texts that span world literature, drama and poetry, religion, philosophy, and politics. Each edition includes perceptive commentary and essential background information to meet the changing needs of readers.*

OXFORD WORLD'S CLASSICS

JANE AUSTEN

# Lady Susan, The Watsons, and Sanditon

## Unfinished Fictions and Other Writings

*Edited with an Introduction and Notes by*
KATHRYN SUTHERLAND

OXFORD
UNIVERSITY PRESS

# OXFORD
UNIVERSITY PRESS

Great Clarendon Street, Oxford, OX2 6DP,
United Kingdom

Oxford University Press is a department of the University of Oxford.
It furthers the University's objective of excellence in research, scholarship,
and education by publishing worldwide. Oxford is a registered trade mark of
Oxford University Press in the UK and in certain other countries

First published as an Oxford World's Classics paperback 2021

Impression: 1

Published in the United States of America by Oxford University Press
198 Madison Avenue, New York, NY 10016, United States of America

British Library Cataloguing in Publication Data

Data available

Library of Congress Control Number: 2021939022

ISBN 978-0-19-883589-9

Printed and bound in Great Britain by
Clays Ltd, Elcograf S.p.A.

# CONTENTS

# INTRODUCTION

THE machinations of a sociopath, the petty spites of the genteel poor, the crazy fantasies of misfits holidaying by the sea — these are the objects of Jane Austen's forensic gaze in her unfinished fictions, *Lady Susan*, *The Watsons*, and *Sanditon*. Experimental, sharp-elbowed comedies, they come as a surprise after the forgiving wit of *Pride and Prejudice* and the poignant renewal of *Persuasion*. Yet there they are, adding pepper and spice and more than a dash of discomfort to our image of the romantic novelist. Left in manuscript, they raise questions: was there an intention to publish; and, if so, in what form? Given their difference in tone, they invite us to reconsider what she was about in the finished works. *Lady Susan* may have been written as early as 1794, when Austen was 18 or 19, soon after the last of the teenage writings and not long before a first draft of 'Elinor and Marianne', the novel that became *Sense and Sensibility* and, in 1811, her first publication.[1] *The Watsons* dates, according to family tradition, from 1804–5, the unsettled years living in Bath when Austen was in her late twenties. *Sanditon*, dated by her own hand to the opening months of 1817, marks the end of Austen's writing career: she died later that same year, in July, aged 41. We cannot dismiss the unfinished fictions as freaks or anomalies without also recognizing that they form a persistent, lifelong thread in her way of working and seeing; they are part of the inheritance of the published fictions.

*Pride and Prejudice*, Austen's most popular novel even in her lifetime, has long been established as *the* most successful romantic comedy in English. It is an aspect of Austen's genius that she persuades us it is the archetypal courtship novel. Particularly satisfying is her use of the cover that romance provides to serve up that most potent of all cocktails: love and money. As one modern critic has keenly observed, Austen writes 'fairy stories in which cash has a real presence'.[2] The Austen we know from her famous six novels makes her art out of romance, and her genius

---

[1] We have Cassandra Austen to thank for leaving a note of the dates of composition of her sister's novels. For *Sense and Sensibility*, *Pride and Prejudice*, and *Northanger Abbey*, there were early drafts preceding final publication by many years. For the note, see *Jane Austen's Fiction Manuscripts*, ed. Kathryn Sutherland, 5 vols (Oxford: Oxford University Press, 2018), vv. 297–9.

[2] Barbara Everett, 'Jane Austen: Hard Romance', The Hilda Hulme Memorial Lecture (London: University of London, 1996), 4.

is non-transgressive. Unlike those great rebel romancers, Emily and
Charlotte Brontë, Austen persuades the reader we can have it all. She
wraps ambition, sex, and money in respectability; the heroine gets the
handsome hero and the big house, and without breaking any social codes.
'Will you tell me how long you have loved him?' Jane Bennet enquires;
and her sister Elizabeth replies: 'It has been coming on so gradually, that
I hardly know when it began. But I believe I must date it from my first
seeing his beautiful grounds at Pemberley' (*Pride and Prejudice*, ch. 59).

The American critic Dorothy Van Ghent long ago observed that the
'general directions of reference taken by Jane Austen's language . . .
are clearly materialistic', reflecting the culture of her own commercial
society with its base, much like ours, in 'acquisitiveness and calculation
and materialism'. It is this 'single materialistic language' that, according to Van Ghent, Austen 'forces—or blandishes or intrigues—into
spiritual duties', through antithesis, irony, and direct and indirect
play.[3] Materialism intrigued into spiritual duties; this is the key to so
much that we find satisfying in Austen's romantic novels, wittily
described by another critic, Marjorie Garber, as 'real estate literature'.[4] The country house and its estate represent both a social and
a moral inheritance that Austen's characters are seen to enhance or
betray and whose effect on the very fabric of identity is explored in
shifting ways from novel to novel. The estate literally and figuratively
is the plot, around which the values and strains within individuals and
community coalesce. Each Austen novel is a study in finding a home,
a place to belong, which is why her heroes are so squarely identified
with their houses: Mr Darcy's best self *is* Pemberley; Mr Knightley
and Donwell Abbey are one. Under Emma Woodhouse's smug observance, Donwell is 'just what it ought to be, and it looked what it was . . .
the residence of a family of such true gentility, untainted in blood
and understanding', fixed in a landscape and with a prospect 'sweet to
the eye and the mind. English verdure, English culture, English
comfort, seen under a sun bright, without being oppressive' (*Emma*,
ch. 42). Mansfield Park, a house in peril, is spiritually renewed in the

---

[3] Dorothy Van Ghent, *The English Novel: Form and Function* (New York: Harper &
Brothers, 1953), 110–11.
[4] Marjorie Garber, 'The Jane Austen Syndrome', in *Quotation Marks* (New York:
Routledge, 2003), 199–200. See, too, the older iteration of this thesis in Alistair
M. Duckworth, *The Improvement of the Estate: A Study of Jane Austen's Novels*
(Baltimore: Johns Hopkins University Press, 1971).

course of the novel that takes its name. The erotic interest of *Pride and Prejudice*, recovered in the posthumously published *Persuasion*, the novel in which the heroine must learn finally to turn her back on home as a physical place, lies in the fact that hero as well as heroine requires education; they grow together *and* towards home—in the latter case, a spiritual rather than material destination.

It is important to have this trajectory clear; for where Austen's finished romances revel in their soft-focus materialism, dispossession, ruin, and transgression haunt the broken structures of the unfinished fictions. We might be tempted to read this as the consequence of our own retrospective encounters—the fact that we come to them only *after* the published novels. This is something the Victorian novelist Anne Thackeray, responding to the publication of *The Watsons* in 1871, described as the work's apparent shadowing of what we already know, detecting in its ingredients the 'anteghosts, if such things exist' of the later fiction.[5] There is some truth in this. *The Watsons* is reminiscent throughout: Lord Osborne, cold and careless, 'out of his Element in a Ball room' (p. 76), is only slightly more dysfunctional in female society than Mr Darcy; Mrs Robert Watson, the desperately genteel linch-pin of the Croydon smart set, is surely launched into print in *Emma* as the vulgar Mrs Augusta Elton; and Emma Watson shares aspects of character and situation with *Mansfield Park*'s Fanny Price. But this effect of reading half-echoes or traces of more familiar texts is not the whole truth: the unsmooth forms of the unfinished fictions are intrinsic to their meaning, essential to the stance they take; to the cynically bifurcated world view of *Lady Susan*, where people divide into manipulators and dupes; to the bleak reality that drags Austen down even as she writes *The Watsons*; to *Sanditon*'s satiric study of a society in fragments, of a town built upon sand. Experiments that probe new areas of invention, all three connect with and push out beyond what we know belongs in a Jane Austen novel. As such, the unfinished fictions provide interpretative tools for, and shed unexpected light on, novels we think we know.

Take the country village, 'such a spot as is the delight of my life . . . the very thing to work on', as Austen, in 1814 and at the height of her powers, confided to her fiction-scribbling niece, Anna.[6] For Lady

---

[5] A[nne] I. T[hackeray], 'Jane Austen', *Cornhill Magazine*, 24 (1871), 159.

[6] *Jane Austen's Letters*, ed. Deirdre Le Faye (4th edn, Oxford: Oxford University Press, 2011), 287. (Subsequent references to frequently cited works are given as in the Abbreviations; in this case, *Letters*.)

Susan it is 'that insupportable spot, a Country Village' (p. 5); for the Watson women, the village has become a muddy prison with no gentleman's house beyond their father's shabby parsonage; while the 'real village' of Sanditon is abandoned in favour of a half-built new town marching perilously towards the cliff edge (p. 120). In the published fictions, Austen's country village implied something permanent and known—'such pictures of domestic Life in Country Villages as I deal in', as she replied when James Stanier Clarke, the Prince Regent's librarian, challenged her to vary her formula.[7] In contrast, the transient inhabitants of the fledgling resort of Sanditon are as changeful as its shoreline. Casting doubt upon her settled village, Austen, the great realist, appears to question the central impulse of her fiction-making, not only in the company of Sanditon's eccentrics and idlers, but in the fretful lives of the Watson women, their youth wasting away day by dull day as they wait in their cramped parlour for the suitors who never materialize. *The Watsons* has something of the powerful, arrested messiness of a Chekhov short story.

Probably begun in the mid-1790s, *Lady Susan* had a longer gestation. We know Austen returned to it, possibly revising and finishing it, in or after 1805, around the time she wrote *The Watsons*.[8] Both are cynical studies of money, sex, and marriage; dark shadows of the

[7] *Letters*, 326.

[8] The composition date of *Lady Susan* has been a topic of considerable critical debate. The material evidence of the 1805 watermark in the manuscript and the mature subject (of a mother's sexual jealousy of her teenage daughter) have been used to place the work as significantly later than the three volumes of teenage writings (datable to 1787–93); on the other hand, Austen's youthful writings show considerable facetious experimentation with sexual subjects, and it is equally possible that *Lady Susan* is a fair copy of an earlier drafted work and the culmination of the epistolary experimentation that marked much of the teenage writing (works like 'Love and Friendship' and 'Lesley-Castle' for example). Within the extended Austen family of the mid-nineteenth century, it was ranked among the 'betweenities' and treated with some caution (written 'when the nonsense [of the teenage writings] was passing away, and before her wonderful talent had found it's [*sic*] proper channel' (J. E. Austen-Leigh, *A Memoir of Jane Austen and Other Family Recollections*, ed. Kathryn Sutherland (Oxford World's Classics; Oxford: Oxford University Press, 2002), 186). This would place the work firmly in the 1790s, with genesis as early as November 1793, not long before a first drafting of 'Elinor and Marianne', also written at this stage as a novel in letters. Brian Southam put forward the possibility of a two-stage dating, across a distance of ten or more years, conjecturing that significant alterations might have been made to the draft during fair-copying and arguing for the late addition of the abrupt 'Conclusion', in or after 1805 (B. C. Southam, *Jane Austen's Literary Manuscripts: A Study of the Novelist's Development through the Surviving Papers* (1964; rev. edn, London: Athlone Press, 2001), 45–52).

finished fictions. Despite differences—the hard social realities of *The Watsons* as against the conscious artifice of the novella-in-letters—they share a synergy: according to one Austen family tradition, the widowed Lady Osborne, 'tho' nearly 50 . . . very handsome' (p. 76), was to become a rival in love to the young Emma Watson, a variation upon Lady Susan's sexual jealousy towards her daughter. Austen's unfinished fictions should be approached warily, with eyes and minds wide open. Like the steel traps, set to catch lady trespassers in one of Austen's teenage stories,[9] the unfinished fictions too can waylay those Austen-lovers who think they know her through and through. Risky in style and subject, they suggest, too, the limitations and responsibilities she imposed on her finished fictions.

Lady Susan is a sophisticated, sardonic socialite and an accomplished sexual predator, whose 'rather romantic' (her term for 'impractical') notions extend no further than the wish to find a rich husband, not too 'contemptibly weak' (p. 4). She merely exposes what lies more artfully submerged inside the published novels—the real limits of women's power and the tricks to which they are reduced to catch a man and secure a comfortable future. Austen's women are wives, mothers, sisters, and at their most vulnerable, unmarriageable dependants. In contrast, her men inherit estates, are baronets and gentlemen farmers, or they make careers in the Navy, the Church, the law. Just occasionally, against the odds, a woman stands on her own ground and claws something back: the comfortable independence of Mrs Jennings, the jolly widow in *Sense and Sensibility*; the vast wealth of Lady Denham, 'who had buried two Husbands, who knew the value of Money', and holds a large chunk of Sanditon real estate 'all at her Disposal' (p. 114); and above all, the females of *Lady Susan*.

In seeming revenge for their sex's meanness of opportunity, even the 'good' women in *Lady Susan* hold their menfolk in low esteem. They, the men, are mere ciphers: the imbecilic Sir James Martin, marriageable by virtue of his cash alone, and the voiceless Charles Vernon, Lady Susan's brother-in-law. He 'rolls in money' (p. 9) and is easily managed into whatever is required of him: 'Mr Vernon who, as it must have already appeared, lived only to do whatever he was desired', comments the narrator in the briskly ordered

---

[9] In 'Jack & Alice', in Jane Austen, *Teenage Writings*, ed. Kathryn Sutherland and Freya Johnston (Oxford World's Classics; Oxford: Oxford University Press, 2017), 18.

'Conclusion' (p. 61). The handsome adulterer Manwaring, whose affair with the newly widowed Lady Susan sets the whole chain of letters and events in motion, never emerges from the wings, unlike his lachrymose wife, who doggedly spies on him from street corners. Young Reginald De Courcy is a mere paper hero, by turns ingenuous, pompous, and melodramatic; he is last seen being 'talked, flattered & finessed' (p. 62) by his mother and sister into marriage to the weedy daughter of the sophisticated cougar he thought he loved. The real power-play is between the women, each of whom is a vivid study in her own right: the wholesome but unillusioned Catherine Vernon, the passive-aggressive Frederica Vernon, the pragmatic Mrs Johnson, to whom 'Facts are such horrid things!' (p. 53), who readily sacrifices her bosom friend and confidante when threatened with her greatest fear—a life in the country—and, above all, the unwaveringly amoral and joyously narcissistic Lady Susan Vernon.

The form Austen chose for *Lady Susan*, the epistolary novel, already in 1795 appeared constrained and passé. Despite the late success of Frances Burney's *Evelina* (1778) and, in French, the deliciously scandalous *Les Liaisons dangereuses* (1782) by Pierre Choderlos de Laclos, it was falling out of favour with those novelists who aimed higher than the pulp fiction of the circulating libraries. Used in conduct books to peddle advice to young ladies and by early practitioners of the novel, the fictional letter was, through the eighteenth century, a vehicle for moral instruction that lent itself readily to subversion in the virtuoso performances of a series of exhibitionists. Lady Susan is in the line of Laclos's protagonists, using seduction as social control. Her pen, like theirs, is at the service of duplicity. This is a far cry from the unguarded openness of 'writing from the heart' that propelled Samuel Richardson into mid-century fame with his prolix, multi-voiced *Clarissa* (1747–8). The novel in letters was ideal for examining the workings of character and for setting narrative in motion as a sequence of immediate responses to events. In its declarative mode of communication, it recast for the page those stage conventions that would later become familiar plot ingredients for Austen—the seductress tainted by city life, the contrast between town and country values (think of Mary Crawford in *Mansfield Park*). This is how the teenage Austen had experimented with the letter in works like 'Love and Friendship' and 'Lesley-Castle', but she was also already satirizing the form's creaking, improbable machinery: 'I have many things to inform you of besides; but my Paper, reminds me of concluding', writes the epistolary scribbler Amelia Webster, only two lines into her letter.[10] *Lady Susan* seems the culmination of a kind of writing Austen apparently wrote herself out of around 1796–7 in the early, discarded drafts of *Sense and Sensibility* and, more especially, *Pride and Prejudice*, whose published form maintains evidence of the importance of letters to its development.

'Oh! the blessing of a female correspondent . . . she will tell me every thing', declares Frank Churchill in *Emma* (ch. 30). Is *Lady Susan* finished or unfinished? As yet, there is no clear moral steer to events: Lady Susan dominates the action, proving an obstacle, despite the flickering interest of the other female portraits, to any apportioning of sympathy among her victims. It matters little: *Lady Susan*, more especially the controlled performance of its central character, tells us all we need to know. With Lady Susan herself back in London and her schemes exposed, correspondence with some is closed off; with others, the letters now serve little practical purpose. The threads of the story may have been hastily tied up at a late date, around 1805, when the fair-copy manuscript was made. The brisk third-person 'Conclusion' introduces a different narrative mode and voice; in it we seem to anticipate the cool tones of the mature novelist intervening to round things off. A series of female psychological sketches, *Lady Susan* is a remarkable apprentice study from a novelist for whom the interplay of voice and character—especially the emotional ambiguity of female character—will become a major concern.

Biography clings to unfinished and unpublished works. *Lady Susan* required excuse and explanation from the extended Austen family, uncomfortable with it as the work of a youthful imagination. Long after Austen's death, her niece, Caroline Austen, described how the family had 'years ago' 'discouraged' the work's publication. One story had it that Lady Susan's behaviour was based in circumstances in the life of Mary Craven, grandmother of Jane Austen's great friend Martha Lloyd. Into the twentieth century, the family biographers were still defending 'the purity of [Austen's] imagination and the delicacy of her taste' from any repetition of such alarming material. Once finished, they declared, the 'wholly sinister figure which occupies the canvas . . . seems . . . to have disappeared entirely from the

---

[10] *Teenage Writings*, 69–119; 'Amelia Webster', *Teenage Writings*, 42.

mind of its creator'; as if, neither in life nor literature, could she possibly have encountered manipulative femmes fatales.[11] Yet letters surviving Cassandra Austen's eagle-eyed cull of her sister's correspondence suggest, like the unfinished fictions, that there are aspects to Jane Austen insufficiently regarded: not only her boast that 'I have a very good eye at an Adultress'; but, contradicting the persistent myth that she was only happy in her beloved Steventon, her village home until she was 25, is her early comment that 'It must not be generally known however that I am not sacrificing a great deal in quitting the Country—or I can expect to inspire no tenderness, no interest in those I leave behind.'[12]

With the composition of *The Watsons*, we may feel we are on securer ground. Yet this is not an idyllic tale of village life: Stanton is a dreary place, home of the equally dreary Watson family. 'Notice how many letters [Stanton] shares with the lost Steventon', remarked the novelist Kate Atkinson.[13] The work's date suggests it was begun with the confidence inspired by the sale of Austen's first manuscript: the publisher Crosby and Co. had bought 'Susan' for £10 in 1803. Though only published posthumously in 1818 as *Northanger Abbey*, at the time 'Susan' must have opened the prospect of a career as professional writer—perhaps even some financial independence.[14] *The Watsons* is a tale of riches to rags, the story of 19-year-old Emma Watson, adopted in childhood by a wealthy aunt and uncle, and now, following the death of her uncle and her aunt's imprudent second marriage, returned after 'an absence of 14 years' (p. 91) to her birth family. Her invalid clergyman father and three unmarried older sisters live in not-so-genteel poverty in their country rectory. Two

[11] *Memoir*, ed. Sutherland, 186; and William Austen-Leigh and Richard Arthur Austen-Leigh, *Jane Austen, Her Life and Letters: A Family Record* (London: Smith, Elder, and Co., 1913), 80–1. Mary Augusta Austen-Leigh, *Personal Aspects of Jane Austen* (London: John Murray, 1920), 100–5, alludes, in veiled terms, to *Lady Susan*'s antecedent in the story of Mary Craven, 'an unnatural and brutal mother'.

[12] *Letters*, 88 and 71.

[13] *The Watsons* (London: Hesperus Press Ltd, 2007), foreword by Kate Atkinson, p. viii.

[14] In terms of the complex chronology of Austen's writing and publishing, and setting aside *Lady Susan*, this makes *The Watsons* Austen's fourth drafted novel, begun after she had written early versions of what would later be published as *Sense and Sensibility* (1811), *Pride and Prejudice* (1813), and *Northanger Abbey* (1818), and before *Mansfield Park* (1814). Crosby asserted his right not to publish 'Susan' (*Northanger Abbey*), which was bought back much later, perhaps in 1816, and finally published posthumously.

brothers—an apprentice surgeon and a lawyer who has been shrewd enough to marry his employer's daughter—are making their way in the world. The character list is full of possibilities: a spirited heroine in Emma, the disappointed heiress and stranger to her own family; her peevish sisters, aware of the years slipping by and increasingly desperate to marry well or at all; their self-satisfied sister in law, Mrs Robert Watson, with her small-town superior airs; and Tom Musgrave, the neighbourhood's eligible bachelor, whom all the sisters have had a crack at. It is a tale of dispossession that encompasses the fading charms of her ageing sisters, Emma's lost prospects, and the deeper economic distress that lies in wait when her father dies.

*The Watsons* opens onto classic Austen territory as Emma Watson prepares for her first ball at the local assembly rooms, in company with her friends the Edwardses. At the ball, Emma attracts the attention of two potential suitors: Lord Osborne, 'a very fine young man; but there was an air of, Coldness, of Carelessness, even of Awkwardness about him . . . he was not fond of Women's company, & he never danced'; and Mr Howard, 'an agreeable-looking Man, a little more than Thirty', a clergyman (pp. 76–7). But the story is barely begun before it is abandoned. The characters are introduced; there is the ball; this is followed by the unwelcome intrusion of Lord Osborne and Tom Musgrave on the Watsons' meagre family dinner; and then by the arrival of Mr and Mrs Robert Watson on a short visit from Croydon: just enough story to point up Emma's discomfort in her surroundings and to hint at the courtship plot. The fragment ends with Emma rejecting an invitation to go back to Croydon with her brother and his wife; its final words: '& the Visitors departed without her' (p. 102).

Balls move the plot along in Austen's novels with their opportunities for observing and animating relations between the sexes. With this in mind, it is fascinating to see how minutely the ball in *The Watsons* is described: twenty closely written pages, almost a quarter of the manuscript, are taken up with the ball itself, and several more with its anticipation and aftermath. There is more detail, more enjoyment in the ball, more ball altogether than we sense the plot needs. There are the preparations for the ball—the dressing and hair arranging; the sharing of girlish confidences and hopes for the evening—what the narrator sums up as 'the happy occupation, the first Bliss of a Ball' (p. 72); the impatient clock-watching and slow pace of dinner, the extra dish of tea and 'additional muffin' (p. 74) to fortify them for the long night's dancing; and finally the ball itself (those twenty pages)—the shame of too early arrival, the cold of the assembly rooms, and those awkward conversations before the dancing begins; the little excitements of seeing and being seen, of eyeing and being eyed (Austen brings out the painful difference), the anxious wait for partners, the thrill of dancing at last, the cramped card tables and refreshment room. Then home, to analyse it all, over the welcome bowl of soup; and finally, we are told, 'Emma went to bed in charming Spirits, her head full of Osbornes, Blakes & Howards' (p. 83).

Would Emma Watson's ball have become, in revision, more tightly subordinated to plot? Would its detail have been pruned; and, if so, which detail might have been lost? The question invites us to consider the difference between manuscript and print—unfinished and finished writings. Until it leaves the writer's laboratory, no part of a manuscript is invulnerable to change; nothing is settled. Austen was a great reviser, each novel a reimagining of the themes and preoccupations of the last. What is fascinating about the ball in *The Watsons* is its excess of observation, excess that belongs as much to the noticing eye of the narrator as to the characters in the story. It is as if fiction is not yet fully ascendant. In its excess and its seeming independence of structural purpose, the detail of the ball stands both inside and outside the story—as if it belongs as much to Austen's memories of balls at the Angel Inn in Basingstoke, now, like her own youth, several years distant,[15] as to Emma Watson's ball in the town of 'D—— in Surry' (p. 65).

*The Watsons* marks a turning point in Austen's way of writing. It suggests, unusually, Austen experimenting with biography as fiction. At the same time, it marks a development in her art towards the greater realism of the mature novels, of *Mansfield Park* and *Emma*. Why, then, was it abandoned? Writing in 1883, Fanny Caroline Lefroy, Jane Austen's great-niece and an important source of information for the first generation of professional, non-family biographers, had this to say: 'Somewhere in 1804 [Jane Austen] began "The Watsons", but her father died early in 1805, and it was never finished.'[16] From the start, it was to be a darker engagement with the harsh circumstances of

---

[15] Described, for example, in *Letters*, 54–5.
[16] [Fanny C. Lefroy], 'Is It Just?', *Temple Bar*, 67 (1883), 277.

dependent women's lives, with little of the romantic illusion we associate with *Sense and Sensibility* and *Pride and Prejudice*. Elizabeth
Watson, the eldest sister, knows that her only hope of escaping desti-
tution or dependence on unwilling relations lies in marriage, and
there is nothing romantic in what she says:

you know we must marry. I could do very well single for my own part A
little Company, & a pleasant Ball now & then, would be enough for me, if
one could be young for ever, but my Father cannot provide for us, & it is
very bad to grow old & be poor and laughed at.—I have lost Purvis, it is
true but very few people marry their first Loves. I should not refuse a man
because he was not Purvis—. (p. 67)

In a manuscript filled with deletions and interlinear additions, with
evidence of second thoughts, this passage flows easily, with almost no
correction.

Before Austen brought her new novel to the domestic crisis that
Mr Watson's death would precipitate, real events overtook fiction. By
late March 1805, the Austen women (two ageing unmarried daughters and their widowed mother) had given up their house in Bath and
moved into cheaper lodgings. From this point to the ends of their
lives they would be dependent for house and security on Jane's brothers' generosity. In 1804–5, a new novel based in the harsh circumstances of women's material lives came unexpectedly close to events
in Austen's own life. What redemptive scope could its story offer once
Austen's own ageing, all-female household had been rendered so vulnerable? The collision of life and fiction is traceable in the letters
Austen wrote from Bath, Lyme Regis, and Southampton during this
unsettled time—letters in which she bemoans the forced sociability
and boredom of small-town life: 'the bold, queerlooking people, just
fit to be Quality at Lyme'; and wryly comments on Mrs Lance, a new
Southampton acquaintance, who 'seemed to like to be rich, and we
gave her to understand that we were far from being so; she will soon
feel therefore that we are not worth her acquaintance'; and elsewhere
reflects, 'What a different set we are now moving in!'[17]

*The Watsons* may have begun as Austen's attempt to assert through
her art some power over her own circumstances: she was in her late
twenties, with a rejection of marriage and the security that represented
recently behind her. That story is well known: in December 1802

[17] *Letters*, 98, 122, 103.

a family friend in very comfortable circumstances, Harris Bigg-Wither, had proposed to Jane and overnight been turned down.[18] Immediately afterwards, or so it seems, she revised 'Susan', sold it, and began *The Watsons*. The dark social criticism of *The Watsons* marks a stage in Austen's maturing as a novelist that must have required her to delve deeper into herself than she had done before. Did it remain unfinished because, with her father's death, life had pushed the experiment too far?

What more was there to say? Her sister Cassandra, after Austen's death in 1817, shared with her nieces 'something of the intended story'. Emma Watson's father

was soon to die; and Emma to become dependent for a home on her narrow-minded sister-in-law and brother [the Croydon smart set]. She was to decline an offer of marriage from Lord Osborne, and much of the interest of the tale was to arise from [the older] Lady Osborne's love for Mr Howard, and his counter affection for Emma, whom he was finally to marry.[19]

There is another possibility: that *The Watsons* simply ran out of fictional steam; that, despite Cassandra's sharing of the 'intended story', it had no real growth left in it. There is something already too determined about the main characters—Emma Watsons's chief disappointment is behind her; other characters lack ambiguity; too much background has been told—awkwardly back-filled rather than lying ahead to be discovered. Is Emma herself too healthy (unlike Fanny Price), too faultless (unlike Emma Woodhouse), and too young and confident (unlike Anne Elliot) to merit deeper acquaintance? This raises another possibility: that *The Watsons* began and ended in experimentation, in twisting familiar ingredients into a new and darker shape but with little certainty of where they might lead. It has not yet assumed the shape of a novel: there are no chapter divisions in the manuscript, which is written continuously. There is a short rule drawn across the page midway through the seventh of its ten tiny booklets, which may suggest a division in the story at this point;

---

[18] For biographical details of this period, see Deirdre Le Faye, *Jane Austen: A Family Record* (2nd edn, Cambridge: Cambridge University Press, 2004), 135–59.

[19] J. E. Austen-Leigh, *A Memoir of Jane Austen, to which is added Lady Susan and Fragments of two other unfinished tales by Miss Austen* (2nd edn, London: Richard Bentley and Son, 1871), 364.

another short rule sits midway through booklet ten; otherwise, no formal structural markings. The manuscript's appearance is, in this respect, quite different from those that survive from *Persuasion* and *Sanditon*, with their clear chapter divisions.

Reading *The Watsons* after *Pride and Prejudice*, *Mansfield Park*, *Emma*, and *Persuasion*, we can do, we indeed glimpse those 'antagonists' that Anne Thackeray saw: of heroines like Fanny Price (*Mansfield Park*) and Anne Elliot (*Persuasion*), outsiders within their unhappy families, seeking solace in the life of the imagination as a compensation for painful reality. Towards the end of *The Watsons*, we are told that Emma prefers sharing the retirement of her father's sick room to the family party downstairs, made painful by her sister Margaret's 'perverseness' and the vulgarity of her sister-in-law:

In *his* chamber, Emma was at peace from the dreadful mortifications of unequal Society, & family Discord—from the immediate endurance of Hard-hearted prosperity, low-minded Conceit, & wrong-headed folly . . . She still suffered from them in the Contemplation of their existence; in memory & in prospect, but for the moment, she ceased to be tortured by their effects.—She was at leisure, she could read & think (p. 101)

This is something new in Austen's style of writing that we encounter more fully in Fanny Price's East room refuge or 'nest of comforts' as the narrator describes it in *Mansfield Park* (ch. 16). Emma Watson promises to be a different kind of heroine, but as yet, there is no hint of an interesting pathology to explore as there will be in Fanny and Anne. But it is worth asking whether Austen could have reached the emotional complexity, the interiority and defensiveness that Fanny Price and Anne Elliot both exhibit, without the experiment in social meanness and the painful reaching into life's depths that *The Watsons* represents.

Where *Lady Susan* has its hastily patched 'Conclusion', *The Watsons* appears to stall, falling victim to its internally mounting malaise. But *Sanditon*, we know with certainty, is a novel in the making, broken off only by illness and death. Again, it opens onto new fictional ground, so extraordinary that its unfinished state is not its most obvious feature. From its first page, *Sanditon* upsets our expectations of an Austen novel. A carriage overturns on a road that leads nowhere. Its occupants, Mr Parker and his wife, are in search of a doctor whom they hope to tempt to set up practice in the new seaside resort they represent: they are Mr and Mrs Parker of Sanditon, and 'everybody has heard of Sanditon' (p. 108). There is no doctor in this out-of-the-way place; the only local family of any gentility, the numerous Heywoods, are robustly and defiantly healthy. But with a sprained ankle the consequence of his carriage accident, Mr Parker now finds himself in need, in earnest, of medical attendance. We might expect a novel or play by Samuel Beckett to begin with such a gesture to the absurd—but from Jane Austen? This is only the first disturbance of our expectations. In gratitude for the hospitality they receive, the Parkers take home with them to Sanditon Miss Charlotte Heywood, 'a very pleasing young woman of two & twenty' (p. 113), who proposes to make an extended visit. In standard Austen, we would now find ourselves eased comfortably into the story of a marriageable young heroine singled out, here on a visit to the seaside, so that we might observe her encounters with several eligible young men, from the charming but worthless to the ultimately worthy, whom she will come to love. But that is not what happens; almost immediately, a bizarre assortment of eccentric characters hijack the reader's attention—chief among them Mr Parker himself.

Mr Parker is 'an Enthusiast' (p. 111); a term that at the time implied obsessive self-delusion. He has abandoned his family estate to sink his funds in the new leisure industry, and with his co-investor, the local great lady, Lady Denham, is speculating on various property developments—specifically, lodging houses and amenities (hotel, library, billiard room) in yet another seaside resort on an oversupplied south coast. On a hilltop looking out across the English Channel, records the narrator, 'the Modern began' (p. 121)—Mr Parker's vision for a fashionable new holiday destination. Mr Parker, too, is a modern type, dislocated by recent events and wishing to make the world anew. We should not forget that Austen was a wartime writer; that for almost the whole of her adult life Britain was at war with France—a war conducted not just on a European but a global scale. Where in earlier novels, Austen figured the national through the personal perspective on war—a family in peril in *Mansfield Park*, in *Persuasion* a love affair renewed in the shadow of Napoleon's final showdown—in *Sanditon* she draws a traumatized post-war society, opening to change after decades of confinement and bearing conflict's mental and emotional scars. England's Channel coast,

anxiously defended against the threat of invasion in *Mansfield Park*'s
Portsmouth scenes, is now in *Sanditon*, eighteen months after
Waterloo (the battle that ended war with France in June 1815), the
site of keen resort wars and an eagerly anticipated invasion from
holidaymakers.

The novel is filled with topical allusion: Mr Parker's regret that
his new-built house, Trafalgar House, is not named Waterloo ('for
Waterloo is more the thing now' (p. 118)) invokes the contemporary
craze for naming buildings after national wartime victories:
London's Strand Bridge, begun in 1811, had been renamed
Waterloo Bridge just one year earlier in 1816. Even a passing men
tion of 'Blue Shoes' (p. 120), casually spotted in a Sanditon shop
window, is not without significance: several contemporary com-
mentators noted the craze for blue garments, in the shade known as
Waterloo blue, after the dye in common use in Flanders. Within
weeks of the battle, trophy-hunting determined the field of Waterloo
as a tourist destination. The collection of relics quickly transformed
the Flanders site into something other; a relatively recent equivalent would be the tourist onslaught following the fall of the Berlin
Wall in November 1989. Almost overnight Waterloo, like the Wall,
shifted from history into myth. Already in *Sanditon*, recent history
has been commodified and packaged—transformed into marketing
opportunities.

And *Sanditon* is all about marketing: from cottages ornés to patent
medicines. The end of war saw a new kind of risk emerging in the
shape of a volatile economy. Rich Lady Denham and her penniless
nephew Sir Edward are each gambling on fast money-making
schemes: she has her supply of asses' milk and a second-hand exercise machine (a chamber horse, lying useless after the death of her
first husband) ready to rent out to sickly visitors; he has his killer
charms, perfectly honed for the seduction of holidaying heiresses.
Who can resist? Bustling, suggestible Mr Parker is caught up in the
frenzy. The difference is that he has a conscience, unlike Lady
Denham, his 'Colleague in speculation' (p. 114), and is concerned
for the claims on his protection of the established village community
(the site of his 'old House—the house of my Forefathers' (p. 117)),
threatened by the sudden expansion of the new town. Speculation is
profiteering, buying, selling, and making money by a rise or fall in
the market without regard for its long-term effects on the local

environment.[20] Readers are not likely to connect Austen with the economic theory of her day, but a conversation between Mr Parker and Lady Denham revises that assumption. They debate the effect of demand on supply and the consequences that a more general diffusion of wealth might bring for their local community. While he welcomes the prospect of free-spending visitors and the rising prices and increased productivity they might stimulate, she is jealous to protect her interests against servants wanting higher wages. Not only does this speak in timely fashion to the state of the national economy, in the grip of post-war depression, it sounds much like Jane Marcet's newly published *Conversations on Political Economy* (1816), a work that successfully explained Adam Smith's influential doctrines for a popular audience. Like Marcet, Austen grasps the change that narrow commercialization will work upon social relations; the dangerous erosion of an older moral economics based on mutual obligation. Again, we look at village life with new eyes.

Speculation of various kinds is set to be a major theme: in only twelve chapters, 'speculation' appears six times and 'speculating' once. The 'two Post chaises', seen by the Parkers and Charlotte crossing the down to the hotel, and described as not only 'a joyful sight' but also 'full of speculation' (p. 145), nicely conflate the imaginative and economic guesswork that occupies their several thoughts. For all the characters assembled in Sanditon are seasoned fantasists; one way or another, all are speculators. Charlotte Heywood, for much of the narrative the reader's eyes and ears on events, is given to speculation as she processes the sights and sounds of a world she witnesses but never really enters. The effect is disorientating; she is repeatedly assailed by the new and the unexpected. In this resort filled with eccentrics, she must regularly reassess: did she really see/hear that? what can she/he mean by it? is this a kind or a cruel/an intelligent or a stupid person? Charlotte is presented as a problem solver; as yet, the novel itself is a mystery.

With *Sanditon* Austen is taking her celebrated naturalism into strange waters. This is not what reality in a novel looks like; not how 'real' people in fiction speak and behave; and certainly not in Austen's realist fictions. It is an accepted realist convention that, inside the

---

[20] Adam Smith, *An Inquiry into the Nature and Causes of the Wealth of Nations*, 2 vols (London, 1776), i. 140 (bk I, ch. 10). See, too, 'speculation', *OED*, sense 8a.

fiction, characters behave as though they are real—even to the point where they might say 'if this were a novel, such and such would happen'. *Sanditon* is unusual in its knowing parade of its fictional credentials; in the way its characters appear to relish and act up to their fictional status. Sir Edward is a thorough fictional construct—turning to pulp fiction for lifestyle advice, he is novel-addled to a remarkable degree. But for Charlotte Heywood, too, fiction provides a handy interpretative tool, seen in her pointed association with the volume of Frances Burney's *Camilla* lying on the counter of Mrs Whitby's circulating library: 'She took up a Book; it happened to be a volume of *Camilla*. She had not *Camilla's* Youth, & had no intention of having her Distress' (p. 126). One consequence of this fictive self-consciousness is a new freedom, openness, and energy. There is freedom in the absurd posturing of Sir Edward, whose passion for Walter Scott's verses brings the enigmatic declaration, 'That Man who can read them unmoved must have the nerves of an Assassin!—Heaven defend me from meeting such a Man un armed' (p. 131). There is frustrated sexual energy in Miss Diana Parker's persistent rubbing, 'six Hours without Intermission', of Mrs Sheldon's coachman's ankle (p. 123). Mr Parker's impassioned niche marketing of Sanditon as a health resort—'a second Wife & 4 Children . . . hardly less Dear—& certainly more engrossing' (p. 112)—lends his enthusiastic riffs the puffed-up style of a guidebook. Here he is extolling the therapeutic effects of the seaside:

The Sea Air & Sea Bathing together were nearly infallible, One or the other of them being a match for every Disorder, of the Stomach, the Lungs or the Blood; They were anti-spasmodic, anti-pulmonary, anti-sceptic, anti-bilious & anti-rheumatic. Nobody could catch cold by the Sea, Nobody wanted appetite by the Sea, Nobody wanted Spirits. Nobody wanted Strength.—They were healing, softing, relaxing—fortifying & bracing—seemingly just as was wanted—sometimes one, sometimes the other.—If the Sea breeze failed, the Sea Bath was the certain corrective;—& where Bathing disagreed, the Sea Breeze alone was evidently designed by Nature for the cure. (p. 112)

Here is a popular guidebook of the time, promoting sea air and bathing at Brighton:

Those who use the cold or warm sea-bath, very soon become sensible how much *the air of the coast* contributes to general health; indeed, in almost every instance, its good effects are far more considerable than is generally supposed. To the young, and those debilitated by years, its influence is often surprising . . . to those in the vigour of life, the stimulus deriveable from wine, or fermented liquors, is amply supplied by the revivifying effects of sea air alone; so much so indeed, as to render their use, in most cases, quite unnecessary. To these general facts may be added, the evidence arising from the health and vigour of the resident inhabitants of the sea-shore, who are strangers to the melancholy catalogue of diseases which annually prevail in inland situations, and who present numerous examples of unusual and vigorous old age.[21]

The mood in *Sanditon* is not just optimistic; it is frenetic and reck-less. Among war's aftershocks is its effect on language and identity. Communication breaks down under assault from the various specu-lators, each trapped inside their bizarre thought bubbles and unique speech habits. Miss Diana Parker's profiteering takes the form of offi-cious acts of charity. A fanatical dualism governs her actions and her belief that 'the World is pretty much divided between the Weak of Mind & the Strong—between those who can act & those who can not, & it is the bounden Duty of the Capable to let no opportunity of being useful escape them' (pp. 141–2). Her bullying interference in other people's business is expressed in paramilitary terms: '[Miss Diana Parker] was now regaling in the delight of opening the first Trenches of an acquaintance with such a powerful discharge of unexpected Obligation' (p. 145). Sir Edward Denham has amassed a complete lexicon of hard, shiny, new words which he lobs into the conversation to the considerable confusion of Charlotte Heywood and the reader. His hyperbolic ravings on the anti-hero, his favourite character in the contemporary novel—'T'were Pseudo-Philosophy to assert that we do not feel more enwraped by the brilliancy of his Career, than by the tranquil & morbid Virtues of any opposing Character'—reduce Charlotte to the Alice-like observation: ' "If I understand you aright"—said Charlotte—"our taste in Novels is not at all the same" ' (pp. 136–7). Verbal idiosyncrasy, like fanaticism, signals a community that has lost its connective glue—society falling apart.

One of the oddest features of *Sanditon* is its unusual air of detach-ment. The distance between Charlotte Heywood and the seaside world she encounters and attempts to analyse is rarely bridged. And

---

[21] [John Feltham], *A Guide to all the Watering and Sea-Bathing Places* (new and improved edn, London, 1815), 130.

those who assume that she is the usual Austen heroine, aligned more closely than any other character with the narrator's perspective, should consider how little Austen relies in this her last novel on the kind of double voicing or intimacy with the heroine that colours *Emma* and *Persuasion*, and the almost equal interplay of the narrator's voice with that of Mr Parker, a leading eccentric. *Sanditon* reads like an experiment in testing the social basis of perception. How do we know whom and what to trust? How will it all turn out? We cannot know. *Sanditon* was left unfinished; in some ways, it is barely begun. With its eccentrics vying for our attention, at odds with Austen's usual steady focus on her heroine's expectations, we are faced with not only a broken tale but also one that leaves so much uncertainty about how it will develop. Nothing as yet has a settled shape. Is this fluidity, this shapelessness, part of the bold experiment that includes her unusually intrusive seaside topography?

By her own dating of the first page, Austen started the new novel on 27 January 1817, setting it aside after twelve chapters, on 18 March 1817. Five days later she wrote to her niece Fanny Knight:

> I certainly have not been well for many weeks, & about a week ago I was very poorly . . . I must not depend upon being ever very blooming again. Sickness is a dangerous Indulgence at my time of Life.[22]

She died just four months later on 18 July, possibly from Addison's disease (at the time, undiagnosed and not in fact described before the mid-nineteenth century). In all, she wrote about 24,000 words of the new work, around one-fifth the length of her usual completed novels.

More than either *Lady Susan* or *The Watsons*, this dying work is attached to its writer's life. Its background of financial speculation and risk has been linked to the post-war failure of Henry Austen's bank in March 1816, the consequent sharp dip in the income of the Austen women, the possible stalling of Jane Austen's plans for further publications, and even the acceleration of the late stages of her degenerative illness.[23] *Sanditon* is a satire about the contemporary craze for seaside holidays; it is also a study of people who imagine they are ill, written by a woman we know was dying. To us she appears to be shadow-boxing with and laughing at death. Diana Parker, second

[22] *Letters*, 350–1.
[23] *Family Record*, 234–48; E. J. Clery, *Jane Austen: The Banker's Sister* (London: Biteback Publishing, 2017), 265 ff.

sister and Hampshire spinster, deluded hypochondriac and martyr to
the same condition, 'Spasmodic Bile' (p. 122), as her author in her
final months, reads like Austen's mad alter ego. The novel is written
in a radically new, impressionistic style. If the ground beneath her
characters' feet appears less secure, her vision is opening out. Was
this deliberate or a distortion caused by illness? Is Austen striking out
in a new direction or failing to establish overall control of a work
which, had she been stronger, would have proceeded on more familiar lines? Unavoidable and unanswerable questions; every reader will
ask them.[24] As light and funny as it is, this unfinished fiction is
Austen's most poignant work.

* * *

In her essay, 'The Selfishness of Art', Cynthia Ozick describes how
'biography . . . attaches to certain writers . . . with the phantom tenacity
of a Doppelganger: history clouding into fable', and that for Jane
Austen this means sitting 'eternally in her parlor, hiding her manuscripts under her blotter when someone intrudes, as someone eternally does'.[25] Defended in life from intrusion, the publication of
Austen's fiction manuscripts—of the teenage writings and the unfinished later fictions—was a slow affair, beginning in the 1870s and
only fully completed in 1954. With the exception of *Lady Susan* and
twelve pages of *The Watsons*, the manuscripts themselves remained in

[24] In an early, classic study, still one of the most sophisticated readings of Austen's
narrative style, Mary Lascelles described it as 'a bold venture in a new way of telling
a story' while acknowledging that though 'an advance beyond its predecessors, none of
them would, if broken off short at the eleventh chapter, have left us in such uncertainty
as to the way in which it was going to develop' (*Jane Austen and Her Art* (London: Oxford
University Press, 1939), 39). To Margaret Drabble, the 'rather unsympathetic, hard,
unsubtle nature of the satire' is 'surely best explained by its author's state of health. She
has returned to an almost eighteenth-century view of man as a being dominated by a rul-
ing passion' (*Lady Susan, The Watsons, Sanditon*, ed. Margaret Drabble (Harmondsworth:
Penguin, 1974), 31). Tony Tanner, in an influential reading, argued for its apparent narrative disintegration as 'a new kind of phenomenological complexity', which Clara Tuite,
formulating as a queer, Gothic extravagance, has described as 'The elusive "newness" . . .
as well as the paradoxical "buoyancy" of this death-bed text' (Tony Tanner, *Jane Austen*
(Basingstoke: Macmillan, 1986), 282; Clara Tuite, *Romantic Austen: Sexual Politics and
the Literary Canon* (Cambridge: Cambridge University Press, 2002), 158). See, too,
D. A. Miller, *Jane Austen, or The Secret of Style* (Princeton: Princeton University Press,
2003), 76–92. The range of interpretation (itself a witness to the imaginative power of
unfinished works) is perhaps greater than for any of the six printed novels.
[25] Cynthia Ozick, 'The Selfishness of Art', in *Letters of Intent: Selected Essays*, ed.
David Miller (London: Atlantic Books, 2017), 31.

family hands until the early 1920s. They have given up their secrets slowly. The tendency of early editors and critics was to minimize their difference from the printed works; to provide an experience more consistent with the expectations raised by the finished writings. The challenge now is to shift perspective and review the style and subject matter of the famous six published novels in the light of these experimental fragments; to read print in the shadow of manuscript.

Not least, there is the evidence manuscripts provide to unlock the secrets of style. Manuscripts look different from print, offering radically changed understandings of writers we think we know. Henry Austen's eulogistic comment on his sister's style, that 'Every thing came finished from her pen; for on all subjects she had ideas as clear as her expressions were well chosen',[26] influenced generations of critics; it has influenced all her readers, as D. A. Miller wittily exposed. According to Miller, Austen's style (unlike that of other writers) is neither container nor embellishment but substance; it is 'absolute style'. We read her early, 'at eleven or twelve, the age when she began writing', and are thereafter lost to 'the siren lure of her voice . . . a truly out-of-body voice, so stirringly free of what it abhorred as "particularity" or "singularity" that it seemed to come from no enunciator at all'. For Miller, the fascination of Austen's work 'most fundamentally consists in *dematerializing* the voice that speaks it'.[27] As Miller goes on to show, Austen represents what is patently impossible: pure, unmediated style; or, we might say, text without the manuscript mess. What else explains the embarrassment, defensiveness, or denial that family biographers and later scholars long expressed in the face of her manuscript fictions: she was too young, too ill, too unhappy when she wrote them; or the manuscripts are not what they appear, they too are not themselves and would have evolved further and looked different. Those who have examined Austen's manuscripts have usually done so wishing to deny or excuse their expressive difference from print.

Another way to look at the evidence is to see draft manuscripts in a writer's hand as giving material form to an intangible concept: writing as the product of labour and as witness to the presence and personality of the writer. Manuscripts encourage us to consider how meaning is made, exposing through correction and revision the

[26] *Memoir*, ed. Sutherland, 141.     [27] Miller, *The Secret of Style*, 1 and 6–7.

workings of the mind in composition. The Textual Notes at the back
of this volume (and there are a lot of them) are designed to give a sense
of Austen's struggle to wrest meaning into shape: of the intensity,
even obsessiveness of the revising hand, and elsewhere the ease with
which some passages hit the paper, almost free of the need for correction. From these notes we gain new insights into the features that
characterize Austen's way of writing and begin to see how disciplined
was her method.

Beginnings rarely come easily to any writer. Too much back-story,
we sense, is crammed into the opening pages of *The Watsons* as
Elizabeth and Emma Watson awkwardly play catch-up during the
short journey to the Edwardses. The manuscript shows Austen struggling with an unusual weight of information, shifting and reshaping
it, but also adding even more:

On the present occasion, ~~one only of the Family f in Stanton Parsonage
could profit by~~ ^as only two of Mr W.'s children were at home, & one was always necessary ~~to him~~ as companion to
himself, for he was sickly & had lost his wife one only could profit by the kindness of their friends; Miss
Emma Watson ~~was to make her first public appearance in the
Neighbourhood; & Miss Watson drove her & all her finery in the old Chair
to D. on the important morning of the Ball; without being able to stay &
share the pleasure herself, because her Father who was an Invalid could not
be left to spend the Eveng alone~~ ^who was very recently returned to her family from the care of an Aunt
who had brought her up was to make her first public appearance in the neighbourhood— ~~& her eldest Sister who had kindly
undertaken~~ her eldest Sister, whose delight in a Ball was not lessened by a ten years Enjoyment, had some merit in chearfully
undertaking to drive her & all her finery in the old Chair to D. on the important morng.— (p. 65)

In *Sanditon*, too, she struggles with the release of information in the
passage where Mr Parker first introduces to Charlotte Heywood
and the reader the outline of his brother Sidney's character (p. 119).
The sketch is considerably reworked as it emerges. The disposition
of deletions, substitutions, and new material suggests the dynamic
interrelation of processes of correction and creation as a struggle to
clarify intention: what is to be Sidney's role? what aspects will define
his character? what to reveal at this stage, in advance of his actual
appearance, and in what order? Significantly, what emerges leaves
Sidney as yet an ambiguous figure—'privileged by superior abilities
or spirits to say anything', 'fashionable', 'with great powers of pleasing', but unfixed. By contrast, when only a few pages later, in chapter 5, Diana Parker's letter offers the chance for her to introduce
herself, she does so openly with her idiosyncrasies all on show, and

the writing flows smoothly with virtually no revision (pp. 122–4). Conversations, more especially, the crazy monologues of *Sanditon*'s eccentrics, appear to flow relatively easily from the tip of Austen's nib; it could be that she formed them in her head before committing them to paper—that she heard them as voices and recorded what she heard. She is, after all, one of our most brilliant conversational novelists.

Something more puzzling (and therefore more interesting) is going on in those places where we see Austen struggling to lock down detail that, superficially, matters little. For example, in the description of the front of Mr Edwards's house:

Mr E's House ~~was of a dull brick colour, & an high Elevation~~ ~~a flight of stone steps to the Door, & two windows~~ ~~flight of stone steps with white posts, & a chain, divided~~ ^was higher than most of its neighbours with two windows on each side the door, & five the windows guarded by ~~a chain & green~~ posts & chain the door approached by a flight of stone steps. (p. 70)

Why, after revision, have we lost the house's 'dull brick colour' and the 'white' and then 'green' of the posts? Why were they there in the first place? It is tempting to see such detail as playing for time, as contributing to a kind of mind-focusing discipline in composition. In describing the approach to Sanditon House the same anxiety to fix the scene as a set of precise phenomena and instructions seems more comprehensible, part of the novel's wider perceptual unease, excused here by the alienating effect of the mist that shrouds the landmarks of the walk:

The ~~approach~~ ^road to Sanditon H. was ~~at first only~~ ^by a broad, handsome, planted ~~road~~ ^approach, between fields, ~~but ending in about a qr of a mile~~ ^of about a qr of a mile's length, & conducting at the end of a qr of a mile through second Gates into the Grounds, which though ^not extensive ~~were~~ had all the Beauty . . . could give. — ~~They were so narrow at the Entrance~~ ^These Entrance Gates were so much in a corner of the Grounds or Paddock, so near one of its Boundaries, that ~~one~~ ^an outside fence was at first almost pressing on the road—till an angle ~~in one~~ ^here, & a curve ~~in the other~~ ^there, ~~gave~~ ^threw them ^to a better distance. The Fence was a proper, Park paling in excellent condition; with ~~vigorous~~ ^rows clusters of fine Elms, or ^rows of old Thorns ~~& Hollies~~ following its ~~course~~ ^line almost every where . . . there were ~~inter-vals~~ vacant spaces—& through one of ~~them~~>se, Charlotte . . . caught a glimpse ^over the pales of something White & Womanish ~~over the pales~~ . . . & very ~~distinctly, though at some distance before her~~ ^decidedly inspite of the Mist; Miss B. seated, not far before her, ~~on~~>at the foot of the ~~sloping~~ bank which sloped down from the outside of the Paling & ~~at~~ which a narrow ~~track~~ ^Path seemed to skirt along (p. 154) xxx					*Introduction*

This kind of writing and the effort to get it in place points to an effect Austen strives for in other ways—an exaggerated reality whose design only gradually becomes clear to her. Sometimes, it is no more than a matter of adjusting names and locations, but she can appear obsessive in this regard. There is a particular attention to naming: in *Sanditon*, 'Old Stringer', the market gardener, was first 'old Salmon'; 'old Sam' was 'old Hannah'; 'Mr Woodcock' was 'young Woodcock'. The 'List of Subscribers' to Mrs Whitby's circulating library requires some effort to earn its description of being 'but commonplace': 'Dr & Mrs Henderson' may not have seemed sufficiently ordinary, since they are altered, first to 'Dr & Mrs Ba[ron?]' and then to 'Dr & Mrs Brown'; while the 'Rev. Mr Hankin' becomes 'Hankins'. Some of these little adjustments contribute to a wider structural purpose, but others remain purely local in effect—signs of a freewheeling creativity that names other subscribers on Mrs Whitby's list 'Miss Scroggs' and 'Miss Merryweather'. In similar fashion, the opening line of *The Watsons* shows Austen settling the town where the winter assembly is to be held as 'L' in 'Sussex'. Subsequently, she deleted and reinscribed 'L' before altering this second 'L' to 'D' and 'Sussex' to 'Surry'. Is 'D' meant as a reference to 'Dorking'? A little later, 'Dorking' was to be the town where Sam Watson is training as a surgeon, later, again, changed to 'Guilford'. Tom Musgrave was originally 'Charles Musgrave'; Penelope Watson is said to be visiting 'Southampton', later altered to 'Chichester'; Emma Watson is newly returned from 'Devonshire' after 'a dozen years', altered to 'Shropshire' after '14' years, at which point the setting of the story is still Sussex. Mary Edwards's admirer is initially 'Captain Carr', later altered to 'Hunter', before 'Carr' is reapportioned as the name of the particular friend of Miss Osborne.[28] Do these adjustments as to names and places give some indication of the struggle and time it cost Austen to get into her stride in writing? If so, is the shifting and eventual settling of detail (Dr Henderson becoming Dr Brown and Devonshire becoming Shropshire) some form of limbering-up exercise in creating reality—fictional reality, that is? Is this how Austen eases herself into this other, imagined world? We learn years later from her letters to her niece Anna how important the mapping of precise details of a local geography and social circle were always to her method of writing:

[28] See Textual Notes to pp. 65, 67, 69, 93, 119, 125.

Lyme will not do. Lyme is towards 40 miles distance from Dawlish & would not be talked of there.—I have put Starcross indeed.—If you prefer *Exeter*, that must always be safe.—I have also scratched out the Introduction between Lord P. & his Brother, & Mr Griffin. A Country Surgeon (don't tell Mr C. Lyford) would not be introduced to Men of their rank.[29]

In other places, revision simply shows Austen having fun, riffing on her eccentric creations to see how far she can take their absurdity; for example, in Diana Parker's medicinally applied friction to Mrs Sheldon's coachman's ankle 'for 4 ^six Hours without intermission' (p. 123), or in turning up the temperature of Sir Edward Denham's critical discourse upon the fictional characters he most esteems, those imbued with 'unconquerable ^indomptible Decision . . . the ^high-toned Machinations of the prime Character, the potent, pervading Hero of the Story', as against the 'morbid Virtues of his Rival ^any opposing Character' (p. 136).

* * *

Jane Austen is a writer of two halves; fictions published in her lifetime and others left unfinished in manuscript at her death. The division is not tidy: within the surviving manuscripts there are stories best described as working drafts in varying stages of development, potential publications never finished—*The Watsons* and *Sanditon*. In contrast, *Lady Susan*, a clean fair copy, may or may not be finished; short by the standards of contemporary publications, it was perhaps destined primarily for reading within a closed circle, but we cannot be certain. Most likely, all three fictions were incubated in the private space of writing that we associate with the great writer. Different again are those manuscript works, shorter, lighter, and occasional in inspiration, which we can be sure were never intended for publication but belong as writing and reading exclusively to habits of amateur composition, made to amuse family and friends. Several generations of the scribbling Austens contributed to and enjoyed such performances: from Jane Austen's mother, a regular comic versifier, to her rather pedantic nephew, the proto-novelist, James Edward. A survey of her own lifelong writing practices makes it clear that there was no simple division for Austen between writing for family enjoyment and writing

[29] *Letters*, 280.

for print; she did not outgrow one as she gained confidence in the other way of writing.

The three teenage notebooks, precociously titled *Volume the First*, *Volume the Second*, and *Volume the Third*, were home-centred collections that also served as apprentice ground for her professional ambitions. Amateur composition persisted long into Austen's professional period in the form of occasional verses (even the most ardent fan cannot believe they merited contemporary publication) and in the comic *Plan of a Novel*, probably written in early 1816, coinciding with the publication of *Emma*. Such home-directed pieces (they include *Opinions of Mansfield Park and Emma*) grow out of and thrive upon the views of a confidential circle, reading, laughing over, and commenting on the author's performance. They benefited from the kind of family 'improvement' (her word) of her latest short poem that she refers to as 'the Steventon Edition' in a letter of 29 November 1812,[30] and that elsewhere she openly acknowledges in the marginal display of sources on the manuscript pages of the *Plan*. From 1817 and the final months of her life there survive both professional and amateur family compositions: the draft twelve chapters of a new novel, *Sanditon*, surely begun bravely with an intention to print; and the verses 'When Winchester races first took their beginning' that James Edward, writing in 1870, now as her biographer Austen-Leigh, tells us she composed three days before she died, to amuse her family 'even in their sadness'.[31]

The endurance of amateur composition alongside steady professionalization through the 1810s witnesses as much to Austen's mounting independence as a writer as to creative symbiosis or dependency: novels gestated in greater seclusion from outside influence in these years (*Mansfield Park*, *Emma*, and *Persuasion*) spawned family comment and 'continuations' only *after* they were published. Once a novel was off the stocks, Austen-Leigh later remembered, 'She would, if asked, tell us many little particulars about the subsequent career of some of her people.'[32] The evidence suggests that by the 1810s Austen maintained simultaneous yet distinct identities as amateur and professional author. Correspondence from 1814 to 1816, when her brief public career was at its height,

---

[30] *Letters*, 205.     [31] *Memoir*, ed. Sutherland, 130–1.
[32] *Memoir*, ed. Sutherland, 119.

shows her advising niece and nephew, Anna and James Edward, on their attempts at fiction. She dusted off her teenage notebooks, inviting them to use her own early stories as inspiration for their creative writing.[33] At the same time, she carefully circumscribed any family influence on her professional development.

'It is not as a celebrated writer that she appears in these pages, but as one of a family group', announced Mary Augusta Austen-Leigh, in publishing a collection of Austen family charades in 1895.[34] Unlike the unfinished fictions, all the verses collected here belong squarely to the world of family entertainment; they are of interest now only because Jane Austen wrote them. Where the unfinished fictions are experiments that shed new light on published novels, the verses are humorous or affectionate responses to particular events and occasions, entailed permanently to biography: a wedding, the present of some handkerchiefs, the birth of a child, the memory of a dead friend, a family card game, a rebellious niece, a headache, politics. Some were written to accompany gifts; others were enclosed in letters; yet others were exercises or contributions to family games in verse. They enlivened the domestic scene. But they are tame stuff, mostly reliant on tired eighteenth-century conventions. One poem only is remarkable: 'When Winchester races first took their beginning'. Its swift, tripping line (anapaestic tetrameter) is light and suited to comedy. Its subject—St Swithin's curse bringing rain upon the ungodly Winchester race-goers—is scarcely serious in tone. In its composition Austen appears to us to be facing down death with a laugh: 'When once we are buried you think we are dead | But behold me Immortal' (p. 181). This is spine-tingling stuff. The next generation of Austens, by then keepers of her flame, were concerned that the publication of such frivolous verses might cast doubt on the Christian piety with which Saint/Aunt Jane faced her end, and so they long delayed their publication. But we cannot for a moment regret that they have been left to us. They speak out of that sudden upsurge of life and lucidity that comes to many, after long illness and just before death. They are intensely moving for this reason.

---

[33] Kathryn Sutherland, 'From Kitty to Catharine: James Edward Austen's Hand in *Volume the Third*', *Review of English Studies*, NS 66 (2014), 124–43.

[34] [Mary Augusta Austen-Leigh], *Charades &c. Written a hundred years ago by Jane Austen and her family* (London: Spottiswoode & Co., 1895), 'Preface', unpaginated.

# NOTE ON THE TEXT

JANE AUSTEN is a writer of two halves: of manuscript and print. There are authorized early print editions for her famous six novels but, apart from a few pages of *Persuasion*, no manuscripts survive. In the case of the three fictions presented here—*Lady Susan*, *The Watsons*, and *Sanditon*—there are manuscripts but no early printed texts. All the works collected into this edition—fictions, poetry, and miscellaneous prose—were left unpublished at Austen's death in 1817. With the exception of some poems and the prayers (the latter not certainly her own compositions), all derive directly from manuscripts in her hand. The first printed editions of *Lady Susan*, *The Watsons*, and *Sanditon*, appeared over fifty years after Austen's death when her nephew James Edward Austen-Leigh included them in the second edition of his *Memoir of Jane Austen*, issued in 1871.[1] It was only then that all three fictions were publicly given the titles we know them by. Even now, in spite of her remarkable world fame, all three are far from familiar to Austen's readers; to some, the fresh perspective they offer on her writing and reputation as established by the six published novels will come as a surprise.

Because there are for these works no early printed texts, all offer challenges for the modern editor: with no lifetime published versions to follow, how might they be presented? Austen's manuscript of *Lady Susan* is a fair copy, neatly formatted to the style of a contemporary novel in letters and reasonably close to what might have been printed at the time. *The Watsons* and *Sanditon*, however, are draft manuscripts, their texts still evolving, filled with deletions and revisions. The modern editor can choose either to follow the textual choices made by previous editors in transforming manuscript into print or turn afresh to the original manuscript forms and make new decisions on how to present them to the reader. In editing direct from manuscript, the choices are these: to stick close to what the manuscripts offer and thus capture some of their idiosyncrasy of expression; or tidy them up as

---

[1] *Memoir* (1871), 167–364. Drafts of the 'cancelled' chapter of *Persuasion* and heavily edited extracts from *Sanditon* are included as chs 12 and 13 within the biography, while *Lady Susan* and *The Watsons* are appended as separate works in their own right. The inclusion of the manuscript fictions more than doubled the length of the biography.

the author might have done in anticipation of publication and as a contemporary printer would certainly have done. The former, taken to extreme, would result in a faithful transcription, recording every erasure and revision as it occurs; but it would not produce a smooth reading text. The other extreme would normalize the text by second-guessing decisions likely to have been made concerning both substance and style by author and printer. While this latter choice would ease things for the reader, by setting aside their manuscript states it would risk losing much that is experimental in the sense and flavour of these fictions.

In practice, the reader is best served by a compromise between the two positions: one that offers a clear text, removing evidence of alteration to the Textual Notes, but that refrains from making the kinds of change that would absorb all signs of manuscript practice into something like the print appearance of Austen's other, published novels. Thanks to the electronic availability of so much of our literary heritage, readers are now far more accustomed to encountering texts in a variety of forms—as images of manuscript pages and early print typefaces—than we were in the relatively recent pre-digital past. Because in a variety of ways the works collected here are, in subject as well as style, unlike print Austen, it is important that they be presented and received as such. Exhibiting a range of experimental writing practices, they open up new ways of reading one of our greatest writers.

There are, then, two Austens, and we should not conflate them into a single entity. In her case, print and manuscript survive from the early nineteenth century to represent the difference. Austen's manuscripts also fall into two categories: they are either unfinished drafts giving insight into her creative processes, or finished writings unintended for print that link her to an informal coterie of domestic and family composition; print marks her entry into public and professional life. *The Watsons* and *Sanditon*, we can assume, were written to traverse that private–public divide, but neither developed that far. Aspects of their rawness—minimal paragraphing, abbreviated names, the collapsing together of different speakers' voices, punctuation by dashes—convey the impressionistic energy of her style in the process of writing. They offer windows onto her methods of composition and food for the reader's imagination. Here, if anywhere, is our best opportunity to understand how she wrote the drafts that became the great printed novels. Other manuscript compositions are rooted in family or amateur practices and were never directed to publication—*Plan of a Novel*, *Opinions of Mansfield Park* and *of Emma*, and the poetry. They allow us to glimpse a contrasting sociable space in which writing grows more directly from the rhythms and events of shared experiences, often blurring a sense of individual authorship. The one work included here that challenges such straightforward categorization is *Lady Susan*. Might it have been intended for publication?

Among the puzzles posed for the reader by Austen's manuscript writings is her liberal use of dashes. The dash is a vital component of Austen's way of composing. Hovering between somatic trace (evidence of where the hand and the pen rested) and punctuation, it is both a mechanical and a stylistic feature. More visceral than conventional punctuation, it challenges interpretation. Unlike a regular punctuation mark, the power of the dash lies in its gesture towards something absent or unfinished. As a mature novelist, Austen appears to recognize that the dash fulfils complex functions: it can substitute for brackets, before and after parenthetical remarks; it can surround a speaker reference (—she said—) within a continuing speech; it can enforce a semicolon or full stop; it can indicate a paragraph break. In dividing the paratactic jottings of Austen's familiar letters, or in capturing the particular effects of voice in conversation in fiction, the dash provides a nervous, taut connector; it can open a rhetorical space, denoting impatience, hesitation, and emotion. In the heavily be-dashed epistolary novel *Lady Susan*, it is just such a rhetorical marker, employed by the various letter writers to simulate the inflections of the speaking voice. In the draft manuscript of *Sanditon*, the expressive and rhythmic force of the dash comes into full play to denote distinctive speech patterns and the supple potential of text as performance. Editing Austen's unfinished fictions in 1974 for Penguin, Margaret Drabble, a fellow novelist, made considerable changes in order to present a modern, print-friendly text, but she resisted tinkering with *Sanditon*'s dashes on the grounds that they 'may have been intentional rather than the effect of fast or unrevised writing'.[2] Austen's early printers also respected her dashing style and recognized its effects: for example, in the strawberry-picking party, in *Emma* (ch. 42), and in Emma and Mr Knightley's broken speech patterns (ch. 49 of

[2] *Lady Susan, The Watsons, Sanditon*, ed. Drabble, 38.

the same novel). Austen's dashes are retained across all the manuscripts presented here.

Even small manuscript details can resonate imaginatively: it would be impossible to decide, for instance, whether in the eccentric society of *Sanditon* every use of 'Mr P.' for 'Mr Parker' and 'Lady D.' for 'Lady Denham' should be expanded or only some (and, if so, which?). They are, of course, a clear feature of manuscript shorthand. But readers of *Emma* will recall that Mrs Elton's occasional references to Mr Elton as 'Mr E.' carry further significance. In Jane Bennet's second 'hurried' letter (*Pride and Prejudice*, ch. 46) disclosing details of Lydia's elopement, similar abbreviated forms survive into print. It therefore seems desirable, where interpretation is not rendered obscure, to retain these distinctive features and effects that print might suppress or regularize but which mark manuscript as working draft.

For this new edition, no changes have been made to Austen's spellings, capitalization, paragraphing, or punctuation, all features that stamp her writings as her own or of her time. When she wrote, spelling, especially in manuscript, was not standardized. Forms such as 'travellor', 'ancle', 'bason', 'stile', 'adeiu', 'beleive', 'cheif', 'neice', 'veiw', 'medecine' not only carry the stamp of Austen's personality as a writer, they were used by many other writers of her time. They have been allowed to stand. Austen regularly uses the forms 'dependant/ance' and 'independant/ance' where we would expect an 'ent/ence' ending (*Lady Susan*, p. 50: 'a state of dependance'; *Sanditon*, p. 116: 'Poverty & Dependance'). She is consistent in favouring 'teize' (for 'tease'), 'atcheive' (for 'achieve'), 'expence' (for 'expense'), and the spellings 'agreable' and 'disagreable', for two of her most regularly employed adjectives. As late as *Sanditon*, she is writing 'simpathy' (p. 135) and 'accomodation' (p. 149). In general, we should see variation in spelling at this time as a sign of the flexibility of the standard or norm within the public printed text as in private usage.[3] In this category might be placed Austen's use of both '-ise' and '-ize' endings

---

[3] Systemic variability was a normal feature of both printer's and author's style well into the nineteenth century. See Philip Gaskell, *From Writer to Reader: Studies in Editorial Method* (Oxford: Clarendon Press, 1978), 7–8. See, too, the examination of inconsistencies in spelling in and between manuscript and first-edition print versions of Walter Scott's *Waverley* (1814), in *Waverley*, ed. P. D. Garside (Edinburgh: Edinburgh University Press, 2007), 399–400; and Lynda Mugglestone, 'English in the Nineteenth Century', in Mugglestone (ed.), *The Oxford History of English* (Oxford: Oxford University Press, 2006), 274–88.

('surprise'/'surprize', 'realise'/'realize', 'recognise'/'recognize'); and
the mixing of older and newer forms, as in 'chuse'/'choose', 'shew'/
'show', 'croud'/'crowd', 'encrease'/'increase', 'cloathes'/'clothes',
'sopha'/'sofa'.

It is startling to realize that paragraphing may have been a feature imposed on the manuscripts only at a late stage, perhaps not
until they reached the printer, and that the scant use of such divisions in *The Watsons* and *Sanditon* was Austen's common practice in
writing. Their tightly filled, unbroken pages convey a raw intensity
whose effect is retained here. Also preserved is Austen's characteristic use of capitalized initial letters for common nouns occurring
mid-sentence and even in some cases for adjectives (habits of writing surviving from the eighteenth century). Capitalizations of this
kind are sprinkled liberally across all her manuscript pages. In print,
they survive abundantly in the first-edition text of *Mansfield Park*
(1814). But she is by no means consistent in her practice: sometimes
in a single sentence the initial letter of one common noun is capitalized and another is not; and in handwriting, where initial letters
often hover ambiguously between what print must determine as
either upper-case (capital) or lower-case forms, editors must interpret the evidence one way or the other. The shift between capitalization and non-capitalization gives an irregular feel and look to text
when translated into print, providing an approximation of the
movement of the hand.

Another feature of early nineteenth-century handwriting, now
obsolete, the long-tailed 's', still in use by Austen's contemporaries,
contributes nothing to meaning and might merely impede the
enjoyment of the modern reader; it is not retained here. By contrast, and in a departure from other modern editors, I have retained
Austen's use of ampersand (&) as a variation upon 'and'. Ampersands
are sprinkled liberally over her manuscripts; no bar to comprehen-
sion, they signal speed and economy of writing. I have retained,
too, some contractions and abbreviations, such as 'Compts' for
'Compliments', 'Yrs affec:ly' for 'Yours affectionately' as contributing to the air of naturalism or colloquialism achieved in several of
the letter-texts collected here. Other standard abbreviations contributing less to fictional characterization or colour, like 'c^d' for
'could', 'B^r' for 'Brother', 'morn^g' for 'morning', are expanded. In
abbreviations, Austen, like her contemporaries, used raised final

letters, writing 'M$^r$.', 'M$^{rs}$.', 'Rev$^d$', and 'S$^t$.', represented here as 'Mr', 'Mrs', 'Revd', 'St'. Austen's floating or absent apostrophes in the so-called Saxon genitive, 'its''/'it's' (meaning 'of it'), and the contracted forms 'sha'nt'/'shan't', 'wo'nt'/'won't' are a challenge; like the variations in her spelling, they contribute to the flavour of her style, though unlike her distinctive spellings they probably represent no more than a kind of casualness or carelessness in pointing text. Where Austen omits the apostrophe altogether ('shant', 'wont'), it is not supplied. Elsewhere and to avoid unnecessary obscurity, her floating apostrophe is regularized to the modern standard ('shan't', 'won't'), even though the irregularity often carried over into print in her time. Her use of the forms 'it's' and 'her's', though now no longer in use, is retained and regularized (as in 'you had no doubt of it's authenticity' (*Lady Susan*, p. 18); 'to make my story as good as her's' (p. 24)).

There are major differences between Austen's paratactic punctuation (closer to the adjustments of the speaking voice) and the syntactic markers distinguishing the structural components of language. Austen's manuscript punctuation can on occasion suggest the pauses in composition and writing. The non-grammatical commas in the following passage from *Lady Susan* possibly indicate pauses in reading aloud: 'Contemptible as a regard founded only on compassion, must make them both, in my eyes, I felt by no means assured that such might not be the consequence' (p. 34). The eccentric placing of commas in the opening description of Lord Osborne—'there was an air of, Coldness, of Carelessness, even of Awkwardness' (*The Watsons*, p. 76)—slow the reader down and invite close inspection. The comma in the pronouncement 'The great Lady of Sanditon, was Lady Denham' (*Sanditon*, p. 113) seems like a marker in composition. These features too survive elsewhere into print. Not only is there a distinction to be observed between standards expected for novelistic discourse and grammatically 'correct' prose, but in reading manuscript it is even more important to resist weighing the evidence against an assumed print norm which may never have been in play. In general, I have held back from 'correcting' what is merely different. Importantly, Austen's lighter punctuation may give the modern reader a better sense of the expressive, conversational style of her writing. In her day, too, conventions for recording speech in novels were still emerging and experimental, with slightly different modes of representation from those in modern use. Reported speech as well as direct speech might be set inside speech marks; speeches broken by a 'he said' or 'she remarked', not usually closed and reopened in manuscript, were, however, becoming more precisely demarcated in print.

In presenting this new edition of the manuscript materials the following minor changes have been made: double quotation marks around speeches have been reduced to single, in line with modern British print style; in those instances where the manuscript omits to close or reopen speech marks, they are silently supplied; words and phrases underlined for emphasis are printed in italics; paragraph indentations and dashes are reduced to a single length (Austen uses many different lengths for both). The formatting of letters of *Lady Susan* has been standardized to a single style derived from Austen's most common usage. I have not, however, separated out speech exchanges in any manuscript to follow the conventions of print then and now. The presentation of conversation as the close interplay of several voices is a significant feature of Austen's way of composing. We *see* as well as *hear* this in the collapsed speech blocks of the adult manuscript. Not only does this represent an important element in her mature compositional method—making her one of the subtlest and most accurately attuned conversational novelists in English—there is little likelihood that the reader will be confused by it. Rather, the text is enlivened by its preservation.

All Austen's revisions, deletions, and additions are recorded in the Textual Notes at the end of the volume. The interested reader will find here the best evidence for the labour she expended in composition. The present edition is based upon work undertaken for the digital edition of Jane Austen's fiction manuscripts, published electronically in 2010 and with fuller critical apparatus in the enhanced five-volume print edition of 2018. Through digitization many new readings have been recovered. The reader interested in testing readings, in inspecting how Jane Austen worked, and in comparing the appearance of manuscript with the print interpretations offered here can do so at < http://www.janeausten.ac.uk>.

Descriptions of the fiction manuscripts represented in this edition are offered below. The shorter verse manuscripts are described briefly at the appropriate point in the Textual Notes at the end of the volume. The text reproduced in every instance, unless otherwise stated, is the manuscript in Jane Austen's hand.

## Lady Susan

*MS. MA 1226, Morgan Library & Museum, New York*

The untitled manuscript, known as *Lady Susan*, from the name of its chief character, Lady Susan Vernon, is a neat fair-copy in Jane Austen's own hand, with little sign of rewriting, made no earlier than 1805 (the date of the paper). Written in letters, it is the only complete manuscript of a novel by Austen known to survive and was first published in 1871, apparently from a further non-authorial copy (since untraced), when James Edward Austen-Leigh appended it with other fragments to the second edition of his *Memoir of Jane Austen*. At this stage it was publicly given the title *Lady Susan*, though it may already have been known by that name within the family. *Lady Susan* was subsequently reprinted in various collected editions of Austen's Works: the Winchester edition (1898) and the Adelphi edition (1923). In 1925, R. W. Chapman edited the manuscript, from the original. Garland Publishing, New York, issued a photo-facsimile of the manuscript, together with Chapman's 1925 print edition, in 1989.[4]

In the division of Jane Austen's surviving manuscripts at her sister Cassandra's death in 1845, *Lady Susan* passed to her niece Fanny Knight, by this time Lady Knatchbull (1793–1882), who also inherited the bulk of Jane Austen's letters to Cassandra. They passed to her son, Edward Knatchbull-Hugessen, Lord Brabourne (1829–93). Brabourne was quick to turn his Austen inheritance to commercial advantage, editing *Letters of Jane Austen*, 2 vols (1884) and sending manuscripts to the auction rooms. After several sales, *Lady Susan* arrived in 1947 at the Morgan Library, New York, where it remains.

Though rebound in the 1890s into a splendid orange morocco album tooled in gold, *Lady Susan*'s original binding can be conjectured from the internal evidence of its gatherings. They show Austen copying into the same kind of quarto notebook as those she used for her three volumes of teenage writings, a form of preservation that may signal there was no intention to print. In 2009 Morgan conservators

---

[4] *Lady Susan* [ed. R. W. Chapman] (Oxford: Clarendon Press, 1925); *Jane Austen's Lady Susan*, with a preface by A. Walton Litz (New York: Garland Publishing, Inc., 1989). The descriptions of the three fiction manuscripts offered here derive from the headnotes attached to each manuscript transcription in *Jane Austen's Fiction Manuscripts*, ed. Sutherland, 5 vols.

removed *Lady Susan* from its late nineteenth-century binding. The manuscript now presents as a series of single leaves, housed in a folder and cloth box.

## The Watsons

*MS. MA 1034, Morgan Library & Museum, New York; MS. Eng. e. 3764, Bodleian Library, Oxford*

The untitled, unfinished, and undated manuscript in Jane Austen's hand is now divided into two parts and is her only known work of fiction surviving in manuscript to have suffered physical separation in this way. Unlike the fair-copy manuscript of *Lady Susan*, this is a draft or working manuscript filled with signs of the struggles of composition. Approximately 17,500 words long, it reads like a substantial beginning to a novel and was given the descriptive title *The Watsons* by Austen-Leigh, 'for the sake of having a title by which to designate it', when he first presented it to the public in the expanded second edition of his *Memoir of Jane Austen* in 1871. According to Austen-Leigh, who was working from family information, it is 'probable, that it was composed at Bath, before she ceased to reside there in 1805'.[5]

Of the two parts, the smaller portion (twelve pages) is held in the Morgan Library, New York; the larger portion (sixty-eight pages) is in the Bodleian Library, Oxford. Both portions are written onto sheets of paper watermarked 1803, folded to form homemade booklets of four to eight pages in length. The manuscript breaks off, unfinished, on the first leaf of booklet 11. There are three loose pieces of paper, previously attached as patches in booklets 7, 9, and 10.

Of all Austen's manuscripts, this is the most challenging to decipher. Its pages are tightly packed with writing, deletions, and revision, interspersed with occasional passages of heavy interlinear correction. There is no pagination, no clear or regular paragraphing, and no separation of speaking parts one from another. (Over a third of *The Watsons* is cast in direct speech.) The manuscript is without chapter divisions, though not without informal division by wider spacing and ruled lines. These rules divide it into three unequal

---

[5] *Memoir* (1871), 295. Austen lived in Bath from May 1801 and did not finally leave until July 1806.

portions, too long for chapter divisions, and represented in the text here as short rules at pp. 88 and 100.

The manuscript descended from Cassandra Austen to her niece Caroline Mary Craven Austen (1805–80), the younger daughter of their eldest brother James. It was in Caroline's possession when first published in 1871 by her brother Austen Leigh. It passed to Caroline Austen's nephew, William Austen-Leigh (1843–1921), and he presented the first six leaves to a 1915 charity sale in aid of the Red Cross Society. In 1925 these six leaves were purchased for the Morgan Library, where they remain. The larger portion of the manuscript was in Austen-Leigh family ownership (though much of the time on deposit in the British Museum) until 1978. Its adventures thereafter include a ten-year sojourn in the British Rail Pension Fund portfolio, followed by private ownership, before its purchase for the nation in 2011 by the Bodleian Library, Oxford.

In 1850, Catherine Hubback (1818–77), daughter of Jane Austen's brother Francis, published a three-decker novel, *The Younger Sister*, the opening five chapters of which are based closely on her aunt's fragment. R. W. Chapman's transcription of the manuscript appeared in 1927. In the following year, 1928, Catherine Hubback's granddaughter Edith Brown published a completion grafted onto a verbatim transcription of the original, paragraphed and punctuated in modern style.[6]

## Sanditon

*No accession number, King's College Cambridge*

The untitled manuscript, written throughout in Jane Austen's hand, is the unfinished draft of a substantial and evolving work of fiction. It is contained in three small gatherings of ordinary writing paper, folded and cut down to form three fat homemade booklets. In total, there are 120 written pages, about 24,000 words, divided into twelve chapters, and perhaps one-fifth of a completed novel. This is a working draft: long passages of smooth flowing, uncorrected or minimally

[6] Mrs [Catherine] Hubback, *The Younger Sister. A Novel*, 3 vols (London: Thomas Cautley Newby, 1850); *The Watsons: A Fragment* [ed. R. W. Chapman] (Oxford: Clarendon Press, 1927); Edith and Francis Brown, *The Watsons* (London: Elkin Mathews and Marrot Ltd, 1928).

corrected text are interspersed with more densely worked and reworked sections. From dates attached to sections of the draft, it was written between 27 January and 18 March 1817.

Austen-Leigh provided a highly selective précis and quotations from the manuscript, under the title 'The Last Work', in the second edition of his *Memoir of Jane Austen*, and R. W. Chapman published the first complete transcription under the title *Fragment of a Novel* in 1925. Yet 'Sanditon' seems to have been an unofficial title used within the Austen family at least from the mid-nineteenth century.[7]

The manuscript passed from Cassandra Austen to her niece Anna Lefroy (1793–1872) and thence to Mary Isabella Lefroy (1860–1939), Anna Lefroy's granddaughter and Jane Austen's great-great-niece. She presented it to King's College Cambridge, in October 1930, where it remains. A copy made by Cassandra Austen had a different descent through Jane's brother Frank's family to Janet Austen, later Sanders. It was from her father that Mrs Sanders got the information, which she communicated to Chapman in February 1925 after the publication of his transcription, that Austen's intended title for the novel was 'The Brothers'.[8] Cassandra Austen's copy of the manuscript, also untitled, is now in Jane Austen's House, Chawton, Hampshire.

## Opinions of Mansfield Park

*Add. MSS 41253A, f.5–f.8, British Library, London.*
Mansfield Park *was published in May 1814.*

*Opinions of Mansfield Park* is written onto two half-sheets of writing paper folded to form a booklet of eight pages, the last three pages being blank.

First referenced in *Memoir* (1870), 192; R. W. Chapman prepared a transcription and facsimile edition of several short manuscripts, including the two sets of *Opinions*, in 1926 (see under *Plan of a Novel*).

Printed here from Jane Austen's manuscript.

---

[7] *Fragment of A Novel written by Jane Austen January–March 1817* [ed. R. W. Chapman] (Oxford: Clarendon Press, 1925); Anna Lefroy refers to the work as 'Sanditon' in a family letter of 1869 (see *Memoir*, ed. Sutherland, 184).

[8] In a letter of 8 February 1925, now housed with the *Sanditon* manuscript; Janet Sanders, 'Sanditon', *Times Literary Supplement*, 19 February 1925, 120.

## Opinions of Emma

*Add. MSS 41253A, f.9–f.10, British Library, London.*
Emma *was published in late December 1815 (dated 1816 on the title page).*

*Opinions of Emma* is written in a single two leaves folded into a booklet of four pages. Evidence of distinctions in paper stocks and the layout of the items in the two collections of *Opinions* point to different transcription dates for each set.

First referenced in *Memoir* (1870), 192; a version of *Opinions of E* only appeared in *Life & Letters*, 328–31.

Printed here from Jane Austen's manuscript.

## Plan of a Novel

*MS. MA 1034.1, Morgan Library & Museum, New York.*

The *Plan* dates from the period of Jane Austen's correspondence with James Stanier Clarke, domestic chaplain and librarian to the Prince Regent; that is, between November 1815 and April 1816. The manuscript, titled in the author's hand '*Plan of a Novel, according to hints from various quarters*', consists of a single piece of paper folded to produce four pages. The paper may be from the same stock as that used in *Opinions of Emma*.

The *Plan* was first printed, in selected form, in *Memoir* (1870), 161–5. It was subsequently published in *Life & Letters*, 338–40; and in [R. W. Chapman, ed.], *Plan of a Novel according to hints from various quarters, by Jane Austen; with opinions on Mansfield Park and Emma* (Oxford: Clarendon Press, 1926).

Printed here from Jane Austen's manuscript.

## Verses

Information about the verse texts appears in the Textual Notes, pp. 240–7.

# SELECT BIBLIOGRAPHY

## Editions

*Fragment of A Novel written by Jane Austen January–March 1817* [*Sanditon*], ed. R. W. Chapman (Oxford: Clarendon Press, 1925).

*Lady Susan*, ed. R. W. Chapman (Oxford: Clarendon Press, 1925).

*The Watsons: A Fragment*, ed. R. W. Chapman (Oxford: Clarendon Press, 1927).

*Minor Works*, vol. vi of *The Works of Jane Austen*, ed. R. W. Chapman (1954); rev. B. C. Southam (Oxford: Oxford University Press, 1969).

*Lady Susan, The Watsons, Sanditon*, ed. Margaret Drabble (Harmondsworth: Penguin, 1974).

*Jane Austen's Lady Susan*, with a preface by A. Walton Litz (New York: Garland Publishing, Inc., 1989).

Jane Austen, *Collected Poems and Verse of the Austen Family*, ed. David Selwyn (Manchester: Carcanet Press, 1996).

*Later Manuscripts*, ed. Janet Todd and Linda Bree, *The Cambridge Edition of the Works of Jane Austen* (Cambridge: Cambridge University Press, 2008).

*Jane Austen's Fiction Manuscripts: A Digital Edition*, ed. Kathryn Sutherland (2010), http://www.janeausten.ac.uk (an open access resource containing full photographic images with transcriptions, descriptions, and provenance details for all Austen's fiction manuscripts); her handwritten manuscripts of *Lady Susan*, *The Watsons*, and *Sanditon* can be read here.

*Jane Austen's Fiction Manuscripts*, ed. Kathryn Sutherland, 5 vols (Oxford: Oxford University Press, 2018).

## Textual Studies

Marshall, Mary Gaither, 'Jane Austen's Manuscripts of the Juvenilia and *Lady Susan*: A History and Description', in J. David Grey (ed.), *Jane Austen's Beginnings: The Juvenilia and Lady Susan* (Ann Arbor: University of Michigan Research Press, 1989), 107–21.

Southam, Brian, *Jane Austen's Literary Manuscripts: A Study of the Novelist's Development through the Surviving Papers* (1964; rev. edn, London: Althone Press, 2001).

Southam, Brian, *Jane Austen: A Students' Guide to the Later Manuscript Works* (London: Concord Books, 2007).

Sutherland, Kathryn, *Jane Austen's Textual Lives: From Aeschylus to Bollywood* (Oxford: Oxford University Press, 2005).

## Biography

*Jane Austen's Letters*, ed. Deirdre Le Faye (4th edn, Oxford: Oxford University Press, 2011).

Austen-Leigh, James Edward, *A Memoir of Jane Austen and Other Family Recollections*, ed. Kathryn Sutherland (Oxford World's Classics; Oxford: Oxford University Press, 2002).

Byrne, Paula, *The Real Jane Austen: A Life in Small Things* (London: HarperPress, 2013).

Clery, E. J., *Jane Austen, The Banker's Sister* (London: Biteback Publishing, 2017).

Fergus, Jan, *Jane Austen: A Literary Life* (Basingstoke: Macmillan, 1991).

Le Faye, Deirdre, *Jane Austen: A Family Record* (2nd edn, Cambridge: Cambridge University Press, 2004).

Nokes, David, *Jane Austen. A Life* (London: Fourth Estate, 1997).

Tomalin, Claire, *Jane Austen: A Life* (Harmondsworth: Viking, 1997).

## Criticism

Gilson, David J., and Grey, J. David, 'Jane Austen's Juvenilia and *Lady Susan*: An Annotated Bibliography', in J. David Grey (ed.), *Jane Austen's Beginnings: The Juvenilia and Lady Susan* (Ann Arbor. University of Michigan Research Press, 1989), 243–62.

Roth, Barry, *An Annotated Bibliography of Jane Austen Studies, 1952–1972* (Charlottesville: University Press of Virginia, 1973) (further volumes cover 1973–83, 1984–94).

The survey of early criticism is supplemented by later online resources, such as *Persuasions On Line*, which since vol. 22 (Winter 2001) provides regularly updated bibliographies (http://www.jasna.org/index.html).

*Persuasions Online*, 38/2 (Spring 2018), the whole issue is dedicated to essays containing recent research on and critical readings of *Sanditon* (http://www.jasna.org/persuasions/on-line/index.html).

Baugh, Victoria, 'Mixed-Race Heiresses in Early Nineteenth-Century Literature: *Sanditon*'s Miss Lambe in Context', *European Romantic Review*, 29 (2018), 449–58.

Bray, Joe, *The Language of Jane Austen* (London: Palgrave Macmillan, 2018).

Darcy, Jane, 'Jane Austen's *Sanditon*, Doctors, and the Rise of Seabathing', *Persuasions Online*, 38/2 (Spring 2018).

Fergus, Jan, and Steele, Elizabeth, ' "There is a great deal in Novelty": The Pleasures of *The Watsons*', *Persuasions*, 32 (2010), 210–23.

Friedman, Emily C., 'Austen Among the Fragments: Understanding the Fate of *Sanditon* (1817)', *Women's Writing*, 20 (2013), 115–29.

Gard, Roger, '*Lady Susan* and the Singular Effect', *Essays in Criticism*, 39 (1989), 305–25.

Harris, Jocelyn, *Satire, Celebrity, and Politics in Jane Austen* (Lewisburg, PA: Bucknell University Press, 2017).

James-Cavan, Kathleen, 'Closure and Disclosure: The Significance of Conversation in Jane Austen's "The Watsons"', *Studies in the Novel*, 29 (1997), 437–52.

Jordan, Elaine, 'Jane Austen Goes to the Seaside: *Sanditon*, English Identity, and the "West Indian" Schoolgirl', in You-Me Park and Rajeswari Sunder Rajan (eds), *The Postcolonial Jane Austen* (London: Routledge, 2000), 29–55.

Miller, D. A., *Jane Austen, or The Secret of Style* (Princeton: Princeton University Press, 2003).

Mulvihill, James, '*Lady Susan*: Jane Austen's Machiavellian Moment', *Studies in Romanticism*, 50 (2011), 619–37.

Pickrel, Paul, '"The Watsons" and the Other Jane Austen', *English Literary History*, 55 (1988), 443–67.

Sabor, Peter, and James-Cavan, Kathleen, 'Anna Lefroy's Continuation of *Sanditon*: Point and Counterpoint', *Persuasions*, 19 (1997), 229–43.

Sutherland, Kathryn, 'Jane Austen: Fragment Artist', *Essays in Criticism*, 68 (2018), 190–210.

Tandon, Bharat, *Jane Austen and the Morality of Conversation* (London: Anthem Press, 2003).

Tanner, Tony, *Jane Austen* (Basingstoke: Macmillan, 1986).

Tuite, Clara, *Romantic Austen: Sexual Politics and the Literary Canon* (Cambridge: Cambridge University Press, 2002).

Tuite, Clara, '*Sanditon*: Austen's Pre-Post Waterloo', *Textual Practice*, 26 (2012), 609–29.

Wiesenfarth, Joseph, '*The Watsons* as Pretext', *Persuasions*, 8 (1986), 101–11.

Wiltshire, *Jane Austen and The Body* (Cambridge: Cambridge University Press, 1992).

Woolf, Virginia, 'Jane Austen', *The Common Reader* (1st ser., London: Hogarth Press, 1925).

## Continuations

FAMILY

Brown, Edith and Francis, *The Watsons* (London: Elkin Mathews and Marrot Ltd, 1928).

Hubback, Mrs [Catherine], *The Younger Sister: A Novel*, 3 vols (London: Thomas Cautley Newby, 1850).

Lefroy, Anna, *Jane Austen's Sanditon: A Continuation by Her Niece*, ed. Mary Gaither Marshall (Chicago: Chiron Press, 1983).

OTHER: GENERAL

Marshall, Mary Gaither, 'Jane Austen's *Sanditon*: Inspiring Continuations, Adaptations, and Spin-Offs for 200 Years', *Persuasions Online*, 38/1 (Winter 2017) offers the most comprehensive listing (http://www. jasna.org/persuasions/on-line/index.html).

Wright, Andrew, 'Jane Austen Adapted', *Nineteenth-Century Fiction*, 30 (1975), 421–33 (including adaptations, completions, and dramatizations of the unfinished fictions, up to 1974).

OTHER: SPECIFIC

Austen, Jane, and Another Lady, *Sanditon* (novel; London: Peter Davies, 1975).

Bushman, Jay, and Dunlap, Margaret, *Welcome to Sanditon* (interactive multiplatform website; Pemberley Digital Production, 2013– ; http:// www.pemberleydigital.com/welcome-to-sanditon).

Cobbett, Alice, *Somehow Lengthened* (novel; London: Ernest Benn, Ltd, 1932).

Stillman, Whit, *Love and Friendship* (screenplay and film based on *Lady Susan*; 2016).

Todd, Janet, *Lady Susan Plays the Game* (novel; London: Bloomsbury, 2013).

Wade, Laura, *The Watsons* (stage play; London: Oberon Books, 2018).

# A CHRONOLOGY OF JANE AUSTEN

| | *Life* | *Historical and Cultural Background* |
|---|---|---|
| 1775 | (16 Dec.) born in Steventon, Hampshire, seventh child of Revd George Austen (1731–1805), Rector of Steventon and Deane, and Cassandra Austen, née Leigh (1739–1827) | American War of Independence begins. |
| 1776 | | American Declaration of Independence; James Cook's third Pacific voyage. |
| 1778 | | France enters war on side of American revolutionaries. Frances Burney, *Evelina* |
| 1779 | Birth of youngest brother, Charles (1779–1852); eldest brother, James (1765–1819), goes to St John's College, Oxford; distant cousin Thomas Knight II and wife, Catherine, of Godmersham in Kent, visit Steventon and take close interest in brother Edward (1767–1852) | Britain at war with Spain; siege of Gibraltar (to 1783); Samuel Crompton's spinning mule revolutionizes textile production. |
| 1781 | Cousin Eliza Hancock (thought by some to be natural daughter of Warren Hastings) marries Jean-François Capot de Feuillide in France | Warren Hastings deposes Raja of Benares and seizes treasure from Nabob of Oudh. |
| 1782 | Austens put on first amateur theatricals at Steventon | Frances Burney, *Cecilia*; William Gilpin, *Observations on the River Wye*; William Cowper, *Poems* |
| 1783 | JA, sister Cassandra (1773–1845), and cousin Jane Cooper are tutored by Mrs Cawley in Oxford then Southampton until they fall ill with typhoid fever; death of aunt Jane Cooper from typhoid; brother Edward formally adopted by the Knights; JA's mentor, Anne Lefroy, moves into neighbourhood | American independence conceded at Peace of Versailles; Pitt becomes Prime Minister. |

|  | Life | Historical and Cultural Background |
|---|---|---|
| 1784 | Performance of Sheridan's *The Rivals* at Steventon | India Act imposes some parliamentary control on East India Company; Prince Regent begins to build Brighton Pavilion; death of Samuel Johnson. |
| 1785 | Attends Abbey House School, Reading, with Cassandra | William Cowper, *The Task* |
| 1786 | Brother Francis (1774–1865) enters Royal Naval Academy, Portsmouth; brother Edward on Grand Tour (to 1790); JA and Cassandra leave school for good | William Gilpin, *Observations, Relative Chiefly to Picturesque Beauty . . . particularly the Mountains, and Lakes of Cumberland, and Westmoreland* |
| 1787 | Starts writing stories collected in three notebooks (to 1793); cousin Eliza de Feuillide visits Steventon; performance of Susannah Centlivre's *The Wonder* at Steventon | American constitution signed. |
| 1788 | JA and Cassandra taken on a trip to Kent and London; *The Chances* and *Tom Thumb* performed at Steventon; brother Henry (1771–1850) goes to St John's College, Oxford; brother Francis sails to East Indies on HMS *Perseverance*; cousins Eliza de Feuillide and Philadelphia Walter attend Hastings's trial | Warren Hastings impeached for corruption in India; George III's first spell of madness. |
| 1789 | James and Henry in Oxford produce periodical, *The Loiterer* (to Mar. 1790); JA begins lifelong friendship with Martha Lloyd and sister Mary when their mother rents Deane Parsonage | Fall of the Bastille marks beginning of French Revolution. |
| 1790 | (June) completes 'Love and Friendship' | Edmund Burke, *Reflections on the Revolution in France*; [Mary Wollstonecraft], *Vindication of the Rights of Men* |
| 1791 | Brother Charles enters Royal Naval Academy, Portsmouth; (Nov.) completes 'The History of England'; Edward marries Elizabeth Bridges and they live at Rowling, Kent | Parliament rejects bill to abolish slave trade. James Boswell, *Life of Johnson*; Ann Radcliffe, *The Romance of the Forest* |

| *Life* | *Historical and Cultural Background* |
|---|---|
| 1792 | Writes 'Lesley-Castle' and 'Evelyn', and begins 'Kitty, or the Bower'; Lloyds leave Deane to make way for James and first wife, Anne Mathew; cousin Jane Cooper marries Capt. Thomas Williams, RN; sister Cassandra engaged to Revd Tom Fowle | France declared a republic; Warren Hastings acquitted. Mary Wollstonecraft; *Vindication of the Rights of Woman*; Clara Reeve, *Plans of Education* |
| 1793 | Birth of eldest nieces, Fanny and Anna, daughters of brothers Edward and James; writes last of entries in the teenage notebooks; brother Henry joins Oxford Militia | Execution of Louis XVI of France and Marie Antoinette: revolutionary 'Terror' in Paris; Britain declares war on France. |
| 1794 | Probably working on *Lady Susan*; cousin Eliza de Feuillide's husband guillotined in Paris | Suspension of Habeas Corpus; 'Treason Trials' of radicals abandoned by government when juries refuse to convict; failure of harvests keeps food prices high. Uvedale Price, *Essays on the Picturesque*; Ann Radcliffe, *The Mysteries of Udolpho* |
| 1795 | Writes 'Elinor and Marianne' (first draft of *Sense and Sensibility*); death of James's wife; JA flirts with Tom Lefroy, as recorded in first surviving letter | George III's coach stoned; Pitt's 'Two Acts' enforce repression of radical dissent. |
| 1796 | Visits Edward at Rowling; (Oct.) begins 'First Impressions'; subscribes to Frances Burney's *Camilla* | Frances Burney, *Camilla*; Regina Maria Roche, *Children of the Abbey*; Jane West, *A Gossip's Story* |
| 1797 | Marriage of James to Mary Lloyd; (Aug.) completes 'First Impressions'; Cassandra's fiancé dies of fever off Santo Domingo; begins revision of 'Elinor and Marianne' into *Sense and Sensibility*; George Austen offers 'First Impressions' to publisher Cadell without success; Catherine Knight gives Edward possession of Godmersham; marriage of Henry and Eliza de Feuillide | Napoleon becomes commander of French army; failure of French attempt to invade by landing in Wales; mutinies in British Navy, leaders hanged. Ann Radcliffe, *The Italian* |

| | Life | Historical and Cultural Background |
|---|---|---|
| 1798 | Starts to write 'Susan' (later *Northanger Abbey*); visits Godmersham; death in driving accident of cousin Lady Williams (Jane Cooper) | Irish Rebellion; defeat of French fleet at Battle of the Nile; French army lands in Ireland; further suspension of Habeas Corpus. Elizabeth Inchbald, *Lovers' Vows* (adaptation of play by Kotzebue. |
| 1799 | Visit to Bath; probably finishes 'Susan'; aunt, Mrs Leigh-Perrot, charged with theft and imprisoned in Ilchester Gaol | Napoleon becomes consul in France. Hannah More, *Strictures on the Modern System of Female Education*; Jane West, *A Tale of the Times* |
| 1800 | Stays with Martha Lloyd at Ibthorpe; trial and acquittal of Mrs Leigh-Perrot | French conquer Italy; British capture Malta; food riots; first iron-frame printing press; copyright law extended to Ireland. Elizabeth Hamilton, *Memoirs of Modern Philosophers* |
| 1801 | Austens move to Bath on George Austen's retirement; James and family move into Stevenson Rectory; first of series of holidays in West Country (to 1804), during one of which thought to have had brief romantic involvement with a man who later died; Henry resigns from Oxford Militia and becomes banker and Army agent in London | Slave rebellion in Santo Domingo led by Toussaint L'Ouverture; Nelson defeats Danes at Battle of Copenhagen; Act of Union joins Britain and Ireland. Maria Edgeworth, *Belinda* |
| 1802 | Visits Godmersham; accepts, then the following morning refuses, proposal of marriage from Harris Bigg-Wither; revises 'Susan' | L'Ouverture's slave rebellion crushed by French; Peace of Amiens with France; founding of William Cobbett's *Political Register* |
| 1803 | With brother Henry's help, 'Susan' sold to publishers Crosby & Co. for £10 | Resumption of war with France. |
| 1804 | Starts writing *The Watsons*; (Dec.) death of Anne Lefroy in riding accident | |
| 1805 | (Jan.) death of George Austen; stops working on *The Watsons* | Battle of Trafalgar. Walter Scott, *The Lay of the Last Minstrel* |

| | Life | Historical and Cultural Background |
|---|---|---|
| 1806 | Austens leave Bath; visit relations at Adlestrop and Stoneleigh; Martha Lloyd becomes member of Austen household after death of her mother; brother Francis marries Mary Gibson; JA, Cassandra, and Mrs Austen take lodgings with them in Southampton | French blockade of continental ports against British shipping; first steam-powered textile mill opens in Manchester. Lady Morgan, *The Wild Irish Girl* |
| 1807 | Brother Charles marries Fanny Palmer in Bermuda | France invades Portugal; slave-trading by British ships outlawed. George Crabbe, *Poems* |
| 1808 | JA visits Godmersham; death of Edward's wife Elizabeth after giving birth to eleventh child | France invades Spain; beginning of Peninsular War. Debrett, *Baronetage* (*Peerage* first published 1802); Hannah More, *Coelebs in Search of a Wife*; Walter Scott, *Marmion* |
| 1809 | (Apr.) attempts unsuccessfully to make Crosby publish 'Susan', writing under pseudonym 'Mrs Ashton Dennis' ('M.A.D.'); visits Godmersham; (July) moves, with Cassandra, Martha, and Mrs Austen, to house owned by Edward at Chawton, Hampshire | British capture Martinique and Cayenne from France. |
| 1810 | Publisher Egerton accepts *Sense and Sensibility* | British capture Guadeloupe, last French West Indian colony; riots in London in support of parliamentary reform. Walter Scott, *The Lady of the Lake* |
| 1811 | (Feb.) begins *Mansfield Park*; stays with Henry and Eliza in London to correct proofs of *Sense and Sensibility*; (Oct.) *Sense and Sensibility*, 'by a Lady', published on commission; revises 'First Impressions' into *Pride and Prejudice* | Prince of Wales becomes Regent; Ludditte anti-machine riots in North and Midlands. Mary Brunton, *Self-Control* |
| 1812 | Copyright of *Pride and Prejudice* sold to Egerton for £110; Edward's family take name of Knight at death of Catherine Knight | United States declare war on Britain; French retreat from Moscow; Lord Liverpool becomes Prime Minister after assassination of Spencer Perceval. |

|  | Life | Historical and Cultural Background |
|---|---|---|
| 1813 | (Jan.) *Pride and Prejudice* published to great acclaim; JA stays in London to nurse Eliza; death of Eliza; in letter, expresses her hatred for Prince Regent; (June) finishes *Mansfield Park*; second editions of *Sense and Sensibility* and *Pride and Prejudice* | British invasion of France after Wellington's success at Battle of Vittoria. Byron, *The Giaour, The Bride of Abydos*; Robert Southey, *Life of Nelson* |
| 1814 | (21 Jan.) begins *Emma*; (Mar. and Nov.) visits brother Henry in London, sees Kean play Shylock; (May) Egerton publishes *Mansfield Park* on commission, sold out in six months; death of Fanny Palmer Austen, brother Charles's wife, after childbirth; marriage of niece Anna Austen to Ben Lefroy | Napoleon defeated and exiled to Elba; George Stevenson builds first steam locomotive; Edmund Kean's first appearance at Drury Lane. Mary Brunton, *Discipline*; Frances Burney, *The Wanderer*; Byron, *The Corsair*; Maria Edgeworth, *Patronage*; Walter Scott, *Waverley* |
| 1815 | (29 Mar.) completes *Emma*; (Aug.) begins *Persuasion*; invited to dedicate *Emma* to the Prince Regent; visits Henry in London; (Dec.) *Emma* published by Murray | Napoleon escapes; finally defeated at Battle of Waterloo and exiled to St Helena; Humphry Davy invents miners' safety lamp. |
| 1816 | 'Susan' bought back from Crosby and revised as 'Catherine'; failure of Henry's bank; second edition of *Mansfield Park*; (Aug.) JA completes *Persuasion*; health beginning to fail | Post-war slump inaugurates years of popular agitation for political and social reform. |
| 1817 | (Jan.–Mar.) works on *Sanditon*; (Apr.) makes her Will; moves, with Cassandra, to Winchester, to be closer to skilled medical care; (15 July) composes last poem 'When Winchester Races'; (18 July, 4.30 a.m.) dies in Winchester; buried in Winchester Cathedral; (Dec.) publication (dated 1818) of *Northanger Abbey* and *Persuasion*, together with brother Henry's 'Biographical Notice' | Attacks on Prince Regent at opening of Parliament; death of his only legitimate child, Princess Charlotte. |

# LADY SUSAN

# LADY SUSAN

## LETTER 1

*Lady Susan Vernon to Mr Vernon.*

LANGFORD, December

My dear Brother*

I can no longer refuse myself the pleasure of profitting by your kind invitation when we last parted, of spending some weeks with you at Churchill, & therefore if quite convenient to you & Mrs Vernon to receive me at present, I shall hope within a few days to be introduced to a Sister, whom I have so long desired to be acquainted with.—My kind friends here are most affectionately urgent with me to prolong my stay, but their hospitable & chearful dispositions lead them too much into society for my present situation & state of mind; & I impatiently look forward to the hour when I shall be admitted into your delightful retirement. I long to be made known to your dear little Children, in whose hearts I shall be very eager to secure an interest.—I shall soon have occasion for all my fortitude, as I am on the point of separation from my own daughter.—The long illness of her dear Father prevented my paying her that attention which Duty & affection equally dictated, & I have but too much reason to fear that the Governess to whose care I consigned her, was unequal to the charge.—I have therefore resolved on placing her at one of the best Private Schools in Town,* where I shall have an opportunity of leaving her myself, in my way to you. I am determined you see, not to be denied admittance at Churchill.—It would indeed give me most painful sensations to know that it were not in your power to receive me.—Yr most obliged & affec: Sister

S. Vernon.*—

## LETTER 2

*Lady Susan to Mrs Johnson.*

LANGFORD

You were mistaken my dear Alicia, in supposing me fixed at this place for the rest of the winter. It greives me to say how greatly you were mistaken, for I have seldom spent three months more agreably than those which have just flown away.—At present nothing goes smoothly.—The Females of the Family are united against me.—You foretold how it would be, when I first came to Langford; & Manwaring is so uncommonly pleasing that I was not without apprehensions myself. I remember saying to myself as I drove to the House, 'I like this Man; pray Heaven no harm come of it!'—But I was determined to be discreet, to bear in mind my being only four months a widow,* & to be as quiet as possible,—and I have been so;—My dear Creature, I have admitted no one's attentions but Manwaring's, I have avoided all general flirtation whatever, I have distinguished no Creature besides of all the Numbers resorting hither, except Sir James Martin, on whom I bestowed a little notice in order to detach him from Miss Manwaring. But if the World could know my motive *there*, they would honour me.—I have been called an unkind Mother, but it was the sacred impulse of maternal affection, it was the advantage of my Daughter that led me on; & if that Daughter were not the greatest simpleton on Earth, I might have been rewarded for my Exertions as I ought.—Sir James did make proposals to me for Frederica—but Frederica, who was born to be the torment of my life, chose to set herself so violently against the match, that I thought it better to lay aside the scheme for the present.—I have more than once repented that I did not marry him myself, & were he but one degree less contemptibly weak I certainly should, but I must own myself rather romantic* in that respect, & that Riches only, will not satisfy me. The event of all this is very provoking.—Sir James is gone, Maria highly incensed, & Mrs Manwaring insupportably jealous;—so jealous in short, & so enraged against me, that in the fury of her temper I should not be surprised at her appealing to her Guardian if she had the liberty of addressing him—but there your Husband stands my friend, & the kindest, most amiable action of his Life was his throwing her off forever on her Marriage.—Keep up his resentment therefore I charge you.—We are now in a sad state; no house was ever more altered; the whole family are at war, & Manwaring scarcely dares speak to me. It is time for me to be gone; I have therefore determined on leaving them, & shall spend I hope a comfortable day with you in Town within this week.—If I am as little in favour with Mr Johnson as ever, you must come to me at No. 10 Wigmore St.* but I hope this may not be the case, for as Mr Johnson with all his faults is a Man to whom that great word 'Respectable' is always given, & I am known to be so intimate with his wife, his slighting me has an awkward Look.—I take Town in my way to that insupportable spot, a Country Village, for I am really going to Churchill.—Forgive me my dear friend, it is my last resource. Were there another place in England open to me, I would prefer it.—Charles Vernon is my aversion, & I am afraid of his Wife.—At Churchill however I must remain till I have something better in veiw. My young Lady accompanies me to Town, where I shall deposit her under the care of Miss Summers in Wigmore Street, till she becomes a little more reasonable. She will make good connections there, as the Girls are all of the best Families.—The price is immense, & much beyond what I can ever attempt to pay.—Adeiu. I will send you a line, as soon as I arrive in Town.—Yours Ever,

S. Vernon.

# LETTER 3

*Mrs Vernon to Lady De Courcy.*

CHURCHILL

My dear Mother

I am very sorry to tell you that it will not be in our power to keep our promise of spending the Christmas with you; & we are prevented that happiness by a circumstance which is not likely to make us any amends.—Lady Susan in a letter to her Brother, has declared her intention of visiting us almost immediately—& as such a visit is in all probability merely an affair of convenience, it is impossible to conjecture it's length. I was by no means prepared for such an event, nor can I now account for her Ladyship's conduct.—Langford appeared so exactly the place for her in every respect, as well from the elegant &

expensive stile of Living there, as from her particular attachment to Mrs Manwaring, that I was very far from expecting so speedy a distinction, tho' I always imagined from her increasing friendship for us since her Husband's death, that we should at some future period be obliged to receive her.—Mr Vernon I think was a great deal too kind to her, when he was in Staffordshire.* Her behaviour to him, independant of her general Character, has been so inexcusably artful & ungenerous since our marriage was first in agitation,* that no one less amiable & mild than himself could have overlooked it at all; & tho' as his Brother's widow & in narrow circumstances it was proper to render her pecuniary assistance, I cannot help thinking his pressing invitation to her to visit us at Churchill perfectly unnecessary.—Disposed however as he always is to think the best of every one, her display of Greif, & professions of regret, & general resolutions of prudence were sufficient to soften his heart, & make him really confide in her sincerity. But as for myself, I am still unconvinced; & plausibly as her Ladyship has now written, I cannot make up my mind, till I better understand her real meaning in coming to us.—You may guess therefore my dear Madam with what feelings I look forward to her arrival. She will have occasion for all those attractive Powers for which she is celebrated, to gain any share of my regard; & I shall certainly endeavour to guard myself against their influence, if not accompanied by something more substantial.—She expresses a most eager desire of being acquainted with me, & makes very gracious mention of my children, but I am not quite weak enough to suppose a woman who has behaved with inattention if not unkindness to her own child, should be attached to any of mine. Miss Vernon is to be placed at a school in Town before her Mother comes to us, which I am glad of, for her sake & my own. It must be to her advantage to be separated from her Mother; & a girl of sixteen who has received so wretched an education would not be a very desirable companion here.—Reginald has long wished I know to see this captivating Lady Susan, & we shall depend on his joining our party soon.—I am glad to hear that my Father continues so well, & am, with best Love &c,

Cath Vernon.—

## LETTER 4

*Mr De Courcy to Mrs Vernon.*

My dear Sister

I congratulate you & Mr Vernon on being about to receive into your family, the most accomplished Coquette* in England.—As a very distinguished Flirt, I have been always taught to consider her; but it has lately fallen in my way to hear some particulars of her conduct at Langford, which prove that she does not confine herself to that sort of honest flirtation which satisfies most people, but aspires to the more delicious gratification of making a whole family miserable.—By her behaviour to Mr Manwaring, she gave jealousy & wretchedness to his wife, & by her attentions to a young Man previously attached to Mr Manwaring's sister, deprived an amiable girl of her Lover.— I learnt all this from a Mr Smith now in this neighbourhood— (I have dined with him at Hurst & Welford)—who is just come from Langford, where he was a fortnight in the house with her Ladyship, & who is therefore well qualified to make the communication.—What a Woman she must be!—I long to see her, & shall certainly accept your kind invitation, that I may form some idea of those bewitching powers which can do so much—engaging at the same time & in the same house the affections of two Men who were neither of them at liberty to bestow them—& all this, without the charm of youth.—I am glad to find that Miss Vernon does not come with her Mother to Churchill, as she has not even manners to recommend her, & according to Mr Smith's account, is equally dull & proud. Where Pride & Stupidity* unite, there can be no dissimulation worthy notice, & Miss Vernon shall be consigned to unrelenting contempt; but by all that I can gather, Lady Susan possesses a degree of captivating Deceit which it must be pleasing to witness & detect. I shall be with you very soon, & am your affec. Brother

R. De Courcy.—

## LETTER 5

*Lady Susan to Mrs Johnson.*

CHURCHILL

I received your note my dear Alicia, just before I left Town, & rejoice to be assured that Mr Johnson suspected nothing of your engagement the evening before; it is undoubtedly better to deceive him entirely;—since he will be stubborn, he must be tricked.— I arrived here in safety, & have no reason to complain of my reception from Mr Vernon; but I confess myself not equally satisfied with the behaviour of his Lady.—She is perfectly well bred indeed, & has the air of a woman of fashion, but her manners are not such as can persuade me of her being prepossessed in my favour.—I wanted her to be delighted at seeing me—I was as amiable as possible on the occasion—but all in vain—she does not like me.—To be sure, when we consider that I *did* take some pains to prevent my Brother-in-law's marrying her, this want of cordiality is not very surprising—& yet it shews an illiberal & vindictive spirit to resent a project which influenced me six years ago, & which never succeeded at last.—I am sometimes half disposed to repent that I did not let Charles buy Vernon Castle when we were obliged to sell it, but it was a trying circumstance, especially as the Sale took place exactly at the time of his marriage—& everybody ought to respect the delicacy of those feelings, which could not endure that my Husband's Dignity should be lessened by his younger brother's having possession of the Family Estate.—Could Matters have been so arranged as to prevent the necessity of our leaving the Castle, could we have lived with Charles & kept him single, I should have been very far from persuading my husband to dispose of it elsewhere;—but Charles was then on the point of marrying Miss De Courcy, & the event has justified me. Here are Children in abundance, & what benefit could have accrued to me from his purchasing Vernon?—My having prevented it, may perhaps have given his wife an unfavourable impression—but where there is a disposition to dislike a motive will never be wanting; & as to money-matters, it has not with-held him from being very useful to me. I really have a regard for him, he is so easily imposed on!

The house is a good one, the Furniture fashionable, & everything announces plenty & Elegance.—Charles is very rich I am sure; when a Man has once got his name in a Banking House* he rolls in money. But they do not know what to do with their fortune, keep very little Company, & never go to Town but on business.—We shall be as stupid as possible.—I mean to win my Sister in law's heart through her Children; I know all their names already, & am going to attach myself with the greatest sensibility* to one in particular, a young Frederic, whom I take on my lap & sigh over for his dear Uncle's sake.—

Poor Manwaring!—I need not tell you how much I miss him—how perpetually he is in my Thoughts.—I found a dismal Letter from him on my arrival here, full of complaints of his wife & sister, & lamentations on the cruelty of his fate. I passed off the letter as his wife's, to the Vernons, & when I write to him, it must be under cover* to you.

Yours Ever, S. V.—

## LETTER 6

*Mrs Vernon to Mr De Courcy.*

CHURCHILL

Well my dear Reginald, I have seen this dangerous creature, & must give you some description of her, tho' I hope you will soon be able to form your own judgement. She is really excessively pretty.—However you may chuse to question the allurements of a Lady no longer young, I must for my own part declare that I have seldom seen so lovely a woman as Lady Susan.—She is delicately fair, with fine grey eyes & dark eyelashes; & from her appearance one would not suppose her more than five & twenty, tho' she must in fact be ten years older.— I was certainly not disposed to admire her, tho' always hearing she was beautiful; but I cannot help feeling that she possesses an uncommon union of Symmetry, Brilliancy & Grace.*—Her address* to me was so gentle, frank & even affectionate, that if I had not known how much she has always disliked me for marrying Mr Vernon, & that we had never met before, I should have imagined her an attached friend.—One is apt I beleive to connect assurance of manner with coquetry, & to expect that an impudent address will necessarily attend an impudent mind;—at least I was myself prepared for an improper degree of confidence in Lady Susan; but her Countenance is absolutely sweet, & her voice & manner winningly mild.—I am sorry it is so, for what is this but Deceit?—Unfortunately one knows her too well.—She is clever & agreable, has all that knowledge of the world which makes conversation easy, & talks very well, with a happy command of Language, which is too often used I beleive to make Black appear White.—She has already almost persuaded me of her being warmly attached to her daughter, tho' I have so long been convinced of the contrary. She speaks of her with so much tenderness & anxiety, lamenting so bitterly the neglect of her education, which she represents however as wholly unavoidable, that I am forced to recollect how many successive Springs her Ladyship spent in Town,* while her daughter was left in Staffordshire to the care of servants or a Governess very little better,* to prevent my beleiving whatever she says.

If her manners have so great an influence on my resentful heart, you may guess how much more strongly they operate on Mr Vernon's generous temper.—I wish I could be as well satisfied as he is, that it was really her choice to leave Langford for Churchill; & if she had not staid three months there before she discovered that her friends manner of Living did not suit her situation or feelings, I might have beleived that concern for the loss of such a Husband as Mr Vernon, to whom her own behaviour was far from unexceptionable, might for a time make her wish for retirement. But I cannot forget the length of her visit to the Manwarings, & when I reflect on the different mode of Life which she led with them, from that to which she must now submit, I can only suppose that the wish of establishing her reputation by following, tho' late, the path of propriety, occasioned her removal from a family where she must in reality have been particularly happy. Your friend Mr Smith's story however cannot be quite true, as she corresponds regularly with Mrs Manwaring;—at any rate it must be exaggerated;—it is scarcely possible that two men should be so grossly deceived by her at once.—

Yrs &c Cath Vernon.

## LETTER 7

*Lady Susan to Mrs Johnson.*

My dear Alicia

You are very good in taking notice of Frederica, & I am grateful for it as a mark of your friendship; but as I cannot have a doubt of the warmth of that friendship, I am far from exacting so heavy a sacrifice. She is a stupid girl, & has nothing to recommend her.—I would not therefore on any account have you encumber one moment of your precious time by sending for her to Edward St.,* especially as every visit is so many hours deducted from the grand affair of Education,* which I really wish to be attended to, while she remains with Miss Summers.—I want her to play & sing with some portion of Taste, & a good deal of assurance, as she has *my* hand & arm,* & a tolerable voice. *I* was so much indulged in my infant years that I was never obliged to attend to any thing, & consequently am without those accomplishments which are now necessary to finish a pretty Woman. Not that I am an advocate for the prevailing fashion of acquiring a perfect knowledge in all the Languages Arts & Sciences;—it is throwing time away;—to be Mistress of French, Italian, German, Music, Singing, Drawing &c. will gain a Woman some applause, but will not add one Lover to her list. Grace & Manner after all are of the greatest importance. I do not mean therefore that Frederica's acquirements should be more than superficial, & I flatter myself that she will not remain long enough at school to understand anything thoroughly.—I hope to see her the wife of Sir James within a twelve-month.—You know on what I ground my hope, & it is certainly a good foundation, for School must be very humiliating to a girl of Frederica's age; & by the bye, you had better not invite her any more on that account, as I wish her to find her situation as unpleasant as possible.—I am sure of Sir James at any time, & could make him renew his application by a Line.—I shall trouble you meanwhile to prevent his forming any other attachment when he comes to Town;—ask him to your House occasionally, & talk to him about Frederica that he may not forget her.—

Upon the whole I commend my own conduct in this affair extremely, & regard it as a very happy mixture of circumspection &

tenderness. Some Mothers would have insisted on their daughter's accepting so great an offer on the first overture, but I could not answer it to myself to force Frederica into a marriage from which her heart revolted; & instead of adopting so harsh a measure, merely propose to make it her own choice by rendering her thoroughly uncomfortable till she does accept him. But enough of this tiresome girl.—

You may well wonder how I contrive to pass my time here—& for the first week, it was most insufferably dull. Now however, we begin to mend;—our party is enlarged by Mrs Vernon's brother, a handsome young Man, who promises me some amusement. There is something about him that rather interests me, a sort of sauciness, of familiarity which I shall teach him to correct. He is lively & seems clever, & when I have inspired him with greater respect for me than his sister's kind offices have implanted, he may be an agreable Flirt.—There is exquisite pleasure in subduing an insolent spirit, in making a person pre-determined to dislike, acknowledge one's superiority.—I have disconcerted him already by my calm reserve; & it shall be my endeavour to humble the Pride of these self-important De Courcies still lower, to convince Mrs Vernon that her sisterly cautions have been bestowed in vain, & to persuade Reginald that she has scandalously belied me. This project will serve at least to amuse me, & prevent my feeling so acutely this dreadful separation from You & all whom I love. Adeiu.

Yours Ever<br>S. Vernon.

## LETTER 8

*Mrs Vernon to Lady De Courcy.*

CHURCHILL

My dear Mother

You must not expect Reginald back again for some time. He desires me to tell you that the present open weather* induces him to accept Mr Vernon's invitation to prolong his stay in Sussex* that they may have some hunting together.—He means to send for his Horses immediately, & it is impossible to say when you may see him in Kent.* I will not disguise my sentiments on this change from you my dear

Madam, tho' I think you had better not communicate them to my Father, whose excessive anxiety about Reginald would subject him to an alarm which might seriously affect his health & spirits. Lady Susan has certainly contrived in the space of a fortnight to make my Brother like her.—In short, I am persuaded that his continuing here beyond the time originally fixed for his return, is occasioned in much by a degree of fascination towards her, as by the wish of hunting with Mr Vernon, & of course I cannot receive that pleasure from the length of his visit which my Brother's company would otherwise give me.— I am indeed provoked at the artifice of this unprincipled Woman. What stronger proof of her dangerous Abilities can be given, than this perversion of Reginald's Judgement, which when he entered the house was so decidedly against her?—In his last letter he actually gave me some particulars of her behaviour at Langford, such as he received from a Gentleman who knew her perfectly well, which if true must raise abhorrence against her, & which Reginald himself was entirely disposed to credit.—His opinion of her I am sure, was as low as of any Woman in England, & when he first came it was evident that he considered her as one entitled neither to Delicacy nor respect, & that he felt she would be delighted with the attentions of any Man inclined to flirt with her.

Her behaviour I confess has been calculated to do away such an idea, I have not detected the smallest impropriety in it,—nothing of Vanity, of pretension, of Levity—& she is altogether so attractive, that I should not wonder at his being delighted with her, had he known nothing of her previous to this personal acquaintance;—but against reason, against conviction, to be so well pleased with her as I am sure he is, does really astonish me.—His admiration was at first very strong, but no more than was natural; & I did not wonder at his being struck by the gentleness & delicacy of her Manners;—but when he has mentioned her of late, it has been in terms of more extraordinary praise, & yesterday he actually said, that he could not be surprised at any effect produced on the heart of Man by such Loveliness & such Abilities; & when I lamented in reply the badness of her disposition, he observed that whatever might have been her errors, they were to be imputed to her neglected Education & early Marriage, & that she was altogether a wonderful Woman.—

This tendency to excuse her conduct, or to forget it in the warmth of admiration vexes me; & if I did not know that Reginald is too much at home at Churchill to need an invitation for lengthening his visit, I should regret Mr Vernon's giving him any.——

Lady Susan's intentions are of course those of absolute coquetry, or a desire of universal admiration. I cannot for a moment imagine that she has anything more serious in veiw, but it mortifies me to see a young Man of Reginald's sense duped by her at all.——I am &c

Cath Vernon.——

## LETTER 9

*Mrs Johnson to Lady Susan.*

EDWARD ST.

My dearest Friend

I congratulate you on Mr De Courcy's arrival, & advise you by all means to marry him; his Father's Estate is we know considerable, & I beleive certainly entailed.*——Sir Reginald is very infirm, & not likely to stand in your way long.——I hear the young Man well spoken of, & tho' no one can really deserve you my dearest Susan, Mr De Courcy may be worth having.——Manwaring will storm of course, but you may easily pacify him. Besides, the most scrupulous point of honour could not require you to wait for *his* emancipation.——I have seen Sir James,——he came to Town for a few days last week, & called several times in Edward Street. I talked to him about you & your daughter, & he is so far from having forgotten you, that I am sure he would marry either of you with pleasure.——I gave him hopes of Frederica's relenting, & told him a great deal of her improvements.—— I scolded him for making Love to Maria Manwaring; he protested that he had been only in joke, & we both laughed heartily at her disappointment, & in short were very agreable.——He is as silly as ever.——Yours faithfully

Alicia.——

# LETTER 10

*Lady Susan to Mrs Johnson.*

I am much obliged to you my dear Friend, for your advice respecting Mr De Courcy, which I know was given with the fullest conviction of it's expediency, tho' I am not quite determined on following it.— I cannot easily resolve on anything so serious as Marriage, especially as I am not at present in want of money, & might perhaps till the old Gentleman's death, be very little benefited by the match. It is true that I am vain enough to beleive it within my reach.—I have made him sensible of my power, & can now enjoy the pleasure of triumphing over a Mind prepared to dislike me, & prejudiced against all my past actions. His sister too, is I hope convinced how little the ungenerous representations of any one to the disadvantage of another will avail, when opposed to the immediate influence of Intellect & Manner.— I see plainly that she is uneasy at my progress in the good opinion of her Brother, & conclude that nothing will be wanting on her part to counteract me;—but having once made him doubt the justice of her opinion of me, I think I may defy her.—

It has been delightful to me to watch his Advances towards intimacy, especially to observe his altered manner in consequence of my repressing by the calm dignity of my deportment, his insolent approach to direct familiarity.—My conduct has been equally guarded from the first, & I never behaved less like a Coquette in the whole course of my Life, tho' perhaps my desire of dominion was never more decided. I have subdued him entirely by sentiment & serious Conversation, & made him I may venture to say at least *half* in Love with me, without the semblance of the most common-place flirtation. Mrs Vernon's consciousness of deserving every sort of revenge that it can be in my power to inflict, for her ill-offices, could alone enable her to perceive that I am actuated by any design in behaviour so gentle & unpretending.—Let her think & act as she chuses however; I have never yet found that the advice of a Sister could prevent a young Man's being in love if he chose it.—We are advancing now towards some kind of confidence, & in short are likely to be engaged in a kind of platonic friendship.—On *my* side, you may be sure of it's never being more, for if I were not already as much attached to another person as I can be to any one, I should make a point of not bestowing my affection on a Man who had dared to think so meanly of me.——

Reginald has a good figure, & is not unworthy the praise you have heard given him, but is still greatly inferior to our friend at Langford.——He is less polished, less insinuating* than Manwaring, & is comparatively deficient in the power of saying those delightful things which put one in good humour with oneself & all the world. He is quite agreable enough however, to afford me amusement, & to make many of those hours pass very pleasantly which would be otherwise spent in endeavouring to overcome my sister in law's reserve, & listening to her Husband's insipid talk.——

Your account of Sir James is most satisfactory, & I mean to give Miss Frederica a hint of my intentions very soon.——Yours &c,

S. Vernon.

## LETTER 11

*Mrs Vernon to Lady De Courcy.*

I really grow quite uneasy my dearest Mother about Reginald, from witnessing the very rapid increase of Lady Susan's influence. They are now on terms of the most particular friendship, frequently engaged in long conversations together, & she has contrived by the most artful Coquetry to subdue his Judgement to her own purposes.——It is impossible to see the intimacy between them, so very soon established, without some alarm, tho' I can hardly suppose that Lady Susan's veiws extend to marriage.——I wish you could get Reginald home again, under any plausible pretence. He is not at all disposed to leave us, & I have given him as many hints of my Father's precarious state of health, as common decency will allow me to do in my own house.——Her power over him must now be boundless, as she has entirely effaced all his former ill-opinion, & persuaded him not merely to forget, but to justify her conduct.——Mr Smith's account of her proceedings at Langford, where he accused her of having made Mr Manwaring & a young Man engaged to Miss Manwaring distractedly in love with her, which Reginald firmly beleived when he came to Churchill, is now he is persuaded only a scandalous invention. He has told me so in a warmth of manner which spoke his regret at having ever beleived the contrary himself.——

How sincerely do I greive that she ever entered this house!—
I always looked forward to her coming with uneasiness—but very far
was it, from originating in anxiety for Reginald.—I expected a most
disagreable companion to myself, but could not imagine that my
Brother would be in the smallest danger of being captivated by
a Woman, with whose principles he was so well acquainted, & whose
Character he so heartily despised. If you can get him away, it will be
a good thing.

Yrs affec:ly,<br>
Cath Vernon.

## LETTER 12

*Sir Reginald De Courcy to his Son.*

PARKLANDS

I know that young Men in general do not admit of any enquiry, even
from their nearest relations, into affairs of the heart; but I hope my dear
Reginald that you will be superior to such as allow nothing for a Father's
anxiety, & think themselves privileged to refuse him their confidence &
slight his advice.—You must be sensible that as an only son & the rep-
resentative of an ancient Family, your conduct in Life is most interesting to* your connections.—In the very important concern of Marriage
especially, there is everything at stake; your own happiness, that of your
Parents, & the credit of your name.—I do not suppose that you would
deliberately form an absolute engagement* of that nature without
acquainting your Mother & myself, or at least without being convinced
that we should approve your choice; but I cannot help fearing that you
may be drawn in by the Lady who has lately attached you, to a Marriage,
which the whole of your Family, far and near, must highly reprobate.

Lady Susan's age is itself a material objection, but her want of
character is one so much more serious, that the difference of even
twelve years becomes in comparison of small account.—Were you
not blinded by a sort of fascination, it would be ridiculous in me to
repeat the instances of great misconduct on her side, so very generally
known.—Her neglect of her husband, her encouragement of other
Men, her extravagance & dissipation were so gross & notorious, that
no one could be ignorant of them at the time, nor can now have

forgotten them.—To our Family, she has always been represented in softened colours by the benevolence of Mr Charles Vernon; & yet inspite of his generous endeavours to excuse her, we know that she did, from the most selfish motives, take all possible pains to prevent his marrying Catherine.—

My Years & increasing Infirmities make me very desirous my dear Reginald, of seeing you settled in the world.—To the Fortune of your wife, the goodness of my own, will make me indifferent; but her family & character must be equally unexceptionable. When your choice is so fixed as that no objection can be made to either, I can promise you a ready & chearful consent; but it is my Duty to oppose a Match, which deep Art only could render probable, & must in the end make wretched.

It is possible that her behaviour may arise only from Vanity, or a wish of gaining the admiration of a Man whom she must imagine to be particularly prejudiced against her; but it is more likely that she should aim at something farther.—She is poor, & may naturally seek an alliance which must be advantageous to herself.—You know your own rights, & that it is out of my power to prevent your inheriting the family Estate.* My Ability of distressing you during my Life, would be a species of revenge to which I should hardly stoop under any circumstances.—I honestly tell you my Sentiments & Intentions. I do not wish to work on your Fears, but on your Sense & Affection.—It would destroy every comfort of my Life, to know that you were married to Lady Susan Vernon. It would be the death of that honest Pride with which I have hitherto considered my son, I should blush to see him, to hear of him, to think of him.—

I may perhaps do no good, but that of releiving my own mind, by this Letter; but I felt it my Duty to tell you that your partiality for Lady Susan is no secret to your friends, & to warn you against her.— I should be glad to hear your reasons for disbeleiving Mr Smith's intelligence;*—you had no doubt of it's authenticity a month ago.—

If you can give me your assurance of having no design beyond enjoying the conversation of a clever woman for a short period, & of yeilding admiration only to her Beauty & Abilities without being blinded by them to her faults, you will restore me to happiness; but if you cannot do this, explain to me at least what has occasioned so great an alteration in your opinion of her.

I am &c<br>Regd De Courcy.

## LETTER 13

*Lady De Courcy to Mrs Vernon.*

My dear Catherine,

Unluckily I was confined to my room when your last letter came, by a cold which affected my eyes so much as to prevent my reading it myself, so I could not refuse your Father when he offered to read it to me, by which means he became acquainted to my great vexation with all your fears about your Brother. I had intended to write to Reginald myself, as soon as my eyes would let me, to point out as well as I could the danger of an intimate acquaintance with so artful a woman as Lady Susan, to a young Man of his age & high expectations. I meant moreover to have reminded him of our being quite alone now, & very much in need of him to keep up our spirits these long winter evenings. Whether it would have done any good, can never be settled now; but I am excessively vexed that Sir Reginald should know anything of a matter which we foresaw would make him so uneasy.—He caught all your fears the moment he had read your Letter, & I am sure has not had the business out of his head since;—he wrote by the same post to Reginald, a long letter full of it all, & particularly asking an explanation of what he may have heard from Lady Susan to contradict the late shocking reports. His answer came this morning, which I shall enclose to you, as I think you will like to see it; I wish it was more satisfactory, but it seems written with such a determination to think well of Lady Susan, that his assurances as to Marriage &c, do not set my heart at ease.— I say all I can however to satisfy your Father, & he is certainly less uneasy since Reginald's letter. How provoking it is my dear Catherine, that this unwelcome Guest of yours, should not only prevent our meeting this Christmas, but be the occasion of so much vexation & trouble.—Kiss the dear Children for me.—Your affec: Mother

C. De Courcy.—

## LETTER 14

*Mr De Courcy to Sir Reginald.*

CHURCHILL

My dear Sir

I have this moment received your Letter, which has given me more astonishment than I ever felt before. I am to thank my Sister I suppose, for having represented me in such a light as to injure me in your opinion, & give you all this alarm.——I know not why she should chuse to make herself & her family uneasy by apprehending an Event, which no one but herself I can affirm, would ever have thought possible. To impute such a design to Lady Susan would be taking from her every claim to that excellent understanding which her bitterest Enemies have never denied her; & equally low must sink my pretensions to common sense, if I am suspected of matrimonial veiws in my behaviour to her.——Our difference of age must be an insuperable objection, & I entreat you my dear Sir to quiet your mind, & no longer harbour a suspicion which cannot be more injurious to your own peace than to our Understandings.

I can have no veiw in remaining with Lady Susan than to enjoy for a short time (as you have yourself expressed it) the conversation of a Woman of high mental powers. If Mrs Vernon would allow something to my affection for herself & her husband in the length of my visit, she would do more justice to us all;——but my Sister is unhappily prejudiced beyond the hope of conviction against Lady Susan.—— From an attachment to her husband which in itself does honour to both, she cannot forgive those endeavours at preventing their union, which have been attributed to selfishness in Lady Susan. But in this case, as well as in many others, the World has most grossly injured that Lady, by supposing the worst, where the motives of her conduct have been doubtful.——

Lady Susan had heard something so materially to the disadvantage of my Sister, as to persuade her that the happiness of Mr Vernon, to whom she was always much attached, would be absolutely destroyed by the marriage. And this circumstance while it explains the true motive of Lady Susan's conduct, & removes all the blame which has been so lavished on her, may also convince us how little the general report of any one ought to be credited, since no Character however upright, can escape the malevolence of slander. If my Sister in the security of retirement, with as little opportunity as inclination to do Evil, could not avoid Censure, we must not rashly condemn those who living in the World & surrounded with temptation, should be accused of Errors which they are known to have the power of committing —

I blame myself severely for having so easily beleived the scandalous tales invented by Charles Smith to the prejudice of Lady Susan, as I am now convinced how greatly they have traduced* her. As to Mrs Manwaring's jealousy, it was totally his own invention; & his account of her attaching Miss Manwaring's Lover was scarcely better founded. Sir James Martin had been drawn in by that young Lady to pay her some attention, & as he is a Man of fortune, it was easy to see that *her* veiws extended to Marriage.—It is well known that Miss Manwaring is absolutely on the catch for* a husband, & no one therefore can pity her, for losing by the superior attractions of another Woman, the chance of being able to make a worthy Man completely miserable.—Lady Susan was far from intending such a conquest, & on finding how warmly Miss Manwaring resented her Lover's defection, determined, inspite of Mr & Mrs Manwaring's most earnest entreaties, to leave the family.—I have reason to imagine that she did receive serious Proposals from Sir James, but her removing from Langford immediately on the discovery of his attachment, must acquit her on that article, with every Mind of common candour.*—You will, I am sure my dear Sir, feel the truth of this reasoning, & will hereby learn to do justice to the character of a very injured Woman.—

I know that Lady Susan in coming to Churchill was governed only by the most honourable & amiable intentions.—Her prudence & economy are exemplary, her regard for Mr Vernon equal even to *his* deserts, & her wish of obtaining my sister's good opinion merits a better return than it has received.—As a Mother she is unexceptionable. Her solid affection for her Child is shewn by placing her in hands, where her Education will be properly attended to; but because she has not the blind & weak partiality of most Mothers, she is accused of wanting Maternal Tenderness.—Every person of Sense however will know how to value & commend her well directed affection, & will join me in wishing that Frederica Vernon may prove more worthy than she has yet done, of her Mother's tender cares.

I have now my dear Sir, written my real Sentiments of Lady Susan; you will know from this Letter, how highly I admire her Abilities, & esteem her Character; but if you are not equally convinced by my full & solemn assurance that your fears have been most idly created, you will deeply mortify & distress me.—I am &c

R. De Courcy.—


## LETTER 15

*Mrs Vernon to Lady De Courcy.*

CHURCHILL

My dear Mother

I return you Reginald's letter, & rejoice with all my heart that my Father is made easy by it. Tell him so, with my congratulations;—but between ourselves, I must own it has only convinced *me* of my Brother's having no *present* intention of marrying Lady Susan—not that he is in no danger of doing so three months hence.—He gives a very plausible account of her behaviour at Langford, I wish it may be true, but his intelligence must come from herself, & I am less disposed to beleive it, than to lament the degree of intimacy subsisting between them, implied by the discussion of such a subject.

I am sorry to have incurred his displeasure, but can expect nothing better while he is so very eager in Lady Susan's justification.—He is very severe against me indeed, & yet I hope I have not been hasty in my judgement of her.—Poor Woman! tho' I have reasons enough for my dislike, I can not help pitying her at present as she is in real distress, & with too much cause.—She had this morning a letter from the Lady with whom she has placed her daughter, to request that Miss Vernon might be immediately removed, as she had been detected in an attempt to run away. Why, or whither she intended to go, does not appear; but as her situation seems to have been unexceptionable, it is a sad thing & of course highly afflicting to Lady Susan.—

Frederica must be as much as sixteen, & ought to know better, but from what her Mother insinuates I am afraid she is a perverse girl. She has been sadly neglected however, & her Mother ought to remember it.—

Mr Vernon set off for Town as soon as she had determined what should be done. He is if possible to prevail on Miss Summers to let Frederica continue with her, & if he cannot succeed, to bring her to Churchill for the present, till some other situation can be found for her.—Her Ladyship is comforting herself meanwhile by strolling along the Shrubbery* with Reginald, calling forth all his tender feelings I suppose on this distressing occasion. She has been talking a great deal about it to me, she talks vastly well,* I am afraid of being ungenerous or I should say she talks *too* well to feel so very deeply. But I will not look for Faults. She may be Reginald's Wife—Heaven forbid it!—but why should I be quicker sighted than any body else?—Mr Vernon declares that he never saw deeper distress than hers, on the receipt of the Letter & is his Judgement inferior to mine?—

She was very unwilling that Frederica should be allowed to come to Churchill, & justly enough, as it seems a sort of reward to Behaviour deserving very differently. But it was impossible to take her any where else, & she is not to remain here long.—

'It will be absolutely necessary,' said she, 'as You my dear Sister must be sensible, to treat my daughter with some severity while she is here;—a most painful necessity, but I will *endeavour* to submit to it.—I am afraid I have been often too indulgent, but my poor Frederica's temper could never bear opposition well. You must support & encourage me—you must urge the necessity of reproof, if you see me too lenient.'

All this sounds very reasonably.—Reginald is so incensed against the poor silly Girl!—Surely it is not to Lady Susan's credit that he should be so bitter against her daughter; his idea of her must be drawn from the Mother's description.—

Well, whatever may be his fate, we have the comfort of knowing that we have done our utmost to save him. We must commit the event to an Higher Power.—Yours Ever &c

Cath Vernon.

## LETTER 16

*Lady Susan to Mrs Johnson.*

CHURCHILL

Never my dearest Alicia, was I so provoked in my life as by a Letter this morning from Miss Summers. That horrid girl of mine has been trying to run away.—I had not a notion of her being such a little Devil before;—she seemed to have all the Vernon Milkiness;* but on receiving the letter in which I declared my intentions about Sir James, she actually attempted to elope;* at least, I cannot otherwise account for her doing it.—She meant I suppose to go to the Clarkes in Staffordshire, for she has no other acquaintance.—But she *shall* be punished, she *shall* have him. I have sent Charles to Town to make matters up if he can, for I do not by any means want her here. If Miss Summers will not keep her, you must find me out another school, unless we can get her married immediately.—Miss S. writes word that she could not get the young Lady to assign any cause for her extraordinary conduct, which confirms me in my own private explanation of it.—

Frederica is too shy I think, & too much in awe of me, to tell tales; but if the mildness of her Uncle *should* get any thing from her, I am not afraid. I trust I shall be able to make my story as good as her's.—If I am vain of any thing, it is of my eloquence. Consideration & Esteem as surely follow command of Language, as Admiration waits on Beauty. And here I have opportunity enough for the exercise of my Talent, as the cheif of my time is spent in Conversation. Reginald is never easy unless we are by ourselves, & when the weather is tolerable we pace the shrubbery for hours together.—I like him on the whole very well, he is clever & has a good deal to say; but he is sometimes impertinent* & troublesome.—There is a sort of ridiculous delicacy about him which requires the fullest explanation of whatever he may have heard to my disadvantage, & is never satisfied till he thinks he has ascertained the beginning & end of everything.—

This is *one* sort of Love—but I confess it does not particularly recommend itself to me. I infinitely prefer the tender & liberal spirit of Manwaring, which impressed with the deepest conviction of my merit, is satisfied that whatever I do must be right; & look* with a degree of Contempt on the inquisitive & doubting Fancies of that

Heart which seems always debating on the reasonableness of it's Emotions. Manwaring is indeed beyond compare superior to Reginald.—superior in every thing but the power of being with me.—Poor fellow! he is quite distracted by Jealousy, which I am not sorry for, as I know no better support of Love.—He has been teizing* me to allow of his coming into this Country, & lodging somewhere near me *incog.*—but I forbid every thing of the kind.—Those women are inexcusable who forget what is due to themselves & the opinion of the World.—

S. Vernon—

## LETTER 17

*Mrs Vernon to Lady De Courcy.*

CHURCHILL

My dear Mother

Mr Vernon returned on Thursday night, bringing his neice with him. Lady Susan had received a line from him by that day's post informing her that Miss Summers had absolutely refused to allow of Miss Vernon's continuance in her Academy. We were therefore prepared for her arrival, & expected them impatiently the whole evening.—They came while we were at Tea,* & I never saw any creature look so frightened in my life as Frederica when she entered the room.—

Lady Susan who had been shedding tears before & shewing great agitation at the idea of the meeting, received her with perfect self–command, & without betraying the least tenderness of spirit.—She hardly spoke to her, & on Frederica's bursting into tears as soon as we were seated, took her out of the room & did not return for some time; when she did, her eyes looked very red, & she was as much agitated as before.—We saw no more of her daughter.—

Poor Reginald was beyond measure concerned to see his fair friend in such distress, & watched her with so much tender solicitude that I, who occasionally caught her observing his countenance with exultation, was quite out of patience.—This pathetic* representation lasted the whole evening, & so ostentatious & artful a display has entirely convinced me that she did in fact feel nothing.—

I am more angry with her than ever since I have seen her daughter.—The poor girl looks so unhappy that my heart aches for her.—Lady Susan is surely too severe, because Frederica does not seem to have the sort of temper to make severity necessary.—She looks perfectly timid, dejected & penitent.—

She is very pretty, tho' not so handsome as her Mother, nor at all like her. Her complexion is delicate, but neither so fair, nor so blooming as Lady Susan's—& she has quite the Vernon cast of countenance, the oval face & mild dark eyes, & there is peculiar sweetness in her look when she speaks either to her Uncle or me, for as we behave kindly to her, we have of course engaged her gratitude.—Her Mother has insinuated that her temper is untractable,* but I never saw a face less indicative of any evil disposition than her's; & from what I now see of the behaviour of each to the other, the invariable severity of Lady Susan, & the silent dejection of Frederica, I am led to beleive as heretofore that the former has no real Love for her daughter & has never done her justice, or treated her affectionately.

I have not yet been able to have any conversation with my neice; she is shy, & I think I can see that some pains are taken to prevent her being much with me.—Nothing satisfactory transpires as to her reason for running away.—Her kind hearted Uncle you may be sure, was too fearful of distressing her, to ask many questions as they travelled.—I wish it had been possible for me to fetch her instead of him;—I think I should have discovered the truth in the course of a Thirty miles Journey.—

The small Pianoforté has been removed within these few days at Lady Susan's request, into her Dressing room, & Frederica spends great part of the day there;—*practising* it is called, but I seldom hear any noise when I pass that way.—What she does with herself there I do not know, there are plenty of books in the room, but it is not every girl who has been running wild the first fifteen years of her life, that can or will read.—Poor Creature! the prospect from her window is not very instructive, for that room overlooks the Lawn you know with the Shrubbery on one side, where she may see her Mother walking for an hour together, in earnest conversation with Reginald.—A girl of Frederica's age must be childish indeed, if such things do not strike her.—Is it not inexcusable to give such an example to a daughter?—Yet Reginald still thinks Lady Susan the best of Mothers—still condemns Frederica as a worthless girl!—He is convinced that her attempt to run away, proceeded from no justifiable cause, & had no provocation.—I am sure I cannot say that it *had*, but while Miss Summers declares that Miss Vernon shewed no sign of Obstinacy or Perverseness during her whole stay in Wigmore St. till she was detected in this scheme, I cannot so readily credit what Lady Susan has made him & wants to make me believe, that it was merely an impatience of restraint, & a desire of escaping from the tuition of Masters which brought on the plan of an elopement.—Oh! Reginald, how is your Judgement enslaved!—He scarcely dares even allow her to be handsome, & when I speak of her beauty, replies only that her eyes have no Brilliancy.

Sometimes he is sure that she is deficient in Understanding, & at others that her temper only is in fault. In short when a person is always to deceive, it is impossible to be consistent. Lady Susan finds it necessary for her own justification that Frederica should be to blame, & probably has sometimes judged it expedient to accuse her of ill-nature & sometimes to lament her want of sense. Reginald is only repeating after her Ladyship.—

I am &c

Cath Vernon

## LETTER 18

*From the same to the same.*

CHURCHILL

My dear Madam

I am very glad to find that my description of Frederica Vernon has interested you, for I do beleive her truly deserving of our regard, & when I have communicated a notion that has recently struck me, your kind impression in her favour will I am sure be heightened. I cannot help fancying that she is growing partial to my brother, I so very often see her eyes fixed on his face with a remarkable expression of pensive admiration!—He is certainly very handsome—& yet more—there is an openness in his manner that must be highly prepossessing, & I am sure she feels it so.—Thoughtful & pensive in general her countenance always brightens with a smile when Reginald says anything amusing; & let the subject be ever so serious that he may be conversing on, I am much mistaken if a syllable of his uttering, escape her.—

I want to make *him* sensible of all this, for we know the power of gratitude on such a heart as his; & could Frederica's artless affection detach him from her Mother, we might bless the day which brought her to Churchill. I think my dear Madam, you would not disapprove of her as a Daughter. She is extremely young to be sure, has had a wretched Education & a dreadful example of Levity in her Mother; but yet I can pronounce her disposition to be excellent, & her natural abilities very good.—

Tho' totally without accomplishment, she is by no means so ignorant as one might expect to find her, being fond of books & spending the cheif of her time in reading. Her Mother leaves her more to herself now than she *did*, & I have her with me as much as possible, & have taken great pains to overcome her timidity. We are very good friends, & tho' she never opens her lips before her Mother, she talks enough when alone with me, to make it clear that if properly treated by Lady Susan she would always appear to much greater advantage. There cannot be a more gentle, affectionate heart; or more obliging manners, when acting without restraint. Her little Cousins are all very fond of her.—Yrs affec:ly

Cath Vernon

## LETTER 19

*Lady Susan to Mrs Johnson.*

CHURCHILL

You will be eager I know to hear something farther of Frederica, & perhaps may think me negligent for not writing before.—She arrived with her Uncle last Thursday fortnight, when of course I lost no time in demanding the reason of her behaviour, & soon found myself to have been perfectly right in attributing it to my own letter.—The purport of it frightened her so thoroughly that with a mixture of true girlish perverseness & folly, without considering that she could not escape from my authority by running away from Wigmore Street, she resolved on getting out of the house; & proceeding directly by the stage* to her friends the Clarkes, & had really got as far as the length of two streets in her journey, when she was fortunately miss'd, pursued, & overtaken.—

Such was the first distinguished exploit of Miss Frederica Susanna Vernon, & if we consider that it was atcheived at the tender age of sixteen we shall have room for the most flattering prognostics* of her future renown.—I am excessively provoked however at the parade of propriety which prevented Miss Summers from keeping the girl; & it seems so extraordinary a peice of nicety,* considering what are my daughter's family connections, that I can only suppose the Lady to be governed by the fear of never getting her money.—Be that as it may however, Frederica is returned on my hands, & having now nothing else to employ her, is busy in pursueing the plan of Romance begun at Langford.—She is actually falling in love with Reginald De Courcy.—To disobey her Mother by refusing an unexceptionable offer is not enough; her affections must likewise be given without her Mother's approbation.—I never saw a girl of her age, bid fairer to be the sport of Mankind. Her feelings are tolerably lively, & she is so charmingly artless in their display, as to afford the most reasonable hope of her being ridiculed & despised by every Man who sees her.—

Artlessness will never do in Love matters, & that girl is born a simpleton who has it either by nature or affectation.—I am not yet certain that Reginald sees what she is about; nor is it of much consequence;—she is now an object of indifference to him, she would be one of contempt were he to understand her Emotions.—Her beauty is much admired by the Vernons, but it has no effect on *him*. She is in high favour with her Aunt altogether—because she is so little like myself of course. She is exactly the companion for Mrs Vernon, who dearly loves to be first, & to have all the sense & all the wit of the Conversation to herself;—Frederica will never eclipse her.— When she first came, I was at some pains to prevent her seeing much of her Aunt, but I have since relaxed, as I beleive I may depend on her observing the rules I have laid down for their discourse.—

But do not imagine that with all this Lenity,* I have for a moment given up my plan of her marriage;—No, I am unalterably fixed on that point, tho' I have not yet quite resolved on the manner of bringing it about.—I should not chuse to have the business brought forward here, & canvassed by the wise heads of Mr and Mrs Vernon;

& I cannot just now afford to go to Town.—Miss Frederica therefore must wait a little.—

Yours Ever

S. Vernon.—

## LETTER 20

*Mrs Vernon to Lady De Courcy.*

CHURCHILL

We have a very unexpected Guest with us at present, my dear Mother.—He arrived yesterday.—I heard a carriage at the door as I was sitting with my Children while they dined, & supposing I should be wanted left the Nursery soon afterwards & was half way down stairs, when Frederica as pale as ashes came running up, & rushed by me into her own room.—I instantly followed, & asked her what was the matter.—'Oh!' cried she, 'he is come, Sir James is come—& what am I to do?'—This was no explanation; I begged her to tell me what she meant. At that moment we were interrupted by a knock at the door;—it was Reginald, who came by Lady Susan's direction to call Frederica down.—'It is Mr De Courcy,' said she, colouring violently, 'Mama has sent for me, & I must go.'—

We all three went down together, & I saw my Brother examining the terrified face of Frederica with surprise.—In the breakfast room we found Lady Susan & a young Man of genteel appearance, whom she introduced to me by the name of Sir James Martin, the very person, as you may remember, whom it was said she had been at pains to detach from Miss Manwaring.—But the conquest it seems was not designed for herself, or she has since transferred it to her daughter, for Sir James is now desperately in love with Frederica, & with full encouragement from Mama.—The poor girl however I am sure dislikes him; & tho' his person & address are very well, he appears both to Mr Vernon & me a very weak young Man.—

Frederica looked so shy, so confused, when we entered the room, that I felt for her exceedingly. Lady Susan behaved with great attention to her Visitor, & yet I thought I could perceive that she had no particular pleasure in seeing him.—Sir James talked a good deal, & made many civil excuses to me for the liberty he had taken in coming

to Churchill, mixing more frequent laughter with his discourse than
the subject required;—said many things over & over again, & told
Lady Susan three times that he had seen Mrs Johnson a few Evenings
before.—He now & then addressed Frederica, but more frequently
her Mother.—The poor girl sat all this time without opening her
lips;—her eyes cast down, & her colour varying every instant, while
Reginald observed all that passed, in perfect silence.—

At length Lady Susan, weary I beleive of her situation, proposed
walking, & we left the two Gentlemen together to put on our
Pelisses.*—

As we went upstairs Lady Susan begged permission to attend me
for a few moments in my Dressing room, as she was anxious to speak
with me in private.—I led her thither accordingly, & as soon as the
door was closed she said, 'I was never more surprised in my life than
by Sir James's arrival, & the suddenness of it requires some apology
to *You* my dear Sister, tho' to *me* as a Mother, it is highly flattering.—
He is so warmly attached to my daughter that he could exist no longer
without seeing her.—Sir James is a young Man of an amiable
disposition, & excellent character; a little too much of the *Rattle**
perhaps, but a year or two will rectify *that*, & he is in other respects so
very eligible a Match for Frederica that I have always observed his
attachment with the greatest pleasure, & am persuaded that you & my
Brother will give the alliance your hearty approbation.—I have never
before mentioned the likelihood of it's taking place to any one, because
I thought that while Frederica continued at school, it had better not
be known to exist;—but now, as I am convinced that Frederica is too
old ever to submit to school confinement, & have therefore begun to
consider her union with Sir James as not very distant, I had intended
within a few days to acquaint yourself & Mr Vernon with the whole
business.—I am sure my dear Sister, you will excuse my remaining
silent on it so long, & agree with me that such circumstances, while
they continue from any cause in suspense, cannot be too cautiously
concealed.—When you have the happiness of bestowing your
sweet little Catherine some years hence on a Man, who in connection
& character is alike unexceptionable, you will know what I feel
now;—tho' Thank Heaven! you cannot have all my reasons for
rejoicing in such an Event.—Catherine will be amply provided for, &
not like my Frederica endebted to a fortunate Establishment* for the
comforts of Life.'—

She concluded by demanding my congratulations.—I gave them somewhat awkwardly I beleive;—for in fact, the sudden disclosure of so important a matter took from me the power of speaking with any clearness.—She thanked me however most affectionately for my kind concern in the welfare of herself & her daughter, & then said,

'I am not apt to deal in professions, my dear Mrs Vernon, & I never had the convenient talent of affecting sensations foreign to my heart; & therefore I trust you will beleive me when I declare that much as I had heard in your praise before I knew you, I had no idea that I should ever love you as I now do;—And I must farther say that your friendship towards me is more particularly gratifying, because I have reason to beleive that some attempts were made to prejudice you against me.—I only wish that They—whoever they are—to whom I am endebted for such kind intentions, could see the terms on which we now are together, & understand the real affection we feel for each other!—But I will not detain you any longer.—God bless you, for your goodness to me & my girl, & continue to you all your present happiness.'

What can one say of such a woman, my dear Mother?—Such earnestness, such solemnity of expression!—And yet I cannot help suspecting the truth of everything she said.—

As for Reginald, I beleive he does not know what to make of the matter.—When Sir James first came, he appeared all astonishment & perplexity. The folly of the young Man, & the confusion of Frederica entirely engrossed him; & tho' a little private discourse with Lady Susan has since had it's effect, he is still hurt I am sure at her allowing of such a Man's attentions to her daughter.—

Sir James invited himself with great composure to remain here a few days;—hoped we would not think it odd, was aware of it's being very impertinent, but he took the liberty of a relation, & concluded by wishing with a laugh, that he might be really one soon.—Even Lady Susan seemed a little disconcerted by this forwardness;—in her heart I am persuaded, she sincerely wishes him gone.—

But something must be done for this poor Girl, if her feelings are such as both her Uncle & I beleive them to be. She must not be sacrificed to Policy or Ambition, she must not be even left to suffer from the dread of it.—The Girl, whose heart can distinguish Reginald De Courcy, deserves, however he may slight her, a better fate than to be Sir James Martin's wife.—As soon as I can get her alone, I will discover the real Truth, but she seems to wish to avoid me.—I hope this does not proceed from any thing wrong, & that I shall not find out I have thought too well of her.—Her behaviour before Sir James certainly speaks the greatest consciousness & Embarrassment; but I see nothing in it more like Encouragement.—

Adieu my dear Madam,

Yrs &c Cath Vernon.—

# LETTER 21

*Miss Vernon to Mr De Courcy.*

Sir,

I hope you will excuse this liberty, I am forced upon it by the greatest distress, or I should be ashamed to trouble you.—I am very miserable about Sir James Martin, & have no other way in the world of helping myself but by writing to you, for I am forbidden ever speaking to my Uncle or Aunt on the subject; and this being the case, I am afraid my applying to you will appear no better than equivocation, & as if I attended only to the letter & not the spirit of Mama's commands, but if *You* do not take my part, & persuade her to break it off, I shall be half-distracted, for I can not bear him.—No human Being but *You* could have any chance of prevailing with her.—If you will therefore have the unspeakable great kindness* of taking my part with her, & persuading her to send Sir James away, I shall be more obliged to you than it is possible for me to express.—I always disliked him from the first, it is not a sudden fancy I assure you Sir, I always thought him silly & impertinent & disagreable, & now he is grown worse than ever.—I would rather work for my bread than marry him.*—I do not know how to apologise enough for this Letter, I know it is taking so great a liberty, I am aware how dreadfully angry it will make Mama, but I must run the risk.—I am Sir, your most Humble Servt.

F. S. V.—

## LETTER 22

*Lady Susan to Mrs Johnson.*

This is insufferable!—My dearest friend, I was never so enraged before, & must relieve myself by writing to you, who I know will enter into all my feelings.—Who should come on Tuesday but Sir James Martin?—Guess my astonishment & vexation—for as you well know, I never wished him to be seen at Churchill. What a pity that you should not have known his intentions!—Not content with coming, he actually invited himself to remain here a few days. I could have poisoned him;—I made the best of it however, & told my story with great success to Mrs Vernon who, whatever might be her real sentiments, said nothing in opposition to mine. I made a point also of Frederica's behaving civilly to Sir James, & gave her to understand that I was absolutely determined on her marrying him.—She said something of her misery, but that was all.—I have for some time been more particularly resolved on the Match, from seeing the rapid increase of her affection for Reginald, & from not feeling perfectly secure that a knowledge of *that* affection might not in the end awaken a return.—Contemptible as a regard founded only on compassion, must make them both, in my eyes, I felt by no means assured that such might not be the consequence.—It is true that Reginald had not in any degree grown cool towards me;—but yet he had lately mentioned Frederica spontaneously & unnecessarily, & once had said something in praise of her person.—

*He* was all astonishment at the appearance of my visitor; & at first observed Sir James with an attention which I was pleased to see not unmixed with jealousy;—but unluckily it was impossible for me really to torment him, as Sir James tho' extremely gallant to me, very soon made the whole party understand that his heart was devoted to my daughter.—

I had no great difficulty in convincing De Courcy when we were alone, that I was perfectly justified, all things considered, in desiring the match; & the whole business seemed most comfortably arranged.— They could none of them help perceiving that Sir James was no Solomon,* but I had positively forbidden Frederica's complaining to Charles Vernon or his wife, & they had therefore no pretence for

Interference, though my impertinent Sister I beleive wanted only opportunity for doing so.—

Everything however was going on calmly & quietly; & tho' I counted the hours of Sir James's stay, my mind was entirely satisfied with the posture of affairs.*—Guess then what I must feel at the sudden disturbance of all my schemes, & that too from a quarter, whence I had least reason to apprehend it.—Reginald came this morning into my Dressing room, with a very unusual solemnity of countenance, & after some preface informed me in so many words, that he wished to reason with me on the Impropriety & Unkindness of allowing Sir James Martin to address my Daughter, contrary to *her* inclination. I was all amazement.—When I found that he was not to be laughed out of his design, I calmly required an explanation, & begged to know by what he was impelled & by whom commissioned to reprimand me.

He then told me, mixing in his speech a few insolent compliments & ill timed expressions of Tenderness to which I listened with perfect indifference, that my daughter had acquainted him with some circumstances concerning herself, Sir James, & me, which gave him great uneasiness.—

In short, I found that she had in the first place actually written to him, to request his interference, & that on receiving her Letter he had conversed with her on the subject of it, in order to understand the particulars & assure himself of her real wishes!—

I have not a doubt but that the girl took this opportunity of making down right Love to him; I am convinced of it, from the manner in which he spoke of her. Much good, may such Love do him!—I shall ever despise the Man who can be gratified by the Passion, which he never wished to inspire, nor solicited the avowal of.—I shall always detest them both.—He can have no true regard for me, or he would not have listened to her;—And she, with her little rebellious heart & indelicate feelings to throw herself into the protection of a young Man with whom she had scarcely ever exchanged two words before. I am equally confounded at *her* Impudence & *his* Credulity.—How dared he beleive what she told him in my disfavour!—Ought he not to have felt assured that I must have unanswerable motives for all that I had done!—Where was his reliance on my Sense or Goodness then; where the resentment which true Love would have dictated against the person defaming me, that person too, a Chit,* a Child, without Talent or Education, whom he had been always taught to despise?—

I was calm for some time, but the greatest degree of Forbearance may be overcome; & I hope I was afterwards sufficiently keen.*—He endeavoured, long endeavoured to soften my resentment, but that woman is a fool indeed who while insulted by accusation, can be worked on by compliments.—At length he left me as deeply provoked as myself, & he shewed his anger *more.*—I was quite cool, but he gave way to the most violent indignation.—I may therefore expect it will the sooner subside; & perhaps his may be vanished for ever, while mine will be found still fresh & implacable.

He is now shut up in his apartment, whither I heard him go, on leaving mine.—How unpleasant, one would think, must his reflections be!—But some people's feelings are incomprehensible.—I have not yet tranquillized myself enough to see Frederica. *She* shall not soon forget the occurrences of this day.—She shall find that she has poured forth her tender Tale of Love in vain, & exposed herself forever to the contempt of the whole world, & the severest Resentment of her injured Mother.—yrs affec:ly

S. Vernon

## LETTER 23

*Mrs Vernon to Lady De Courcy.*

CHURCHILL

Let me congratulate you, my dearest Mother. The affair which has given us so much anxiety is drawing to a happy conclusion. Our prospect is most delightful;—And since matters have now taken so favourable a turn, I am quite sorry that I ever imparted my apprehensions to you; for the pleasure of learning that the Danger is over, is perhaps dearly purchased by all that you have previously suffered.—

I am so much agitated by Delight that I can scarcely hold a pen, but am determined to send you a few lines by James, that you may have some explanation of what must so greatly astonish you, as that Reginald should be returning to Parklands.—

I was sitting about half an hour ago with Sir James in the Breakfast parlour, when my Brother called me out of the room.—I instantly saw that something was the matter;—his complexion was raised, & he spoke with great emotion.—You know his eager manner, my dear Madam, when his mind is interested.—

'Catherine,' said he, 'I am going home today. I am sorry to leave you, but I must go.—It is a great while since I have seen my Father & Mother—I am going to send James forward with my Hunters*
immediately, if you have any Letter therefore he can take it.—I shall not be at home myself till Wednesday or Thursday, as I shall go through London, where I have business.—But before I leave you,' he continued, speaking in a lower voice & with still greater energy, 'I must warn you of one thing.—Do not let Frederica Vernon be made unhappy by that Martin.—He wants to marry her—her Mother promotes the Match—but *She* cannot endure the idea of it.—Be assured that I speak from the fullest conviction of the Truth of what I say.—I *know* that Frederica is made wretched by Sir James' continuing here.—She is a sweet girl, & deserves a better fate.—Send him away immediately. *He* is only a fool—but what her Mother can mean, Heaven only knows!—Good bye,' he added shaking my hand with earnestness—'I do not know when you will see me again. But remember what I tell you of Frederica;—you *must* make it your business to see justice done her.—She is an amiable girl, & has a very superior mind to what we have ever given her credit for.—'

He then left me & ran upstairs.—I would not try to stop him, for I knew what his feelings must be; the nature of mine, as I listened to him, I need not attempt to describe.—For a minute or two I remained in the same spot, overpowered by wonder—of a most agreable sort indeed; yet it required some consideration to be tranquilly happy.—

In about ten minutes after my return to the parlour, Lady Susan entered the room.—I concluded of course that she & Reginald had been quarrelling, & looked with anxious curiosity for a confirmation of my beleif in her face.—Mistress of Deceit however, she appeared perfectly unconcerned, & after chatting on indifferent subjects for a short time, said to me,

'I find from Wilson that we are going to lose Mr De Courcy.—Is it true that he leaves Churchill this morning?'—

I replied that it was.—

'He told us nothing of all this last night,' said she laughing, 'or even this morning at Breakfast. But perhaps he did not know it himself.—Young Men are often hasty in their resolutions—& not more sudden in forming, than unsteady in keeping them.—I should not be surprised if he were to change his mind at last, & not go.'—

She soon afterwards left the room.—I trust however my dear Mother, that we have no reason to fear an alteration of his present plan; things have gone too far.—They must have quarrelled, & about Frederica too.—Her calmness astonishes me.—What delight will be yours in seeing him again, in seeing him still worthy your Esteem, still capable of forming your Happiness!

When I next write, I shall be able I hope to tell you that Sir James is gone, Lady Susan vanquished, & Frederica at peace.—We have much to do, but it shall be done.—I am all impatience to know how this astonishing change was effected.—I finish as I began, with the warmest congratulations.—Yrs Ever,

Cath Vernon.

## LETTER 24

*From the same to the same.*

CHURCHILL

Little did I imagine my dear Mother, when I sent off my last letter, that the delightful perturbation of spirits I was then in, would undergo so speedy, so melancholy a reverse!—I never can sufficiently regret that I wrote to you at all.—Yet who could have foreseen what has happened? My dear Mother, every hope which but two hours ago made me so happy, is vanished. The quarrel between Lady Susan & Reginald is made up, & we are all as we were before. One point only is gained; Sir James Martin is dismissed.—What are we now to look forward to?—I am indeed disappointed. Reginald was all but gone; his horse was ordered, & almost brought to the door!—Who would not have felt safe?—

For half an hour I was in momentary expectation of his departure.—After I had sent off my Letter to you, I went to Mr Vernon & sat with him in his room, talking over the whole matter.—I then determined to look for Frederica, whom I had not seen since breakfast.—I met her on the Stairs & saw that she was crying.

'My dear Aunt,' said she, 'he is going, Mr De Courcy is going, & it is all my fault. I am afraid you will be angry, but indeed I had no idea it would end so.'—

'My Love,' replied I, 'do not think it necessary to apologize to me on that account.—I shall feel myself under an obligation to any one who in the means of sending my brother home;—because, (recollecting myself) I know my Father wants very much to see him. But what is it that *you* have done to occasion all this?'—

She blushed deeply as she answered, 'I was so unhappy about Sir James that I could not help—I have done something very wrong I know—but you have not an idea of the misery I have been in, & Mama had ordered me never to speak to you or my Uncle about it,— and—'

'You therefore spoke to my Brother, to engage *his* interference;'— said I, wishing to save her the explanation.—

'No—but I wrote to him.—I did indeed.—I got up this morning before it was light—I was two hours about it—& when my Letter was done, I thought I never should have courage to give it.—After breakfast however, as I was going to my own room I met him in the passage, & then as I knew that every thing must depend on that moment, I forced myself to give it.—He was so good as to take it immediately;—I dared not look at him—& ran away directly.—I was in such a fright that I could hardly breathe.—My dear Aunt, you do not know how miserable I have been.'

'Frederica,' said I, 'you ought to have told *me* all your distresses.— You would have found in me a friend always ready to assist you.—Do you think that your Uncle & I should not have espoused your cause as warmly as my Brother?'—

'Indeed I did not doubt your goodness,' said she colouring again, 'but I thought that Mr De Courcy could do anything with my Mother;—but I was mistaken;—they have had a dreadful quarrel about it, & he is going.—Mama will never forgive me, & I shall be worse off than ever.'—

'No, you shall not,' replied I.—'In such a point as this, your Mother's prohibition ought not to have prevented your speaking to me on the subject. She has no right to make you unhappy, & she shall *not* do it.—Your applying however to Reginald can be productive only of Good to all parties.—I beleive it is best as it is.—Depend upon it that you shall not be made unhappy any longer.'

At that moment, how great was my astonishment at seeing Reginald come out of Lady Susan's Dressing room. My heart misgave me instantly. His confusion on seeing me was very evident.—Frederica immediately disappeared. 'Are you going?'—said I. 'You will find Mr Vernon in his own room.'—

'No Catherine', replied he.—'I am *not* going.—Will you let me speak to you a moment?'

We went into my room. 'I find,' continued he, his confusion increasing as he spoke, 'that I have been acting with my usual foolish Impetuosity.—I have entirely misunderstood Lady Susan, & was on the point of leaving the house under a false impression of her conduct.—There has been some very great mistake—we have been all mistaken I fancy.—Frederica does not know her Mother—Lady Susan means nothing but her Good—but Frederica will not make a friend of her.—Lady Susan therefore does not always know what will make her daughter happy.—Besides *I* could have no right to interfere—Miss Vernon was mistaken in applying to me.—In short Catherine, every thing has gone wrong—but it is now all happily settled.—Lady Susan I beleive wishes to speak to you about it, if you are at leisure.'—

'Certainly;' replied I, deeply sighing at the recital of so lame a story.—I made no remarks however, for words would have been vain. Reginald was glad to get away, & I went to Lady Susan; curious indeed to hear her account of it.—

'Did not I tell you,' said she with a smile, 'that your Brother would not leave us after all?'

'You did indeed,' replied I very gravely, 'but I flattered myself that you would be mistaken.'

'I should not have hazarded such an opinion,' returned she, 'if it had not at that moment occurred to me, that his resolution of going might be occasioned by a Conversation in which we had been this morning engaged, & which had ended very much to his Dissatisfaction from our not rightly understanding each other's meaning.—This idea struck me at the moment, & I instantly determined that an accidental dispute in which I might probably be as much to blame as himself, should not deprive you of your Brother.—If you remember, I left the room almost immediately.—I was resolved to lose no time in clearing up these mistakes as far as I could.—The case was this.— Frederica had set herself violently against marrying Sir James'—

'And can your Ladyship wonder that she should?' cried I with some warmth.—'Frederica has an excellent Understanding, & Sir James has none.'

'I am at least very far from regretting it, my dear Sister,' said she; 'on the contrary, I am grateful for so favourable a sign of my Daughter's sense. Sir James is certainly under par* (his boyish manners make him appear the worse)—& had Frederica possessed the penetration, the abilities, which I could have wished in my daughter, or had I even known her to possess so much as she does, I should not have been anxious for the match.'

'It is odd that you alone should be ignorant of your Daughter's sense.'

'Frederica never does justice to herself;—her manners are shy & childish.—She is besides afraid of me; she scarcely loves me.—During her poor Father's life she was a spoilt child; the severity which it has since been necessary for me to shew, has entirely alienated her affection;—neither has she any of that Brilliancy of Intellect, that Genius,* or vigour of Mind which will force itself forward.'

'Say rather that she has been unfortunate in her Education.'

'Heaven knows my dearest Mrs Vernon, how fully I am aware of *that*; but I would wish to forget every circumstance that might throw blame on the memory of one, whose name is sacred with me.'

Here she pretended to cry.—I was out of patience with her.—'But what,' said I, 'was your Ladyship going to tell me about your disagreement with my Brother?'—

'It originated in an action of my Daughter's, which equally marks her want of Judgement, & the unfortunate Dread of me I have been mentioning.—She wrote to Mr De Courcy.'—

'I know she did.—You had forbidden her speaking to Mr Vernon or to me on the cause of her distress;—what could she do therefore but apply to my Brother?'—

'Good God!'—she exclaimed, 'what an opinion must you have of me!—Can you possibly suppose that I was aware of her unhappiness? that it was my object to make my own Child miserable, & that I had forbidden her speaking to you on the subject, from a fear of your interrupting the Diabolical scheme?—Do you think me destitute of every honest, every natural feeling?—Am I capable of consigning *her* to everlasting Misery, whose welfare it is my first Earthly Duty to promote?'—

'The idea is horrible.—What then was your intention when you insisted on her silence?'—

'Of what use my dear Sister, could be any application to you, however the affair might stand? Why should I subject you to entreaties, which I refused to attend to myself?—Neither for your sake, for hers, nor for my own, could such a thing be desireable.—Where my own resolution was taken, I could not wish for the interference, however friendly, of another person.—I was mistaken it is true, but I beleived myself to be right.'—

'But what was this mistake, to which your Ladyship so often alludes? From whence arose so astonishing a misapprehension of your Daughter's feelings?—Did not you know that she disliked Sir James?'—

'I knew that he was not absolutely the Man whom she would have chosen.—But I was persuaded that her objections to him did not arise from any perception of his Deficiency.—You must not question me however my dear Sister, too minutely on this point'—continued she, taking me affectionately by the hand.—'I honestly own that there is something to conceal.—Frederica makes me very unhappy.—Her applying to Mr De Courcy hurt me particularly.'

'What is it that you mean to infer' said I, 'by this appearance of mystery?—If you think your daughter at all attached to Reginald, her objecting to Sir James could not less deserve to be attended to, than if the cause of her objecting had been a consciousness of his folly.—And why should your Ladyship at any rate quarrel with my brother for an interference which you must know, it was not in his nature to refuse, when urged in such a manner?'

'His disposition you know is warm,* & he came to expostulate with me, his compassion all alive for this ill-used Girl, this Heroine in distress!—We misunderstood each other. He beleived me more to blame than I really was; I considered his interference as less excusable than I now find it. I have a real regard for him, & was beyond expression mortified to find it as I thought so ill bestowed. We were both warm, & of course both to blame.—His resolution of leaving Churchill is consistent with his general eagerness;—when I understood his intention however, & at the same time began to think that we had perhaps been equally mistaken in each other's meaning, I resolved to have an explanation before it were too late.—For any Member of your Family I must always feel a degree of affection, & I own it would have sensibly hurt me, if my acquaintance with Mr De Courcy had ended so gloomily. I have now only to say farther, that as I am convinced of Frederica's having a reasonable dislike to Sir James, I shall instantly inform him that he must give up all hope of her.— I reproach myself for having ever, tho' so innocently, made her unhappy on that score. She shall have all the satisfaction* in my power to make; if she value her own happiness as much as I do, if she judge wisely & command herself as she ought, she may now be easy.—Excuse me, my dearest Sister, for thus trespassing on your time, but I owed it to my own Character; & after this explanation I trust I am in no danger of sinking in your opinion.'

I could have said 'Not much indeed;'—but I left her almost in silence.—It was the greatest stretch of Forbearance I could practise. I could not have stopped myself, had I begun.—Her assurance, her Deceit—but I will not allow myself to dwell on them;—they will strike you sufficiently. My heart sickens within me.—

As soon as I was tolerably composed, I returned to the Parlour. Sir James's carriage was at the door, & he, merry as usual, soon afterwards took his leave.—How easily does her Ladyship encourage, or dismiss a Lover!—

In spite of this release, Frederica still looks unhappy, still fearful perhaps of her Mother's anger, & tho' dreading my Brother's departure jealous, it may be, of his staying.—I see how closely she observes him & Lady Susan.—Poor Girl, I have now no hope for her. There is not a chance of her affection being returned.—He thinks very differently of her, from what he used to do, he does her some justice, but his reconciliation with her Mother precludes every dearer hope.—

Prepare my dear Madam, for the worst.—The probability of their marrying is surely heightened. He is more securely her's than ever.—When that wretched Event takes place, Frederica must belong wholly to us.—

I am thankful that my last Letter will precede this by so little, as every moment that you can be saved from feeling a Joy which leads only to disappointment is of consequence.—

yrs Ever, Cath Vernon.

## LETTER 25

*Lady Susan to Mrs Johnson.*

CHURCHILL

I call on you dear Alicia, for congratulations. I am again myself;—gay & triumphant.— When I wrote to you the other day, I was in truth in high irritation, & with ample cause.—Nay, I know not whether I ought to be quite tranquil now, for I have had more trouble in restoring peace than I ever intended to submit to.—This Reginald has a proud spirit of his own!—A spirit too, resulting from a fancied sense of superior Integrity which is peculiarly insolent.—I shall not easily forgive him I assure you. He was actually on the point of leaving Churchill!—I had scarcely concluded my last, when Wilson brought me word of it.—I found therefore that something must be done, for I did not chuse to have my character at the mercy of a Man whose passions were so violent & resentful.—It would have been trifling with my reputation, to allow of his departing with such an impression in my disfavour;—in this light, condescension* was necessary.—

I sent Wilson to say that I desired to speak with him before he went.—He came immediately. The angry emotions which had marked every feature when we last parted, were partially subdued. He seemed astonished at the summons, & looked as if half wishing & half fearing to be softened by what I might say.—

If my Countenance expressed what I aimed at, it was composed & dignified—& yet with a degree of pensiveness which might convince him that I was not quite happy.—

'I beg your pardon Sir, for the liberty I have taken in sending to you,' said I; 'but as I have just learnt your intention of leaving this place today, I feel it my duty to entreat that you will not on my account shorten your visit here, even an hour.—I am perfectly aware that after what has passed between us, it would ill suit the feelings of either to remain longer in the same house.—So very great, so total a change from the intimacy of Friendship, must render any future intercourse the severest punishment;—& your resolution of quitting Churchill is undoubtedly in unison with our situation & with those lively feelings which I know you to possess.—But at the same time, it is not for me to suffer such a sacrifice, as it must be, to leave Relations to whom you are so much attached & are so dear. My remaining here cannot give that pleasure to Mr & Mrs Vernon which your society must;—& my visit has already perhaps been too long. My removal therefore, which must at any rate take place soon, may with perfect convenience be hastened;—& I make it my particular request that I may not in any way be instrumental in separating a family so affectionately attached ~~to each other.~~ ~~Whom I am, is of no consequence to any one, of very~~ little to myself; but *you* are of importance to all your connections.'

Here I concluded, & I hope you will be satisfied with my speech.—It's effect on Reginald justifies some portion of vanity, for it was no less favourable than instantaneous.—Oh! how delightful it was, to watch the variations of his Countenance while I spoke, to see the struggle between returning Tenderness & the remains of Displeasure.—There is something agreable in feelings so easily worked on. Not that I envy him their possession, nor would for the world have such myself, but they are very convenient where one wishes to influence the passions of another. And yet this Reginald, whom a very few words from me softened at once into the utmost submission, & rendered more tractable, more attached, more devoted than ever, would have left me in the first angry swelling of his proud heart, without deigning to seek an explanation!—

Humbled as he now is, I cannot forgive him such an instance of Pride; & am doubtful whether I ought not to punish him, by dismissing him at once after this our reconciliation, or by marrying & teizing him for ever.—But these measures are each too violent to be adopted without some deliberation. At present my Thoughts are fluctuating between various schemes.—I have many things to compass.—I must punish Frederica, & pretty severely too, for her application to Reginald;—I must punish him for receiving it so favourably, & for the rest of his conduct. I must torment my Sister-in-law for the insolent triumph of her Look & Manner since Sir James has been dismissed—for in reconciling Reginald to me, I was not able to save that ill-fated young Man;—& I must make myself amends for the humiliations to which I have stooped within these few days.—To effect all this I have various plans.—I have also an idea of being soon in Town, & whatever may be my determination as to the rest, I shall probably put *that* project in execution—for London will be always the fairest field of action, however my veiws may be directed, & at any rate, I shall there be rewarded by your society & a little Dissipation for a ten weeks penance at Churchill.—

I beleive I owe it to my own Character, to complete the match between my daughter & Sir James, after having so long intended it.—Let me know your opinion on this point.—Flexibility of Mind, a Disposition easily biassed by others, is an attribute which you know I am not very desirous of obtaining;—nor has Frederica any claim to the indulgence of her whims, at the expence of her Mother's inclination.—Her idle Love for Reginald too;—it is surely my duty to discourage such romantic nonsense.—All things considered therefore, it seems encumbent on me to take her to Town, & marry her immediately to Sir James.

When my own will is effected, contrary to his, I shall have some credit in being on good terms with Reginald, which at present in fact I have not, for tho' he is still in my power, I have given up the very article by which our quarrel was produced, & at best, the honour of victory is doubtful.—

Send me your opinion on all these matters, my dear Alicia, & let me know whether you can get Lodgings to suit me within a short distance of you.—Yr most attached

S. Vernon.

## LETTER 26

*Mrs Johnson to Lady Susan.*

EDWARD ST.

I am gratified by your reference, & this is my advice; that you come to Town yourself without loss of time, but that you leave Frederica behind. It would surely be much more to the purpose to get yourself well established by marrying Mr De Courcy, than to irritate him & the rest of his family, by making her marry Sir James.—You should think more of yourself, & less of your Daughter.—She is not of a disposition to do you credit in the World, & seems precisely in her proper place, at Churchill with the Vernons;—but *you* are fitted for Society, & it is shameful to have you exiled from it.—Leave Frederica therefore to punish herself for the plague she has given you, by indulging that romantic tender-heartedness which will always ensure her misery enough; & come yourself to Town, as soon as you can.—

I have another reason for urging this.—Manwaring came to Town last week, & has contrived, in spite of Mr Johnson, to make opportunities of seeing me.—He is absolutely miserable about you, & jealous to such a degree of De Courcy, that it would be highly unadvisable for them to meet* at present; & yet if you do not allow him to see you here, I cannot answer for his not committing some great imprudence—such as going to Churchill for instance, which would be dreadful.—Besides, if you take my advice, & resolve to marry De Courcy, it will be indispensably necessary for you to get Manwaring out of the way, & you only can have influence enough to send him back to his wife.—

I have still another motive for your coming. Mr Johnson leaves London next Tuesday. He is going for his health to Bath,* where if the waters are favourable to his constitution & my wishes, he will be laid up with the Gout many weeks.—During his absence we shall be able to chuse our own Society, & have true enjoyment.—I would ask you to Edward St. but that he once forced from me a kind of promise never to invite you to my house. Nothing but my being in the utmost distress for Money, could have extorted it from me.—I can get you however a very nice Drawing room-apartment in Upper Seymour St.,* & we may be always together, there or here, for I consider my promise to Mr Johnson as comprehending only (at least in his absence) your not sleeping in the House.—

Poor Manwaring gives me such histories of his wife's jealousy!— Silly Woman, to expect Constancy from so charming a Man!—But she was always silly; intolerably so, in marrying him at all. She, the Heiress of a large Fortune, he without a shilling!—*One* Title I know she might have had, besides Baronets.*—Her folly in form-ing the connection was so great, that tho' Mr Johnson was her Guardian & I do not in general share his feelings, I never can forgive her.—

Adeiu. Yours, Alicia.—

## LETTER 27

*Mrs Vernon to Lady De Courcy.*

CHURCHILL

This Letter my dear Mother, will be brought you by Reginald. His long visit is about to be concluded at last, but I fear the separation takes place too late to do us any good.—*She* is going to Town, to see her particular friend, Mrs Johnson. It was at first her intention that Frederica should accompany her for the benefit of Masters,* but we over-ruled her there.— Frederica was wretched in the idea of going, & I could not bear to have her at the mercy of her Mother. Not all the Masters in London could compensate for the ruin of her comfort. I should have feared too for her health, & for every thing in short but her Principles; *there* I beleive she is not to be injured, even by her Mother, or all her Mother's friends;—but with those friends (a very bad set I doubt not) she must have mixed, or have been left in total solitude, & I can hardly tell which would have been worse for her.—If she is with her Mother moreover, she must alas! in all probability be with Reginald—and that would be the greatest evil of all.—

Here, we shall in time be at peace.—Our regular employments, our Books & conversation, with Exercise, the Children, & every domestic pleasure in my power to procure her, will, I trust, gradually overcome this youthful attachment. I should not have a doubt of it, were she slighted for any other woman in the world, than her own Mother.—

How long Lady Susan will be in Town, or whether she returns here again, I know not.—I could not be cordial in my invitation; but if she chuses to come, no want of cordiality on my part will keep her away.—

I could not help asking Reginald if he intended being in Town this winter, as soon as I found that her Ladyship's steps would be bent thither; & tho' he professed himself quite undetermined, there was a something in his Look & voice as he spoke, which contradicted his words.—I have done with Lamentation.—I look upon the Event as so far decided, that I resign myself to it in despair. If he leaves you soon for London, every thing will be concluded.—

Yours affec:ly<br>Cath Vernon.

# LETTER 28

*Mrs Johnson to Lady Susan.*

EDWARD ST.

My dearest Friend,

I write in the greatest distress; the most unfortunate event has just taken place. Mr Johnson has hit on the most effectual manner of plaguing us all.—He had heard I imagine by some means or other, that you were soon to be in London, & immediately contrived to have such an attack of the Gout, as must at least delay his journey to Bath, if not wholly prevent it.—I am persuaded the Gout is brought on, or kept off at pleasure; it was the same, when I wanted to join the Hamiltons to the Lakes;* & three years ago when *I* had a fancy for Bath, nothing could induce him to have a Gouty symptom.

I have received yours, & have engaged the Lodgings in consequence.—I am pleased to find that my Letter had so much effect on you, & that De Courcy is certainly your own.—Let me hear from you as soon as you arrive, & in particular tell me what you mean to do with Manwaring.—It is impossible to say when I shall be able to see you. My confinement must be great. It is such an abominable trick, to be ill here, instead of at Bath, that I can scarcely command myself at all.—At Bath, his old Aunts would have nursed him, but here it all falls upon me—& he bears pain with such patience that I have not the common excuse for losing my temper.

Yrs Ever, Alicia.

# LETTER 29

*Lady Susan to Mrs Johnson.*

UPPER SEYMOUR ST.

My dear Alicia

There needed not this last fit of the Gout to make me detest Mr Johnson; but now the extent of my aversion is not to be estimated.— To have you confined, a Nurse, in his apartment!—My dear Alicia, of what a mistake were you guilty in marrying a Man of his age!—just old enough to be formal, ungovernable & to have the Gout—too old to be agreable, & too young to die.

I arrived last night about five, & had scarcely swallowed my dinner when Manwaring made his appearance.—I will not dissemble what real pleasure his sight afforded me, nor how strongly I felt the contrast between his person & manners, & those of Reginald, to the infinite disadvantage of the latter.—For an hour or two, I was even stagger'd in my resolution of marrying him—& tho' this was too idle & nonsensical an idea to remain long on my mind, I do not feel very eager for the conclusion of my marriage, or look forward with much impatience to the time when Reginald according to our agreement is to be in Town.—I shall probably put off his arrival, under some pretence or other. He must not come till Manwaring is gone.

I am still doubtful at times, as to Marriage.—If the old Man would die, I might not hesitate; but a state of dependance on the caprice of Sir Reginald, will not suit the freedom of my spirit;—and if I resolve to wait for that event, I shall have excuse enough at present, in having been scarcely ten months a Widow.*

I have not given Manwaring any hint of my intention—or allowed him to consider my acquaintance with Reginald as more than the commonest flirtation;—& he is tolerably appeased.—Adeiu till we meet.—I am enchanted with my Lodgings.—Yrs Ever,

S. Vernon.—

# LETTER 30

*Lady Susan to Mr De Courcy.**

UPPER SEYMOUR ST.

I have received your Letter; & tho' I do not attempt to conceal that I am gratified by your impatience for the hour of meeting, I yet feel myself under the necessity of delaying that hour beyond the time originally fixed.—Do not think me unkind for such an exercise of my power, or accuse me of Instability, without first hearing my reasons.— In the course of my journey from Churchill, I had ample leisure for reflection on the present state of our affairs, & every reveiw has served to convince me that they require a delicacy & cautiousness of conduct, to which we have hitherto been too little attentive.—We have been hurried on by our feelings to a degree of Precipitance which ill accords with the claims of our Friends, or the opinion of the World.—We have been unguarded in forming this hasty Engagement; but we must not complete the imprudence by ratifying it, while there is so much reason to fear the Connection would be opposed by those Friends on whom you depend.

It is not for us to blame any expectation on your Father's side of your marrying to advantage; where possessions are so extensive as those of your Family, the wish of increasing them, if not strictly reasonable, is too common to excite surprise or resentment.—He has a right to require a woman of fortune in his daughter in law; & I am sometimes quarreling with myself for suffering you to form a connection so imprudent.—But the influence of reason is often acknowledged too late by those who feel like me.—

I have now been but a few months a widow; & however little endebted to my Husband's memory for any happiness derived from him during an Union of some years, I cannot forget that the indelicacy of so early a second marriage, must subject me to the censure of the World, & incur what would be still more insupportable, the displeasure of Mr Vernon.—I might perhaps harden myself in time against the injustice of general reproach; but the loss of *his* valued Esteem, I am as you well know, ill fitted to endure;—and when to this, may be added the consciousness of having injured you with your Family, how am I to support myself.—With feelings so poignant as mine, the conviction of having divided the son from his Parents, would make me, even with *You,* the most miserable of Beings.—

It will surely therefore be advisable to delay our Union, to delay it till appearances are more promising, till affairs have taken a more favourable turn.—To assist us in such a resolution, I feel that absence will be necessary. We must not meet.—Cruel as this sentence may appear, the necessity of pronouncing it, which can alone reconcile it to myself, will be evident to you when you have considered our situation in the light in which I have found myself imperiously* obliged to place it.—You may be, you must be well assured that nothing but the strongest conviction of Duty, could induce me to wound my own feelings by urging a lengthened separation; & of Insensibility to yours, you will hardly suspect me.—Again therefore I say that we ought not, we must not yet meet.—By a removal for some months from each other, we shall tranquillize the sisterly fears of Mrs Vernon, who, accustomed herself to the enjoyment of riches, considers Fortune as necessary every where, & whose Sensibilities are not of a nature to comprehend ours.——

Let me hear from you soon, very soon. Tell me that you submit to my Arguments, & do not reproach me for using such.——I cannot bear reproaches. My spirits are not so high as to need being repressed.—— I must endeavour to seek amusement abroad,* & fortunately many of my Friends are in Town—among them, the Manwarings.——You know how sincerely I regard both Husband & wife.——I am Ever, Faithfully Yours

S. Vernon——

LETTER 31

*Lady Susan to Mrs Johnson.*

UPPER SEYMOUR ST.

My dear Friend,

That tormenting Creature Reginald is here. My Letter, which was intended to keep him longer in the Country, has hastened him to Town. Much as I wish him away however, I cannot help being pleased with such a proof of attachment. He is devoted to me, heart & soul.——He will carry this note himself, which is to serve as an Introduction to you, with whom he longs to be acquainted. Allow him to spend the Evening with you, that I may be in no danger of his returning here.——I have told him that I am not quite well, & must be alone—& should he call again there might be confusion, for it is impossible to be sure of servants.——Keep him therefore I entreat you in Edward St.——You will not find him a heavy companion, & I allow you to flirt with him as much as you like. At the same time do not forget my real interest;—say all that you can to convince him that I shall be quite wretched if he remain here;—you know my reasons— Propriety & so forth.——I would urge them more myself, but that I am impatient to be rid of him, as Manwaring comes within half an hour.

Adeiu. SV.——

# LETTER 32

*Mrs Johnson to Lady Susan.*

EDWARD ST.

My dear Creature,

I am in agonies, & know not what to do, nor what *you* can do.—Mr De Courcy arrived, just when he should not. Mrs Manwaring had that instant entered the House, & forced herself into her Guardian's presence, tho' I did not know a syllable of it till afterwards, for I was out when both she & Reginald came, or I would have sent him away at all events; but *she* was shut up with Mr Johnson, while *he* waited in the Drawing room for me.—

She arrived yesterday in pursuit of her Husband;—but perhaps you know this already from himself.—She came to this house to entreat my Husband's interference, & before I could be aware of it, everything that you could wish to be concealed, was known to him; & unluckily she had wormed out of Manwaring's servant that he had visited you every day since your being in Town, & had just watched him to your door herself!—What could I do?—Facts are such horrid things!—All is by this time known to De Courcy, who is now alone with Mr Johnson.—Do not accuse me;—indeed it was impossible to prevent it.—Mr Johnson has for some time suspected De Courcy of intending to marry you, & would speak with him alone, as soon as he knew him to be in the House.—

That detestable Mrs Manwaring, who for your comfort, has fretted herself thinner & uglier than ever, is still here, & they have been all closeted together. What can be done?—If Manwaring is now with you, he had better be gone.—At any rate I hope he will plague his wife more than ever.—With anxious wishes, Yrs faithfully

Alicia.

## LETTER 33

*Lady Susan to Mrs Johnson.*

UPPER SEYMOUR ST.

This Eclaircissement* is rather provoking.—How unlucky that you should have been from home!—I thought myself sure of you at 7.—I am undismayed however. Do not torment yourself with fears on my account.—Depend upon it, I can make my own story good with Reginald. Manwaring is just gone; he brought me the news of his wife's arrival. Silly Woman! what does she expect by such manœuvres?*—Yet, I wish she had staid quietly at Langford.—

Reginald will be a little enraged at first, but by Tomorrow's Dinner, every thing will be well again.—Adeiu. SV.

## LETTER 34

*Mr De Courcy to Lady Susan.*

HOTEL

I write only to bid you Farewell.—The spell is removed. I see you as you are.—Since we parted yesterday, I have received from indisputable authority, such an history of you as must bring the most mortifying conviction of the Imposition I have been under, & the absolute necessity of an immediate & eternal separation from you.—You cannot doubt to what I allude;—Langford—Langford—that word will be sufficient.—I received my information in Mr Johnson's house, from Mrs Manwaring herself.—

You know how I have loved you, you can intimately judge of my present feelings; but I am not so weak as to find indulgence in describing them to a woman who will glory in having excited their anguish, but whose affection they have never been able to gain.

R De Courcy.

## LETTER 35

*Lady Susan to Mr De Courcy.*

UPPER SEYMOUR ST.

I will not attempt to describe my astonishment on reading the note, this moment received from you.— I am bewilder'd in my endeavours to form some rational conjecture of what Mrs Manwaring can have told you, to occasion so extraordinary a change in your sentiments.— Have I not explained everything to you with respect to myself which could bear a doubtful meaning, & which the illnature of the world had interpreted to my Discredit?—What can you *now* have heard to stagger your Esteem for me?—Have I ever had a concealment from you?—Reginald, you agitate me beyond expression.—I cannot suppose that the old story of Mrs Manwaring's jealousy can be revived again, or at least, be *listened* to again.—Come to me immediately, & explain what is at present absolutely incomprehensible.—Beleive me, the single word of *Langford* is not of such potent intelligence, as to supersede the necessity of more.—If we *are* to part, it will at least be handsome to take your personal Leave.—But I have little heart to jest; in truth, I am serious enough—for to be sunk, tho' but an hour, in your opinion, is an humiliation to which I know not how to submit. I shall count every moment till your arrival.

S. V.

## LETTER 36

*Mr De Courcy to Lady Susan.*

HOTEL

Why would you write to me?—Why do you require particulars?— But since it must be so, I am obliged to declare that all the accounts of your misconduct during the life & since the death of Mr Vernon which had reached me in common with the World in general, & gained my entire beleif before I saw you, but which you by the exertion of your perverted Abilities had made me resolve to disallow, have been unanswerably proved to me.—Nay, more—I am assured that a Connection, of which I had never before entertained a thought, has for some time existed, & still continues to exist between you & the Man, whose family you robbed of it's Peace, in return for the hospitality with which you were received into it!—That you have corresponded with him ever since your leaving Langford—not with his wife—but with him—& he now visits you every day.—Can you, dare you deny it?—And all this at the time when I was an encouraged, an accepted Lover!—From what have I not escaped!—I have only to be grateful.—Far from me be all Complaint, & every sigh of regret. My own Folly had endangered me, my Preservation I owe to the kindness, the Integrity of another.—But the unfortunate Mrs Manwaring, whose agonies while she related the past, seem'd to threaten her reason—how is *she* to be consoled?

After such a discovery as this, you will scarcely affect farther wonder at my meaning in bidding you Adeiu.—My Understanding is at length restored, & teaches me no less to abhor the Artifices which had subdued me, than to despise myself for the weakness, on which their strength was founded.—

R De Courcy.—


## LETTER 37

*Lady Susan to Mr De Courcy.*

UPPER SEYMOUR ST.

I am satisfied—& will trouble you no more when these few Lines are dismissed.*—The Engagement which you were eager to form a fortnight ago, is no longer compatible with your veiws, & I rejoice to find that the prudent advice of your Parents has not been given in vain.—Your restoration to Peace will, I doubt not, speedily follow this act of filial Obedience, & I flatter myself with the hope of surviving *my* share in this disappointment.

SV.

## LETTER 38

*Mrs Johnson to Lady Susan.*

EDWARD ST.

I am greived, tho' I cannot be astonished at your rupture with Mr De Courcy;—he has just informed Mr Johnson of it by letter. He leaves London he says to day.—Be assured that I partake in all your feelings, & do not be angry if I say that our intercourse even by Letter must soon be given up.—It makes me miserable—but Mr Johnson vows that if I persist in the Connection, he will settle in the Country for the rest of his life—& you know it is impossible to submit to such an extremity while any other alternative remains.—

You have heard of course that the Manwarings are to part;*—I am afraid Mrs M. will come home to us again. But she is still so fond of her Husband & frets so much about him that perhaps she may not live long.—

Miss Manwaring is just come to Town to be with her Aunt, & they say, that she declares she will have Sir James Martin before she leaves London again.—If I were you, I would certainly get him myself.—I had almost forgot to give you my opinion of De Courcy, I am really delighted with him, he is full as handsome I think as Manwaring, & with such an open, good humoured Countenance that one cannot help loving him at first sight.—Mr Johnson & he are the greatest friends in the World. Adeiu, my dearest Susan.—I wish matters did not go so perversely. That unlucky visit to Langford!—But I dare say you did all for the best, & there is no defying Destiny.—

Yr sincerely attached

Alicia.

## LETTER 39

*Lady Susan to Mrs Johnson.*

UPPER SEYMOUR ST.

My dear Alicia

I yeild to the necessity which parts us. Under such circumstances you could not act otherwise. Our friendship cannot be impaired by it; &

in happier times, when your situation is as independant as mine, it will unite us again in the same Intimacy as ever.—For this, I shall impatiently wait; & meanwhile can safely assure you that I never was more at ease, or better satisfied with myself & every thing about me, than at the present hour.—Your Husband I abhor—Reginald I despise—& I am secure of never seeing either again. Have I not reason to rejoice?—Manwaring is more devoted to me than ever; & were he at liberty, I doubt if I could resist even Matrimony offered by *him*. This Event, if his wife live with you, it may be in your power to hasten. The violence of her feelings, which must wear her out, may be easily kept in irritation.—I rely on your friendship for this.—I am now satisfied that I never could have brought myself to marry Reginald; & am equally determined that Frederica never *shall*. To-morrow I shall fetch her from Churchill, & let Maria Manwaring tremble for the consequence. Frederica shall be Sir James's wife before she quits my house. *She* may whimper, & the Vernons may storm;—I regard them not. I am tired of submitting my will to the Caprices of others—of resigning my own Judgement in deference to those, to whom I owe no Duty, & for whom I feel no respect.—I have given up too much—have been too easily worked on; but Frederica shall now find the difference.—

Adeiu, dearest of Friends. May the next Gouty Attack be more favourable—& may you always regard me as unalterably yours
S. Vernon.—

# LETTER 40

*Lady De Courcy to Mrs Vernon.*

PARKLANDS

My dear Catherine

I have charming news for you, & if I had not sent off my Letter this morning, you might have been spared the vexation of knowing of Reginalds being gone to Town, for he is returned, Reginald is returned, not to ask our consent to his marrying Lady Susan, but to tell us that they are parted forever!—He has been only an hour in the House, & I have not been able to learn particulars, for he is so very low, that I have not the heart to ask questions; but I hope we shall soon know all.—This is the most joyful hour he has ever given us, since the day of his birth. Nothing is wanting but to have you here, & it is our particular wish & entreaty that you would come to us as soon as you can. You have owed us a visit many long weeks.—I hope nothing will make it inconvenient to Mr Vernon, & pray bring all my Grand Children, & your dear Niece is included of course, I long to see her.—It has been a sad heavy winter hitherto, without Reginald, & seeing nobody from Churchill; I never found the season so dreary before, but this happy meeting will make us young again.—Frederica runs much in my thoughts, & when Reginald has recovered his usual good spirits, (as I trust he soon will) we will try to rob him of his heart once more, & I am full of hopes of seeing their hands joined at no great distance.

Yr affec: Mother

C. De Courcy.

## LETTER 41

*Mrs Vernon to Lady De Courcy.*

CHURCHILL

My dear Madam

Your Letter has surprised me beyond measure. Can it be true that they are really separated—& for ever?—I should be overjoyed if I dared depend on it, but after all that I have seen, how can one be secure?—And Reginald really with you!—My surprise is the greater, because on Wednesday, the very day of his coming to Parklands, we had a most unexpected & unwelcome visit from Lady Susan, looking all chearfulness & good humour, & seeming more as if she were to marry him when she got back to Town, than as if parted from him for ever.—She staid nearly two hours, was as affectionate & agreable as ever, & not a syllable, not a hint was dropped of any Disagreement or Coolness between them. I asked her whether she had seen my Brother since his arrival in Town—not as you may suppose with any doubt of the fact—but merely to see how she looked.—She immediately answered without any embarrassment that he had been kind enough to call on her on Monday, but she beleived he had already returned home—which I was very far from crediting.—

Your kind invitation is accepted by us with pleasure, & on Thursday next, we & our little ones will be with you.—Pray Heaven! Reginald may not be in Town again by that time!—

I wish we could bring dear Frederica too, but I am sorry to add that her Mother's errand hither was to fetch her away; & miserable as it made the poor Girl, it was impossible to detain her. I was thoroughly unwilling to let her go, & so was her Uncle; & all that could be urged, we *did* urge. But Lady Susan declared that as she was now about to fix herself in Town for several months she could not be easy if her Daughter were not with her, for Masters &c.—Her Manner, to be sure, was very kind & proper—& Mr Vernon beleives that Frederica will now be treated with affection. I wish I could think so too!—

The poor girl's heart was almost broke at taking leave of us. I charged her to write to me very often, & to remember that if she were in any distress, we should be always her friends.—I took care to see her alone, that I might say all this, & I hope made her a little more comfortable.—But I shall not be easy till I can go to Town & judge of her Situation myself.—

I wish there were a better prospect than now appears, of the Match, which the conclusion of your Letter declares your expectation of.—At present it is not very likely.—

Yrs &c<br>
Cath Vernon.

## CONCLUSION

This Correspondence, by a meeting between some of the Parties & a separation between the others, could not, to the great detriment of the Post office Revenue,* be continued longer.—Very little assistance to the State could be derived from the Epistolary Intercourse of Mrs Vernon & her neice, for the former soon perceived by the stile of Frederica's Letters that they were written under her Mother's inspection, & therefore deferring all particular enquiry till she could make it personally in Town, ceased writing minutely or often.—

Having learnt enough in the meanwhile from her open-hearted Brother, of what had passed between him & Lady Susan to sink the latter lower than ever in her opinion, she was proportionably more anxious to get Frederica removed from such a Mother, & placed under her own care; & tho' with little hope of success, was resolved to leave nothing unattempted that might offer a chance of obtaining her Sister in law's consent to it.—Her anxiety on the subject made her press for an early visit to London; & Mr Vernon who, as it must have already appeared, lived only to do whatever he was desired, soon found some accommodation. Thoroughly in full love thither.—With a heart full of the Matter, Mrs Vernon waited on Lady Susan, shortly after her arrival in Town; & was met with such an easy & chearful affection as made her almost turn from her with horror.—No remembrance of Reginald, no consciousness of Guilt, gave one look of embarrassment.—She was in excellent spirits, & seemed eager to shew at once, by every possible attention to her Brother & Sister, her sense of their kindness, & her pleasure in their society.

Frederica was no more altered than Lady Susan;—the same restrained Manners, the same timid Look in the presence of her Mother as heretofore, assured her Aunt of her situation's being uncomfortable, & confirmed her in the plan of altering it.—No unkindness however on the part of Lady Susan appeared. Persecution on the subject of Sir James was entirely at an end—his name merely mentioned to say that he was not in London; and in all her conversation she was solicitous only for the welfare & improvement of her Daughter, acknowledging in terms of grateful delight that Frederica was now growing every day more & more what a Parent could desire.—

Mrs Vernon surprised & incredulous, knew not what to suspect, & without any change in her own veiws, only feared greater difficulty in accomplishing them. The first hope of anything better was derived from Lady Susan's asking her whether she thought Frederica looked quite as well as she had done at Churchill, as she must confess herself to have sometimes an anxious doubt of London's perfectly agreeing with her.—

Mrs Vernon encouraging the doubt, directly proposed her Neice's returning with them into the Country. Lady Susan was unable to express her sense of such kindness; yet knew not from a variety of reasons how to part with her Daughter; & as, tho' her own plans were not yet wholly fixed, she trusted it would ere long be in her power to take Frederica into the Country herself, concluded by declining entirely to profit by such unexampled attention.—Mrs Vernon however persevered in the offer of it; & tho' Lady Susan continued to resist, her resistance in the course of a few days seemed somewhat less formidable.

The lucky alarm of an Influenza,* decided what might not have been decided quite so soon.—Lady Susan's maternal fears were then too much awakened for her to think of anything but Frederica's removal from the risk of infection. Above all Disorders in the World, she most dreaded the Influenza for her daughter's constitution. Frederica returned to Churchill with her Uncle & Aunt, & three weeks afterwards Lady Susan announced her being married to Sir James Martin.—

Mrs Vernon was then convinced of what she had only suspected before, that she might have spared herself all the trouble of urging a removal, which Lady Susan had doubtless resolved on from the first.—Frederica's visit was nominally for six weeks;—but her Mother, tho' inviting her to return in one or two affectionate Letters, was very ready to oblige the whole Party by consenting to a prolongation of her stay, & in the course of two months ceased to write of her absence, & in the course of two more, to write to her at all.

Frederica was therefore fixed in the family of her Uncle & Aunt, till such time as Reginald De Courcy could be talked, flattered & finessed* into an affection for her—which, allowing leisure for the conquest of his attachment to her Mother, for his abjuring all future attachments & detesting the Sex, might be reasonably looked for in the course of a Twelvemonth. Three Months might have done it in general, but Reginald's feelings were no less lasting than lively.—

Whether Lady Susan was, or was not happy in her second Choice— I do not see how it can ever be ascertained—for who would take her assurance of it, on either side of the question?—The World must judge from Probability.—She had nothing against her, but her Husband & her Conscience.

Sir James may seem to have drawn an harder Lot than mere Folly merited.—I leave him therefore to all the Pity that anybody can give him. For myself, I confess that *I* can pity only Miss Manwaring, who coming to Town & putting herself to an expence in Cloathes, which impoverished her for two years, on purpose to secure him, was defrauded of her due by a Woman ten years older than herself.

FINIS.

# THE WATSONS

# THE WATSONS

The first winter assembly* in the Town of D—— in Surry* was to
be held on Tuesday October the 13th,* & it was generally expected to
be a very good one; a long list of Country Families* was confidently
run over as sure of attending, & sanguine hopes were entertained that
the Osbornes themselves would be there.—The Edwardes' invitation
to the Watsons followed of course. The Edward's were people of fortune who lived in the Town & kept their Coach; the Watsons inhabited
a village about 3 miles distant, were poor & had no close carriage;* &
ever since there had been Balls in the place, the former were accustomed to invite the Latter* to dress dine & sleep at their House, on
every monthly return* throughout the winter.—On the present occasion, as only two of Mr W.'s children were at home, & one was always
necessary as companion to himself, for he was sickly & had lost his
wife one only could profit by the kindness of their friends; Miss
Emma Watson who was very recently returned to her family from the
care of an Aunt who had brought her up was to make her first public
appearance in the neighbourhood—& her eldest Sister, whose delight
in a Ball was not lessened by a ten years Enjoyment, had some merit
in chearfully undertaking to drive her & all her finery in the old
Chair* to D. on the important morning.—

As they splashed along the dirty Lane Miss Watson* thus in-
structed & cautioned her inexperienc'd sister.—'I dare say it will be
a very good Ball, & among so many officers, you will hardly want partners. You will find Mrs Edwards' maid very willing to help you, and
I would advise you to ask Mary Edwards's opinion if you are at all at
a loss for she has a very good Taste.—If Mr E. does not lose his
money at Cards, you will stay as late as you can wish for; if he does, he
will hurry you home perhaps—but you are sure of some comfortable
Soup.—I hope you will be in good looks—. I should not be surprised
if you were to be thought one of the prettiest girls in the room, there
is a great deal in Novelty. Perhaps Tom Musgrave* may take notice of
you—but I would advise you by all means not to give him any encouragement. He generally pays attention to every new girl, but he is
a great flirt & never means anything serious.' 'I think I have heard you

speak of him before,' said Emma. 'Who is he?' 'A young Man of very good fortune, quite independant,* & remarkably agreable, an universal favourite wherever he goes. Most of the girls hereabouts are in love with him, or have been. I beleive I am the only one among them that have escaped with a whole heart, and yet I was the first he paid attention to, when he came into this Country,* six years ago; and very great attention indeed did he pay me. Some people say that he has never seemed to like any girl so well since, tho' he is always behaving in a particular way to one or another.'—

'And how came *your* heart to be the only cold one?'—said Emma smiling. 'There was a reason for that'—replied Miss W. changing colour.—'I have not been very well used Emma among them, I hope you will have better luck.'—'Dear Sister, I beg your pardon, if I have unthinkingly given you pain.'—'When first we knew Tom Musgrave,' continued Miss W. without seeming to hear her, 'I was very much attached to a young Man of the name of Purvis* a particular freind of Robert's, who used to be with us a great deal. Every body thought it would have been a Match.' A sigh accompanied these words, which Emma respected in silence—but her Sister after a short pause, went on—'You will naturally ask why it did not take place, & why he is married to another Woman, while I am still single.—But you must ask him—not me—you must ask Penelope.—Yes Emma, Penelope was at the bottom of it all.—She thinks everything fair for a Husband; I trusted her, she set him against me, with a veiw of gaining him herself, & it ended in his discontinuing his visits & soon after marrying somebody else.—Penelope makes light of her conduct, but *I* think such Treachery very bad. It has been the ruin of my happiness. I shall never love any Man as I loved Purvis. I do not think Tom Musgrave should be named with him in the same day.—' 'You quite shock me by what you say of Penelope'—said Emma. 'Could a sister do such a thing?—Rivalry, Treachery between Sisters!—I shall be afraid of being acquainted with her—but I hope it was not so. Appearances were against her'—'You do not know Penelope.—There is nothing she would not do to get married—she would as good as tell you so herself.—Do not trust her with any secrets of your own, take warning by me, do not trust her; she has her good qualities, but she has no Faith, no Honour, no Scruples, if she can promote her own advantage.—I wish with all my heart she was well married. I declare I had rather have her well-married than myself.'—'Than Yourself!—Yes

I can suppose so. A heart, wounded like yours can have little inclination for Matrimony.'—'Not much indeed—but you know we must marry.—I could do very well single for my own part—A little Company, & a pleasant Ball now & then, would be enough for me, if one could be young for ever, but my Father cannot provide for us, & it is very bad to grow old & be poor & laughed at.— I have lost Purvis, it is true but very few people marry their first Loves. I should not refuse a man because he was not Purvis—. Not that I can ever quite forgive Penelope.'—Emma shook her head in acquiescence.— 'Penelope however has had her Troubles'—continued Miss W.—'she was sadly disappointed in Tom Musgrave, who afterwards transferred his attentions from me to her, & whom she was very fond of;—but he never means anything serious, & when he had trifled with her long enough, he began to slight her for Margaret, & poor Penelope was very wretched—. And since then, she has been trying to make some match at Chichester; she wont tell us with whom, but I beleive it is a rich old Dr Harding, Uncle to the friend she goes to see;—& she has taken a vast deal of trouble about him & given up a great deal of Time to no purpose as yet.——When she went away the other day, she said it should be the last time.—I suppose you did not know what her particular Business was at Chichester—nor guess at the object that could take her away, from Stanton just as you were coming home after so many years absence.'—'No indeed, I had not the smallest suspicion of it. I considered her engagement to Mrs Shaw just at that time as very unfortunate for me. I had hoped to find all my Sisters at home; to be able to make an immediate friend of each.'—'I suspect the Dr to have had an attack of the Asthma,* & that she was hurried away on that account—The Shaws are quite on her side.—At least I beleive so—but she tells me nothing. She professes to keep her own counsel; she says, & truly enough, that "Too many Cooks spoil the Broth".'— 'I am sorry for her anxieties,' said Emma,—'but I do not like her plans or her opinions. I shall be afraid of her.—She must have too masculine & bold a temper.—To be so bent on Marriage—to pursue a Man merely for the sake of Situation—is a sort of thing that shocks me; I cannot understand it. Poverty is a great Evil, but to a woman of Education & feeling it ought not, it cannot be the greatest.—I would rather be Teacher at a school* (and I can think of nothing worse) than marry a Man I did not like.—' 'I would rather do any thing than be Teacher at a school'—said her sister. '*I* have been at school,* Emma,

& know what a Life they lead; *you* never have.—I should not like marrying a disagreable Man any more than yourself,—but I do not think there *are* many very disagreable Men;—I think I could like any good humoured Man with a comfortable Income.—I suppose my Aunt brought you up to be rather refined.' 'Indeed I do not know.—My Conduct must tell you how I have been brought up. I am no judge of it my self. I cannot compare my Aunt's method with any other persons, because I know no other.'—'But I can see in a great many things that you are very refined. I have observed it ever since you came home, & I am afraid it will not be for your happiness. Penelope will laugh at you very much.' '*That* will not be for my happiness I am sure.—If my opinions are wrong, I must correct them—if they are above my Situation, I must endeavour to conceal them.—But I doubt whether Ridicule,—Has Penelope much wit?'—'Yes—she has great spirits, & never cares what she says.'—'Margaret is more gentle I imagine?'—'Yes—especially in company; she is all gentleness & mildness when anybody is by.—But she is a little fretful & perverse* among ourselves.—Poor Creature!—she is possessed with the notion of Tom Musgrave's being more seriously in love with her, than he ever was with any body else, & is always expecting him to come to the point. This is the second time within this twelvemonth that she has gone to spend a month with Robert & Jane on purpose to egg him on, by her absence—but I am sure she is mistaken, & that he will no more follow her to Croydon* now than he did last March.—He will never marry unless he can marry somebody very great; Miss Osborne perhaps, or something in that stile.—' 'Your account of this Tom Musgrave, Elizabeth, gives me very little inclination for his acquaintance.' 'You are afraid of him, I do not wonder at you.'—'No indeed—I dislike & despise him.'—'Dislike & Despise Tom Musgrave! No, *that* you never can. I defy you not to be delighted with him if he takes notice of you.—I hope he will dance with you—& I dare say he will, unless the Osbornes come with a large party, & then he will not speak to any body else.—' 'He seems to have most engaging manners!'—said Emma.—'Well, we shall see how irresistable Mr Tom Musgrave & I find each other.—I suppose I shall know him as soon as I enter the Ball-room; he *must* carry some of his Charms in his face.'—'You will not find him in the Ball room I can tell you, You will go early that Mrs Edwards may get a good place by the fire, & he never comes till late; & if the Osbornes are coming, he will wait in the

Passage, & come in with them.—I should like to look in upon you Emma. If it was but a good day with my Father, I would wrap my self up, & James should drive me over, as soon as I had made Tea for him, & I should be with you by the time the Dancing began.' 'What! would you come late at night in this Chair?'—'To be sure I would.—There, I said you were very serious; & that's an instance of it.' Emma for a moment made no answer—at last she said—'I wish Elizabeth, you had not made a point of my going to this Ball, I wish you were going instead of me. Your pleasure would be greater than mine. I am a stranger here, & know nobody but the Edwardses;—my Enjoyment therefore must be very doubtful. Yours among all your acquaintance would be certain.—It is not too late to change. Very little apology could be requisite to the Edwardses, who must be more glad of your company than of mine, & I should most readily return to my Father; & should not be at all afraid to drive this quiet old Creature home. Your Cloathes I would undertake to find means of sending to you.'—'My dearest Emma' cried Elizabeth warmly—'do you think I would do such a thing?—Not for the Universe—but I shall never forget your goodnature in proposing it. You must have a sweet temper indeed!—I never met with any thing like it—And would you really give up the Ball, that I might be able to go to it!—Beleive me Emma, I am not so selfish as that comes to. No, tho' I am nine years older than you are, I would not be the means of keeping you from being seen.—You are very pretty, & it would be very hard that you should not have as fair a chance as we have all had, to make your fortune.—No Emma, whoever stays at home this winter, it shan't be you. I am sure I should never have forgiven the person who kept me from a Ball at 19.' Emma expressed her gratitude, & for a few minutes they jogged on in silence.—Elizabeth first spoke.—'You will take notice who Mary Edwards dances with.'—'I will remember her partners if I can—but you know they will be all strangers to me.' 'Only observe whether she dances with Captain Hunter, more than once; I have my fears in that quarter. Not that her Father or Mother like officers,* but if she does you know, it is all over with poor Sam.—And I have promised to write him word who she dances with.' 'Is Sam attached to Miss Edwardses?'—'Did not you know *that*?'—'How should I know it?—How should I know in Shropshire,* what is passing of that nature in Surry?—It is not likely that circumstances of such delicacy should make any part of the scanty communication which passed between you & me for the last 14 years;' 'I wonder I never mentioned it when I wrote. Since you have been at home, I have been so busy with my poor Father & our great wash* that I have had no leisure to tell you anything—but indeed I concluded you knew it all.—He has been very much in love with her these two years, & it is a great disappointment to him that he cannot always get away to our Balls—but Mr Curtis won't often spare him, & just now it is a sickly time at Guilford—' 'Do you suppose Miss Edwardes inclined to like him?' 'I am afraid not: You know she is an only Child, & will have at least ten thousand pounds.'*—'But still she may like our Brother.' 'Oh! no—. The Edwardes look much higher. Her Father & Mother would never consent to it. Sam is only a Surgeon* you know.—Sometimes I think she does like him. But Mary Edwardes is rather prim & reserved; I do not always know what she would be at.'—'Unless Sam feels on sure grounds with the Lady herself, It seems a pity to me that he should be encouraged to think of her at all.'—'A young Man must think of somebody,' said Elizabeth—'& why should not he be as lucky as Robert, who has got a good wife & six thousand pounds?' 'We must not all expect to be individually lucky' replied Emma. 'The Luck of one member of a Family is Luck to all.—' 'Mine is all to come I am sure'—said Elizabeth giving another sigh to the remembrance of Purvis.—'I have been unlucky enough, & I cannot say much for you, as my Aunt married again so foolishly.—Well—you will have a good Ball I dare say. The next turning will bring us to the Turnpike.* You may see the Church Tower over the hedge, & the White Hart is close by it.—I shall long to know what you think of Tom Musgrave.' Such were the last audible sounds of Miss Watson's voice, before they passed thro' the Turnpike gate & entered on the pitching* of the Town—the jumbling & noise of which made farther Conversation most thoroughly undesirable.—The old Mare trotted heavily on, wanting no direction of the reins to take the right Turning, & making only one Blunder, in proposing to stop at the Milleners, before she drew up towards Mr Edward's door.—Mr E. lived in the best house in the Street, & the best in the place, if Mr Tomlinson the Banker might be indulged in calling his newly erected House at the end of the Town with a shrubbery & sweep* in the Country.—Mr E.'s House was higher than most of its neighbours with windows on each side the door, the windows guarded by posts & chain the door approached by a flight of stone steps.*—'Here we are'—said Elizabeth—as the

Carriage ceased moving—'safely arrived;—& by the Market Clock, we have been only five & thirty minutes coming.—which *I* think is doing pretty well, tho' it would be nothing for Penelope.—Is not it a nice Town?—The Edwards' have a noble house you see, & they live quite in stile. The door will be opened by a Man in Livery with a pow-der'd head, I can tell you.'

Emma had seen the Edwardses only one morning at Stanton, they were therefore all but Strangers to her, & tho' her spirits were by no means insensible to the expected joys of the Evening, she felt a little uncomfortable in the thought of all that was to precede them. Her conversation with Elizabeth too giving her some very unpleasant feel ings, with respect to her own family, had made her more open to dis-agreeable impressions from any other cause, & encreased her sense of the awkwardness of rushing into Intimacy on so slight an acquaint-ance.—There was nothing in the manners of Mrs or Miss Edwardes to give immediate change to these Ideas; the Mother tho' a very friendly woman, had a reserved air, & a great deal of formal Civility—& the daughter, a genteel looking girl of 22, with her hair in papers,* seemed very naturally to have caught something of the Stile of the Mother who had brought her up.—Emma was soon left to know what they could be, by Elizabeth's being obliged to hurry away—& some very, very languid remarks on the probable Brilliancy of the Ball, were all that broke at intervals a silence of half an hour before they were joined by the Master of the house.—Mr Edwards had a much easier, & more communicative air than the Ladies of the Family; he was fresh from the Street, & he came ready to tell what-ever might interest.—After a cordial reception of Emma, he turned to his daughter with 'Well Mary, I bring you good news.—The Osbornes will certainly be at the Ball tonight.—Horses for two Carriages are ordered from the White Hart, to be at Osborne Castle by 9.—' 'I am glad of it'—observed Mrs E., 'because their coming gives a credit to our Assemblies. The Osbornes being known to have been at the first Ball, will dispose a great many people to attend the second.—It is more than they deserve for in fact they add nothing to the pleasure of the Evening, they come so late, & go so early;—but Great People have always their charm.'—Mr Edwards proceeded to relate every other little article of news which his morning's lounge* had supplied him with, & they chatted with greater briskness, till Mrs E.'s moment for dressing arrived, & the young Ladies were carefully recommended to lose no time.—Emma was shewn to a very comfortable apartment, & as soon as Mrs E.'s civilities could leave her to herself, the happy occupation, the first Bliss of a Ball began.—The girls, dressing in some measure together, grew unavoidably better acquainted; Emma found in Miss E.—the shew of good sense, a modest unpretending mind, & a great wish of obliging—& when they returned to the parlour where Mrs E. was sitting respectably attired in one of the two Sattin gowns which went thro' the winter, & a new Cap* from the Milliners, they entered it with much easier feelings & more natural smiles than they had taken away.—Their dress was now to be examined; Mrs Edwards acknowledged herself too old-fashioned to approve of every modern extravagance however sanctioned—& tho' complacently veiwing her daughter's good looks, would give but a qualified admiration; & Mr E. not less satisfied with Mary, paid some Compliments of good humoured Gallantry to Emma at her expence.—The discussion led to more intimate remarks, & Miss Edwardes gently asked Emma if she were not often reckoned very like her youngest brother.—Emma thought she could perceive a faint blush accompany the question, & there seemed something still more suspicious in the manner in which Mr E. took up the subject.—'You are paying Miss Emma no great compliment I think Mary,' said he hastily—. 'Mr Sam Watson is a very good sort of young man, & I dare say a very clever Surgeon, but his complexion has been rather too much exposed to all weathers, to make a likeness to him very flattering.' Mary apologized in some confusion. 'She had not thought a strong Likeness at all incompatible with very different degrees of Beauty.—There might be resemblance in Countenance; & the complexion, & even the features be very unlike.'—'I know nothing of my Brother's Beauty,' said Emma, 'for I have not seen him since he was 7 years old*—but my father reckons us alike.' 'Mr Watson!'—cried Mr Edwardes, 'Well, you astonish me.—There is not the least likeness in the world; your brother's eyes are grey, yours are brown, He has a long face, & a wide mouth.—My dear, do *you* perceive the least resemblance?'—'Not the least.—Miss Emma Watson puts me very much in mind of her eldest Sister, & sometimes I see a look of Miss Penelope—& once or twice there has been a glance of Mr Robert—but I cannot perceive any likeness to Mr Samuel.' 'I see the likeness between her & Miss Watson,' replied Mr E.—, 'very strongly—but I am not sensible of the others.—I do not much think she is like any of the Family *but* Miss Watson; but I am very sure there is no resemblance between her & Sam.'—

This matter was settled, & they went to Dinner.—'Your Father, Miss Emma, is one of my oldest friends'—said Mr Edwardes, as he helped her to wine, when they were drawn round the fire to enjoy their Desert, 'We must drink to his better health.—It is a great concern to me I assure you that he should be such an Invalid.—I know nobody who likes a game of cards in a social way, better than he does;—& very few people that play a fairer rubber.*—It is a thousand pities that he should be so deprived of the pleasure. For now we have a quiet little Whist club that meets three times a week at the White Hart, & if he could but have his health, how much he would enjoy it.' 'I dare say he would Sir   & I wish with all my heart he were equal to it.' 'Your Club would be better fitted for an Invalid,' said Mrs E. 'if you did not keep it up so late.'—This was an old greivance.—'So late, my dear, what are you talking of;' cried the Husband with sturdy pleasantry—. 'We are always at home before midnight. They would laugh at Osborne Castle to hear you call *that* late; they are but just rising from dinner at midnight.'*—'That is nothing to the purpose.'—retorted the Lady calmly. 'The Osbornes are to be no rule for us. You had better meet every night, & break up two hours sooner.' So far, the subject was very often carried;—but Mr & Mrs Edwards were so wise as never to pass that point; & Mr Edwards now turned to something else.—He had lived long enough in the Idleness of a Town to become a little of a Gossip, & having some curiosity to know more of the Circumstances of his young Guest than had yet reached him, he began with, 'I think Miss Emma, I remember your Aunt very well about 30 years ago; I am pretty sure I danced with her in the old rooms at Bath,* the year before I married—. She was a very fine woman then—but like other people I suppose she is grown somewhat older since that time.—I hope she is likely to be happy in her second choice.'

'I hope so, I beleive so, Sir'—said Emma in some agitation.—'Mr Turner had not been dead a great while I think?' 'About 2 years Sir.' 'I forget what her name is now?'—'O'brien.' 'Irish! Ah! I remember—& she is gone to settle in Ireland.—I do not wonder that you should not wish to go with her into *that* Country* Miss Emma—but it must be a great deprivation to her, poor Lady!—After bringing you up like a Child of her own.'—'I was not so ungrateful Sir,' said Emma warmly, 'as to wish to be any where but with her.—It did not suit them, it did not suit Captain O'brien that I should be of the party.—' 'Captain!'—repeated Mrs E., 'the Gentleman is in the army then?' 'Yes Ma'am.'—'Aye—there is nothing like your officers for captivating the Ladies, Young or Old.—There is no resisting a Cockade* my dear.'—'I hope there is.'—said Mrs E. gravely, with a quick glance at her daughter;—and Emma had just recovered from her own perturbation in time to see a blush on Miss E.'s cheek, & in remembering what Elizabeth had said of Captain Hunter, to wonder & waver between his influence and her brother's.—

'Elderly Ladies should be careful how they make a second choice.' observed Mr Edwardes.—'Carefulness—Discretion—should not be confined to Elderly Ladies, or to a second choice' added his wife. 'It is quite as necessary to young Ladies in their first.'—'Rather more so, my dear' replied he—'because young Ladies are likely to feel the effects of it longer. When an old Lady plays the fool, it is not in the course of nature that she should suffer from it many years.' Emma drew her hand across her eyes—& Mrs Edwards on perceiving it, changed the subject to one of less anxiety to all.—

With nothing to do but to expect the hour of setting off, the afternoon was long to the two young Ladies; & tho' Miss Edwards was rather discomposed at the very early hour which her mother always fixed for going, that early hour itself was watched for with some eagerness.—The entrance of the Tea things* at 7 o'clock was some releif—& luckily Mr & Mrs Edwards always drank a dish extraordinary,* & ate an additional muffin when they were going to sit up late, which lengthened the ceremony almost to the wished for moment. At a little before 8, the Tomlinsons carriage was heard to go by, which was the constant signal for Mrs Edwards to order hers to the door; & in a very few minutes, the party were transported from the quiet warmth of a snug parlour, to the bustle, noise & draughts of air of the broad Entrance-passage of an Inn. Mrs Edwards carefully guarding her own dress, while she attended with yet greater Solicitude to the proper security of her young Charges' Shoulders & Throats,* led the way up the wide staircase, while no sound of a Ball but the first Scrape of one violin, blessed the ears of her followers, & Miss Edwards on hazarding the anxious enquiry of whether there were many people come yet, was told, by the Waiter as she knew she should, that 'Mr Tomlinson's family were in the room.' In passing along a short gallery to the Assembly-room, brilliant in lights before them,

They were accosted* by a young Man in a morning dress* & Boots, who was standing in the doorway of a Bedchamber, apparently on purpose to see them go by.—'Ah! Mrs E.—how do you do?—How do you do Miss E.?'—he cried, with an easy air;—'You are determined to be in good time I see, as usual.—The Candles are but this moment lit—' 'I like to get a good seat by the fire you know, Mr Musgrave,' replied Mrs E. 'I am this moment going to dress,' said he—'I am waiting for my stupid fellow.—We shall have a famous Ball, The Osbornes are certainly coming; you may depend upon *that* for I was with Lord Osborne this morning—.'

The party passed on—Mrs E's sattin gown swept along the clean floor of the Ball-room, to the fire place at the upper end, where one party only were formally seated, while three or four Officers were lounging together, passing in & out from the adjoining card-room.— A very stiff meeting between these near neighbours ensued—& as soon as they were all duely placed again, Emma in the low whisper which became the solemn scene, said to Miss Edwardes, 'The gentleman we passed in the passage, was Mr Musgrave, then.—He is reckoned remarkably agreable I understand. ' Miss E. answered hesitatingly—'Yes—he is very much liked by many people.—But *we* are not very intimate.'—'He is rich, is not he?—' 'He has about 8 or 900£ a year* I beleive.—He came into possession of it, when he was very young, & my Father & Mother think it has given him rather an unsettled turn.—He is no favourite with them.'—The cold & empty appearance of the Room & the demure air of the small cluster of Females, at one end of it began soon to give way; the inspiriting sound of other Carriages was heard, & continual accessions of portly Chaperons,* & strings of smartly-dressed girls were received, with now & then a fresh, gentleman straggler, who if not enough in Love to station himself near any fair Creature seemed glad to escape into the Card-room.—Among the increasing numbers of Military Men, one now made his way to Miss Edwards, with an air of Empressément,* which decidedly said to her Companion 'I am Captain Hunter.'—& Emma, who could not but watch her at such a moment, saw her looking rather distressed, but by no means displeased, & heard an engagement formed for the two first dances,* which made her think her Brother Sam's a hopeless case.—

Emma in the mean while was not unobserved, or unadmired herself.—A new face & a very pretty one, could not be slighted—her name was whispered from one party to another, & no sooner had the signal been given, by the Orchestra's striking up a favourite air, which seemed to call the young Men to their duty, & people to the centre of the room, than she found herself engaged to dance with a Brother officer, introduced by Captain Hunter.—Emma Watson was not more than of the middle height—well made & plump, with an air of healthy vigour.—Her skin was very brown,* but clear, smooth and glowing—; which with a lively Eye, a sweet smile, & an open Countenance, gave beauty to attract, & expression to make that beauty improve on acquaintance.—Having no reason to be dissatisfied with her partner, the Evening began very pleasantly to her; & her feelings perfectly coincided with the re-iterated observation of others, that it was an excellent Ball.—The two first dances were not quite over, when the returning sound of Carriages after a long interruption, called general notice, & 'the Osbornes are coming, the Osbornes are coming'—was repeated round the room.—After some minutes of extraordinary bustle without, & watchful curiosity within, the important Party, preceded by the attentive Master of the Inn to open a door which was never shut, made their appearance. They consisted of Lady Osborne, her son Lord Osborne, her daughter Miss Osborne; Miss Carr, her daughter's friend, Mr Howard formerly Tutor to Lord Osborne, now Clergyman of the Parish in which the Castle stood, Mrs Blake, a widow-sister who lived with him, her son a fine boy of 10 years old, & Mr Tom Musgrave; who probably imprisoned within his own room, had been listening in bitter impatience to the sound of the Music, for the last half hour. In their progress up the room, they paused almost immediately behind Emma, to receive the Compliments of some acquaintance, & she heard Lady Osborne observe that they had made a point of coming early for the gratification of Mrs Blake's little boy, who was uncommonly fond of dancing.—Emma looked at them all as they passed—but cheifly & with most interest on Tom Musgrave, who was certainly a genteel, good looking young man.—Of the females, Lady Osborne had by much the finest person;—tho' nearly 50, she was very handsome, & had all the Dignity of Rank.—Lord Osborne was a very fine young man; but there was an air of, Coldness, of Carelessness, even of Awkwardness about him, which seemed to speak him out of his Element in a Ball room. He came in fact only because it was judged expedient for him to please the Borough*—he was not fond of Women's company, & he never danced.—Mr Howard was an agreable-looking Man, a little more than Thirty.—

At the conclusion of the two Dances, Emma found herself, she knew not how, seated amongst the Osborne Set; & she was immediately struck with the fine Countenance & animated gestures of the little boy, as he was standing before his Mother, wondering when they should begin.—'You will not be surprised at Charles's impatience,' said Mrs Blake, a lively pleasant-looking little Woman of 5 or 6 & 30, to a Lady who was standing near her, 'when you know what a partner he is to have. Miss Osborne has been so very kind as to promise to dance the two 1st dances with him.' 'Oh! yes—we have been engaged this week,' cried the boy, '& we are to dance down every couple.'*—On the other side of Emma, Miss Osborne, Miss Carr, & a party of young Men were standing engaged in very lively consultation—& soon afterwards she saw the smartest officer of the Sett, walking off to the Orchestra to order the dance,* while Miss Osborne passing before her, to her little expecting Partner* hastily said—'Charles, I beg your pardon for not keeping my engagement,* but I am going to dance these two dances with Colonel Beresford. I know you will excuse me, & I will certainly dance with you after Tea.' And without staying for an answer, she turned again to Miss Carr, & in another minute was led by Colonel Beresford to begin the Set. If the poor little boy's face had in it's happiness been interesting* to Emma, it was infinitely more so under this sudden reverse;—he stood the picture of disappointment, with crimson'd cheeks, quivering lips, & eyes bent on the floor. His mother, stifling her own mortification, tried to sooth his, with the prospect of Miss Osborne's second promise; but tho' he contrived to utter with an effort of Boyish Bravery 'Oh! I do not mind it'—it was very evident by the unceasing agitation of his features that he minded it as much as ever.—Emma did not think, or reflect;—she felt & acted—. 'I shall be very happy to dance with you Sir, if you like it.' said she, holding out her hand with the most unaffected good humour.—The Boy in one moment restored to all his first delight—looked joyfully at his Mother and stepping forward with an honest & simple 'Thank you Maam' was instantly ready to attend his new acquaintance.—The Thankfulness of Mrs Blake was more diffuse;—with a look, most expressive of unexpected pleasure, & lively Gratitude, she turned to her neighbour with repeated & fervent acknowledgements of so great & condescending* a kindness to her boy.—Emma with perfect truth could assure her that she could not be giving greater pleasure than she felt herself—& Charles being provided with his gloves* & charged to keep them on, they joined the Set which was now rapidly forming, with nearly equal complacency.*—It was a Partnership which could not be noticed without surprise. It gained her a broad stare from Miss Osborne & Miss Carr as they passed her in the dance. 'Upon my word Charles you are in luck,' (said the former as she turned him) 'you have got a better partner than me'—to which the happy Charles answered 'Yes.'—Tom Musgrave who was dancing with Miss Carr, gave her many inquisitive glances; & after a time Lord Osborne himself came & under pretence of talking to Charles, stood to look at his part-ner.—Tho' rather distressed by such observation, Emma could not repent what she had done, so happy had it made both the boy & his Mother; the latter of whom was continually making opportunities of addressing her with the warmest civility.—Her little partner she found, tho' bent cheifly on dancing, was not unwilling to speak, when her questions or remarks gave him any thing to say; & she learnt, by a sort of inevitable enquiry that he had two brothers & a sister, that they & their Mama all lived with his Uncle at Wickstead, that his Uncle taught him Latin, that he was very fond of riding, & had a horse of his own given him by Lord Osborne; & that he had been out once already with Lord Osborne's Hounds.—At the end of these Dances Emma found they were to drink tea;—Miss E. gave her a caution to be at hand, in a manner which convinced her of Mrs E.'s holding it very important to have them both close to her when she moved into the Tearoom; & Emma was accordingly on the alert to gain her proper station. It was always the pleasure of the company to have a little bustle & croud when they thus adjourned for refresh-ment;—The Tea room was a small room within the Card room, & in passing thro' the latter, where the passage was straightened* by Tables, Mrs E. & her party were for a few moments hemmed in. It happened close by Lady Osborne's Cassino* Table; Mr Howard who belonged to it spoke to his Nephew; & Emma on perceiving herself the object of attention both to Lady O. & him, had just turned away her eyes in time, to avoid seeming to hear her young companion delightedly whisper aloud—'Oh! Uncle, do look at my partner. She is so pretty!' As they were immediately in motion again however, Charles was hurried off without being able to receive his Uncle's suffrage.\*—On entering the Tea room, in which two long Tables were prepared, Lord Osborne was to be seen quite alone at the end of one, as if retreating as far as he could from the Ball, to enjoy his own thoughts, & gape\* without restraint.—Charles instantly pointed him out to Emma—'There's Lord Osborne—Let you & I go & sit by him '—'No, no,' said Emma laughing 'you must sit with my friends.' Charles was now free enough to hazard a few questions in his turn. 'What o'clock was it?'—'Eleven.'—'Eleven!—And I am not at all sleepy. Mama said I should be asleep before ten.—Do you think Miss Osborne will keep her word with me, when Tea is over?' 'Oh! yes.—I suppose so.'—tho' she felt that she had no better reason to give than that Miss Osborne had *not* kept it before.—'When shall you come to Osborne Castle?'—'Never, probably.—I am not acquainted with the family.' 'But you may come to Wickstead & see Mama, & she can take you to the Castle.—There is a monstrous curious stuff'd Fox there, & a Badger—any body would think they were alive. It is a pity you should not see them.'—

On rising from Tea, there was again a scramble for the pleasure of being first out of the room, which happened to be increased by one or two of the card parties having just broken up & the players being disposed to move exactly the different way. Among these was Mr Howard—his Sister leaning on his arm—& no sooner were they within reach of Emma, than Mrs B. calling her notice by a friendly touch, said 'Your goodness to Charles, my dear Miss Watson, brings all his family upon you. Give me leave to introduce my Brother—Mr H.' Emma curtsied, the gentleman bowed—made a hasty request for the honour of her hand in the two next dances, to which as hasty an affirmative was given, & they were immediately impelled in opposite directions.—Emma was very well pleased with the circumstance;—there was a quietly-chearful, gentlemanlike air in Mr H. which suited her—& in a few minutes afterwards, the value of her Engagement increased, when as she was sitting in the Card room somewhat screened by a door, she heard Lord Osborne, who was lounging on a vacant Table near her, call Tom Musgrave towards him & say, 'Why do not you dance with that beautiful Emma Watson?—I want you to dance with her—& I will come & stand by you.'—'I was determining on it this very moment my Lord; I'll be introduced & dance with her directly.'—'Aye do—& if you find she does not want much Talking to, you may introduce me by & bye.'—'Very well my

Lord—. If she is like her Sisters, she will only want to be listened
to.—I will go this moment. I shall find her in the Tea room. That stiff
old Mrs E. has never done tea.'—Away he went—Lord Osborne
after him—& Emma lost no time in hurrying from her corner, exactly
the other way, forgetting in her haste that she left Mrs Edwardes
behind.—'We had quite lost you'—said Mrs E.—who followed her
with Mary, in less than five minutes.—'If you prefer this room to the
other, there is no reason why you should not be here, but we had better all be together.' Emma was saved the Trouble of apologizing, by
their being joined at the moment by Tom Musgrave, who requesting
Mrs E. aloud to do him the honour of presenting him to Miss Emma
Watson, left that good Lady without any choice in the business, but
that of testifying by the coldness of her manner that she did it unwill-
ingly. The honour of dancing with her, was solicited without loss of
time—& Emma, however she might like to be thought a beautiful girl
by Lord or Commoner, was so little disposed to favour Tom Musgrave
himself, that she had considerable satisfaction in avowing her prior
Engagement.—He was evidently surprised & discomposed.—The
stile of her last partner had probably led him to beleive her not overpowered with applications.—'My little friend Charles Blake,' he
cried, 'must not expect to engross you the whole evening. We can
never suffer this—It is against the rules of the Assembly*—& I am
sure it will never be patronised by our good friend here Mrs E.; She
is by much too nice a judge of Decorum to give her license to such
a dangerous Particularity.'—'I am not going to dance with Master
Blake Sir.' The Gentleman a little disconcerted, could only hope he
might be more fortunate another time—& seeming unwilling to leave
her, tho' his friend Lord Osborne was waiting in the Doorway for
the result, as Emma with some amusement perceived—he began to
make civil enquiries after her family.—'How comes it, that we have
not the pleasure of seeing your Sisters here this Evening?—Our
Assemblies have been used to be so well treated by them, that we do
not know how to take this neglect.'—'My eldest Sister is the only one
at home—& she could not leave my Father'—'Miss Watson the only
one at home!—You astonish me!—It seems but the day before yesterday that I saw them all three in this Town. But I am afraid I have been
a very sad neighbour* of late. I hear dreadful complaints of my negli-
gence wherever I go, & I confess it is a shameful length of time since
I was at Stanton.—But I shall *now* endeavour to make myself amends

for the past.'—Emma's calm curtsey in reply must have struck him as very unlike the encouraging warmth he had been used to receive from her Sisters, & gave him probably the novel sensation of doubting his own influence, & of wishing for more attention than she bestowed.—

The dancing now recommenced; Miss Carr being impatient to *call*,* everybody was required to stand up—& Tom Musgrave's curiosity was appeased, on seeing Mr Howard come forward & claim Emma's hand—'That will do as well for *me*'—was Lord Osborne's remark, when his friend carried him the news—& he was continually at Howard's Elbow during the two dances.—The frequency of his appearance there, was the only unpleasant part of her engagement, the only objection she could make to Mr Howard.—In himself, she thought him as agreable as he looked; tho' chatting on the commonest topics he had a sensible, unaffected, way of expressing himself, which made them all worth hearing, & she only regretted that he had not been able to make his pupil's Manners as unexceptionable as his own.—The two dances seemed very short, & she had her partner's authority for considering them so.—At their conclusion the Osbornes & their Train were all on the move. 'We are off at last,' said his Lordship to Tom—'How much longer do *you* stay in this Heavenly place?—till Sunrise?'—'No faith! my Lord, I have had quite enough of it; I assure you—I shall not shew myself here again when I have had the honour of attending Lady Osborne to her Carriage. I shall retreat in as much secrecy as possible to the most remote corner of the House, where I shall order a Barrel of Oysters, & be famously snug.' 'Let us see you soon at the Castle; & bring me word how she looks by daylight.'—Emma & Mrs Blake parted as old acquaintance, & Charles shook her by the hand & wished her 'goodbye' at least a dozen times. From Miss Osborne & Miss Carr she received something like a jerking curtsey as they passed her; even Lady Osborne gave her a look of complacency—& his Lordship actually came back after the others were out of the room, to 'beg her pardon', & look in the window seat behind her for the gloves which were visibly compressed in his hand.—

As Tom Musgrave was seen no more, we may suppose his plan to have succeeded, & imagine him mortifying with his Barrel of Oysters, in dreary solitude—or gladly assisting the Landlady in her Bar to make fresh Negus* for the happy Dancers above. Emma could not help missing the party, by whom she had been, tho' in some respects unpleasantly, distinguished, & the two Dances which followed & concluded the Ball, were rather flat, in comparison with the others.—Mr E. having play'd with good luck, they were some of the last in the room—'Here we are, back again I declare'—said Emma sorrowfully, as she walked into the Dining room, where the Table was prepared, & the neat Upper maid* was lighting the Candles—'My dear Miss Edwards—how soon it is at an end!—I wish it could all come over again!—' A great deal of kind pleasure was expressed in her having enjoyed the Evening so much—& Mr Edwards was as warm as herself, in praise of the fullness, brilliancy & Spirit of the Meeting tho' as he had been fixed the whole time at the same Table in the same Room, with only one change of Chairs, it might have seemed a matter scarcely perceived.—But he had won 4 rubbers out of 5, & every thing went well. His daughter felt the advantage of this gratified state of mind, in the course of the remarks & retrospections which now ensued, over the welcome Soup.—'How came you not to dance with either of the Mr Tomlinsons, Mary?'—said her Mother. 'I was always engaged when they asked me.' 'I thought you were to have stood up with Mr James, the last two dances; Mrs Tomlinson told me he was gone to ask you—& I had heard you say two minutes before that you were *not* engaged.—' 'Yes—but—there was a mistake—I had misunderstood—I did not know I was engaged.—I thought it had been for the 2 Dances after, if we staid so long—but Captain Hunter assured me it was for those very Two.—'

'So, you ended with Captain Hunter Mary, did you?' said her Father. 'And who did you begin with?' 'Captain Hunter.' was repeated, in a very humble tone—'Hum!—That is being constant however. But who else did you dance with?' 'Mr Norton, & Mr Styles.' 'And who are they?' 'Mr Norton is a Cousin of Captain Hunter's.'—'And who is Mr Styles?' 'One of his particular friends.'—'All in the same Regiment' added Mrs E.—'Mary was surrounded by Red coats the whole Evening. I should have been better pleased to see her dancing with some of our old Neighbours I confess.—' 'Yes, yes, we must not neglect our old Neighbours—. But if these soldiers are quicker than other people in a Ball room, what are young Ladies to do?' 'I think there is no occasion for their engaging themselves so many Dances before hand, Mr Edwards.'—'No—perhaps not—but I remember my dear when you & I did the same.'—Mrs E. said no more, & Mary

breathed again.—A great deal of goodhumoured pleasantry followed—& Emma went to bed in charming Spirits, her head full of
Osbornes, Blakes & Howards.—

The next morning brought a great many visitors. It was the way of
the place always to call on Mrs E. on the morning after a Ball, & this
neighbourly inclination was increased in this present instance by
a general spirit of curiosity on Emma's account, as Everybody wanted
to look again at the girl who had been admired the night before by
Lord Osborne.—Many were the eyes, & various the degrees of approbation with which she was examined. Some saw no fault, & some no
Beauty—. With some her brown skin was the annihilation of every
grace, & others could never be persuaded that she were half so handsome as Elizabeth Watson had been ten years ago —The morning
passed quickly away in discussing the merits of the Ball with all this
succession of Company—& Emma was at once astonished by finding
it Two o'clock, & considering that she had heard nothing of her
Father's Chair. After this discovery she had walked twice to the window to examine the Street, & was on the point of asking leave to ring
the bell & make enquiries, when the light sound of a Carriage driving
up to the door set her heart at ease. She stepd again to the window—but instead of the convenient but very un-smart Family
Equipage perceived a neat Curricle.*—Mr Musgrave was shortly
afterwards announced;—& Mrs Edwards put on her very stiffest look
at the sound.—Not at all dismayed however by her chilling air, he
paid his Compliments to each of the Ladies with no unbecoming
Ease, & continuing to address Emma, presented her a note, which he
had 'the honour of bringing from her Sister; But to which he must
observe that a verbal postscript from himself would be requisite.—'

The note, which Emma was beginning to read rather *before* Mrs
Edwards had entreated her to use no ceremony, contained a few lines
from Elizabeth importing that their Father in consequence of being
unusually well had taken the sudden resolution of attending the visitation* that day, & that as his Road lay quite wide from R.,* it was
impossible for her to come home till the following morning, unless
the Edwardses would send her which was hardly to be expected, or
she could meet with any chance conveyance, or did not mind walking
so far.—She had scarcely run her eye thro' the whole, before she
found herself obliged to listen to Tom Musgrave's farther account.
'I received that note from the fair hands of Miss Watson only ten

minutes ago,' said he—'I met her in the village of Stanton, whither
my good Stars prompted me to turn my Horses heads—she was at
that moment in quest of a person to employ on the Errand, & I was
fortunate enough to convince her that she could not find a more willing or speedy Messenger than myself—. Remember, I say nothing of
my Disinterestedness.—My reward is to be the indulgence of con-
veying you to Stanton in my Curricle.—Tho' they are not written
down, I bring your Sister's orders for the same.—' Emma felt distressed; she did not like the proposal—she did not wish to be on
terms of intimacy with the Proposer—& yet fearful of encroaching
on the Edwardes', as well as wishing to go home herself, she was at
a loss how entirely to decline what he offered—Mrs E. continued
silent, either not understanding the case, or waiting to see how the
young Lady's inclination lay. Emma thanked him—but professed
herself very unwilling to give him so much trouble. 'The Trouble was
of course, Honour, Pleasure, Delight. What had he or his Horses to
do?'—Still she hesitated. 'She beleived she must beg leave to decline
his assistance—she was rather afraid of the sort of carriage—. The
distance was not beyond a walk.—' Mrs E. was silent no longer. She
enquired into the particulars—& then said 'We shall be extremely
happy Miss Emma, if you can give us the pleasure of your company
till tomorrow—but if you can not conveniently do so, our Carriage is
quite at your Service, & Mary will be pleased with the opportunity of
seeing your Sister.'—This was precisely what Emma had longed
for, & she accepted the offer most thankfully; acknowledging that as
Elizabeth was entirely alone, it was her wish to return home to dinner.—The plan was warmly opposed by their visitor. 'I cannot suffer
it indeed. I must not be deprived of the happiness of escorting you.
I assure you there is not a possibility of fear with my Horses. You
might guide them yourself. *Your Sisters* all know how quiet they are;
They have none of them the smallest scruple in trusting themselves
with me, even on a Race-Course.—Beleive me'—added he lowering
his voice—'*You* are quite safe, the danger is only *mine*.'—Emma was
not more disposed to oblige him for all this.—'And as to Mrs
Edwardes' carriage being used the day after a Ball, it is a thing quite
out of rule I assure you—never heard of before—the old Coachman
will look as black as his Horses—. Won't he Miss Edwards?'—No
notice was taken. The Ladies were silently firm, & the gentleman
found himself obliged to submit.

'What a famous Ball we had last night!'—he cried, after a short pause. 'How long did you keep it up, after the Osbornes & I went away?'—'We had two dances more.'—'It is making it too much of a fatigue I think, to stay so late.—I suppose your Set was not a very full one.—' 'Yes, quite as full as ever, except the Osbornes. There seemed no vacancy anywhere— & Everybody danced with uncommon spirit to the very last.—' Emma said this—tho' against her conscience.—'Indeed! perhaps I might have looked in upon you again, if I had been aware of as much;—for I am rather fond of dancing than not.—Miss Osborne is a charming girl, is not she?' 'I do not think her handsome.' replied Emma, to whom all this was cheifly addressed. 'Perhaps she is not critically handsome,* but her Manners are delightful. And Fanny Carr is a most interesting little creature. You can imagine nothing more *naive* or *piquante*;* & What do you thing of *Lord Osborne* Miss Watson?' 'That he would be handsome even, tho' he were *not* a Lord—& perhaps—better bred; more desirous of pleasing, & shewing himself pleased in a right place.—' 'Upon my word, you are severe upon my friend!—I assure you Lord Osborne is a very good fellow.—' 'I do not dispute his virtues—but I do not like his careless air.—' 'If it were not a breach of confidence,' replied Tom with an important look, 'perhaps I might be able to win a more favourable opinion of poor Osborne.—' Emma gave him no Encouragement, & he was obliged to keep his friend's secret.—He was also obliged to put an end to his visit—for Mrs Edwards' having ordered her Carriage, there was no time to be lost on Emma's side in preparing for it.—Miss Edwards accompanied her home, but as it was Dinner hour at Stanton, staid with them only a few minutes.—'Now my dear Emma, said Miss W., as soon as they were alone, you must talk to me all the rest of the day, without stopping, or I shall not be satisfied. But first of all Nanny shall bring in the dinner. Poor thing!—You will not dine as you did yesterday, for we have nothing but some fried beef.—How nice Mary Edwards looks in her new pelisse!*—And now tell me how you like them all, & what I am to say to Sam. I have begun my Letter, Jack Stokes is to call for it tomorrow, for his Uncle is going within a mile of Guilford the next day.—' Nanny brought in the dinner;—'We will wait upon ourselves,' continued Elizabeth '& then we shall lose no time.—And so, you would not come home with Tom Musgrave?'—'No. You had said so much against him that I could not wish either for the obligation, or the

Intimacy which the use of his Carriage must have created—. I should not even have liked the appearance of it.—' 'You did very right; tho' I wonder at your forbearance, & I do not think I could have done it myself.—He seemed so eager to fetch you, that I could not say no, tho' it rather went against me to be throwing you together, so well as I knew his Tricks;—but I did long to see you, & it was a clever way of getting you home; Besides—it won't do, to be too nice.—Nobody could have thought of the Edwards' letting you have their Coach,—after the Horses being out so late.—But what am I to say to Sam?'—'If you are guided by me, you will not encourage him to think of Miss Edwards.—The Father is decidedly against him, the Mother shews him no favour, & I doubt his having any interest with Mary. She danced twice with Captain Hunter, & I think shews him in general as much Encouragement as is consistent with her disposition, & the circumstances she is placed in.—She once mentioned Sam, & certainly with a little confusion—but that was perhaps merely oweing to the consciousness of his liking her, which may very probably have come to her knowledge.'—'Oh! dear. Yes—she has heard enough of that from us all. Poor Sam!—He is out of luck as well as other people. For the life of me Emma, I cannot help feeling for those that are cross'd in Love.—Well—now begin, & give me an account of every thing as it happened.—' Emma obeyed her—& Elizabeth listened with very little interruption till she heard of Mr H. as a partner.—'Dance with Mr H.—Good Heavens! You don't say so!—Why—he is quite one of the great & Grand ones;—Did not you find him very high?—' 'His manners are of a kind to give *me* much more Ease & confidence than Tom Musgrave's.' 'Well—go on. I should have been frightened out of my wits, to have had anything to do with the Osborne's set.'—Emma concluded her narration.—'And so, you really did not dance with Tom M. at all?—But you must have liked him, you must have been struck with him altogether.'—'I do *not* like him, Elizabeth—. I allow his person & air to be good—& that his manners to a certain point—his address* rather—is pleasing.—But I see nothing else to admire in him.—On the contrary, he seems very vain, very conceited, absurdly anxious for Distinction, & absolutely contemptible in some of the measures he takes for becoming so.—There is a ridiculousness about him that entertains me—but his company gives me no other agreable Emotion.'

'My dearest Emma!—You are like nobody else in the world.—It is well Margaret is not by.—You do not offend *me*, tho' I hardly know

how to beleive you. But Margaret would never forgive such words.'
'I wish Margaret could have heard him profess his ignorance of her
being out of the Country;* he declared it seemed only two days since
he had seen her.—' 'Aye—that is just like him, & yet this is the Man,
she *will* fancy so desperately in love with her.—He is no favourite of
mine, as you well know, Emma;—but you must think him agreable.
Can you lay your hand on your heart, & say you do not?'—'Indeed
I can. Both Hands; & spread to their widest extent.'—'I should like to
know the man you *do* think agreable.' 'His name is Howard.' 'Howard!
Dear me. I cannot think of *him*, but as playing cards with Lady
Osborne, & looking proud.—I must own however that it *is* a releif to
me, to find you can speak as you do, of Tom Musgrave; my heart did
misgive me that you would like him too well. You talked so stoutly
beforehand, that I was sadly afraid your Brag would be punished.—
I only hope it will last; & that he will not come on to pay you much
attention; it is a hard thing for a woman to stand against the flattering
ways of a Man, when he is bent upon pleasing her.—' As their quietly-
sociable little meal concluded, Miss Watson could not help observing
how comfortably it had passed. 'It is so delightful to me,' said she, 'to
have Things going on in peace & goodhumour. Nobody can tell how
much I hate quarrelling. Now, tho' we have had nothing but fried
beef, how good it has all seemed.—I wish everybody were as easily
satisfied as you—but poor Margaret is very snappish, & Penelope
owns she had rather have Quarrelling going on, than nothing at
all.'—Mr Watson returned in the Evening, not the worse for the
exertion of the day, & consequently pleased with what he had done, &
glad to talk of it, over his own Fireside.—

Emma had not foreseen any interest to herself in the occurrences
of a visitation—but when she heard Mr Howard spoken of as the
Preacher, & as having given them an excellent Sermon, she could not
help listening with a quicker Ear.—'I do not know when I have heard
a Discourse more to my mind'—continued Mr W. 'or one better
delivered.—He reads extremely well, with great propriety & in a very
impressive manner; & at the same time without any Theatrical grim-
ace or violence.—I own, I do not like much action in the pulpit*—
I do not like the studied air & artificial inflexions of voice, which your
very popular & most admired Preachers generally have.—A simple
delivery is much better calculated to inspire Devotion, & shews a much
better Taste.—Mr H. read like a Scholar & a gentleman.'—'And

what had you for dinner Sir?—' said his eldest Daughter.—He related the Dishes & told what he had ate himself. 'Upon the whole,' he added, 'I have had a very comfortable day; my old friends were quite surprised to see me amongst them—& I must say that everybody paid me great attention, & seemed to feel for me as an Invalid.—They would make me sit near the fire, & as the partridges were pretty high,* Dr Richards would have them sent away to the other end of the Table, that they might not offend Mr Watson—which I thought very kind of him.—But what pleased me as much as anything was Mr Howard's attention;—There is a pretty steep flight of steps up to the room we dine in—which do not quite agree with my gouty foot—& Mr Howard walked by me from the bottom to the top, & would make me take his arm.—It struck me as very becoming in so young a Man, but I am sure I had no claim to expect it; for I never saw him before in my Life.—By the bye, he enquired after one of my Daughters, but I do not know which. I suppose you know among yourselves.'—

On the 3$^d$ day after the Ball, as Nanny at five minutes before three, was beginning to bustle into the parlour with the Tray & the Knife-case, she was suddenly called to the front door, by the sound of as smart a rap as the end of a riding-whip could give—& tho' charged by Miss W. to let nobody in, returned in half a minute, with a look of awkward dismay, to hold the parlour door open for Lord Osborne & Tom Musgrave.—The Surprise of the young Ladies may be imagined. No visitors would have been welcome at such a moment; but such visitors as these—such a one as Lord Osborne at least, a nobleman & a stranger, was really distressing.—He looked a little embarrassed himself,—as, on being introduced by his easy, voluble friend, he muttered something of doing himself the honour of waiting on Mr Watson.—Tho' Emma could not but take the compliment of the visit to herself, she was very far from enjoying it. She felt all the inconsistency of such an acquaintance with the very humble stile in which they were obliged to live; & having in her Aunt's family been used to many of the Elegancies of Life, was fully sensible of all that must be open to the ridicule of Richer people in her present home.—Of the pain of such feelings, Elizabeth knew very little;—her simpler Mind, or juster reason saved her from such mortification—& tho' shrinking under a general sense of Inferiority, she felt no particular Shame.—Mr Watson, as the Gentlemen had already heard from Nanny, was not well enough to be down stairs;—With much concern they took their seats—Lord Osborne near Emma, & the convenient Mr Musgrave in high spirits at his own importance, on the other side of the fireplace with Elizabeth.—*He* was at no loss for words, but when Lord Osborne had hoped that Emma had not caught cold at the Ball, he had nothing more to say for some time, & could only gratify his Eye by occasional glances at his fair neighbour.—Emma was not inclined to give herself much trouble for his Entertainment—& after hard labour of mind, he produced the remark of it's being a very fine day, & followed it up with the question of, 'Have you been walking this morning?' 'No, my Lord. We thought it too dirty' 'You should wear half-boots.'—After another pause, 'Nothing sets off a neat ancle more than a half-boot; nankin galoshed with black* looks very well.—Do not you like Half-boots?' 'Yes—but unless they are so stout as to injure their beauty, they are not fit for Country walking.'—'Ladies should ride in dirty weather.—Do you ride?' 'No my Lord.' 'I wonder every Lady does not.—A woman never looks better than on horseback.—' 'But every woman may not have the inclination, or the means.' 'If they knew how much it became them, they would all have the inclination—& I fancy Miss Watson—when once they had the inclination, the means would soon follow.'—'Your Lordship thinks* we always have our own way.—*That* is a point on which Ladies & Gentlemen have long disagreed—But without pretending to decide it, I may say that there are some circumstances which even *Women* cannot controul.—Female Economy* will do a great deal my Lord, but it cannot turn a small income into a large one.'—Lord Osborne was silenced. Her manner had been neither Sententious nor sarcastic, but there was a something in it's mild seriousness, as well as in the words themselves which made his Lordship think;—and when he addressed her again, it was with a degree of considerate propriety, totally unlike the half-awkward, half-fearless stile of his former remarks.—It was a new thing with him to wish to please a woman; it was the first time that he had ever felt what was due to a woman, in Emma's situation.—But as he wanted neither Sense nor a good disposition, he did not feel it without effect.—'You have not been long in this Country I understand,' said he in the tone of a Gentleman. 'I hope you are pleased with it.'—He was rewarded by a gracious answer, & a more liberal full veiw of her face than she had yet bestowed. Unused to exert himself, & happy in contemplating her, he then sat in silence for some minutes longer, while Tom Musgrave was chattering to Elizabeth, till they were interrupted by Nanny's approach, who half opening the door & putting in her head, said 'Please Ma'am, Master wants to know why he ben't to have* his dinner.'—The Gentlemen, who had hitherto disregarded every symptom, however positive, of the nearness of that Meal, now jumped up with apologies, while Elizabeth called briskly after Nanny 'to tell Betty to take up the Fowls.'—'I am sorry it happens so'—she added, turning goodhumouredly towards Musgrave—'but you know what early hours we keep.—' Tom had nothing to say for himself, he knew it very well, & such honest simplicity, such shameless Truth rather bewildered him.—Lord Osborne's parting Compliments took some time, his inclination for speech seeming to increase with the shortness of the term for indulgence.—He recommended Exercise in defiance of dirt—spoke again in praise of Half-boots—begged that his Sister might be allow'd to send Emma the name of her Shoemaker—& concluded with saying, 'My Hounds will be hunting this Country next week—I beleive they will throw off* at Stanton Wood on Wednesday at 9 o'clock.—I mention this, in hopes of your being drawn out to see what's going on.*—If the morning's tolerable, pray do us the honour of giving us your good wishes in person.—'

The Sisters looked on each other with astonishment, when their visitors had withdrawn. 'Here's an unaccountable Honour!' cried Elizabeth at last. 'Who would have thought of Lord Osborne's coming to Stanton.*—He is very handsome;—but Tom Musgrave looks all to nothing, the smartest & most fashionable man of the two. I am glad he did not say anything to me; I would not have had to talk to such a great man for the world. Tom was very agreable, was not he?—But did you hear him ask where Miss Penelope & Miss Margaret were, when he first came in?—It put me out of patience.—I am glad Nanny had not laid the Cloth however, it would have looked so awkward;—just the Tray did not signify.—' To say that Emma was not flattered by Lord Osborne's visit, would be to assert a very unlikely thing, & describe a very odd young Lady; but the gratification was by no means unalloyed; His coming was a sort of notice which might please her vanity, but did not suit her pride, & she would rather have known that he wished the visit without presuming to make it, than have seen him at Stanton.—Among other unsatisfactory feelings it once occurred to her to wonder why Mr Howard had not taken the same privilege of coming, & accompanied his Lordship—but she was willing to suppose that he had either known nothing about it, or had declined any share in a measure which carried quite as much Importance in it's form as Goodbreeding. Mr W. was very far from being delighted, when he heard what had passed;—a little peevish under immediate pain, & illdisposed to be pleased, he only replied—'Phoo! Phoo!—What occasion could there be for Lord O.'s coming. I have lived here 14 years without being noticed by any of the family. It is some foolery of that idle fellow T. Musgrave. I cannot return the visit.—I would not if I could.' And when T. Musgrave was met with again, he was commissioned with a message of excuse to Osborne Castle, on the too-sufficient plea of Mr Watson's infirm state of health.—

A week or ten days rolled quietly away after this visit, before any new bustle arose to interrupt even for half a day, the tranquil & affectionate intercourse of the two Sisters, whose mutual regard was increasing with the intimate knowledge of each other which such intercourse produced.—The first circumstance to break in on this serenity, was the receipt of a letter from Croydon to announce the speedy return of Margaret, & a visit of two or three days from Mr and Mrs Robert Watson who undertook to bring her home & wished to see their Sister Emma.—It was an expectation to fill the thoughts of the Sisters at Stanton, & to busy the hours of one of them at least—for as Jane had been a woman of fortune, the preparations for her entertainment were considerable, & as Elizabeth had at all times more good will than method in her guidance of the house, she could make no change without a Bustle.—An absence of 14 years had made all her Brothers & Sisters Strangers to Emma, but in her expectation of Margaret there was more than the awkwardness of such an Alienation; she had heard things which made her dread her return; & the day which brought the party to Stanton seemed to her the probable conclusion of almost all that had been comfortable in the house.—Robert Watson was an Attorney at Croydon, in a good way of Business; very well satisfied with himself for the same, & for having married the only daughter of the Attorney to whom he had been Clerk, with a fortune of six thousand pounds.*—Mrs Robert was not less pleased with herself for having had that six thousand pounds, & for being now in possession of a very smart house in Croydon, where she gave genteel parties, & wore fine Cloathes.—In her person there was nothing remarkable; her manners were pert & conceited.—Margaret was not without beauty; she had a slight, pretty figure, & rather wanted Countenance* than good features;—but the sharp & anxious expression of her face made her beauty in general little felt.—On meeting her long-absent Sister, as on every occasion of shew, her manner was all affection & her voice all gentleness; continual smiles & a very slow articulation being her constant resource when determined on pleasing.—

She was now so 'delighted to see dear, dear Emma', that she could hardly speak a word in a minute.—'I am sure we shall be great friends—' she observed, with much sentiment, as they were sitting together.—Emma scarcely knew how to answer such a proposition—& the manner in which it was spoken, she could not attempt to equal. Mrs R. W. eyed her with much familiar curiosity & Triumphant Compassion;—the loss of the Aunt's fortune was uppermost in her mind, at the moment of meeting;—& she could not but feel how much better it was to be the daughter of a gentleman of property in Croydon, than the neice of an old woman who threw herself away on an Irish Captain.—Robert was carelessly kind, as became a prosperous Man & a brother; more intent on settling with the Post-Boy, inveighing against the Exorbitant advance in Posting,* & pondering over a doubtful halfcrown,* than on welcoming a Sister, who was no longer likely to have any property for him to get the direction of.—'Your road through the village is infamous, Elizabeth;' said he; 'worse than ever it was. By Heaven! I would endite* it if I lived near you. Who is Surveyor* now?'—There was a little neice at Croydon, to be fondly enquired after by the kind-hearted Elizabeth, who regretted very much her not being of the party.—'You are very good'—replied her Mother—'& I assure you it went very hard with Augusta* to have us come away without her. I was forced to say we were only going to Church & promise to come back for her directly.—But you know it would not do, to bring her without her maid, & I am as particular as ever in having her properly attended to.' 'Sweet little Darling!'—cried Margaret—'It quite broke my heart to leave her.—' 'Then why was you in such a hurry to run away from her?' cried Mrs R.—'You are a sad shabby* girl.—I have been quarrelling with you all the way we came, have not I?—Such a visit as this,

I never heard of!—You know how glad we are to have any of you with us;—if it be for months together.—& I am sorry, (with a witty smile) we have not been able to make Croydon agreable this Autumn.'—'My dearest Jane—do not overpower me with your raillery.—You know what inducements I had to bring me home—Spare me, I entreat you.—I am no match for your wickedness.'—'Well, I only beg you will not set your Neighbours against the place.—Perhaps Emma may be tempted to go back with us, & stay till Christmas, if you don't put in your word.'—Emma was greatly obliged. 'I assure you we have very good society at Croydon.—I do not much attend the Balls, they are rather too mixed,*—but our parties are very select & good.— I had seven Tables* last week in my Drawingroom.—Are you fond of the Country? How do you like Stanton?—' 'Very much'—replied Emma, who thought a comprehensive answer, most to the purpose.—She saw that her Sister in law despised her immediately.—Mrs R. W. was indeed wondering what sort of a home Emma could possibly have been used to in Shropshire, & setting it down as certain that the Aunt could never have had six thousand pounds. 'How charming Emma is!—' whispered Margaret to Mrs Robert in her most languishing tone.—Emma was quite distress'd by such behaviour;—& she did not like it better when she heard Margaret 5 minutes afterwards say to Elizabeth in a sharp quick accent, totally unlike the first—'Have you heard from Pen. since she went to Chichester?—I had a letter the other day.—I don't find she is likely to make anything of it. I fancy she'll come back "Miss Penelope" as she went.—'

Such, she feared would be Margaret's common voice, when the novelty of her own appearance were over; the tone of artificial Sensibility was not recommended by the idea.—The Ladies were invited upstairs to prepare for dinner. 'I hope you will find things tolerably comfortable Jane'—said Elizabeth as she opened the door of the spare-bedchamber.—'My good creature,' replied Jane, 'use no ceremony with me, I intreat you. I am one of those who always take things as they find them. I hope I can put up with a small apartment for two or three nights, without making a peice of work. I always wish to be treated quite "en famille" when I come to see you—& now I do hope you have not been getting a great dinner for us.—Remember we never eat Suppers.'—'I suppose,' said Margaret rather quickly to Emma, 'you & I are to be together; Elizabeth always takes care to have

a room to herself.'—'No—Elizabeth gives me half her's.'—'Oh!'—(in
a soften'd voice, & rather mortified to find that she was not ill used)
'I am sorry I am not to have the pleasure of your company—
especially as it makes me nervous to be much alone.'

Emma was the first of the females in the parlour again; on entering
it she found her brother alone.—'So Emma,' said he, 'you are quite
the Stranger at home. It must seem odd enough to you to be here.—
A pretty peice of work your Aunt Turner has made of it!—By Heaven!
a woman should never be trusted with money. I always said she ought
to have settled something on you, as soon as her Husband died.' 'But
*that* would have been trusting *me* with money,' replied Emma, '&
*I* am a woman too.—' 'It might have been secured to your future use,
without your having any power over it now.—What a blow it must
have been upon you!—To find yourself, instead of Heiress of 8 or
9000£, sent back a weight upon your family, without a sixpence.—
I hope the old woman will smart for it.' 'Do not speak disrespectfully
of her—She was very good to me; & if she has made an imprudent
choice, she will suffer more from it herself, than *I* can possibly do.'
'I do not mean to distress you, but you know every body must think
her an old fool.—I thought Turner had been reckoned an extraordinary sensible, clever man.—How the Devil came he to make such
a will?'—'My Uncle's sense is not at all impeached in my opinion, by
his attachment to my Aunt. She had been an excellent wife to him.
The most Liberal & enlightened minds are always the most confid-
ing.—The event has been unfortunate, but my Uncle's memory is if
possible endeared to me by such a proof of tender respect for my
Aunt.'—'That's odd sort of Talking!—He might have provided
decently for his widow, without leaving every thing that he had to
dispose of, or any part of it at her mercy.—' 'My Aunt may have
erred'—said Emma warmly—'she *has* erred—but my Uncle's conduct was faultless. I was her own Neice, & he left to herself the power &
the pleasure of providing for me.'—'But unluckily she has left the
pleasure of providing for you, to your Father, & without the
power.—That's the long & the short of the business. After keeping
you at a distance from your family for such a length of time as must
do away all natural affection among us & breeding you up (I suppose)
in a superior stile, you are returned upon their hands without a sixpence.' 'You know,' replied Emma struggling with her tears, 'my
Uncle's melancholy state of health.—He was a greater Invalid than

my father. He could not leave home.' 'I do not mean to make you cry.'—said Robert rather softened—& after a short silence, by way of changing the subject, he added—'I am just come from my Father's room, he seems very indifferent. It will be a sad break-up when he dies. Pity, you can none of you get married!—You must come to Croydon as well as the rest, & see what you can do there. I believe if Margaret had had a thousand or fifteen hundred pounds, there was a young man who would have thought of her.' Emma was glad when they were joined by the others; it was better to look at her Sister in law's finery, than listen to Robert, who had equally irritated & greived her.—Mrs Robert exactly as smart as she had been at her own party, came in with apologies for her dress—'I would not make you wait,' said she, 'so I put on the first thing I met with. I am afraid I am a sad figure.—My dear Mr W.—(to her husband) you have not put any fresh powder in your hair.'*—'No—I do not intend it.—I think there is powder enough in my hair for my wife & Sisters.—' 'Indeed you ought to make some alteration in your dress before dinner when you are out visitting, tho' you do not at home.' 'Nonsense.—' 'It is very odd you should not like to do what other gentlemen do. Mr Marshall & Mr Hemmings change their dress every day of their Lives before dinner. And what was the use of my putting up* your last new Coat, if you are never to wear it.'—'Do be satisfied with being fine yourself, & leave your husband alone.'—To put an end to this altercation, & soften the evident vexation of her Sister in law, Emma (tho' in no Spirits to make such nonsense easy) began to admire her gown.—It produced immediate complacency.—'Do you like it?'—said she.—'I am very happy.—It has been excessively admired;—but sometimes I think the pattern too large.—I shall wear one tomorrow that I think you will prefer to this.—Have you seen the one I gave Margaret?'—

Dinner came, & except when Mrs R. looked at her husband's head, she continued gay & flippant, chiding Elizabeth for the profusion on the Table, & absolutely protesting against the entrance of the roast Turkey—which formed the only exception to 'You see your dinner'.—'I do beg & entreat that no Turkey may be seen to day. I am really frightened out of my wits with the number of dishes we have already. Let us have no Turkey I beseech you.'—'My dear,' replied Elizabeth 'the Turkey is roasted, & it may just as well come in, as stay in the Kitchen. Besides if it is cut, I am in hopes my Father may be

tempted to eat a bit, for it is rather a favourite dish.' 'You may have it
in my dear, but I assure you *I* shan't touch it.'—

Mr Watson had not been well enough to join the party at dinner,
but was prevailed on to come down & drink tea with them.—'I wish
we may be able to have a game of cards tonight,' said Elizabeth to
Mrs R. after seeing her father comfortably seated in his arm
chair.—'Not on my account my dear, I beg. You know I am no card
player. I think a snug chat infinitely better. I always say cards are very
well sometimes, to break a formal circle, but one never wants them
among freinds.' 'I was thinking of it's being something to amuse my
father,' answered Elizabeth—'if it was not disagreable to you. He says
his head won't bear Whist—but perhaps if we make a round game*
he may be tempted to sit down with us.'—'By all means my dear
Creature. I am quite at your service. Only do not oblige me to chuse
the game, that's all. *Speculation** is the only round game at Croydon
now, but I can play any thing.—When there is only one or two of you
at home, you must be quite at a loss to amuse him—why do not you
get him to play at Cribbage?*—Margaret & I have played at Cribbage,
most nights that we have not been engaged.'—A sound like a distant
Carriage was at this moment caught; every body listened; it became
more decided; it certainly drew nearer.—It was an unusual sound in
Stanton at any time of the day, for the Village was on no very public
road, & contained no gentleman's family but the Rector's.—The
wheels rapidly approached;—in two minutes the general expectation
was answered; they stopped beyond a doubt at the garden gate of the
Parsonage. 'Who could it be?—it was certainly a postchaise.*—Penelope
was the only creature to be thought of. She might perhaps have met
with some unexpected opportunity of returning.'—A pause of suspense ensued.—Steps were distinguished, first along the paved
Footway which led under the windows of the house to the front door,
& then within the passage. They were the Steps of a man. It could not
be Penelope. It must be Samuel.—The door opened, & displayed
Tom Musgrave in the wrap* of a Travellor.—He had been in London &
was now on his way home, & he had come half a mile out of his road
merely to call for ten minutes at Stanton. He loved to take people by
surprise, with sudden visits at extraordinary seasons; & in the present
instance had had the additional motive of being able to tell the Miss
Watsons, whom he depended on finding sitting quietly employed
after tea, that he was going home to an 8 o'clock dinner.*—As it

happened however, he did not give more surprise than he received, when instead of being shewn into the usual little sitting room, the door of the best parlour a foot larger each way than the other was thrown open, & he beheld a circle of smart people whom he could not immediately recognise arranged with all the honours of visiting round the fire, & Miss Watson sitting at the best Pembroke Table, with the best Tea things before her. He stood a few seconds, in silent amazement.—'Musgrave!'—ejaculated Margaret in a tender voice.—He recollected himself, & came forward, delighted to find such a circle of Friends, & blessing his good fortune for the unlooked-for Indulgence.—He shook hands with Robert, bowed & smiled to the Ladies, & did every thing very prettily; but as to any particularity of address or Emotion towards Margaret, Emma who closely observed him, perceived nothing that did not justify Elizabeth's opinions tho' Margaret's modest smiles imported that she meant to take the visit to herself.—He was persuaded without much difficulty to throw off his great coat, & drink tea with them. 'For whether he dined at 8 or 9, as he observed, was a matter of very little consequence.'—and without seeming to seek, he did not turn away from the chair close to Margaret which she was assiduous in providing him.—She had thus secured him from her Sisters—but it was not immediately in her power to preserve him from her Brother's claims, for as he came avowedly from London, & had left it only 4 hours ago, the last current report as to public news, & the general opinion of the day must be understood, before Robert could let his attention be yeilded to the less national, & important demands of the Women.—At last however he was at liberty to hear Margaret's soft address, as she spoke her fears of his having had a most terrible, cold, dark dreadful Journey.—'Indeed you should not have set out so late.—' 'I could not be earlier,' he replied. 'I was detained chatting at the Bedford,* by a friend.—All hours are alike to me.—How long have you been in the Country Miss Margaret?'—'We came only this morning.—My kind Brother & Sister brought me home this very morning.—'Tis singular is it not?' 'You were gone a great while, were not you? a fortnight I suppose?'—'*You* may call a fortnight a great while Mr Musgrave,' said Mrs Robert smartly—'but *we* think a month very little. I assure you we bring her home at the end of a month, much against our will.' 'A month! have you really been gone a month! 'tis amazing how Time flies.—' 'You may imagine,' said Margaret in a sort of Whisper, 'what are my Sensations in finding myself once more at Stanton. You know what a sad visitor I make.—And I was so excessively impatient to see Emma;—I dreaded the meeting, & at the same time longed for it.—Do not you comprehend the sort of feeling?'—'Not at all,' cried he aloud. 'I could never dread a meeting with Miss Emma Watson,—or any of her Sisters.' It was lucky that he added that finish.—'Were you speaking to me?—' said Emma, who had caught her own name.—'Not absolutely'—he answered—'but I was thinking of you,—as many at a greater distance are probably doing at this moment.—Fine open weather* Miss Emma!—Charming season for Hunting.'

'Emma is delightful, is not she?'—whispered Margaret. 'I have found her more than answer my warmest hopes.—Did you ever see any thing more perfectly beautiful?—I think even *you* must be a convert to a brown complexion.'—He hesitated; Margaret was fair herself, & he did not particularly want to compliment her; but Miss Osborne & Miss Carr were likewise fair, & his devotion to them carried the day. 'Your Sister's complexion,' said he at last, 'is as fine as a dark complexion can be, but I still profess my preference of a white skin. You have seen Miss Osborne?—she is my model for a truly feminine complexion, & she is very fair.'—'Is she fairer than me?'—Tom made no reply.—'Upon my Honour Ladies,' said he, giving a glance over his own person, 'I am highly endebted to your Condescension for admitting me, in such Dishabille,* into your Drawing room. I really did not consider how unfit I was to be here, or I hope I should have kept my distance. Lady Osborne would tell me that I were growing as careless as her son, if she saw me in this condition.'—The Ladies were not wanting in civil returns; & Robert Watson stealing a veiw of his own head in an opposite glass,—said with equal civility, 'You cannot be more in dishabille than myself.—We got here so late, that I had not time even to put a little fresh powder in my hair.'—Emma could not help entering into what she supposed her Sister in law's feelings at that moment.—

When the Tea things were removed, Tom began to talk of his Carriage—but the old Card Table being set out, & the fish & counters, with a tolerably clean pack* brought forward from the beaufet* by Miss Watson, the general voice was so urgent with him to join their party, that he agreed to allow himself another quarter of an hour. Even Emma was pleased that he would stay, for she was beginning to feel that a family party might be the worst of all parties; & the others were delighted.—'What's your Game?'—cried he, as they stood round the Table.—'Speculation I beleive,' said Elizabeth—'My sister recommends it, & I fancy we all like it. I know *you* do, Tom.'—'It is the only round game played at Croydon now,' said Mrs Robert—'we never think of any other. I am glad it is a favourite with you.'—'Oh! me!' cried Tom, 'Whatever you decide on, will be a favourite with *me*.—I have had some pleasant hours at Speculation in my time—but I have not been in the way of it now for a long while.—Vingt-un* is the game at Osborne Castle; I have played nothing but Vingt-un of late. You would be astonished to hear the noise we make there.—The fine old, Lofty Drawing-room rings again. Lady Osborne sometimes declares she cannot hear herself speak.—Lord Osborne enjoys it famously & he makes the best Dealer without exception that I ever beheld—such quickness & spirit! he lets nobody dream over their cards.—I wish you could see him overdraw himself on both his own cards—it is worth any thing in the world!'—'Dear me!'—cried Margaret 'why should not we play at vingt un?—I think it is a much better game than Speculation. I cannot say I am very fond of Speculation.' Mrs Robert offered not another word in support of the game.—She was quite vanquished, & the fashions of Osborne-Castle carried it over the fashions of Croydon.—

'Do you see much of the Parsonage-family at the Castle, Mr Musgrave?—' said Emma, as they were taking their seats.—'Oh! yes—they are almost always there. Mrs Blake is a nice little good-humoured Woman, She & I are sworn friends; & Howard's a very Gentlemanlike good sort of fellow!—You are not forgotten I assure you by any of the party. I fancy you must have a little cheek-glowing now & then Miss Emma. Were not you rather warm last Saturday about 9 or 10 o'clock in the Evening—? I will tell you how it was.— I see you are dieing to know.—Says Howard to Lord Osborne—' At this interesting moment he was called on by the others, to regulate the game & determine some disputable point; & his attention was so totally engaged in the business & afterwards by the course of the game as never to revert to what he had been saying before;—& Emma, tho' suffering a good deal from Curiosity, dared not remind him.—He proved a very useful addition at their Table; without him, it would have been a party of such very near relations as could have felt little Interest, & perhaps maintained little complaisance,* but his presence gave variety & secured good manners.—He was in fact excellently

qualified to shine at a round Game; & few situations made him appear
to greater advantage. He played with Spirit & had a great deal to say, &
tho' with no wit himself, could sometimes make use of the wit of an
absent friend; & had a lively way of retailing a commonplace, or saying a mere nothing, that had great effect at a Card Table. The ways, &
good Jokes of Osborne Castle were now added to his ordinary means
of Entertainment; he repeated the smart sayings of one Lady, detailed
the oversights of another, & indulged them even with a copy of Lord
Osborne's stile of overdrawing himself on both cards.—The Clock
struck nine, while he was thus agreably occupied; & when Nanny
came in with her Master's Bason of Gruel,* he had the pleasure of
observing to Mr Watson that he should leave him at supper, while he
went home to dinner himself.—The Carriage was ordered to the
door—& no entreaties for his staying longer could now avail,—for he
well knew, that if he staid he must sit down to supper in less than ten
minutes—which to a Man whose heart had been long fixed on calling
his next meal a Dinner, was quite insupportable.—

On finding him determined to go, Margaret began to wink & nod
at Elizabeth to ask him to dinner for the following day; & Elizabeth at
last not able to resist hints, which her own hospitable, social temper
more than half seconded, gave the invitation. 'Would he give Robert
the meeting,* they should be very happy.' 'With the greatest pleasure'—was his first reply. In a moment afterwards—'That is, if I can
possibly get here in time—but I shoot with Lord Osborne, & therefore must not engage—You will not think of me unless you see
me.'—And so, he departed, delighted with the uncertainty in which
he had left it.—

Margaret in the joy of her heart under circumstances, which she
chose to consider as peculiarly propitious, would willingly have made
a confidante of Emma when they were alone for a short time the next
morning; & had proceeded so far as to say—'The young man who was
here last night my dear Emma & returns to day, is more interesting to
me, than perhaps you may be aware—' but Emma pretending to
understand nothing extraordinary in the words, made some very
inapplicable reply, & jumping up, ran away from a subject which was
odious to her feelings.—

As Margaret would not allow a doubt to be repeated of Musgrave's
coming to dinner, preparations were made for his Entertainment

much exceeding what had been deemed necessary the day
before;—and taking the office of Superintendance entirely from her
Sister, she was half the morning in the Kitchen, herself directing &
scolding.—After a great deal of indifferent Cooking, & anxious
Suspense however they were obliged to sit down without their
Guest.—T. Musgrove never came, & Margaret was at no pains to
conceal her vexation under the disappointment, or repress the peev-
ishness of her Temper—. The Peace of the party for the remainder of
that day, & the whole of the next, which comprised the length of
Robert & Jane's visit, was continually invaded by her fretful displeasure, & querulous attacks. Elizabeth was the usual object of both.
Margaret had just respect enough for her Brother and Sister's opinion, to behave properly by *them,* but Elizabeth & the maids could
never do any thing right—& Emma, whom she seemed no longer to
think about, found the continuance of the gentle voice beyond her
calculation short. Eager to be as little among them as possible, Emma
was delighted with the alternative of sitting above, with her father, &
warmly entreated to be his constant Companion each Evening—& as
Elizabeth loved company of any kind too well, not to prefer being
below, at all risks as She had rather talk of Croydon to Jane, with every
interruption of Margaret's perverseness, than sit with only her father,
who frequently could not endure Talking at all, the affair was so settled, as soon as she could be persuaded to beleive it no sacrifice on her
Sister's part. To Emma, the Exchange was most acceptable, &
delightful. Her father, if ill, required little more than gentleness &
silence; &, being a man of Sense & Education, was if able to converse,
a welcome companion.—In *his* chamber, Emma was at peace from
the dreadful mortifications of unequal Society, & family Discord—
from the immediate endurance of Hard-hearted prosperity, low-
minded Conceit, & wrong-headed folly, engrafted on an untoward
Disposition.—She still suffered from them in the Contemplation of
their existence; in memory & in prospect,* but for the moment, she
ceased to be tortured by their effects.—She was at leisure, she could
read & think,—tho' her situation was hardly such as to make reflection very soothing. The Evils arising from the loss of her Uncle, were
neither trifling, nor likely to lessen; & when Thought had been freely
indulged, in contrasting the past & the present, the employment of
mind, the dissipation of unpleasant ideas which only reading could
produce, made her thankfully turn to a book.—The change in her

home society, & stile of Life in consequence of the death of one freind
& the imprudence of another had indeed been striking.—From being
the first object of Hope & Solicitude to an Uncle who had formed her
mind with the care of a Parent, & of Tenderness to an Aunt whose
amiable temper had delighted to give her every indulgence, from
being the Life & Spirit of a House, where all had been comfort &
Elegance, & the expected Heiress of an easy Independance, she was
become of importance to no one, a burden on those, whose affection
she could not expect, an addition in an house, already overstocked,
surrounded by inferior minds with little chance of domestic comfort,
& as little hope of future support.—It was well for her that she was
naturally chearful;—for the Change had been such as might have
plunged weak spirits in Despondence.—

   She was very much pressed by Robert & Jane to return with them
to Croydon, & had some difficulty in getting a refusal accepted; as
they thought too highly of their own kindness & situation, to suppose
the offer could appear in a less advantageous light to anybody
else.—Elizabeth gave them her interest, tho' evidently against her
own, in privately urging Emma to go—'You do not know what you
refuse Emma'—said she—'nor what you have to bear at home.—
I would advise you by all means to accept the invitation; there is
always something lively going on at Croydon, you will be in company
almost every day, & Robert & Jane will be very kind to you.—As for
me, I shall be no worse off without you, than I have been used to be;
but poor Margaret's disagreable ways are new to *you*, & they would
vex you more than you think for, if you stay at home.—' Emma was of
course un-influenced, except to greater esteem for Elizabeth, by such
representations—& the Visitors departed without her.—

# SANDITON

# SANDITON

## CHAPTER 1

A Gentleman & Lady travelling from Tunbridge towards that part of the Sussex Coast which lies between Hastings & E. Bourne,* being induced by Business to quit the high road, & attempt a very rough Lane, were overturned in toiling up it's long ascent half rock, half sand.—The accident happened just beyond the only Gentleman's House near the Lane—a House, which their Driver on being first required to take that direction, had conceived to be necessarily their object, & had with most unwilling Looks been constrained to pass by—. He had grumbled, & shaken his Shoulders so much indeed, and pitied & cut his Horses so sharply; that he might have been open to the suspicion of overturning them on purpose (especially as the Carriage was not his Masters but the Gentleman's own*) if the road had not indisputably become considerably worse than before, as soon as the premises of the said House were left behind—expressing with a most intelligent portentous countenance that beyond it no wheels but cart wheels could safely proceed. The severity of the fall was broken by their slow pace & the narrowness of the Lane, & the Gentleman having scrambled out & helped out his companion, they neither of them at first felt more than shaken & bruised. But the Gentleman had in the course of the extrication sprained his foot—& soon becoming sensible of it, was obliged in a few moments to cut short, both his remonstrance to the Driver & his congratulations to his wife & himself—& sit down on the bank, unable to stand.—

'There is something wrong here,' said he—putting his hand to his ancle—'But never mind, my Dear—(looking up at her with a smile)—It could not have happened, you know, in a better place.—Good out of Evil—. The very thing perhaps to be wished for. We shall soon get releif. —*There*, I fancy lies my cure'—pointing to the neat-looking end of a Cottage, which was seen romantically situated among wood on a high Eminence at some little Distance—'Does not *that* promise to be the very place?—' His wife fervently hoped it was—but stood, terrified & anxious, neither able to do or suggest anything—& receiving her first real comfort from the sight of several persons now coming to their assistance. The accident had been discerned from a Hay field adjoining the House they had passed—& the persons who approached, were a well-looking Hale, Gentlemanlike Man, of middle age, the Proprietor of the Place, who happened to be among his Haymakers at the time, & three or four of the ablest of them summoned to attend their Master—to say nothing of all the rest of the field, Men, Women & Children—not very far off.—Mr Heywood, such was the name of the said Proprietor, advanced with a very civil salutation—much concern for the accident—some surprise at any body's attempting that road in a Carriage—& ready offers of assistance. His courtesies were received with Goodbreeding & Gratitude & while one or two of the Men lent their help to the Driver in getting the Carriage upright again, the Travellor said—'You are extremely obliging Sir, & I take you at your word.—The injury to my Leg is I dare say very trifling, but it is always best in these cases to have a Surgeon's opinion without loss of time; & as the road does not seem at present in a favourable state for my getting up to his house myself, I will thank you to send off one of these good People for the Surgeon.'* 'The Surgeon Sir!'—replied Mr Heywood—'I am afraid you will find no Surgeon at hand here, but I dare say we shall do very well without him.'—'Nay Sir, if *he* is not in the way, his Partner will do just as well—or rather better—. I would rather see his Partner indeed—I would prefer the attendance of his Partner.—One of these good people can be with him in three minutes I am sure. I need not ask whether I see the House; (looking towards the Cottage), for excepting your own, we have passed none in this place, which can be the Abode of a Gentleman.'—

Mr H. looked very much astonished & replied—'What Sir! are you expecting to find a Surgeon in that Cottage?—We have neither Surgeon nor Partner in the Parish I assure you.'—'Excuse me Sir'—replied the other. 'I am sorry to have the appearance of contradicting you—but though from the extent of the Parish or some other cause you may not be aware of the fact;—Stay—Can I be mistaken in the place?—Am I not in Willingden?—Is not this Willingden?' 'Yes Sir, this is certainly Willingden.' 'Then Sir, I can bring proof of your having a Surgeon in the Parish—whether you may know it or not. Here Sir—(taking out his Pocket book—) if you will do me the favour of casting your eye over these advertisements, which I cut out myself

from the Morning Post & the Kentish Gazette,* only yesterday morning in London—I think you will be convinced that I am not speaking
at random. You will find it an advertisement Sir, of the dissolution of
a Partnership in the Medical Line—in your own Parish—extensive
Business—undeniable Character—respectable references—wishing
to form a separate Establishment. You will find it at full length
Sir'—offering him the two little oblong extracts. 'Sir' said
Mr Heywood with a good humoured smile—'if you were to shew me
all the Newspapers that are printed in one week throughout the
Kingdom, you would not persuade me of there being a Surgeon in
Willingden,—for having lived here ever since I was born, Man & Boy
57 years, I think I must have *known* of such a person, at least I may
venture to say that he has not *much Business*;—To be sure, if Gentlemen
were to be often attempting this Lane in Postchaises,* it might not be
a bad Speculation for a Surgeon to get a House at the top of the
Hill.—But as to that Cottage, I can assure you Sir that it is in
fact—(inspite of its spruce air at this distance—) as indifferent a double
Tenement as any in the Parish, and that my Shepherd lives at one
end, & three old women at the other.' He took the peices of paper as he
spoke—& having looked them over, added—'I beleive I can explain it
Sir.—Your mistake is in the place.—There are two Willingdens in this
Country—& your advertisements refer to the other—which is Great
Willingden, or Willingden Abbots, & lies 7 miles off, on the other side
of Battel—quite down in the Weald. And *we* Sir—' (speaking rather
proudly) 'are not in the Weald.'—'Not *down* in the Weald I am sure
Sir,' replied the Travellor, pleasantly. 'It took us half an hour to climb
your Hill.—Well Sir—I dare say it is as you say, & I have made an
abominably stupid Blunder.—All done in a moment;—the advertisements did not catch my eye till the last half hour of our being in
Town—; when everything was in the hurry & confusion which always
attend a short stay there—One is never able to complete anything in
the way of Business you know till the Carriage is at the door—and
accordingly satisfying myself with a breif enquiry, & finding we were
actually to pass within a mile or two of a *Willingden*, I sought no farther.—My Dear—(to his wife) I am very sorry to have brought you
into this Scrape. But do not be alarmed about my Leg. It gives me no
pain while I am quiet,—and as soon as these good people have succeeded in setting the Carriage to rights & turning the Horses round,
the best thing we can do will be to measure back our steps into the

Turnpike road* & proceed to Hailsham, & so Home, without attempting anything farther.—Two hours take us home, from Hailsham—And
when once at home, we have our remedy at hand you know.—A little
of our own Bracing Sea Air will soon set me on my feet again.—Depend
upon it my Dear, it is exactly a case for the Sea. Saline air & immersion* will be the very thing.—My Sensations tell me so already.'—

In a most friendly manner Mr Heywood here interposed, entreat-
ing them not to think of proceeding till the ancle had been examined, &
some refreshment taken, & very cordially pressing them to make
use of his House for both purposes.—'We are always well stocked,'
said he, 'with all the common remedies for Sprains & Bruises—&
I will answer for the pleasure it will give my wife & daughters to be of
service to you & this Lady, in every way in their power.—' A twinge
or two, in trying to move his foot disposed the Travellor to think
rather more as he had done at first of the benefit of immediate assistance—& consulting his wife in the few words of 'Well my Dear,
I beleive it will be better for us—' turned again to Mr H. &
said—'Before we accept your Hospitality Sir,—& in order to do away
any unfavourable impression which the sort of wild goose-chase you
find me in, may have given rise to—allow me to tell you who we are.
My name is Parker.—Mr Parker of Sanditon;—this Lady, my wife
Mrs Parker.—We are on our road home from London;—*My* name
perhaps—tho' I am by no means the first of my Family, holding
Landed Property in the Parish of Sanditon, may be unknown at this
distance from the Coast—but Sanditon itself—everybody has heard
of Sanditon,—the favourite—for a young & rising Bathing-place,
certainly the favourite spot of all that are to be found along the Coast
of Sussex;—the most favoured by Nature, & promising to be the
most chosen by Man.'—'Yes—I have heard of Sanditon.' replied
Mr H.—'Every five years, one hears of some new place or other starting up by the Sea, & growing the fashion.—How they can half of
them be filled, is the wonder! *Where* People can be found with Money
or Time to go to them!—Bad things for a Country;—sure to raise the
price of Provisions & make the Poor good for nothing—as I dare say
you find, Sir.' 'Not at all Sir, not at all'—cried Mr Parker eagerly.
'Quite the contrary I assure you.—A common idea—but a mistaken
one. It may apply to your large, overgrown Places, like Brighton, or
Worthing, or East Bourne*—but *not* to a small Village like Sanditon,
precluded by its size from experiencing any of the evils of Civilization,

while the growth of the place, the Buildings, the Nursery Grounds,* the demand for every thing, & the sure resort of the very best Company, those regular, steady, private Families of thorough Gentility & Character, who are a blessing every where, excite the industry of the Poor and diffuse comfort & improvement among them of every sort.* "No Sir, I assure you, Sanditon is not a place—' 'I do not mean to take exceptions to any place in particular Sir,' answered Mr H.—'I only think our Coast is too full of them altogether—But had not we better try to get you'—'Our Coast too full'—repeated Mr P.—'On that point perhaps we may not totally disagree;—At least there are *enough*. Our Coast is abundant enough; it demands no more.—Everybody's Taste & every body's finances may be suited—And those good people who are trying to add to the number, are in my opinion excessively absurd, & must soon find themselves the Dupes of their own fallacious Calculations.—Such a place as Sanditon Sir, I may say was wanted, was called for.—Nature had marked it out—had spoken in most intelligible Characters—The finest, purest Sea Breeze on the Coast—acknowledged to be so—Excellent Bathing  fine hard Sand—Deep Water 10 yards from the Shore—no Mud—no Weeds—no slimey rocks—Never was there a place more palpably designed by Nature for the resort of the Invalid—the very Spot which Thousands seemed in need of.—The most desirable distance from London!* One complete, measured mile nearer than East Bourne. Only conceive Sir, the advantage of saving a whole Mile, in a long Journey. But Brinshore Sir, which I dare say you have in your eye—the attempts of two or three speculating People* about Brinshore, this last year, to raise that paltry Hamlet, lying, as it does between a stagnant marsh, a bleak Moor & the constant effluvia* of a ridge of putrifying Sea weed, can end in nothing but their own Disappointment. What in the name of Common Sense is to *recommend* Brinshore?—A most insalubrious Air—Roads proverbially detestable—Water Brackish beyond example, impossible to get a good dish of Tea within 3 miles of the place—& as for the Soil—it is so cold & ungrateful that it can hardly be made to yeild a Cabbage.—Depend upon it Sir, that this is a faithful Description of Brinshore—not in the smallest degree exaggerated—& if you have heard it differently spoken of—' 'Sir I never heard it spoken of in my Life before,' said Mr Heywood. 'I did not know there was such a place in the World.'— 'You did not!—There my Dear—(turning with exultation to his

Wife)—you see how it is. So much for the Celebrity of Brinshore!—This Gentleman did not know there was such a place in the World.—Why, in truth Sir, I fancy we may apply to Brinshore, that line of the Poet Cowper* in his description of the religious Cottager, as opposed to Voltaire—"*She*, never heard of half a mile from home." '—'With all my Heart Sir—Apply any Verses you like to it—But I want to see something applied to your Leg—& I am sure by your Lady's countenance that she is quite of my opinion & thinks it a pity to lose any more time—And here come my Girls to speak for themselves & their Mother, (two or three genteel looking young women, followed by as many Maid Servants, were now seen issueing from the House)—I began to wonder the Bustle should not have reached *them.*—A thing of this kind soon makes a Stir in a lonely place like ours.—Now Sir, let us see how you can be best conveyed into the House.'—The young Ladies approached & said every thing that was proper to recommend their Father's offers; & in an unaffected manner calculated to make the Strangers easy—And as Mrs P. was exceedingly anxious for releif—and her Husband by this time, not much less disposed for it—a very few Civil Scruples were enough—especially as the Carriage being now set up, was discovered to have received such Injury on the fallen side as to be unfit for present use.—Mr Parker was therefore carried into the House, & his Carriage wheeled off to a vacant Barn.—

## CHAPTER 2

The acquaintance, thus oddly begun, was neither short nor unimportant. For a whole fortnight the Travellors were fixed at Willingden; Mr P.'s sprain proving too serious for him to move sooner.—He had fallen into very good hands. The Heywoods were a thoroughly respectable family, & every possible attention was paid in the kindest & most unpretending manner, to both Husband & wife. *He* was waited on & nursed, & *she* cheered & comforted with unremitting kindness—and as every office of Hospitality & friendliness was received as it ought—as there was not more good will on one side than Gratitude on the other—nor any deficiency of generally pleasant manners on either, they grew to like each other in the course of that fortnight, exceedingly well.—Mr Parker's Character & History were soon unfolded. All that he understood of himself, he readily told, for he was very openhearted;—& where he might be himself in the dark, his conversation was still giving information, to such of the Heywoods as could observe.—By such he was perceived to be an Enthusiast;*—on the subject of Sanditon, a complete Enthusiast.—Sanditon,—the success of Sanditon as a small, fashionable Bathing Place, was the object, for which he seemed to live. A very few years ago, & it had been a quiet Village of no pretensions;* but some natural advantages in its position & some accidental circumstances having suggested to himself, & the other principal Land Holder, the probability of it's becoming a profitable Speculation, they had engaged in it, & planned & built, & praised & puffed,* & raised it to a Something of young Renown—and Mr Parker could now think of very little besides. The Facts, which in more direct communication, he laid before them were that he was about 5 & 30—had been married,—very happily married 7 years—& had 4 sweet Children at home;—that he was of a respectable Family, & easy though not large fortune;—no Profession—succeeding as eldest son to the Property which 2 or 3 Generations had been holding & accumulating before him; that he had 2 Brothers & 2 Sisters—all single & all independant—the eldest of the two former indeed, by collateral Inheritance,* quite as well provided for as himself.—His object in quitting the high road, to hunt for an advertising Surgeon, was also plainly stated;—it had not proceeded from any intention of spraining his ancle or doing himself any other Injury for the good of such Surgeon—nor (as Mr H. had been apt to suppose) from any design of entering into Partnership with him—; it was merely in consequence of a wish to establish some medical Man at Sanditon, which the nature of the Advertisement induced him to expect to accomplish in Willingden.—He was convinced that the advantage of a medical Man at hand would very materially promote the rise & prosperity of the Place—would in fact tend to bring a pro-digious influx;—nothing else was wanting. He had *strong* reason to beleive that *one* family had been deterred last year from trying Sanditon on that account—& probably very many more—and his own Sisters who were sad Invalids, & whom he was very anxious to get to Sanditon this Summer, could hardly be expected to hazard themselves in a place where they could not have immediate medical advice.—Upon the whole, Mr P. was evidently an amiable, family-man, fond of Wife, Children, Brothers & Sisters—& generally kind-hearted;—Liberal, gentlemanlike, easy to please;—of a sanguine turn of mind, with more Imagination than Judgement. And Mrs P. was as evidently a gentle, amiable, sweet tempered Woman, the properest wife in the World for a Man of strong Understanding, but not of capacity to supply the cooler reflection which her own Husband sometimes needed, & so entirely waiting to be guided on every occasion, that whether he were risking his Fortune or spraining his Ancle, she remained equally useless.—Sanditon was a second Wife & 4 Children to him—hardly less Dear—& certainly more engrossing.—He could talk of it for ever.—It had indeed the highest claims;—not only those of Birth place, Property, and Home,—it was his Mine, his Lottery, his Speculation & his Hobby Horse;* his Occupation his Hope & his Futurity.*—He was extremely desirous of drawing his good friends at Willingden thither; and his endeavours in the cause, were as grateful & disinterested, as they were warm.—He wanted to secure the promise of a visit—to get as many of the Family as his own house would contain, to follow him to Sanditon as soon as possible—and healthy as they all undeniably were—foresaw that every one of them would be benefited by the Sea.—He held it indeed as certain, that no person could be really well, no person, (however upheld for the present by fortuitous aids of exercise & spirits in a semblance of Health) could be really in a state of secure & permanent Health without spending at least 6 weeks by the Sea every year.—The Sea Air & Sea Bathing together were nearly infallible, One or the other of them being a match for every Disorder, of the Stomach, the Lungs or the Blood; They were anti-spasmodic, anti-pulmonary, anti-sceptic, anti-bilious & anti-rheumatic.* Nobody could catch cold by the Sea, Nobody wanted appetite by the Sea, Nobody wanted Spirits. Nobody wanted Strength.*—They were healing, softing,* relaxing—fortifying & bracing—seemingly just as was wanted—sometimes one, sometimes the other.—If the Sea breeze failed, the Sea-Bath was the certain corrective;—& where Bathing disagreed, the Sea Breeze alone was evidently designed by Nature for the cure.—His eloquence however could not prevail. Mr & Mrs H. never left home. Marrying early & having a very numerous Family, their movements had been long limitted to one small circle; & they were older in Habits than in Age.—Excepting two Journeys to London in the year, to receive his Dividends,* Mr H. went no farther than his feet, or his well-tried old Horse could carry him, and Mrs Heywood's Adventurings were only now & then to visit her Neighbours, in the old Coach which had been new when they married & fresh lined on their Eldest Son's coming of age 10 years ago.—They had very pretty Property—enough, had their family been of reasonable Limits to have allowed them a very gentlemanlike share of Luxuries & Change—enough for them to have indulged in a new Carriage & horses, an occasional month at Tunbridge Wells, & symptoms of the Gout and a Winter at Bath;*—but the maintenance, Education & fitting out of 14 Children demanded a very quiet, settled, careful course of Life—& obliged them to be stationary & healthy at Willingden. What Prudence had at first enjoined, was now rendered pleasant by Habit. They never left home, & they had a gratification in saying so.—But very far from wishing their Children to do the same, they were glad to promote *their* getting out into the World, as much as possible. *They* staid at home, that their Children *might* get out;—and while making that home extremely comfortable, welcomed every change from it which could give useful connections or respectable acquaintance to Sons or Daughters. When Mr & Mrs. Parker therefore ceased from soliciting a family-visit, and bounded their veiws to carrying back one Daughter with them, no difficulties were started. It was general pleasure & consent.—Their invitation was to Miss Charlotte Heywood, a very pleasing young woman of two & twenty, the eldest of the Daughters at home, & the one, who under her Mother's directions had been particularly useful & obliging to them; who had attended them most, & knew them best.—Charlotte was to go,—with excellent health, to bathe & be better if she could—to receive every possible pleasure which Sanditon could be made to supply by the gratitude of those she went with—& to buy new Parasols, new Gloves, & new Broches, for her Sisters & herself at the Library,* which Mr P. was anxiously wishing to support.—All that Mr Heywood himself could be persuaded to promise was, that he would send everyone to Sanditon, who asked his advice, & that nothing should ever induce him (as far as the future could be answered for) to spend even 5 Shillings* at Brinshore.—

## CHAPTER 3

Every Neighbourhood should have a great Lady.—The great Lady of Sanditon, was Lady Denham;* & in their Journey from Willingden

*Sanditon*

to the Coast, Mr Parker gave Charlotte a more detailed account of her, than had been called for before.—She had been necessarily often mentioned at Willingden,—for being his Colleague in speculation, Sanditon itself could not be talked of long, without the introduction of Lady Denham & that she was a very rich old Lady, who had buried two Husbands, who knew the value of Money, was very much looked up to & had a poor Cousin living with her, were facts already well known, but some further particulars of her history & her Character served to lighten the tediousness of a long Hill, or a heavy bit of road, and to give the visiting young Lady* a suitable knowledge of the Person with whom she might now expect to be daily associating.—Lady D. had been a rich Miss Brereton, born to Wealth but not to Education. Her first Husband had been a Mr Hollis, a man of considerable Property in the Country, of which a large share of the Parish of Sanditon, with Manor & Mansion House made a part. He had been an elderly Man when she married him;—her own age about 30.—Her motives for such a Match could be little understood at the distance of 40 years, but she had so well nursed & pleased Mr Hollis, that at his death he left her everything—all his Estates, & all at her Disposal.* After a widowhood of some years, she had been induced to marry again. The late Sir Harry Denham, of Denham Park in the Neighbourhood of Sanditon had succeeded in removing her & her large Income to his own Domains, but he could not succeed in the veiws of permanently enriching his family, which were attributed to him. She had been too wary to put anything out of her own Power—and when on Sir Harry's Decease she returned again to her own House at Sanditon, she was said to have made this boast to a friend 'that though she had *got* nothing but her Title from the Family, still she had *given* nothing for it.'—For the Title, it was to be supposed that she had married—& Mr P. acknowledged there being just such a degree of value for it apparent now, as to give her conduct that natural explanation.—'There is at times,' said he—'a little self-importance—but it is not offensive;—& there are moments, there are points, when her Love of Money is carried greatly too far. But she is a goodnatured Woman, a very goodnatured Woman;—a very obliging, friendly Neighbour; a chearful, independant, valuable character.—and her faults may be entirely imputed to her want of Education. She has good natural Sense, but quite uncultivated.—She has a fine active mind, as well as a fine healthy frame for a Woman of 70, &

enters into the improvement of Sanditon with a spirit truly admirable—though now & then, a Littleness *will* appear. She cannot look forward quite as I would have her—& takes alarm at a trifling present expence, without considering what returns it *will* make her in a year or two. That is—we think *differently*, we now & then, see things *differently, Miss H.—'Those who tell their own Story, you know must be* listened to with Caution.  When you see us in contact, you will judge for yourself.'—Lady D. was indeed a great Lady beyond the common wants of Society—for she had many Thousands a year to bequeath, & three distinct sets of People to be courted by; her own relations, who might very reasonably wish for her Original Thirty Thousand Pounds* among them, the legal Heirs of Mr Hollis, who must hope to be more endebted to *her* sense of Justice than he had allowed them to be to *his,* and those Members of the Denham Family, whom her 2$^d$ Husband had hoped to make a good Bargain for.—By all of these, or by Branches of them, she had no doubt been long, & still continued to be, well attacked;—and of these divisions, Mr P. did not hesitate to say that Mr Hollis' Kindred were the *least* in favour and Sir Harry Denham's the *most*.—The former he beleived, had done themselves irremediable harm by expressions of very unwise & unjustifiable resentment at the time of Mr Hollis's death;—the Latter, to the advantage of being the remnant of a Connection which she certainly valued, joined those of having been known to her from their Childhood & of being always at hand to preserve their interest by reasonable attention. Sir Edward, the present Baronet, nephew to Sir Harry, resided constantly at Denham Park; & Mr P. had little doubt, that he & his Sister Miss D. who lived with him, would be principally remembered in her Will. He sincerely hoped it.—Miss Denham had a very small provision—& her Brother was a poor Man for his rank in Society. 'He is a warm friend to Sanditon'—said Mr Parker—'& his hand would be as liberal as his heart, had he the Power.—He would be a noble Coadjutor!*—As it is, he does what he can—& is running up a tasteful little Cottage Ornèe,* on a strip of waste Ground Lady D. has granted him, which I have no doubt we shall have many a Candidate for, before the end even of *this* Season.' Till within the last twelvemonth, Mr P. had considered Sir Edward as standing without a rival, as having the fairest chance of succeeding to the greater part of all that she had to give—but there was now another person's claims to be taken into the account, those of the young female relation, whom Lady D. had been induced to receive into her Family. After having always protested against any such addition, and long & often enjoyed the repeated defeats she had given to every attempt of her relations to introduce this young Lady, or that young Lady as a Companion* at Sanditon House, she had brought back with her from London last Michaelmas a Miss Brereton, who bid fair by her Merits to vie in favour with Sir Edward, & to secure for herself & her family that share of the accumulated Property which they had certainly the best right to inherit.—Mr Parker spoke warmly of Clara Brereton, & the interest of his Story increased very much with the introduction of such a Character. Charlotte listened with more than amusement now;—it was solicitude & Enjoyment, as she heard her described to be lovely, amiable, gentle, unassuming, conducting herself uniformly with great good Sense, & evidently gaining by her innate worth, on the affections of her Patroness.—Beauty, Sweetness, Poverty & Dependance, do not want the imagination of a Man to operate upon. With due exceptions—Woman feels for Woman very promptly & compassionately.—He gave the particulars which had led to Clara's admission at Sanditon, as no bad exemplification of that mixture of Character, that union of Littleness with Kindness with Good Sense with even Liberality which he saw in Lady D.—After having avoided London for many years, principally on account of these very Cousins, who were continually writing, inviting & tormenting her, & whom she was determined to keep at a distance, she had been obliged to go there last Michaelmas* with the certainty of being detained at least a fort-night.—She had gone to an Hotel—living by her own account, as prudently as possible, to defy the reputed expensiveness of such a home, & at the end of three Days calling for her Bill, that she might judge of her state.—It's amount was such as determined her on stay-ing not another hour in the House, & she was preparing in all the anger & perturbation which a beleif of very gross imposition *there*, & an ignorance of *where* to go for better usage, to leave the Hotel at all hazards, when the Cousins, the politic & lucky Cousins, who seemed always to have a spy on her, introduced themselves at this important moment, & learning her situation, persuaded her to accept such a home for the rest of her Stay as their humbler house in a very inferior part of London, could offer.—She went; was delighted with her welcome & the hospitality & attention she received from every body—found her good Cousins the B.s beyond her expectation worthy people—& finally was impelled by a personal knowledge of their narrow Income & pecuniary difficulties, to invite one of the girls of the family to pass the Winter with her. The invitation was to *one*, for six months—with the probability of another being then to take her place;—but in *selecting* the one, Lady D. had shewn the good part of her Character—for passing by the actual *daughters* of the House, she had chosen Clara, a Neice—, more helpless & more pitiable of course than any—a dependant on Poverty—an additional Burthen on an encumbered Circle—& one, who had been so low in every worldly veiw, as with all her natural endowments & powers, to have been preparing for a situation little better than a Nursery Maid. Clara had returned with her—& by her good sense & merit had now, to all appearance secured a very strong hold in Lady D.'s regard. The six months had long been over—& not a syllable was breathed of any change, or exchange.—She was a general favourite;—the influence of her steady conduct & mild, gentle Temper was felt by everybody. The prejudices which had met her at first in some quarters, were all dissipated. She was felt to be worthy of Trust—to be the very companion who would guide & soften Lady D.—who would enlarge her mind & open her hand.—She was as thoroughly amiable as she was lovely—& since having had the advantage of their Sanditon Breezes that Loveliness was complete.

## CHAPTER 4

'And whose very snug-looking Place is this?'—said Charlotte, as in a sheltered Dip within 2 miles of the Sea, they passed close by a moderate-sized house, well fenced & planted, & rich in the Garden, Orchard & Meadows which are the best embellishments of such a Dwelling. 'It seems to have as many comforts about it as Willingden.'—'Ah'—said Mr P.—'This is my old House—the house of my Forefathers—the house where I & all my Brothers & Sisters were born & bred—and where my own 3 eldest Children were born—where Mrs P. & I lived till within the last 2 years—till our new House was finished.—I am glad you are pleased with it.—It is an honest old Place—and Hillier keeps it in very good order. I have given it up you know to the Man who occupies the cheif of my Land. *He* gets a better House by it—& I, a rather better situation!—one

other Hill brings us to Sanditon—modern Sanditon—a beautiful
Spot.—Our Ancestors, you know always built in a hole.—Here were
we, pent down in this little contracted Nook, without Air or Veiw, only
one mile & 3 quarters from the noblest expanse of Ocean between the
South foreland & the Land's end,* & without the smallest advantage
from it. You will not think I have made a bad exchange, when we reach
Trafalgar House—which by the bye, I almost wish I had not named
Trafalgar—for Waterloo is more the thing now. However, Waterloo is
in reserve—& if we have encouragement enough this year for a little
Crescent to be ventured on—(as I trust we shall) then, we shall be
able to call it Waterloo Crescent*—& the name joined to the form of
the Building, which always takes, will give us the command of
Lodgers—. In a good Season we should have more applications than
we could attend to.'—'It was always a very comfortable House'—said
Mrs Parker—looking at it through the back window with something
like the fondness of regret.—'And such a nice Garden—such an
excellent Garden.' 'Yes, my Love, but *that* we may be said to carry
with us.—*It* supplies us, as before, with all the fruit & vegetables we
want; & we have in fact all the comfort of an excellent Kitchen
Garden, without the constant Eyesore of its formalities; or the yearly
nuisance of its decaying vegetation.—Who can endure a Cabbage
Bed in October?' 'Oh! dear—yes—We are quite as well off for
Gardenstuff as ever we were—for if it is forgot to be brought at any
time, we can always buy what we want at Sanditon-House.—The
Gardiner there, is glad enough to supply us—. But it was a nice place
for the Children to run about in. So Shady in Summer!—' 'My dear,
we shall have shade enough on the Hill & more than enough in the
course of a very few years;—The Growth of my Plantations is a general astonishment. In the mean while we have the Canvas Awning,
which gives us the most complete comfort within doors—& you can
get a Parasol* at Whitby's for little Mary at any time, or a large Bonnet
at Jebb's—And as for the Boys, I must say I would rather *them* run
about in the Sunshine than not. I am sure we agree my dear, in wishing our Boys to be as hardy as possible.'—'Yes indeed, I am sure we
do—& I will get Mary a little Parasol, which will make her as proud
as can be. How Grave she will walk about with it, and fancy herself
quite a little Woman.—Oh! I have not the smallest doubt of our being
a great deal better off where we are now. If we any of us want to bathe,
we have not a quarter of a mile to go.—But you know, (still looking

back) one loves to look at an old friend, at a place where one has been happy.—The Hilliers did not seem to feel the Storms last Winter at all.—I remember seeing Mrs Hillier after one of those dreadful Nights, when *we* had been literally rocked in our bed, and she did not seem at all aware of the Wind being anything more than common.' 'Yes, yes—that's likely enough. We have all the Grandeur of the Storm,* with less real danger, because the Wind meeting with nothing to oppose or confine it around our House, simply rages & passes on—while down in this Gutter—nothing is known of the state of the Air, below the Tops of the Trees—and the Inhabitants may be taken totally unawares, by one of those dreadful Currents which do more mischeif in a Valley, when they *do* arise than an open Country ever experiences in the heaviest Gale.—But my dear Love—as to Gardenstuff;—you were saying that any accidental omission is supplied in a moment by Lady D.'s Gardiner—but it occurs to me that we ought to go else where upon such occasions—& that old Stringer & his son have a higher claim. I encouraged him to set up—& am afraid he does not do very well—that is, there has not been time enough yet.—He *will* do very well beyond a doubt—but at first it is Up hill work; and therefore we must give him what Help we can—& when any Vegetables or fruit happen to be wanted—& it will not be amiss to have them often wanted, to have something or other forgotten most days;—Just to have a nominal supply you know, that poor old Andrew may not lose his daily Job—but in fact to buy the cheif of our consumption of the Stringers.—' 'Very well my Love, that can be easily done—& Cook will be satisfied—which will be a great comfort, for she is always complaining of old Andrew now, & says he never brings her what she wants.—There—now the old House is quite left behind.—What is it, your Brother Sidney says about it's being a Hospital?'* 'Oh! my dear Mary, merely a Joke of his. He pretends to advise me to make a Hospital of it. He pretends to laugh at my Improvements.* Sidney says any thing you know. He has always said what he chose of & to us, all. Most Families have such a member among them I beleive Miss Heywood.—There is a someone in most families privileged by superior abilities or spirits to say anything.—In ours, it is Sidney; who is a very clever young Man,—and with great powers of pleasing.—He lives too much in the World to be settled; that is his only fault.—He is here & there & every where. I wish we may get him to Sanditon. I should like to have you acquainted with

him.—And it would be a fine thing for the Place!—Such a young
Man as Sidney, with his neat equipage* & fashionable air,—You &
I Mary, know what effect it might have. Many a respectable Family,
many a careful Mother, many a pretty Daughter, might it secure us,
to the prejudice of E. Bourne & Hastings.'—They were now
approaching the Church & real village of Sandition, which stood at
the foot of the Hill they were afterwards to ascend—a Hill, whose
side was covered with the Woods & enclosures of Sandition House
and whose Height ended in an open Down where the new Buildings
might soon be looked for. A branch only, of the Valley, winding more
obliquely towards the Sea, gave a passage to an inconsiderable Stream,
& formed at its mouth, a 3ᵈ Habitable Division, in a small cluster of
Fisherman's Houses.—The Village contained little more than
Cottages, but the Spirit of the day had been caught, as Mr P. observed
with delight to Charlotte, & two or three of the best of them were
smartened up with a white Curtain & 'Lodgings to let'—, and farther
on, in the little Green Court of an old Farm House, two Females in
elegant white were actually to be seen with their books & camp-
stools—and in turning the corner of the Baker's shop, the sound of
a Harp* might be heard through the upper Casement.—Such sights
& sounds were highly Blissful to Mr P.—Not that he had any personal concern in the success of the Village itself; for considering it as
too remote from the Beach, he had done nothing there—but it was
a most valuable proof of the increasing fashion of the place altogether.
If the *Village* could attract, the Hill might be nearly full.—He anticipated an amazing Season.—At the same time last year, (late in July)
there had not been a single Lodger in the Village!—nor did he
remember any during the whole Summer, excepting one family of
children who came from London for sea air after the hooping Cough,*
and whose Mother would not let them be nearer the shore, for fear of
their tumbling in.—'Civilization, Civilization indeed!'—cried Mr P.,
delighted—. 'Look my dear Mary—Look at William Heeley's windows.—Blue Shoes, & nankin Boots!*—Who would have expected
such a sight at a Shoemaker's in old Sanditon!—This is new within
the month. There was no blue Shoe when we passed this way a month
ago.—Glorious indeed!—Well, I think I *have* done something in my
Day.—Now, for our Hill, our health-breathing Hill.—' In ascending,
they passed the Lodge-Gates of Sanditon House, & saw the top of the
House itself among its Groves. It was the last Building of former

Days in that line of the Parish. A little higher up, the Modern began; & in crossing the Down, a Prospect House, a Bellevue Cottage, & a Denham Place were to be looked at by Charlotte with the calmness of amused Curiosity, & by Mr P. with the eager eye which hoped to see scarcely any empty houses.——More Bills at the Window than he had calculated on,——and a smaller show of company on the Hill—Fewer Carriages, fewer Walkers. He had fancied it just the time of day for them to be all returning from their Airings to dinner—But the Sands & the Terrace always attracted some—. and the Tide must be flowing—about half-Tide now.——He longed to be on the Sands, the Cliffs, at his own House, & every where out of his House at once. His Spirits rose with the very sight of the Sea & he could almost feel his Ancle getting stronger already.——Trafalgar House, on the most elevated spot on the Down was a light elegant Building, standing in a small Lawn with a very young plantation round it, about an hundred yards from the brow of a steep, but not very lofty Cliff—and the nearest to it, of every Building, excepting one short row of smart-looking Houses, called the Terrace, with a broad walk in front, aspiring to be the Mall of the Place.† In this row were the best Milliner's shop & the Library—a little detached from it, the Hotel & Billiard room—Here began the Descent to the Beach, & to the Bathing Machines*—& this was therefore the favourite spot for Beauty & Fashion.——At Trafalgar House, rising at a little distance behind the Terrace, The Travellors were safely set down, & all was happiness & Joy between Papa & Mama & their Children; while Charlotte having received possession of her apartment, found amusement enough in standing at her ample, venetian window,* & looking over the miscellaneous foreground of unfinished Buildings, waving Linen, & tops of Houses, to the Sea, dancing & sparkling in sun shine & Freshness.——

## CHAPTER 5

When they met before dinner, Mr P. was looking over Letters.——'Not a Line from Sidney!' said he.——'He is an idle fellow.——I sent him an account of my accident from Willingden, & thought he would have vouchsafed me an Answer.——But perhaps it implies that he is coming himself.——I trust it may.——But here is a Letter from one of my Sisters. *They* never fail me.——Women are the only Correspondents to be depended on.—Now Mary, (smiling at his Wife)—before I open it, what shall we guess as to the state of health of those it comes from—or rather what would Sidney say if he were here?—Sidney is a saucy fellow, Miss H.—And you must know, he will have it there is a good deal of Imagination in my two Sisters' complaints—but it really is not so—or very little—They have wretched health, as you have heard us frequently say, & are subject to a variety of very serious Disorders.*—Indeed, I do not beleive they know what a day's health is;—& at the same time, they are such excellent useful Women* & have so much energy of character that, where any Good is to be done, they force themselves on exertions which to those who do not thoroughly know them, have an extraordinary appearance.—But there is really no affectation about them. They have only weaker constitutions & stronger minds than are often met with, either separate or together.—And our youngest Brother—who lives with them, & who is not much above 20, I am sorry to say, is almost as great an Invalid as themselves.—He is so delicate that he can engage in no Profession.—Sidney laughs at him—but it really is no Joke—though Sidney often makes me laugh at them all inspite of myself.—Now, if he were here, I know he would be offering odds, that either Susan Diana or Arthur would appear by this Letter to have been at the point of death within the last month.'—Having run his eye over the Letter, he shook his head & began, 'No chance of seeing them at Sanditon I am sorry to say.—A very indifferent account of them indeed. Seriously, a *very* indifferent account.—Mary, you will be quite sorry to hear how ill they have been & are.—Miss H., if you will give me leave, I will read Diana's Letter aloud.—I like to have my friends acquainted with each other—& I am afraid this is the only sort of acquaintance I shall have the means of accomplishing between you.—And I can have no scruple on Diana's account—for her Letters shew her exactly as she is, the most active, friendly, warmhearted Being in existence, & therefore must give a good impression.' He read.—'My dear Tom, We were all much greived at your accident, & if you had not described yourself as fallen into such very good hands, I should have been with you at all hazards the day after the receipt of your Letter, though it found me suffering under a more severe attack than usual of my old greivance, Spasmodic Bile* & hardly able to crawl from my Bed to the Sofa.—But how were you treated?—Send me more Particulars in your next.—If indeed a simple Sprain, as you

denominate it, nothing would have been so judicious as Friction,*
Friction by the hand alone, supposing it could be applied
*instantly*.—Two years ago I happened to be calling on Mrs Sheldon
when her Coachman sprained his foot as he was cleaning the Carriage
& could hardly limp into the House—but by the immediate use of
Friction alone, steadily persevered in, (& I rubbed his Ancle with my
own hand for six Hours without Intermission)—he was well in three
days.—Many Thanks my dear Tom, for the kindness with respect to
us, which had so large a share in bringing on your accident.—But
pray: never run into Peril again, in looking for an Apothecary on our
account, for had you the most experienced Man in his Line settled at
Sanditon, it would be no recommendation to us. We have entirely
done with the whole Medical Tribe We have consulted Physician
after Physician in vain, till we are quite convinced that they can do
nothing for us & that we must trust to our own knowledge of our own
wretched Constitutions for any releif.—But if you think it advisable
for the interest of the *Place*, to get a Medical Man there, I will undertake the commission with pleasure, & have no doubt of succeeding.—
I could soon put the necessary Irons in the fire. As for getting to
Sanditon myself, it is quite an Impossibility. I greive to say that I dare
not attempt it, but my feelings tell me too plainly that in my present
state, the Sea air would probably be the death of me.—And neither of
my dear Companions will leave me, or I would promote their going
down to you for a fortnight. But in truth, I doubt whether Susan's
nerves would be equal to the effort. She has been suffering much from
the Headache, and Six Leaches* a day for 10 days together releived her
so little that we thought it right to change our measures—and being
convinced on examination that much of the Evil lay in her Gum,
I persuaded her to attack the disorder there. She has accordingly had
3 Teeth drawn*, & is decidedly better, but her Nerves are a good deal
deranged. She can only speak in a whisper—and fainted away twice
this morning on poor Arthur's trying to suppress a cough. He, I am
happy to say is tolerably well—tho' more languid than I like—&
I fear for his Liver.—I have heard nothing of Sidney since your being
together in Town, but conclude his scheme to the I. of Wight* has not
taken place, or we should have seen him in his way.—Most sincerely
do we wish you a good Season at Sanditon, & though we cannot contribute to your Beau Monde* in person, we are doing our utmost to
send you Company worth having; & think we may safely reckon on

securing you two large Families, one a rich West Indian* from Surry, the other, a most respectable Girls Boarding School, or Academy, from Camberwell.*—I will not tell you how many People I have employed in the business—Wheel within wheel.—But Success more than repays.—Yours most affect:ly—&c' 'Well'—said Mr P.—as he finished. 'Though I dare say Sidney might find something extremely entertaining in this Letter & make us laugh for half an hour together, I declare *I* by myself, can see nothing in it but what is either very pitiable or very creditable.—With all their sufferings, you perceive, how much they are occupied in promoting the Good of others!—So anxious for Sanditon! Two large Families—One, for Prospect House probably, the other, for No. 2. Denham Place—or the end house of the Terrace,—& extra Beds at the Hotel.—I told you my Sisters were excellent Women, Miss H.' 'And I am sure they must be very extraordinary ones.'—said Charlotte. 'I am astonished at the chearful style of the Letter, considering the state in which both Sisters appear to be.—Three Teeth drawn at once!—frightful!—Your Sister Diana seems almost as ill as possible, but those 3 Teeth of your Sister Susan's, are more distressing than all the rest.—' 'Oh!—they are so used to the operation—to every operation—& have such Fortitude!—' 'Your Sisters know what they are about, I dare say, but their Measures seem to touch on Extremes.—I feel that in any illness, *I* should be so anxious for Professional advice, so very little venturesome for myself, or any body I loved!—But then, *we* have been so healthy a family, that I can be no Judge of what the habit of self-doctoring may do.—' 'Why to own the truth,' said Mrs P.—'I *do* think the Miss Parkers carry it too far sometimes—& so do you my Love, you know.—You often think they would be better, if they would leave themselves more alone—& especially Arthur. I know you think it a great pity they should give *him* such a turn for being ill.—' 'Well, well—my dear Mary—I grant you, it *is* unfortunate for poor Arthur, that, at his time of Life he should be encouraged to give way to Indisposition. It *is* bad;—it *is* bad that he should be fancying himself too sickly for any Profession—& sit down at 1 & 20, on the interest of his own little Fortune, without any idea of attempting to improve it, or of engaging in any occupation that may be of use to himself or others.—But let us talk of pleasanter things.—These two large Families are just what we wanted—But—here is something at hand, pleasanter still—Morgan, with his "Dinner on Table." '—

## CHAPTER 6

The Party were very soon moving after Dinner. Mr P. could not be satisfied without an early visit to the Library, & the Library Subscription book,* & Charlotte was glad to see as much, & as quickly as possible, where all was new. They were out in the very quietest part of a Watering-place Day, when the important Business of Dinner or of sitting after Dinner was going on in almost every inhabited Lodging;—here & there a solitary Elderly Man might be seen, who was forced to move early & walk for health—but in general, it was a thorough pause of Company, it was Emptiness & Tranquillity on the Terrace, the Cliffs, & the Sands.—The Shops were deserted—the Straw Hats & pendant Lace seemed left to their fate both within the House & without, and Mrs Whitby at the Library was sitting in her inner room, reading one of her own Novels, for want of Employment.— The List of Subscribers was but commonplace. The Lady Denham, Miss Brereton, Mr and Mrs P.—Sir Edward Denham & Miss Denham, whose names might be said to lead off the Season, were followed by nothing better than—Mrs Mathews—Miss Mathews, Miss E. Mathews, Miss H. Mathews.—Dr & Mrs Brown—Mr Richard Pratt.—Lieut. Smith R.N. Capt. Little,—Limehouse.—Mrs Jane Fisher. Miss Fisher. Miss Scroggs.—Rev. Mr Hankins. Mr Beard—Solicitor, Grays Inn.—Mrs Davis. & Miss Merryweather.—Mr P. could not but feel that the List was not only without Distinction, but less numerous than he had hoped. It was but July however, & August & September were the Months;—And besides, the promised large Families from Surry & Camberwell, were an ever-ready consolation.—Mrs Whitby came forward without delay from her Literary recess, delighted to see Mr Parker again, whose manners recommended him to every body, & they were fully occupied in their various Civilities & Communications, while Charlotte having added her name to the List as the first offering to the success of the Season, was busy in some immediate purchases for the further good of Everybody, as soon as Miss Whitby could be hurried down from her Toilette, with all her glossy Curls & smart Trinkets, to wait on her.—The Library of course, afforded every thing; all the useless things in the World that could not be done without, & among so many pretty Temptations, & with so much good will for Mr P. to encourage Expenditure, Charlotte began to feel that she must check herself—or rather she reflected that at two & Twenty there could be no excuse for her doing otherwise—& that it would not do for her to be spending all her Money the very first Evening. She took up a Book; it happened to be a volume of *Camilla*.* She had not *Camilla's* Youth, & had no intention of having her Distress,—so, she turned from the Drawers of rings & Broches repressed farther solicitation & paid for what she bought.—For her particular gratification, they were then to take a Turn on the Cliff—but as they quitted the Library they were met by two Ladies whose arrival made an alteration necessary, Lady Denham & Miss Brereton.—They had been to Trafalgar House, & been directed thence to the Library, & though Lady D. was a great deal too active to regard the walk of a mile as anything requiring rest, & talked of going home again directly, the Parkers knew that to be pressed into their House, & obliged to take her Tea with them, would suit her best,—& therefore the stroll on the Cliff gave way to an immediate return home.—'No, no,' said her Ladyship—'I will not have you hurry your Tea on my account.—I know you like your Tea late.—My early hours are not to put my Neighbours to inconvenience. No, no, Miss Clara & I will get back to our own Tea.—We came out with no other Thought.—We wanted just to see you & make sure of your being really come—, but we get back to our own Tea.'—She went on however towards Trafalgar House & took possession of the Drawing room very quietly—without seeming to hear a word of Mrs P.'s orders to the Servant as they entered, to bring Tea directly. Charlotte was fully consoled for the loss of her walk, by finding herself in company with those, whom the conversation of the morning had given her a great curiosity to see. She observed them well.—Lady D. was of middle height, stout, upright & alert in her motions with a shrewd eye, & self-satisfied air—but not an unagreable Countenance—& tho' her manner was rather downright & abrupt, as of a person who valued herself on being free-spoken, there was a good humour & cordiality about her—a civility & readiness to be acquainted with Charlotte herself, & a heartiness of welcome towards her old friends, which was inspiring the Good will she seemed to feel;—And as for Miss Brereton, her appearance so completely justified Mr P.'s praise that Charlotte thought she had never beheld a more lovely, or more Interesting young Woman.*—Elegantly tall, regularly handsome, with great delicacy of complexion & soft Blue Eyes, a sweetly modest & yet naturally Graceful Address,* Charlotte could see in her only the most perfect representation of whatever Heroine might be most beautiful & bewitching, in all the numerous volumes they had left behind them on Mrs Whitby's shelves.—Perhaps it might be partly oweing to her having just issued from a Circulating Library—but she could not separate the idea of a complete Heroine from Clara Brereton. Her situation with Lady Denham so very much in favour of it!—She seemed placed with her on purpose to be ill-used.—Such Poverty & Dependance joined to such Beauty & Merit, seemed to leave no choice in the business.—These feelings were not the result of any spirit of Romance in Charlotte herself.—No, she was a very sober-minded young Lady, sufficiently well-read in Novels to supply her Imagination with amusement, but not at all unreasonably influenced by them; & while she pleased herself the first 5 minutes with fancying the Persecutions which *ought* to be the Lot of the interesting Clara, especially in the form of the most barbarous conduct on Lady Denham's side, she found no reluctance to admit from subsequent observation, that they appeared to be on very comfortable Terms.—She could see nothing worse in Lady Denham, than the sort of oldfashioned formality of always calling her *Miss Clara*—nor any thing objectionable in the degree of observance & attention which Clara paid.—On one side it seemed protecting kindness, on the other grateful & affectionate respect.—The Conversation turned entirely upon Sanditon, its present number of Visitants, & the Chances of a good Season. It was evident that Lady D. had more anxiety, more fears of loss, than her Coadjutor. She wanted to have the Place fill faster, & seemed to have many harassing apprehensions of the Lodgings being in some instances underlet.—Miss Diana Parker's two large Families were not forgotten. 'Very good, very good,' said her Ladyship.—'A West Indy Family & a school. That sounds well. That will bring Money.'—'No people spend more freely, I beleive, than W. Indians.' observed Mr Parker.—'Aye—so I have heard—and because they have full Purses, fancy themselves equal, may be, to your old Country Families. But then, they who scatter their Money so freely, never think of whether they may not be doing mischeif by raising the price of Things—And I have heard that's very much the case with your West-ingines—and if they come among us to raise the price of our necessaries of Life, we shall not much thank them Mr Parker.—' 'My dear Madam, They can only raise the price of consumeable Articles, by such an extraordinary Demand for them &

such a diffusion of Money among us, as must do us more Good than harm.*—Our Butchers & Bakers & Traders in general cannot get rich without bringing Prosperity to *us*.—If *they* do not gain, our rents must be insecure—& in proportion to their profit must be ours eventually in the increased value of our Houses.' 'Oh!—well.—But I should not like to have Butcher's meat raised, though—& I shall keep it down as long as I can.—Aye—that young Lady smiles I see;—I dare say she thinks me an odd sort of a Creature,—but *she* will come to care about such matters herself in time. Yes, yes, my Dear, depend upon it, you will be thinking of the price of Butcher's meat in time—tho' you may not happen to have quite such a Servants Hall to feed, as I have.—And I do beleive *those* are best off, that have fewest Servants.—I am not a Woman of Parade, as all the World knows, & if it was not for what I owe to poor Mr Hollis's memory, I should never keep up Sanditon House as I do;—it is not for my own pleasure.—Well Mr Parker—and the other is a Boarding school, a French Boarding School,* is it?—No harm in that.—They'll stay their six weeks.—And out of such a number, who knows but some may be consumptive & want Asses milk*—& I have two Milch asses at this present time.—But perhaps the little Misses may hurt the Furniture.—I hope they will have a good sharp Governess to look after them.'—Poor Mr Parker got no more credit from Lady D. than he had from his Sisters, for the object which had taken him to Willingden. 'Lord! my dear Sir,' she cried, 'how could you think of such a thing? I am very sorry you met with your accident, but upon my word you deserved it.—Going after a Doctor!—Why, what should we do with a Doctor here? It would be only encouraging our Servants & the Poor to fancy themselves ill, if there was a Doctor at hand.—Oh! pray, let us have none of the Tribe at Sanditon. We go on very well as we are. There is the Sea & the Downs & my Milch-asses—& I have told Mrs Whitby that if any body enquires for a Chamber Horse,* they may be supplied at a fair rate—(poor Mr Hollis's Chamber Horse, as good as new)—and what can People want for, more?—Here have I lived 70 good years in the world & never took Physic above twice—and never saw the face of a Doctor in all my Life, on my *own* account.—And I verily beleive if my poor dear Sir Harry had never seen one neither, he would have been alive now.—Ten fees, one after another, did the Man take who sent *him* out of the World.—I beseech you Mr Parker, no Doctors here.'—The Tea things were brought in.—'Oh! my dear Mrs Parker—you should not indeed—why would you do so? I was just upon the point of wishing you good Evening. But since you are so very neighbourly, I beleive Miss Clara & I must stay.'—

## CHAPTER 7

The popularity of the Parkers brought them some visitors the very next morning;—amongst them, Sir Edward Denham & his Sister, who having been at Sanditon House drove on to pay their Compliments; & the duty of Letter-writing being accomplished, Charlotte was settled with Mrs P. in the Drawing room in time to see them all.—The Denhams were the only ones to excite particular attention. Charlotte was glad to complete her knowledge of the family by an introduction to them, & found them, the better half at least—(for while single, the *Gentleman* may sometimes be thought the better half, of the pair)—not unworthy notice.—Miss D. was a fine young woman, but cold & reserved, giving the idea of one who felt her consequence with Pride & her Poverty with Discontent, & who was immediately gnawed by the want of an handsomer Equipage than the simple Gig* in which they travelled, & which their Groom was leading about still in her sight.—Sir Edward was much her superior in air & manner; certainly handsome, but yet more to be remarked for his very good address & wish of paying attention & giving pleasure.—He came into the room remarkably well, talked much—& very much to Charlotte, by whom he chanced to be placed—& she soon perceived that he had a fine Countenance, a most pleasing gentleness of voice, & a great deal of Conversation. She liked him.—Sober-minded as she was, she thought him agreable, & did not quarrel with the suspicion of his finding her equally so, which *would* arise from his evidently disregarding his Sister's motion to go, & per-sisting in his station & his discourse.—I make no apologies for my Heroine's vanity.—If there are young Ladies in the World at her time of Life, more dull of Fancy & more careless of pleasing, I know them not, & never wish to know them.—At last, from the low French win-dows of the Drawing room which commanded the road & all the Paths across the Down, Charlotte & Sir Edward as they sat, could not but observe Lady D. and Miss B. walking by—& there was instantly a slight change in Sir Edward's countenance—with an anxious glance after them as they proceeded—followed by an early proposal to his Sister—not merely for moving, but for walking on together to the Terrace—which altogether gave an hasty turn to Charlotte's fancy, cured her of her halfhour's fever, & placed her in a more capable state of judging, when Sir Edward was gone, of *how* agreable he had actually been.—'Perhaps there was a good deal in his Air & Address; And his Title did him no harm.'

She was very soon in his company again. The first object of the Parkers, when their House was cleared of morning visitors was to get out themselves;—the Terrace was the attraction to all;—Every body who walked, must begin with the Terrace, & there, seated on one of the two Green Benches by the Gravel walk, they found the united Denham Party;—but though united in the Gross, very distinctly divided again—the two superior Ladies being at one end of the bench, & Sir Edward & Miss B. at the other.—Charlotte's first glances told her that Sir Edward's air was that of a Lover.—There could be no doubt of his Devotion to Clara.—How Clara received it, was less obvious—but she was inclined to think not very favourably; for tho' sitting thus apart with him (which probably she might not have been able to prevent) her Air was calm & grave.—That the young Lady at the other end of the Bench was doing Penance, was indubitable. The difference in Miss Denham's countenance, the change from Miss Denham sitting in cold Grandeur in Mrs Parker's Drawing-room to be kept from silence by the efforts of others, to Miss D. at Lady D.'s Elbow, listening & talking with smiling attention or solicitous eagerness, was very striking—and very amusing—or very melancholy, just as Satire or Morality might prevail.—Miss Denham's Character was pretty well decided with Charlotte. Sir Edward's required longer Observation. He surprised her by quitting Clara immediately on their all joining & agreeing to walk, & by addressing his attentions entirely to herself.—Stationing himself close by her, he seemed to mean to detach her as much as possible from the rest of the Party & to give her the whole of his Conversation. He began, in a tone of great Taste & Feeling, to talk of the Sea & the Sea shore—& ran with Energy through all the usual Phrases employed in praise of their Sublimity, & descriptive of the *undescribable* Emotions they excite in the Mind of Sensibility.*—The terrific Grandeur of the Ocean in a Storm, its glassy surface in a calm, it's Gulls & its Samphire, & the deep fathoms of it's Abysses, it's quick vicissitudes, it's direful Deceptions, it's Mariners tempting it in Sunshine & overwhelmed by the sudden Tempest, All were eagerly & fluently touched;—rather commonplace perhaps—but doing very well from the Lips of a handsome Sir Edward,—and she could not but think him a Man of Feeling* till he began to stagger her by the number of his Quotations, & the bewilderment of some of his sentences.—'Do you remember,' said he, 'Scott's beautiful Lines on the Sea?—Oh! what a description they convey!—They are never out of my Thoughts when I walk here.—That Man who can read them unmoved must have the nerves of an Assassin!—Heaven defend me from meeting such a Man un-armed.'—'What description do you mean?'—said Charlotte. 'I remember none at this moment, of the Sea, in either of Scott's Poems.'*—'Do not you indeed?—Nor can I exactly recall the beginning at this moment—But—you cannot have forgotten his description of Woman.—

"Oh! Woman in our Hours of Ease—"

Delicious! Delicious!—Had he written nothing more, he would have been Immortal. And then again, that unequalled, unrivalled Address to Parental affection—

"Some feelings are to Mortals given
With less of Earth in them than Heaven" &c

But while we are on the subject of Poetry, what think you Miss H. of Burns Lines to his Mary?*—Oh! there is Pathos to madden one!—If ever there was a Man who *felt*, it was Burns.—Montgomery has all the Fire of Poetry, Wordsworth has the true soul of it—Campbell* in his pleasures of Hope has touched the extreme of our Sensations—

"Like Angel's visits, few & far between."

Can you conceive any thing more subduing, more melting, more fraught with the deep Sublime than that Line?—But Burns—I confess my sense of his Pre-eminence Miss H.—If Scott *has* a fault, it is the want of Passion.—Tender, Elegant, Descriptive—but *Tame*.—The Man who cannot do justice to the attributes of Woman is my contempt.—Sometimes indeed a flash of feeling seems to irradiate him—as in the Lines we were speaking of—"Oh! Woman in our hours of Ease"—. But Burns is always on fire.—His Soul was the Altar in which lovely Woman sat enshrined, his Spirit truly breathed the immortal Incence which is her Due.'—'I have read several of Burns' Poems with great delight,' said Charlotte as soon as she had time to speak, 'but I am not poetic enough to separate a Man's Poetry entirely from his Character;—& poor Burns's known Irregularities, greatly interrupt my enjoyment of his Lines.—I have difficulty in depending on the *Truth* of his Feelings as a Lover. I have not faith in the *sincerity* of the affections of a Man of his Description. He felt & he wrote & he forgot.' 'Oh! no no'—exclaimed Sir Edward in an extasy. 'He was all ardour & Truth!—His Genius & his Susceptibilities might lead him into some Aberrations—But who is perfect?—It were Hyper-criticism, it were Pseudo-philosophy to expect from the soul of high toned Genius, the grovellings of a common mind.—The Coruscations of Talent, elicited by impassioned feeling in the breast of Man, are perhaps incompatible with some of the prosaic Decencies of Life;—nor can you, loveliest Miss Heywood (speaking with an air of deep sentiment)—nor can any Woman be a fair Judge of what a Man may be propelled to say, write or do, by the sovereign impulses of illimitable Ardour.' This was very fine;—but if Charlotte understood it at all, not very moral—& being moreover by no means pleased with his extraordinary stile of compliment, she gravely answered 'I really know nothing of the matter.—This is a charming day. The Wind I fancy must be Southerly.' 'Happy, happy Wind, to engage Miss Heywood's Thoughts!—' She began to think him downright silly.—His chusing to walk with her, she had learnt to understand. It was done to pique Miss Brereton. She had read it, in an anxious glance or two on his side—but why he should talk so much Nonsense, unless he could do no better, was unintelligible.—He seemed very sentimental, very full of some Feelings or other, & very much addicted to all the newest-fashioned hard words—had not a very clear Brain she presumed, & talked a good deal by rote.—The Future might explain him further—but when there was a proposition for going into the Library she felt that she had had quite enough of Sir Edward for one morning, & very gladly accepted Lady D.'s invitation of remaining on the Terrace with her.—The others all left them, Sir Edward with looks of very gallant despair in tearing himself away, & they united their agreableness—that is, Lady Denham like a true great Lady, talked & talked only of her own concerns, & Charlotte listened—amused in considering the contrast between her two companions.—Certainly, there was no strain of doubtful Sentiment, nor any phrase of difficult interpretation in Lady D's discourse. Taking hold of Charlotte's arm with the ease of one who felt that any notice from her was an Honour, & communicative, from the influence of the same conscious Importance or a natural love of talking, she immediately said in a tone of great satisfaction—& with a look of arch sagacity—'Miss Esther wants me to invite her & her Brother to spend a week with me at Sanditon House, as I did last Summer—but I shan't.—She has been trying to get round me every way, with her praise of this, & her praise of that; but I saw what she was about.—I saw through it all.—I am not very easily taken-in my Dear.' Charlotte could think of nothing more harmless to be said, than the simple enquiry of—'Sir Edward & Miss Denham?'—'Yes, my Dear. *My young Folks*, as I call them sometimes, for I take them very much by the hand. I had them with me last Summer, about this time, for a week; from Monday to Monday; and very delighted & thankful they were.—For they are very good young People my Dear. I would not have you think that I *only* notice them, for poor dear Sir Harry's sake. No, no; they are very deserving themselves, or trust me, they would not be so much in *my* Company.—I am not the Woman to help any body blindfold.— I always take care to know what I am about & who I have to deal with, before I stir a finger.—I do not think I was ever over-reached in my Life; & That is a good deal for a woman to say that has been married twice.—Poor dear Sir Harry (between ourselves) thought at first to have got more.—But (with a bit of a sigh) He is gone, & we must not find fault with the Dead. Nobody could live happier together than us—& he was a very honourable Man, quite the Gentleman of ancient Family.—And when he died, I gave Sir Edward his Gold Watch.—' She said this with a look at her Companion which implied it's right to produce a great Impression—& seeing no rapturous astonishment in Charlotte's countenance, added quickly—'He did not bequeath it to his Nephew, my dear—It was no bequest. It was not in the Will. He only told me, & *that* but once, that he should wish his Nephew to have his Watch; but it need not have been binding, if I had not chose it.—' 'Very kind indeed! very Handsome!'—said Charlotte, absolutely forced to affect admiration.—'Yes, my dear—& it is not the *only* kind thing I have done by him.—I have been a very liberal friend to Sir Edward. And poor young Man, he needs it bad enough;—For though I am *only* the *Dowager* my Dear, & he is the *Heir*,* things do not stand between us in the way they commonly do between those two parties.—Not a shilling do I receive from the Denham Estate. Sir Edward has no Payments to make *me*. He don't stand uppermost, beleive me.—It is *I* that help *him*.' 'Indeed!— He is a very fine young Man;—particularly Elegant in his Address.'—This was said cheifly for the sake of saying some-thing—but Charlotte directly saw that it was laying her open to sus-picion by Lady D.'s giving a shrewd glance at her & replying—'Yes, yes, he is very well to look at—& it is to be hoped that some Lady of large fortune will think so—for Sir Edward *must* marry for Money.—He & I often talk that matter over.—A handsome young fellow like him, will go smirking & smiling about & paying girls Compliments, but he knows he *must* marry for Money.—And Sir Edward is a very steady young Man in the main, & has got very good notions.' 'Sir Edward Denham,' said Charlotte, 'with such personal Advantages may be almost sure of getting a Woman of fortune, if he chuses it.'—This glorious sentiment seemed quite to remove suspi-cion. 'Aye my Dear—That's very sensibly said' cried Lady D—'And if we could but get a young Heiress to S.! But Heiresses are mon-strous scarce! I do not think we have had an Heiress here, or even a Co-* since Sanditon has been a public place. Families come after Families, but as far as I can learn, it is not one in an hundred of them that have any real Property, Landed or Funded.*—An Income per-haps, but no Property. Clergymen may be, or Lawyers from Town, or Half pay officers,* or Widows with only a Jointure.* And what good can such people do anybody?—except just as they take our empty Houses—and (between ourselves) I think they are great fools for not staying at home. Now, if we could get a young Heiress to be sent here for her health—(and if she was ordered to drink asses milk I could supply her)—and as soon as she got well, have her fall in love with Sir Edward!'—'That would be very fortunate indeed.' 'And Miss Esther must marry somebody of fortune too—She must get a rich Husband. Ah! young Ladies that have no Money are very much to be pitied!—But'—after a short pause—'if Miss Esther thinks to talk me into inviting them to come & stay at Sanditon House, she will find herself mistaken.—Matters are altered with me since last Summer you know—. I have Miss Clara with me now, which makes a great difference.' She spoke this so seriously, that Charlotte instantly saw in it the evidence of real penetration & prepared for some fuller remarks—but it was followed only by—'I have no fancy for having my House as full as an Hotel. I should not chuse to have my 2 Housemaids Time taken up all the morning, in dusting out Bed rooms.—They have Miss Clara's room to put to rights as well as my own every day.—If they had hard Places, they would want Higher wages.—' For objections of this Nature, Charlotte was not prepared, & she found it so impossible even to affect simpathy, that she could say nothing.—Lady D. soon added, with great glee—'And besides all this my Dear, am I to be filling my House to the prejudice of Sanditon?—If People want to be by the Sea, why dont they take Lodgings?—Here are a great many empty Houses—3 on this very Terrace; no fewer than three Lodging Papers staring us in the face at this very moment, Numbers 3, 4 & 8. 8, the Corner House may be too large for them, but either of the two others are nice little snug Houses, very fit for a young Gentleman & his Sister—And so, my dear, the next time Miss Esther begins talking about the dampness of Denham Park, & the Good Bathing always does her, I shall advise them to come & take one of these Lodgings for a fortnight.—Don't you think that will be very fair?—Charity begins at home you know.'—Charlotte's feelings were divided between amusement & indignation—but indignation had the larger & the increasing share.—She kept her Countenance & she kept a civil Silence. She could not carry her forbearance farther; but without attempting to listen longer, & only conscious that Lady D. was still talking on in the same way, allowed her Thoughts to form themselves into such a Meditation as this.—'She is thoroughly mean. I had not expected anything so bad.—Mr P. spoke too mildly of her.—His Judgement is evidently not to be trusted.—His own Goodnature misleads him. He is too kind hearted to see clearly.—I must judge for myself.—And their very *connection* prejudices him.—He has persuaded her to engage in the same Speculation—& because their object in that Line is the same, he fancies she feels like him in others.—But she is very, very mean.—I can see no Good in her.—Poor Miss Brereton!—And she makes every body mean about her.—This poor Sir Edward & his Sister,—how far Nature meant them to be respectable I cannot tell,—but they are *obliged* to be Mean in their Servility to her.—And I am Mean too, in giving her my attention, with the appearance of coinciding with her.—Thus it is, when Rich People are Sordid.'—

## CHAPTER 8

The two Ladies continued walking together till rejoined by the others, who as they issued from the Library were followed by a young Whitby running off with 5 volumes under his arm to Sir Edward's Gig—and Sir Edward approaching Charlotte, said 'You may perceive what has been our occupation. My Sister wanted my Counsel in the selection of some books.—We have many leisure hours, & read a great deal.— I am no indiscriminate Novel-Reader. The mere Trash of the common Circulating Library, I hold in the highest contempt. You will never hear me advocating those puerile Emanations which detail nothing but discordant Principles incapable of Amalgamation, or those vapid tissues of ordinary occurrences from which no useful Deductions can be drawn.—In vain may we put them into a literary Alembic;*—we distil nothing which can add to Science.—You understand me I am sure?' 'I am not quite certain that I do.—But if you will describe the sort of Novels which you *do* approve, I dare say it will give me a clearer idea.' 'Most willingly, Fair Questioner.—The Novels which I approve are such as display Human Nature with Grandeur—such as shew her in the Sublimities of intense Feeling—Such as exhibit the progress of strong Passion from the first Germ of incipient Susceptibility to the utmost Energies of Reason half-dethroned,—where we see the strong spark of Woman's Captivations elicit such Fire in the Soul of Man as leads him—(though at the risk of some Aberration from the strict line of Primitive Obligations)—to hazard all, dare all, atcheive all, to obtain her.—Such are the Works which I peruse with delight, & I hope I may say, with Amelioration. They hold forth the most splendid Portraitures of high Conceptions, Unbounded Veiws, illimitable ardour, indomptible Decision—and even where the Event is mainly anti-prosperous to the high-toned Machinations of the prime Character, the potent, pervading Hero of the Story, it leaves us full of Generous Emotions for him;—our Hearts are paralized—. T'were Pseudo-Philosophy to assert that we do not feel more enwraped by the brilliancy of his Career, than by the tranquil & morbid Virtues of any opposing Character. Our approbation of the Latter is but Eleemosynary.—These are the Novels which enlarge the primitive Capabilities of the Heart, & which it cannot impugn the Sense or be any Dereliction of the character, of the most anti-puerile Man,* to be conversant with.'—

'If I understand you aright'—said Charlotte—'our taste in Novels is not at all the same.' And here they were obliged to part—Miss D. being too much tired of them all, to stay any longer.—The truth was that Sir Edward whom Circumstances had confined very much to one spot had read more sentimental Novels than agreed with him. His fancy had been early caught by all the impassioned, & most exceptionable parts of Richardsons; & such Authors as have since appeared to tread in Richardson's steps, so far as Man's determined pursuit of Woman in defiance of every opposition of feeling & convenience is concerned, had since occupied the greater part of his literary hours, & formed his Character.—With a perversity of Judgement, which must be attributed to his not having by Nature a very strong head, the Graces, the Spirit, the Ingenuity, & the Perseverance, of the Villain of the Story outweighed all his absurdities & all his Atrocities with Sir Edward. With him, such Conduct was Genius, Fire & Feeling.—It interested & inflamed him; & he was always more anxious for its Success & mourned over its Discomfitures with more Tenderness than could ever have been contemplated by the Authors.—Though he owed many of his ideas to this sort of reading, it were unjust to say that he read nothing else, or that his Language were not formed on a more general knowledge of modern Literature.—He read all the Essays, Letters, Tours & Criticisms of the day—& with the same ill-luck which made him derive only false Principles from Lessons of Morality, & incentives to Vice from the History of it's Overthrow, he gathered only hard words & involved sentences from the style of our most approved Writers.—

Sir Edward's great object in life was to be seductive.—With such personal advantages as he knew himself to possess, & such Talents as he did also give himself credit for, he regarded it as his Duty.—He felt that he was formed to be a dangerous Man—quite in the line of the Lovelaces.*—The very name of Sir Edward, he thought, carried some degree of fascination with it.—To be generally gallant & assiduous about the fair, to make fine speeches to every pretty Girl, was but the inferior part of the Character he had to play.—Miss Heywood, or any other young Woman with any pretensions to Beauty, he was entitled (according to his own veiws of Society) to approach with high Compliment & Rhapsody on the slightest acquaintance; but it was Clara alone on whom he had serious designs; it was Clara whom he meant to seduce.—Her seduction was quite determined on. Her

Situation in every way called for it. She was his rival in Lady D.'s favour, she was young, lovely & dependant.—He had very early seen the necessity of the case, & had now been long trying with cautious assiduity to make an impression on her heart, and to undermine her Principles.—Clara saw through him, & had not the least intention of being seduced—but she bore with him patiently enough to confirm the sort of attachment which her personal Charms had raised.— A greater degree of discouragement indeed would not have affected Sir Edward—. He was armed against the highest pitch of Disdain or Aversion.—If she could not be won by affection, he must carry her off. He knew his Business.—Already had he had many Musings on the Subject. If he *were* constrained so to act, he must naturally wish to strike out something new, to exceed those who had gone before him—and he felt a strong curiosity to ascertain whether the neighbourhood of Tombuctoo* might not afford some solitary House adapted for Clara's reception;—but the Expence alas! of Measures in that masterly style was ill-suited to his Purse, & Prudence obliged him to prefer the quietest sort of ruin & disgrace for the object of his Affections, to the more renowned.—

## CHAPTER 9

One day, soon after Charlotte's arrival at Sanditon, she had the pleasure of seeing just as she ascended from the Sands to the Terrace, a Gentleman's Carriage with Post Horses* standing at the door of the Hotel, as very lately arrived, & by the quantity of Luggage taking off, bringing it might be hoped, some respectable family determined on a long residence.—Delighted to have such good news for Mr & Mrs P., who had both gone home some time before, she proceeded for Trafalgar House with as much alacrity as could remain, after having been contending for the last 2 hours with a very fine wind blowing directly on shore; but she had not reached the little Lawn, when she saw a Lady walking nimbly behind her at no great distance; and convinced that it could be no acquaintance of her own, she resolved to hurry on & get into the House if possible before her. But the Stranger's pace did not allow this to be accomplished;—Charlotte was on the Steps & had rung, but the door was not opened, when the other crossed the Lawn;—and when the Servant appeared, they were just equally ready for entering the House.—The ease of the Lady, her 'How do you do Morgan?—' & Morgan's Looks on seeing her, were a moment's astonishment—but another moment brought Mr P. into the Hall to welcome the Sister he had seen from the Drawing room, & she was soon introduced to Miss Diana Parker. There was a great deal of surprise but still more pleasure in seeing her.—Nothing could be kinder than her reception from both Husband and Wife. 'How did she come? & with whom?—And they were so glad to find her equal to the Journey!—And that she was to belong to *them*, was a thing of course.' Miss Diana P. was about 4 & 30, of middling height & slender;—delicate looking rather than sickly; with an agreable face, & a very animated eye;—her manners resembling her Brother's in their ease & frankness, though with more decision & less mildness in her Tone. She began an account of herself without delay.—Thanking them for their Invitation, but '*that* was quite out of the question, for they were all three come, & meant to get into Lodgings & make some stay.'—'All three come!—What!—Susan & Arthur!—Susan able to come too!—This was better & better.' 'Yes—we are actually all come. Quite unavoidable—Nothing else to be done.—You shall hear all about it.—But my dear Mary, send for the Children;—I long to see them.'—'And how has Susan born the Journey?—& how is Arthur?—& why do not we see him here with you?'—'Susan has born it wonderfully. She had not a wink of sleep either the night before we set out, or last night at Chichester,* and as this is not so common with her as with *me*, I have had a thousand fears for her—but she had kept up wonderfully.—had no Hysterics of consequence till we came within sight of poor old Sanditon—and the attack was not very violent—nearly over by the time we reached your Hotel—so that we got her out of the Carriage extremely well, with only Mr Woodcock's assistance—& when I left her she was directing the Disposal of the Luggage, & helping old Sam uncord the Trunks.—She desired her best Love, with a thousand regrets at being so poor a Creature that she could not come with me. And as for poor Arthur, he would not have been unwilling himself, but there is so much Wind that I did not think he could safely venture,—for I am *sure* there is Lumbago hanging about him—and so I helped him on with his great Coat & sent him off to the Terrace, to take us Lodgings.— Miss Heywood must have seen our Carriage standing at the Hotel.— I knew Miss Heywood the moment I saw her before me on the

Down.—My dear Tom I am so glad to see you walk so well. Let me feel your Ancle.—That's right; all right & clean. The play of your Sinews a *very* little affected:—barely perceptible.—Well—now for the explanation of my being here.—I told you in my Letter, of the two considerable Families, I was hoping to secure for you—the West Indians, & the Seminary.*—' Here Mr P. drew his Chair still nearer to his Sister, & took her hand again most affectionately as he answered 'Yes, Yes;—How active & how kind you have been!'—'The Westindians,' she continued, 'whom I look upon as the *most* desirable of the two—as the Best of the Good—prove to be a Mrs Griffiths & her family. I know them only through others.—You must have heard me mention Miss Capper, the particular friend of *my* very particular friend Fanny Noyce;—now, Miss Capper is extremely intimate with a Mrs Darling, who is on terms of constant correspondence with Mrs Griffiths herself.—Only a *short* chain, you see, between us, & not a Link wanting. Mrs G. meant to go to the Sea, for her young People's benefit—had fixed on the coast of Sussex, but was undecided as to the where, wanted something Private, & wrote to ask the opinion of her friend Mrs Darling.—Miss Capper happened to be staying with Mrs D. when Mrs G.'s Letter arrived, & was consulted on the question; *she* wrote the same day to Fanny Noyce and mentioned it to her—& Fanny all alive for *us*, instantly took up her pen & forwarded the circumstance to me—except as to *Names*—which have but lately transpired.—There was but *one* thing for *me* to do.—I answered Fanny's Letter by the same Post & pressed for the recommendation of Sanditon. Fanny had feared your having no house large enough to receive such a Family.—But I seem to be spinning out my story to an endless length.—You see how it was all managed. I had the pleasure of hearing soon afterwards by the same simple link of connection that Sanditon *had been* recommended by Mrs Darling, & that the Westindians were very much disposed to go thither.—This was the state of the case when I wrote to you;—but two days ago;—yes, the day before yesterday—I heard again from Fanny Noyce, saying that *she* had heard from Miss Capper, who by a Letter from Mrs Darling understood that Mrs G. has expressed herself in a letter to Mrs D. more doubtingly on the subject of Sanditon.—Am I clear?—I would be anything rather than not clear.'—'Oh! perfectly, perfectly. Well?'—'The reason of this hesitation, was her having no connections in the place, & no means of ascertaining that she should have good accomodations on arriving there;—and she was particularly careful & scrupulous on all those matters more on account of a certain Miss Lambe a young Lady (probably a Neice) under her care, than on her own account or her Daughters.—Miss Lambe has an immense fortune—richer than all the rest—& very delicate health.—One sees clearly enough by all this, the *sort* of Woman Mrs G. must be—as helpless & indolent, as Wealth & a Hot Climate are apt to make us. But we are not all born to equal Energy.—What was to be done?—I had a few moments indecision;—Whether to offer to write *to you*,—or to Mrs Whitby to secure them a House?—but neither pleased me.—I hate to employ others, when I am equal to act myself—and my conscience told me that this was an occasion which called for me. Here was a family of helpless Invalides whom I might essentially serve.—I sounded Susan—the same Thought had occurred to her.—Arthur made no difficulties— our plan was arranged immediately, we were off yesterday morning at 6—, left Chichester at the same hour to day—& here we are.—' 'Excellent—Excellent!—' cried Mr Parker.—'Diana, you are unequall'd in serving your friends & doing Good to all the World.—I know nobody like you.—Mary, my Love, is not she a wonderful Creature?—Well—and now, what House do you design to engage for them?—What is the size of their family?—' 'I do not at all know' replied his Sister 'have not the least idea;—never heard any particulars;—but I am very sure that the largest house at Sanditon cannot be *too* large. They are more likely to want a second.—I shall take only one however, & that, but for a week certain.—Miss Heywood, I astonish you.—You hardly know what to make of me.—I see by your Looks, that you are not used to such quick measures.'—The words 'Unaccountable Officiousness!—Activity run mad!'—had just passed through Charlotte's mind—but a civil answer was easy. 'I dare say I do look surprised,' said she—'because these are very great exertions, & I know what Invalides both you & your Sister are.' 'Invalides indeed.—I trust there are not three People in England who have so sad a right to that appellation!—But my dear Miss Heywood, we are sent into this World to be as extensively useful as possible, & where some degree of Strength of Mind is given, it is not a feeble body which will excuse us—or incline us to excuse ourselves.—The World is pretty much divided between the Weak of Mind & the Strong—between those who can act & those who can not, & it is the bounden Duty of the Capable to let no opportunity of being useful escape them.—My Sister's Complaints & mine are happily not often of a nature, to threaten Existence *immediately*—& as long as we *can* exert ourselves to be of use to others, I am convinced that the Body is the better, for the refreshment the Mind receives in doing it's Duty.—While I have been travelling, with this object in veiw, I have been perfectly well.'—The entrance of the Children ended this little panegyric on her own Disposition—& after having noticed & caressed them all,—she prepared to go.—'Cannot you dine with us?—Is not it possible to prevail on you to dine with us?' was then the cry; and *that* being absolutely negatived, it was 'And when shall we see you again? and how can we be of use to you?'—and Mr P. warmly offered his assistance in taking the house for Mrs G.—'I will come to you the moment I have dined,' said he, '& we will go about together.'—But this was immediately declined.—'No, my dear Tom, upon no account in the World, shall you stir a step on any business of mine.—Your Ancle wants rest. I see by the position of your foot, that you have used it too much already.—No, I shall go about my House-taking directly. Our Dinner is not ordered till six—& by that time I hope to have completed it. It is now only 1/2 past 4.—As to seeing *me* again to day—I cannot answer for it; the others will be at the Hotel all the Evening, & delighted to see you at any time, but as soon as I get back I shall hear what Arthur has done about our own Lodgings, & probably the moment Dinner is over, shall be out again on business relative to them, for we hope to get into some Lodgings or other & be settled after breakfast tomorrow.—I have not much confidence in poor Arthur's skill for Lodging-taking, but he seemed to like the commission.—' 'I think you are doing too much,' said Mr P. 'You will knock yourself up. You should not move again after Dinner.' 'No, indeed you should not,' cried his wife, 'for Dinner is such a mere *name* with you all, that it can do you no good.—I know what your appetites are.—' 'My appetite is very much mended I assure you lately. I have been taking some Bitters of my own decocting,* which have done wonders. Susan never eats I grant you—& just at present *I* shall want nothing; I never eat for about a week after a Journey—but as for Arthur, he is only too much disposed for Food.* We are often obliged to check him.'—'But you have not told me anything of the *other* Family coming to Sanditon,' said Mr P. as he walked with her to the door of the House—'the Camberwell Seminary; have we a good chance of *them*?—' 'Oh! Certain—quite certain.—I had forgotten them for the moment, but I had a letter 3 days ago from my friend Mrs Charles Dupuis which assured me of Camberwell. Camberwell will be here to a certainty, & very soon.—*That* good Woman (I do not know her name) not being so wealthy & independent as Mrs G.—can travel & chuse for herself.—I will tell you how I got at *her*. Mrs Charles Dupuis lives almost next door to a Lady who has a relation lately settled at Clapham, who actually attends the Seminary and gives lessons on Eloquence and Belles Lettres* to some of the Girls.—I got that Man a Hare from one of Sidney's friends—and he recommended Sanditon;—Without *my* appearing however.— Mrs Charles Dupuis managed it all.—'

# CHAPTER 10

It was not a week, since Miss Diana Parker had been told by her feelings, that the Sea Air would probably in her present state, be the death of her, and now she was at Sanditon, intending to make some Stay, & without appearing to have the slightest recollection of having written or felt any such thing.—It was impossible for Charlotte not to suspect a good deal of fancy in such an extraordinary state of health.—Disorders & Recoveries so very much out of the common way, seemed more like the amusement of eager minds in want of employment than of actual afflictions & releif. The Parkers, were no doubt a family of Imagination & quick feelings—and while the eldest Brother found vent for his superfluity of sensation as a Projector,* the Sisters were perhaps driven to dissipate theirs in the invention of odd complaints.—The *whole* of their mental vivacity was evidently not so employed; Part was laid out in a Zeal for being useful.—It should seem that they must either be very busy for the Good of others, or else extremely ill themselves. Some natural delicacy of Constitution in fact, with an unfortunate turn for medecine, especially quack Medecine, had given them an early tendency at various times, to various Disorders;—the rest of their sufferings was from Fancy, the love of Distinction & the love of the Wonderful.—They had Charitable hearts & many amiable feelings—but a spirit of restless activity,* & the glory of doing more than anybody else, had their share in every exertion of Benevolence—and there was Vanity in all they did, as well as in all they endured.—

Mr & Mrs P. spent a great part of the Evening at the Hotel; but Charlotte had only two or three veiws of Miss Diana posting* over the Down after a House for this Lady whom she had never seen, & who had never employed her. She was not made acquainted with the others till the following day, when, being removed into Lodgings & all the party continuing quite well, their Brother & Sister & herself were entreated to drink tea with them.—They were in one of the Terrace Houses—& she found them arranged for the Evening in a small neat Drawing room, with a beautiful veiw of the Sea if they had chosen it,—but though it had been a very fair English Summer-day,—not only was there no open window, but the Sopha & the Table, & the Establishment in general was all at the other end of the room by a brisk fire.—Miss P. whom, remembering the three Teeth drawn in one day, Charlotte approached with a peculiar degree of respectful Compassion, was not very unlike her Sister in person or manner—tho' more thin & worn by Illness & Medecine, more relaxed in air, & more subdued in voice. She talked however, the whole Evening, as incessantly as Diana—& excepting that she sat with salts in her hand, took Drops two or three times from one, out of the several Phials already at home on the Mantlepeice,—& made a great many odd faces & contortions, Charlotte could perceive no symptoms of illness which she, in the boldness of her own good health, would not have undertaken to cure, by putting out the fire, opening the Window, & disposing of the Drops & the Salts by means of one or the other. She had had considerable curiosity to see Mr Arthur Parker; & having fancied him a very puny, delicate-looking young Man, the smallest very materially of not a robust Family, was astonished to find him quite as tall as his Brother & a great deal Stouter—Broad made & Lusty*—and with no other look of an Invalide, than a sodden* complexion.—Diana was evidently the cheif of the family; principal mover & Actor;—she had been on her Feet the whole morning, on Mrs G.'s business or their own, & was still the most alert of the three.—Susan had only superintended their final removal from the Hotel, bringing two heavy Boxes herself, & Arthur had found the air so cold that he had merely walked from one House to the other, as nimbly as he could,—& boasted much of sitting by the fire till he had cooked up a very good one.—Diana, whose exercise had been too domestic to admit of calculation, but who, by her own account, had not once sat down during the space of seven hours, confessed herself a little tired. She had been too successful however for much fatigue; for not only had she by walking & talking down a thousand difficulties at last secured a proper House at 8 Guineas per week for Mrs G.—; she had also opened so many Treaties with Cooks, Housemaids, Washerwomen & Bathing Women,* that Mrs G. would have little more to do on her arrival, than to name her hand & collect them around her for Choice.—Her concluding effort in the cause, had been a few polite lines of Information to Mrs G. herself—time not allowing for the circuitous train of intelligence which had been hitherto kept up,—and she was now regaling in the delight of opening the first Trenches of an acquaintance with such a powerful discharge of unexpected Obligation. Mr & Mrs P. & Charlotte had seen two Post chaises crossing the Down to the Hotel as they were setting off,— a joyful sight—& full of speculation.—The Miss P.s & Arthur had also seen something;—they could distinguish from their window that there *was* an arrival at the Hotel, but not its amount. Their Visitors answered for two Hack-Chaises.*—Could it be the Camberwell Seminary?—No—No.—Had there been a 3$^d$ carriage, perhaps it might; but it was very generally agreed that two Hack chaises could never contain a Seminary.—Mr P. was confident of another new Family.—When they were all finally seated, after some removals to look at the Sea & the Hotel, Charlotte's place was by Arthur, who was sitting next to the Fire with a degree of Enjoyment which gave a good deal of merit to his civility in wishing her to take his Chair.—There was nothing dubious in her manner of declining it, & he sat down again with much satisfaction. She drew back her Chair to have all the advantage of his Person as a screen, & was very thankful for every inch of Back & Shoulders beyond her pre-conceived idea. Arthur was heavy in Eye as well as figure, but by no means indisposed to talk;—and while the other 4 were cheifly engaged together, he evidently felt it no penance to have a fine young Woman next to him, requiring in common Politeness some attention—as his Brother, who felt the decided want of some motive for action, some Powerful object of animation for him, observed with considerable pleasure.—Such was the influence of Youth & Bloom that he began even to make a sort of apology for having a Fire. 'We should not have one at home,' said he, 'but the Sea air is always damp. I am not afraid of anything so much as Damp.—' 'I am so fortunate,' said C. 'as never to know whether the air is damp or dry. It has always some property that is wholesome & invigorating to me,—' '*I* like the Air too, as well as any-body can;' replied Arthur, 'I am very fond of standing at an open window when there is no Wind—but unluckily a Damp air does not like *me*.—It gives me the Rheumatism.—You are not rheumatic I suppose?—' 'Not at all.' 'That's a great blessing.—But perhaps you are nervous.' 'No—I beleive not. I have no idea that I am.'—'*I* am very nervous.—To say the truth—Nerves are the worst part of my Complaints in *my* opinion. My Sisters think me Bilious, but I doubt it.—' 'You are quite in the right, to doubt it as long as you possibly can, I am sure.—' 'If I were Bilious,' he continued, 'you know Wine would disagree with me, but it always does me good.—The more Wine I drink (in moderation) the better I am.—I am always best of an Evening.—If you had seen me to day before Dinner, you would have thought me a very poor creature.—' Charlotte could beleive it—. She kept her countenance however, & said—'As far as I can under-stand what nervous complaints are, I have a great idea of the efficacy of Air & exercise for them:—daily, regular Exercise;—and I should recommend rather more of it to *you* than I suspect you are in the habit of taking.—' 'Oh! I am very fond of exercise myself'—he replied—'& mean to walk a great deal while I am here, if the Weather is temperate. I shall be out every morning before breakfast & take several turns upon the Terrace, & you will often see me at Trafalgar House.'—'But you do not call a walk to Trafalgar House much exercise?—' 'Not, as to mere distance, but the Hill is so steep!—Walking up that Hill, in the middle of the day, would throw me into such a Perspiration!—You would see me all in a Bath, by the time I got there!—I am very subject to Perspiration, and there cannot be a surer sign of Nervousness.—' They were now advancing so deep in Physics,* that Charlotte veiwed the entrance of the Servant with the Tea things, as a very fortunate Interruption.—It produced a great & immediate change. The young Man's attentions were instantly lost. He took his own Cocoa from the Tray,—which seemed provided with almost as many Teapots &c as there were persons in company, Miss P. drinking one sort of Herb-Tea & Miss Diana another, & turning completely to the Fire, sat cod-dling & cooking it to his own satisfaction & toasting some Slices of Bread, brought up ready-prepared in the Toast rack—and till it was all done, she heard nothing of his voice but the murmuring of a few broken sentences of self-approbation & success.—When his Toils were over however, he moved back his Chair into as gallant a Line as ever, & proved that he had not been working only for himself, by his earnest invitation to her to take both Cocoa & Toast.—She was already helped to Tea—which surprised him—so totally self-engrossed had he been.—'I thought I should have been in time,' said he, 'but Cocoa takes a great deal of Boiling.'—'I am much obliged to you,' replied Charlotte.—'But I prefer Tea.' 'Then I will help myself,' said he.—'A large Dish of rather weak Cocoa every evening agrees with me better than anything.'—It struck her however, as he poured out this rather weak Cocoa, that it came forth in a very fine, dark coloured Stream—and at the same moment, his Sisters both crying out—'Oh! Arthur, you get your Cocoa stronger & stronger every Evening'—, with Arthur's somewhat conscious reply of '*T*is rather stronger than it should be tonight'—convinced her that Arthur was by no means so fond of being starved as they could desire, or as he felt proper himself.—He was certainly very happy to turn the conversation on dry Toast, & hear no more of his Sisters.—'I hope you will eat some of this Toast,' said he, 'I reckon myself a very good Toaster; I never burn my Toasts—I never put them too near the Fire at first—& yet, you see, there is not a Corner but what is well browned.—I hope you like dry Toast.—' 'With a reasonable quantity of Butter spread over it, very much'—said Charlotte—'but not otherwise.—' 'No more do I'—said he exceedingly pleased—'We think quite alike there.—So far from dry Toast being wholesome, *I* think it a very bad thing for the Stomach. Without a little butter to soften it, it hurts the Coats of the Stomach.* I am sure it does.—I will have the pleasure of spreading some for you directly—& afterwards I will spread some for myself.—Very bad indeed for the Coats of the Stomach—but there is no convincing *some* people.—It irritates & acts like a nutmeg grater.—' He could not get the command of the Butter however, without a struggle; His Sisters accusing him of eating a great deal too much, & declaring he was not to be trusted; and he maintaining that he only eat enough to secure the Coats of his Stomach;—& besides, he only wanted it now for Miss Heywood.—Such a plea must prevail, he got the butter & spread away for her with an accuracy of Judgement which at least delighted himself; but when her Toast was done, & he took his own in hand, Charlotte could hardly contain herself as she saw him watching his Sisters, while he scrupulously scraped off almost as much butter as he put on, & then seize an odd moment for adding a great dab just before it went into his Mouth.—Certainly,

Mr Arthur P.'s enjoyments in Invalidism were very different from his
Sisters—by no means so spiritualized.—A good deal of Earthy Dross
hung about him. Charlotte could not but suspect him of adopting
that line of Life, principally for the indulgence of an indolent
Temper—& to be determined on having no Disorders but such as
called for warm rooms & good Nourishment.—In one particular
however, she soon found that he had caught something from
*them.*—'What!' said he—'Do you venture upon two dishes of strong
Green Tea in one Evening?—What Nerves you must have!—How
I envy you.—Now, if *I* were to swallow only one such dish—what do
you think it's effect would be upon me?—' 'Keep you awake perhaps
all night'—replied Charlotte, meaning to overthrow his attempts at
Surprise, by the Grandeur of her own Conceptions.—'Oh! if that
were all!'—he exclaimed.—'No—it acts on me like Poison and would
entirely take away the use of my right side, before I had swallowed it
5 minutes.—It sounds almost incredible—but it has happened to me
so often that I cannot doubt it.—The use of my right Side is entirely
taken away for several hours!' 'It sounds rather odd to be sure'—
answered Charlotte coolly—'but I dare say it would be proved to be
the simplest thing in the World, by those who have studied right
sides & Green Tea scientifically & thoroughly understand all the possibilities of their action on each other.'—Soon after Tea, a Letter
was brought to Miss D. P. from the Hotel.—'From Mrs Charles
Dupuis'—said she.—'some private hand.'—And having read a few
lines, exclaimed aloud 'Well, this is very extraordinary! very extraordinary indeed!—That both should have the same name.—Two Mrs
Griffiths!—This is a Letter of recommendation & introduction to
me, of the Lady from Camberwell—& *her* name happens to be
Griffiths too.—' A few lines more however, and the colour rushed
into her Cheeks, & with much Perturbation she added—'The oddest
thing that ever was!—a Miss Lambe too!—a young Westindian of
large Fortune.—But it *cannot* be the same.—Impossible that it should
be the same.'—She read the Letter aloud for comfort.—It was merely
to 'introduce the Bearer, Mrs G. from Camberwell, & the three young
Ladies under her care, to Miss D. P.'s notice.—Mrs G. being
a stranger at Sanditon, was anxious for a respectable Introduction—&
Mrs C. Dupuis therefore, at the instance of the intermediate friend,
provided her with this Letter, knowing that she could not do her dear
Diana a greater kindness than by giving her the means of being

useful.—Mrs G.'s cheif solicitude would be for the accomodation & comfort of one of the young Ladies under her care, a Miss Lambe, a young W. Indian of large Fortune, in delicate health.'—'It was very strange!—very remarkable!—very extraordinary' but they were all agreed in determining it to be *impossible* that there should not be two Families, each so totally distinct out of people no more concerned in the reports of each, made that matter quite certain. There *must* be two Families.—Impossible to be otherwise.—'Impossible' & 'Impossible', was repeated over & over again with great fervour.—An accidental resemblance of Names & circumstances, however striking at first, involved nothing really incredible and so it was settled.—Miss Diana herself derived an immediate advantage to counterbalance her Perplexity. She must put her shawl over her shoulders, & be running about again. Tired as she was, she must instantly repair to the Hotel, to investigate the truth & offer her Services.—

## CHAPTER 11

It would not do.—Not all that the whole Parker race could say among themselves, could produce a happier catastrophé* than that the Family from Surry & the Family from Camberwell were one & the same.—The rich Westindians, & the young Ladies Seminary had all entered Sanditon in those two Hack chaises. The Mrs G. who in her friend Mrs Darling's hands, had wavered as to coming & been unequal to the Journey, was the very same Mrs G. whose plans were at the same period (under another representation) perfectly decided, & who was without fears or difficulties.—All that had the appearance of Incongruiety in the reports of the two, might very fairly be placed to the account of the Vanity, the Ignorance, or the blunders of the many engaged in the cause by the vigilance & caution of Miss Diana P.—*Her* intimate friends must be officious like herself, & the subject had supplied Letters & Extracts & Messages enough to make everything appear what it was not. Miss D. probably felt a little awkward on being first obliged to admit her mistake. A long Journey from Hampshire taken for nothing—a Brother disappointed—an expensive House on her hands for a week, must have been some of her immediate reflections—& much worse than all the rest, must have been the sort of sensation of being less clear-sighted & infallible than she had beleived herself.—No part of it however seemed to trouble her long. There were so many to share in the shame & the blame, that probably when she had divided out their proper portions to Mrs Darling, Miss Capper, Fanny Noyce, Mrs C. Dupuis & Mrs C. D.'s Neighbour, there might be a mere trifle of reproach remaining for herself.—At any rate, she was seen all the following morning walking about after Lodgings with Mrs G. as alert as ever.—Mrs G. was a very well-behaved, genteel kind of Woman, who supported herself by receiving such great girls & young Ladies, as wanted either Masters for finishing their Education, or a home for beginning their Displays—She had several more under her care than the three who were now come to Sanditon, but the others all happened to be absent.—Of these three, & indeed of all, Miss Lambe was beyond comparison the most important & precious, as she paid in proportion to her fortune.—She was about 17, half-mulatto,* chilly & tender, had a maid of her own, was to have the best room in the Lodgings, & was always of the first consequence in every plan of Mrs G.—The other Girls, two Miss Beauforts were just such young Ladies as may be met with, in at least one family out of three, throughout the Kingdom; they had tolerable complexions, shewey figures, an upright decided carriage & an assured Look;—they were very accomplished & very Ignorant, their time being divided between such pursuits as might attract admiration, & those Labours & Expedients of dexterous Ingenuity, by which they could dress in a stile much beyond what they *ought* to have afforded; they were some of the first in every change of fashion—& the object of all, was to captivate some Man of much better fortune than their own.—Mrs G. had preferred a small, retired place, like Sanditon, on Miss Lambe's account—and the Miss B.s, though naturally preferring anything to Smallness & Retirement, yet having in the course of the Spring been involved in the inevitable expence of six new Dresses each for a three days visit, were constrained to be satisfied with Sanditon also, till their circumstances were retreived. There, with the hire of a Harp for one, & the purchase of some Drawing paper for the other & all the finery they could already command, they meant to be very economical, very elegant & very secluded; with the hope on Miss Beaufort's side, of praise & celebrity from all who walked within the sound of her Instrument, & on Miss Letitia's, of curiosity & rapture in all who came near her while she sketched—and to Both, the consolation of meaning to be the most stylish Girls in the Place.—The particular introduction of Mrs G. to Miss Diana Parker, secured them immediately an acquaintance with the Trafalgar House-family, & with the Denhams;—and the Miss Beauforts were soon satisfied with 'the Circle in which they moved in Sanditon' to use a proper phrase, for every body must now 'move in a Circle', to the prevalence of which rototary motion,* is perhaps to be attributed the Giddiness & false steps of many.—

Lady Denham had other motives for calling on Mrs G. besides attention to the Parkers.—In Miss Lambe, here was the very young Lady, sickly & rich, whom she had been asking for; & she made the acquaintance for Sir Edward's sake, & the sake of her Milch asses. How it might answer with regard to the Baronet, remained to be proved, but as to the Animals, she soon found that all her calculations of Profit would be vain. Mrs G. would not allow Miss L. to have the smallest symptom of a Decline, or any complaint which Asses milk could possibly releive. 'Miss L. was under the constant care of an experienced Physician;—and his Prescriptions must be their rule'—and except in favour of some Tonic Pills,* which a Cousin of her own had a Property in, Mrs G. did never deviate from the strict medecinal page.—The corner house of the Terrace was the one in which Miss D. P. had the pleasure of settling her new friends, & considering that it commanded in front the favourite Lounge of all the Visitors at Sanditon, & on one side, whatever might be going on at the Hotel, there could not have been a more favourable spot for the seclusions of the Miss Beauforts. And accordingly, long before they had suited themselves with an Instrument, or with Drawing paper, they had, by the frequency of their appearance at the low Windows upstairs, in order to close the blinds, or open the Blinds, to arrange a flower pot on the Balcony, or look at nothing through a Telescope, attracted many an eye upwards, & made many a Gazer gaze again.—A little novelty has a great effect in so small a place; the Miss Beauforts, who would have been nothing at Brighton, could not move here without notice;—and even Mr Arthur Parker, though little disposed for supernumerary exertion, always quitted the Terrace, in his way to his Brothers by this corner House, for the sake of a glimpse of the Miss B.s, though it was 1/2 a quarter of a mile round-about, & added two steps to the ascent of the Hill.

## CHAPTER 12

Charlotte had been 10 days at Sanditon without seeing Sanditon
House, every attempt at calling on Lady D. having been defeated by
meeting with her beforehand. But now it was to be more resolutely
undertaken, at a more early hour, that nothing might be neglected of
attention to Lady D. or amusement to Charlotte.—'And if you should
find a favourable opening my Love,' said Mr P. (who did not mean to
go with them)—'I think you had better mention the poor Mullins's
situation, & sound her Ladyship as to a Subscription for them. I am
not fond of charitable subscriptions in a place of this kind—It is
a sort of tax upon all that come—Yet as their distress is very great &
I almost promised the poor Woman yesterday to get something done
for her, I beleive we must set a subscription on foot—& therefore the
sooner the better,—& Lady Denham's name at the head of the List
will be a very necessary beginning.—You will not dislike speaking to
her about it, Mary?—' 'I will do whatever you wish me,' replied his
wife—'but you would do it so much better yourself. I shall not know
what to say.'—'My dear Mary,' cried he, 'it is impossible you can be
really at a loss. Nothing can be more simple. You have only to state the
present afflicted situation of the family, their earnest application to
me, & my being willing to promote a little subscription for their releif,
provided it meet with her approbation.—' 'The easiest thing in the
World'—cried Miss Diana Parker who happened to be calling on
them at the moment—. 'All said & done, in less time than you have
been talking of it now.—And while you are on the subject of subscriptions Mary, I will thank you to mention a very melancholy case to
Lady D., which has been represented to me in the most affecting
terms.—There is a poor Woman in Worcestershire,* whom some
friends of mine are exceedingly interested about, & I have undertaken
to collect whatever I can for her. If you would mention the circumstance to Lady Denham!—Lady Denham *can* give, if she is properly
attacked—& I look upon her to be the sort of Person who, when once
she is prevailed on to undraw her Purse, would as readily give 10
Guineas as 5.—And therefore, if you find her in a Giving mood, you
might as well speak in favour of another Charity which I & a few
more, have very much at heart—the establishment of a Charitable
Repository* at Burton on Trent.—And then,—there is the family of
the poor Man who was hung last assizes at York,* tho' we really *have*

raised the sum we wanted for putting them all out;* yet if you *can* get a Guinea from her on their behalf, it may as well be done.—' 'My dear Diana!' exclaimed Mrs P.—'I could no more mention these things to Lady D. than I could fly.'—'Where's the difficulty?—I wish I could go with you myself—but in 5 minutes I must be at Mrs G. to encourage Miss Lambe in taking her first Dip. She is so frightened, poor Thing, that I promised to come & keep up her Spirits, & go in the Machine with her if she wished it—and as soon as that is over, I must hurry home, for Susan is to have Leeches at one o'clock—which will be a three hours business,—therefore I really have not a moment to spare—besides that (between ourselves) I ought to be in bed myself at this present time, for I am hardly able to stand—and when the Leeches have done, I dare say we shall both go to our rooms for the rest of the day.'—'I am sorry to hear it, indeed; but if this is the case I hope Arthur will come to us.'—'If Arthur takes my advice, he will go to bed too, for if he stays up by himself, he will certainly eat & drink more than he ought;—but you see Mary, how impossible it is for me to go with you to Lady Denham's.'—'Upon second thoughts Mary,' said her husband, 'I will not trouble you to speak about the Mullins's.—I will take an opportunity of seeing Lady D. myself.— *I* know how little it suits you to be pressing matters upon a Mind at all unwilling.'—*His* application thus withdrawn, his Sister could say no more in support of hers, which was his object, as he felt all their impropriety & all the certainty of their ill effect upon his own better claim.—Mrs P. was delighted at this release, & set off very happy with her friend & her little girl, on this walk to Sanditon House.—It was a close, misty morning, & when they reached the brow of the Hill, they could not for some time make out what sort of Carriage it was, which they saw coming up. It appeared at different moments to be everything from the Gig to the Pheaton,—from one horse to 4; & just as they were concluding in favour of a Tandem,* little Mary's young eyes distinguished the Coachman & she eagerly called out, 'T'is Uncle Sidney Mama, it is indeed.' And so it proved.—Mr Sidney Parker driving his Servant in a very neat Carriage was soon opposite to them; & they all stopped for a few minutes. The manners of the Parkers were always pleasant among themselves—& it was a very friendly meeting between Sidney & his Sister in law, who was most kindly taking it for granted that he was on his way to Trafalgar House. This he declined however. 'He was just come from Eastbourne,

proposing to spend two or three days, as it might happen, at
Sanditon—but the Hotel must be his Quarters—He was expecting
to be joined there by a friend or two.'—The rest was common enquiries & remarks, with kind notice of little Mary, & a very well-bred Bow
& proper address to Miss Heywood on her being named to him—and
they parted, to meet again within a few hours.—Sidney Parker was
about 7 or 8 & 20, very good-looking, with a decided air of Ease &
Fashion, and a lively countenance.—This adventure afforded agreable discussion for some time. Mrs P. entered into all her Husband's
joy on the occasion, & exulted in the credit which Sidney's arrival
would give to the place. The road to Sanditon H. was a broad, handsome, planted approach, between fields, & conducting at the end of
a quarter of a mile through second Gates into the Grounds, which
though not extensive had all the Beauty & Respectability which an
abundance of very fine Timber could give.—These Entrance Gates
were so much in a corner of the Grounds or Paddock, so near one of
its Boundaries, that an outside fence was at first almost pressing on
the road—till an angle *here*, & a curve there, threw them to a better
distance. The Fence was a proper, Park paling* in excellent condition;
with clusters of fine Elms, or rows of old Thorns following its line
almost every where.—*Almost* must be stipulated—for there were
vacant spaces—& through one of these, Charlotte as soon as they
entered the Enclosure, caught a glimpse over the pales of something
White & Womanish in the field on the other side;—it was a something which immediately brought Miss B. into her head—& stepping
to the pales, she saw indeed—& very decidedly inspite of the Mist;
Miss B. seated, not far before her, at the foot of the bank which sloped
down from the outside of the Paling & which a narrow Path seemed to
skirt along;—Miss Brereton seated, apparently very composedly—&
Sir E. D. by her side.—They were sitting so near each other &
appeared so closely engaged in gentle conversation, that Charlotte
instantly felt she had nothing to do but to step back again, & say not
a word.—Privacy was certainly their object.—It could not but strike
her rather unfavourably with regard to Clara;—but hers was a situation which must not be judged with severity.—She was glad to perceive that nothing had been discerned by Mrs Parker. If Charlotte
had not been considerably the tallest of the two, Miss B.'s white ribbons might not have fallen within the ken of *her* more observant
eyes.—Among other points of moralising reflection which the sight

of this Tete a Tete produced, Charlotte could not but think of the extreme difficulty which secret Lovers must have in finding a proper spot for their stolen Interveiws.—Here perhaps they had thought themselves so perfectly secure from observation!—the whole field open before them—a steep bank & Pales never crossed by the foot of Man at their back—and a great thickness of air, in aid— Yet here she had seen them. They were really ill-used.—The House was large & handsome; two Servants appeared, to admit them, & every thing had a suitable air of Property & Order.—Lady D. valued herself upon her liberal Establishment, & had great enjoyment in the order and the Importance of her style of living.—They were shewn into the usual sitting room, well-proportioned & well-furnished;—tho' it was Furniture rather originally good & extremely well kept, than new or shewey—and as Lady D. was not there, Charlotte had leisure to look about, & to be told by Mrs P. that the whole-length Portrait of a stately Gentleman, which placed over the Mantlepeice, caught the eye immediately, was the picture of Sir H. Denham—and that one among many miniatures in another part of the room, little conspicuous, represented Mr Hollis.—Poor Mr Hollis!—It was impossible not to feel him hardly used; to be obliged to stand back in his own House & see the best place by the fire constantly occupied by Sir H. D.

# OPINIONS OF MANSFIELD PARK

'We certainly do not think it as a *whole*, equal to P. & P.—but it has many & great beauties. Fanny is a delightful Character! and Aunt Norris is a great favourite of mine. The Characters are natural & well supported, & many of the Dialogues excellent.—You need not fear the publication being considered as discreditable to the talents of it's Author.' F. W. A.*

Not so clever as P. & P.—but pleased with it altogether. Liked the character of Fanny. Admired the Portsmouth Scene.—Mr K.*—

Edward & George.*—Not liked it near so well as P. & P.—

Edward admired Fanny—George disliked her.—George interested by nobody but Mary Crawford.—Edward pleased with Henry C.—Edmund objected to, as cold & formal.—Henry C.s going off with Mrs R.—at such a time, when so much in love with Fanny, thought unnatural by Edward.—

Fanny Knight.*—Liked it, in many parts, very much indeed, delighted with Fanny;—but not satisfied with the end—wanting more Love between her & Edmund—& could not think it natural that Edmund should be so much attached to a woman without Principle like Mary C.—or promote Fanny's marrying Henry.—

Anna* liked it better than P. & P.—but not so well as S. & S.—could not bear Fanny. Delighted with Mrs Norris, the scene at Portsmouth, & all the humourous parts.—

Mrs James Austen,* very much pleased. Enjoyed Mrs Norris particularly, & the scene at Portsmouth. Thought Henry Crawford's going off with Mrs Rushworth, very natural.—

Miss Clewes's* objections much the same as Fanny's.—

Miss Lloyd* preferred it altogether to either of the others.—Delighted with Fanny.—Hated Mrs Norris.—

My Mother*—not liked it so well as P. & P.—Thought Fanny insipid.—Enjoyed Mrs Norris.—

Cassandra*—thought it quite as clever, tho' not so brilliant as P. & P.—Fond of Fanny.—Delighted much in Mr Rushworth's stupidity.—

My Eldest Brother*—a warm admirer of it in general.—Delighted with the Portsmouth Scene.

Edward*—Much like his Father.—Objected to Mrs Rushworth's Elopement as unnatural.

Mr B. L.*—Highly pleased with Fanny Price—& a warm admirer of the Portsmouth Scene.—Angry with Edmund for not being in love with her, & hating Mrs Norris for teazing her.—

Miss Burdett*—Did not like it so well as P. & P.

Mrs James Tilson*—Liked it better than P. & P.

Fanny Cage*—did not much like it—not to be compared to P. & P.—nothing interesting in the Characters—Language poor.— Characters natural & well supported—Improved as it went on.—

Mr & Mrs Cooke*—very much pleased with it—particularly with the manner in which the Clergy are treated.—Mr Cooke called it 'the most sensible Novel he had ever read.'—Mrs Cooke wished for a good Matronly Character.—

Mary Cooke*—quite as much pleased with it, as her Father & Mother; seemed to enter into Lady B.'s character, & enjoyed Mr Rushworth's folly. Admired Fanny in general; but thought she ought to have been more determined on overcoming her own feelings, when she saw Edmund's attachment to Miss Crawford.—

Miss Burrel*—admired it very much—particularly Mrs Norris & Dr Grant.—

Mrs Bramstone*—much pleased with it; particularly with the character of Fanny, as being so very natural. Thought Lady Bertram like herself.—Preferred it to either of the others—but imagined *that* might be her want of Taste—as she does not understand Wit.—

Mrs Augusta Bramstone*—owned that she thought S. & S.—and P. & P. downright nonsense, but expected to like MP. better, & having finished the 1st vol.—flattered herself she had got through the worst.

The families at Deane*—all pleased with it.—Mrs Anna Harwood delighted with Mrs Norris & the green Curtain.

The Kintbury Family*—very much pleased with it;—preferred it to either of the others.—

Mr Egerton the Publisher*—praised it for it's Morality, & for being so equal a Composition.—No weak parts.

Lady Robert Kerr* wrote—'You may be assured I read every line with the greatest interest & am more delighted with it than my humble pen can express. The excellent delineation of Character, sound sense, Elegant Language & the pure morality with which it abounds, makes it a most desirable as well as useful work, & reflects the highest honour &c &c.—Universally admired in Edinburgh, by all the *wise ones.*—Indeed, I have not heard a single fault given to it.'—

Miss Sharpe*—'I think it excellent—& of it's good sense & moral Tendency there can be no doubt.—Your Characters are drawn to the Life—so *very, very* natural & just—but as you beg me to be perfectly honest, I must confess I prefer P. & P.'—

Mrs Carrick.*—'All who think deeply & feel much will give the Preference to Mansfield Park.'

Mr J. Plumptre.*—'I never read a novel which interested me so very much throughout, the characters are all so remarkably well kept up & so well drawn, & the plot is so well contrived that I had not an idea till the end which of the two would marry Fanny, H. C. or Edmund. Mrs Norris amused me particularly, & Sir Thomas is very clever, & his conduct proves admirably the defects of the modern system of Education.'—Mr J. P. made *two* objections, but only one of them was remembered, the want of some character more striking & interesting to the generality of Readers, than Fanny was likely to be.—

Sir James Langham & Mr H. Sanford,* having been told that it was much inferior to P. & P.—began it expecting to dislike it, but were very soon extremely pleased with it—& I *beleive,* did not think it at all inferior.—

Alethea Bigg.*—'I have read MP. & heard it very much talked of, very much praised, I like it myself & think it very good indeed, but as I never say what I do not think, I will add that although it is superior in a great many points in my opinion to the other two Works, I think it has not the Spirit of P. & P., except perhaps the *Price* family at Portsmouth, & they are delightful in their way.'—

Charles*—did not like it near so well as P. & P.—thought it wanted Incident.—

Mrs Dickson.*—'I have bought MP.—but it is not equal to P. & P.'—

Mrs Lefroy*—liked it, but thought it a mere Novel.—

Mrs Portal*—admired it very much—objected cheifly to Edmund's not being brought more forward.—

Lady Gordon* wrote 'In most novels you are amused for the time with a set of Ideal People whom you never think of afterwards or whom you the least expect to meet in common life, whereas in Miss A–s works, & especially in MP. you actually *live* with them, you fancy yourself one of the family; & the scenes are so exactly descriptive, so perfectly natural, that there is scarcely an Incident a conversation, or a person that you are not inclined to imagine you have at one time or other in your Life been a witness to, born a part in, & been acquainted with.'

Mrs Pole* wrote, 'There is a particular satisfaction in reading all Miss A—s works—they are so evidently written by a Gentlewoman— most Novellists fail & betray themselves in attempting to describe familiar scenes in high Life, some little vulgarism escapes & shews that they are not experimentally acquainted with what they describe, but here it is quite different. Everything is natural, & the situations & incidents are told in a manner which clearly evinces the Writer to *belong* to the Society whose Manners she so ably delineates.' Mrs Pole also said that no Books had ever occasioned so much canvassing & doubt, & that everybody was desirous to attribute them to some of their own friends, or to some person of whom they thought highly.—

Admiral Foote*—surprised that I had the power of drawing the Portsmouth-Scenes so well.—

Mrs Creed*—preferred S & S. and P & P.—to Mansfield Park.

# OPINIONS OF EMMA

Captain Austen *—liked it extremely, observing that though there might be more Wit in P & P—& an higher Morality in MP—yet altogether, on account of it's peculiar air of Nature throughout, he preferred it to either.

Mrs F. A.*—liked & admired it very much indeed, but must still prefer P. & P.

Mrs J. Bridges*—preferred it to all the others.

Miss Sharp*—better than MP.—but not so well as P. & P.—pleased with the Heroine for her Originality, delighted with Mr K—& called Mrs Elton beyond praise.—dissatisfied with Jane Fairfax.

Cassandra*—better than P. & P.—but not so well as M. P.—

Fanny K.*—not so well as either P. & P. or MP.—could not bear *Emma* herself.—Mr Knightley delightful.—Should like J. F.—if she knew more of her.—

Mr & Mrs J. A.*—did not like it so well as either of the 3 others. Language different from the others; not so easily read.—

Edward*—preferred it to MP.—*only*.—Mr K. liked by everybody.

Miss Bigg*—not equal to either P & P.—or MP.—objected to the sameness of the subject (Match making) all through.—Too much of Mr Elton & H. Smith. Language superior to the others.—

My Mother*—thought it more entertaining than MP.—but not so interesting as P. & P.—No characters in it equal to Lady Catherine & Mr Collins.—

Miss Lloyd*—thought it as *clever* as either of the others, but did not receive so much pleasure from it as from P. & P—& MP.—

Mrs & Miss Craven*—liked it very much, but not so much as the others.—

Fanny Cage*—liked it very much indeed & classed it between P & P.—& MP.—

Mr Sherer*—did not think it equal to either MP—(which he liked the best of all) or P. & P.—Displeased with my pictures of Clergymen.—

Miss Bigg—on reading it a second time, liked Miss Bates much better than at first, & expressed herself as liking all the people of

Highbury in general, except Harriet Smith—but could not help still thinking *her* too silly in her Loves.

The family at Upton Gray—all very much amused with it.—Miss Bates a great favourite with Mrs Beaufoy.*

Mr & Mrs Leigh Perrot*—saw many beauties in it, but could not think it equal to P. & P.—Darcy & Elizabeth had spoilt them for anything else.—Mr K. however, an excellent Character; Emma better luck than a Matchmaker often has.—Pitied Jane Fairfax—thought Frank Churchill better treated than he deserved.—

Countess Craven*—admired it very much, but did not think it equal to P & P.—which she ranked as the very first of it's sort.—

Mrs Guiton*—thought it too natural to be interesting.

Mrs Digweed*—did not like it so well as the others, in fact if she had not known the Author, could hardly have got through it.—

Miss Terry*—admired it very much, particularly Mrs Elton.

Henry Sanford*—very much pleased with it—delighted with Miss Bates, but thought Mrs Elton the best drawn Character in the Book.—Mansfield Park however, still his favourite.

Mr Haden*—*quite* delighted with it. Admired the Character of Emma.—

Miss Isabella Herries*—did not like it—objected to my exposing the sex in the character of the Heroine—convinced that I had meant Mrs & Miss Bates for some acquaintance of theirs—People whom I never heard of before.—

Miss Harriet Moore*—admired it very much, but M. P. still her favourite of all.—

Countess Morley*—delighted with it.—

Mr Cockerell*—liked it so little, that Fanny would not send me his opinion.—

Mrs Dickson*—did not much like it—thought it *very* inferior to P. & P.—Liked it the less, from there being a Mr & Mrs Dixon in it.—

Mrs Brandreth*—thought the 3$^d$ vol: superior to anything I had ever written—quite beautiful!—

Mr B. Lefroy*—thought that if there had been more Incident, it would be equal to any of the others.—The Characters quite as well drawn & supported as in any, & from being more Everyday ones, the more entertaining.—Did not like the Heroine so well as any of

the others. Miss Bates excellent, but rather too much of her. Mr &
Mrs Elton admirable & John Knightley a sensible Man.—

Mrs B. Lefroy*—rank'd *Emma* as a composition with S & S.—not so
*Brilliant* as P. & P—nor so *equal* as MP.—Preferred Emma herself
to all the heroines.—The Characters like all the others admirably
well drawn & supported—perhaps rather less *strongly marked* than
some, but only the more natural for that reason.—Mr Knightley
Mrs Elton & Miss Bates her favourites.—Thought one or two of
the conversations too long.—

Mrs Lefroy*—preferred it to MP—but liked MP. the least of all.

Mr Fowle*—read only the first & last Chapters, because he had heard
it was not interesting.—

Mrs Lutley Sclater*—liked it very much, better than MP—&
thought I had 'brought it all about very cleverly in the last volume.'—

Mrs C. Cage* wrote thus to Fanny—'A great many thanks for the
loan of *Emma*, which I am delighted with. I like it better than any.
Every character is thoroughly kept up. I must enjoy reading it
again with Charles. Miss Bates is incomparable, but I was nearly
killed with those precious treasures! They are Unique, & really
with more fun than I can express. I am at Highbury all day, &
I can't help feeling I have just got into a new set of acquaintance.
No one writes such good sense & so very comfortable.

Mrs Wroughton*—did not like it so well as P. & P.—Thought the
Authoress wrong, in such times as these, to draw such clergymen
as Mr Collins & Mr Elton.

Sir J. Langham*—thought it much inferior to the others.—

Mr Jeffrey* (of the Edinburgh Review) was kept up by it three nights.

Miss Murden*—certainly inferior to all the others.

Captain C. Austen* wrote—'Emma arrived in time to a moment.
I am delighted with her, more so I think than even with my favourite
Pride & Prejudice, & have read it three times in the Passage.'

Mrs D. Dundas*—thought it very clever, but did not like it so well as
either of the others.

# PLAN OF A NOVEL, ACCORDING TO HINTS FROM VARIOUS QUARTERS

Scene to be in the Country, Heroine the Daughter of a [1]Clergyman, one who after having lived much in the World had retired from it, & settled on a Curacy, with a very small fortune of his own.—He, the most excellent Man that can be imagined, perfect in Character, Temper & Manners—without the smallest drawback or peculiarity to prevent his being the most delightful companion to his Daughter from one year's end to the other.—Heroine a [2]faultless Character herself—, perfectly good, with much tenderness & sentiment, & not the least [3]Wit—very highly [4]accomplished, understanding modern Languages & (generally speaking) everything that the most accomplished young Women learn, but particularly excelling in Music—her favourite pursuit—& playing equally well on the Piano Forte & Harp—& singing in the first stile. Her Person, quite beautiful—[5]dark eyes & plump cheeks.*—Book to open with the description of Father & Daughter—who are to converse in long speeches, elegant Language—& a tone of high, serious sentiment.—The Father to be induced, at his Daughter's earnest request, to relate to her the past events of his Life.* This Narrative will reach through the greatest part of the 1st vol.—as besides all the circumstances of his attachment to her Mother & their Marriage, it will comprehend his going to sea as [6]Chaplain to a distinguished Naval Character about the Court, his going afterwards to Court himself, which introduced him to a great variety of Characters & involved him in many interesting situations, concluding with his opinion of the Benefits to result from Tythes* being done away, & his having buried his own Mother (Heroine's lamented Grandmother) in consequence of the High Priest of the Parish in which she died, refusing to pay her Remains the respect due to them. The Father to be of a very literary turn, an Enthusiast in Literature, nobody's Enemy but his own*—at the same time most zealous in the discharge of his Pastoral Duties, the model of an [7]exemplary Parish Priest.—The heroine's friendship to be

---

[1] Mr Gifford.*      [2] Fanny Knight.*      [3] Mary Cooke.*      [4] Fanny K.
[5] Mary Cooke.      [6] Mr Clarke.*      [7] Mr Sherer.*

sought after by a young Woman in the same Neighbourhood, of [8]Talents & Shrewdness, with light eyes & a fair skin, but having a considerable degree of Wit, Heroine shall shrink from the acquaintance.—From this outset, the Story will proceed, & contain a striking variety of adventures.* Heroine & her Father never above a [9]fortnight together in one place, *he* being driven from his Curacy by the vile arts of some totally unprincipled & heart-less young Man, desperately in love with Heroine, & pursueing her with unrelenting passion—no sooner settled in one Country of Europe than they are necessitated to quit it & retire to another—always making new acquaintance, & always obliged to leave them.—This will of course exhibit a wide variety of Characters—But there will be no mixture; the scene will be for ever shifting from one Set of People to another—but All the [10]Good will be unexceptionable in every respect—and there will be no foibles or weaknesses but with the Wicked, who will be completely depraved & infamous, hardly a resemblance of Humanity left in them.—Early in her career, in the progress of her first removals, Heroine must meet with the Hero—all [11]perfection of course—& only prevented from paying his addresses to her, by some excess of refinement.—Wherever she goes, somebody falls in love with her, & she receives repeated offers of Marriage—which she always refers wholly to her Father, exceedingly angry that [12]*he* should not be first applied to.—Often carried away by the anti-hero,* but rescued either by her Father or the Hero—often reduced to support herself & her Father by her Talents, & work for her Bread;*—continually cheated & defrauded of her hire, worn down to a Skeleton, & now & then starved to death—. At last, hunted out of civilized Society, denied the poor Shelter of the humblest Cottage, they are compelled to retreat into Kamschatka* where the poor Father, quite worn down, finding his end approaching, throws himself on the Ground, & after 4 or 5 hours of tender advice & parental Admonition to his miserable Child, expires in a fine burst of Literary Enthusiasm, intermingled with Invectives against Holders of Tythes.—Heroine inconsolable for some time—but afterwards crawls back towards her former Country—having at least 20 narrow escapes of falling into the hands of Anti-hero—& at last in the very nick of time, turning a corner to

[8] Mary Cooke.    [9] Many Critics.    [10] Mary Cooke.
[11] Fanny Knight.    [12] Mrs Pearse of Chilton-Lodge*

avoid him, runs into the arms of the Hero himself, who having just shaken off the scruples which fetter'd him before, was at the very moment setting off in pursuit of her.—The Tenderest & completest Eclaircissement* takes place, & they are happily united.—Throughout the whole work, Heroine to be in the most [13]elegant Society & living in high style. The name of the work not to be 'Emma' but of the same sort as [15]S & S. and P & P.

[13] Fanny Knight.    [14] Mrs Craven.*    [15] Mr H. Sanford.*

# THE VERSES OF JANE AUSTEN

## This little bag

This little bag I hope will prove
    To be not vainly made—
For, if you thread & needle want
    It will afford you aid.

And as we are about to part
    T'will serve another end,
For when you look upon the Bag
    You'll recollect your freind.

                Jan:ry 1792

## Miss Lloyd has now sent to Miss Green

Miss Lloyd has now sent to Miss Green,*
As, on opening the box, may be seen,
Some yards of a Black Ploughman's Gauze,*
To be made up directly, because
Miss Lloyd must in mourning appear
For the death of a Relative dear—
Miss Lloyd must expect to receive
This license to mourn & to grieve,
Complete, ere the end of the week—
It is better to write than to speak.

## Oh! Mr Best you're very bad

Oh! Mr Best, you're very bad
    And all the world shall know it;
Your base behaviour shall be sung
    By me, a tuneful Poet.—

You used to go to Harrowgate*
    Each summer as it came,
And why I pray should you refuse
    To go this year the same?—

The way's as plain, the road's as smooth,
    The Posting* not increased;

You're scarcely stouter* than you were,
    Not younger Sir at least.——

If e'er the waters were of use
    Why now their use forego?
You may not live another year,
    All's mortal here below.——

It is your duty Mr Best
    To give your health repair.
Vain else your Richard's pills* will be,
    And vain your Consort's care.

But yet a nobler Duty calls
    You now towards the North.
Arise ennobled—as Escort
    Of Martha Lloyd stand forth.

She wants your aid—she honours you
    With a distinguish'd call.
Stand forth to be the friend of her
    Who is the friend of all.

Take her, & wonder at your luck,
    In having such a Trust.
Her converse sensible & sweet
    Will banish heat and dust.——

So short she'll make the journey seem
    You'll bid the Chaise stand still.
T'will be like driving at full speed
    From Newb'ry to Speen Hill.*——

Convey her safe to Morton's wife*
    And I'll forget the past,
And write some verses in your praise
    As finely & as fast.

But if you still refuse to go
    I'll never let your rest,
But haunt you with reproachful song
    Oh! wicked Mr Best!——

                J. A.
            Clifton 1806

## See they come, post haste from Thanet

See they come, post haste from Thanet,*
  Lovely couple, side by side;
They've left behind them Richard Kennet*
  With the Parents of the Bride!

Canterbury they have passed through;
  Next succeeded Stamford-bridge;
Chilham village* they came fast through;
  Now they've mounted yonder ridge.

Down the hill they're swift proceeding,
  Now they skirt the Park around;
Lo! The Cattle sweetly feeding
  Scamper, startled at the sound!

Run, my Brothers,* to the Pier gate!*
  Throw it open, very wide!
Let it not be said that we're late
  In welcoming my Uncle's Bride!

To the house the chaise advances;
  Now it stops—They're here, they're here!
How d'ye do, my Uncle Francis?
  How does do your Lady dear?

## On Sir Home Popham's sentence—April *1807*

Of a Ministry pitiful, angry, mean,*
A Gallant Commander the victim is seen;
For Promptitude, Vigour, Success—does he stand*
Condemn'd to receive a severe reprimand!
To his Foes I could wish a resemblance in fate;
That they too may suffer themselves soon or late
The injustice they warrant—but vain is my Spite,
*They* cannot so suffer, who never do right.—

## Happy the Lab'rer

Happy the Lab'rer in his Sunday Cloathes!—
In light-drab* coat, smart waistcoat, well-darn'd Hose

And hat upon his head to Church he goes;—
As oft with conscious pride he downward throws
A glance upon the ample Cabbage rose*
Which stuck in Buttonhole, regales his nose,
He envies not the gayest London Beaux.—
In Church he takes his seat among the rows,*
Pays to the Place the reverence he owes,
Likes best the Prayers whose meaning least he knows,
Lists to the Sermon in a softening Doze,
And rouses joyous at the welcome close.—

## Cambrick! with grateful blessings would I pay

Cambrick!* with grateful blessings would I pay
The pleasure given me in sweet employ:—
Long may'st thou serve my Friend without decay,
And have no tears to wipe, but tears of joy!
                              J.A.—Aug:st 26.—1808—

## On the same occasion—but not sent.— Cambrick! thou'st been to me a good

Cambrick! thou'st been to me a good
And I would bless thee if I could.
Go, serve thy Mistress with delight,
Be small in compass, soft & white;
Enjoy thy fortune, honour'd much
To bear her name* & feel her touch;
And that thy worth may last for years,
Slight be her Colds & few her Tears!—

## To the Memory of Mrs Lefroy, who died Dec:r 16—my Birthday.—written 1808

The day returns again, my natal day;
What mix'd emotions with the Thought arise!
Beloved friend, four years have pass'd away
Since thou wert snatch'd forever from our eyes.—

The day, commemorative of my birth
Bestowing Life & Light & Hope on me,
Brings back the hour which was thy last on Earth.
Oh! bitter pang of torturing Memory!—

Angelic Woman! past my power to praise
In Language meet, thy Talents, Temper, Mind,
Thy solid Worth, thy captivating Grace!—
Thou friend & ornament of Humankind!—

At Johnson's death* by Hamilton t'was said,
'Seek we a substitute—Ah! vain the plan,
No second best remains to Johnson dead—
None can remind us even of the Man.'*

So we of thee—unequall'd in thy race
Unequall'd thou, as he the first of Men.
Vainly we search around the vacant place,
We ne'er may look upon thy like again.

Come then fond Fancy, thou indulgent Power,—
—Hope is desponding, chill, severe to thee!—
Bless thou, this little portion of an hour,
Let me behold her as she used to be.

I see her here, with all her smiles benign,
Her looks of eager Love, her accents sweet.
That voice & Countenance almost divine!—
Expression, Harmony, alike complete.—

I listen—'tis not sound alone—'tis sense,
'Tis Genius, Taste & Tenderness of soul.
'Tis genuine warmth of heart without pretence
And purity of Mind that crowns the whole.

She speaks; 'tis Eloquence—that grace of Tongue
So rare, so lovely!—Never misapplied
By *her* to palliate Vice, or deck a Wrong,
She speaks & reasons but on Virtue's side.

Her's is the Energy of soul sincere.
Her Christian Spirit, ignorant to feign,
Seeks but to comfort, heal, enlighten, chear,
Confer a pleasure, or prevent a pain.—

Can ought enhance such Goodness?—Yes, to me,
Her partial favour from my earliest years
Consummates all.—Ah! Give me yet to see
Her smile of Love.—the Vision disappears.

'Tis past & gone—We meet no more below.
Short is the Cheat of Fancy o'er the Tomb.
Oh! might I hope to equal Bliss to go!
To meet thee Angel! in thy future home!—

Fain would I feel an union in thy fate,
Fain would I seek to draw an Omen fair
From this connection in our Earthly date.
Indulge the harmless weakness—Reason, spare.—

                                                    J. A.

## Alas! poor Brag, thou boastful Game!

'Alas! poor Brag,* thou boastful Game! What now avails
    thine empty name?
Where now thy more distinguish'd fame?—My day is o'er,
    & Thine the same.—
For thou like me art thrown aside, At Godmersham, this
    Christmas Tide;
And now across the Table wide, Each Game save Brag or
    Spec: is tried.'—
'Such is the mild Ejaculation, Of tender hearted
    Speculation.'*—

## My dearest Frank, I wish you Joy

                                        Chawton, July 26—1809

        My dearest Frank, I wish you Joy
        Of Mary's safety with a boy,
        Whose birth has given little pain,
        Compared with that of Mary Jane.*—
        May he a growing Blessing prove,
        And well deserve his Parents Love!
        Endow'd with Art's & Nature's Good,
        Thy name possessing with thy Blood,

In him, in all his ways, may we
Another Francis William see!—
Thy infant days may he inherit,
Thy warmth, nay insolence of spirit;—
We would not with one fault dispense
To weaken the resemblance.
May he revive thy Nursery sin,
Peeping as daringly within,
(His curley Locks but just descried)
With, 'Bet, my be not come to bide.'*
Fearless of danger, braving pain,
And threaten'd very oft in vain,
Still may one Terror daunt his soul
One needful engine of controul
Be found in this sublime array,
A neighbouring Donkey's aweful Bray!—
So may his equal faults as Child
Produce Maturity as mild,
His saucy words & fiery ways
In early Childhood's pettish days,
In Manhood, shew his Father's mind
Like him considerate & kind;
All Gentleness to those around,
And eager only not to wound.
Then like his Father too, he must,
To his own former struggles just,
Feel his Deserts with honest Glow,
And all his Self-improvement know.—
A native fault may thus give birth
To the best blessing, conscious worth.—

      As for ourselves, we're very well,
As unaffected prose will tell.
Cassandra's pen will give our state
The many comforts that await
Our Chawton home*—how much we find
Already in it to our mind,
And how convinced that when complete,
It will all other Houses beat,

That ever have been made or mended,
With rooms concise or rooms distended.

You'll find us very snug next year;
Perhaps with Charles & Fanny* near—
For now it often does delight us
To fancy them just over right us.*

J. A.—

## *In measured verse I'll now rehearse*

### 1

In measured verse* I'll now rehearse
  The charms of lovely Anna:
And, first, her mind is unconfined
  Like any vast savannah.*

### 2

Ontario's lake* may fitly speak
  Her fancy's ample bound:
Its circuit may, on strict survey,
  Five hundred miles be found.

### 3

Her wit descends on foes and friends
  Like famed Niagara's Fall;*
And travellers gaze in wild amaze,
  And listen, one and all.

### 4

Her judgment sound, thick, black, profound,
  Like transatlantic groves,*
Dispenses aid, and friendly shade
  To all that in it roves.

### 5

If thus her mind to be defined
  America exhausts,

And all that's grand in that great land
    In similes it costs—

6

Oh how can I her person try
    To image and portray?
How paint the face, the form how trace
    In which those virtues lay?

7

Another world must be unfurled,
    Another language known,
Ere tongue or sound can publish round
    Her charms of flesh and bone.

## I've a pain in my head

I've a pain in my head
    Said the suffering Beckford,
To her Doctor so dread.
    Oh! what shall I take for't?

Said this Doctor so dread
    Whose name it was Newnham.
For this pain in your head
    Ah! What can you do Ma'am?

Said Miss Beckford, Suppose
    If you think there's no risk,
I take a good Dose
    Of calomel* brisk.—

What a praise-worthy notion.
    Replied Mr Newnham.
You shall have such a potion
    And so will I too Ma'am.—

                                            Feby 1811

## On the Marriage of Mr Gell of East Bourn to Miss Gill.—

Of Eastbourn, Mr Gell
From being perfectly well
Became dreadfully ill
For the Love of Miss Gill.
So he said with some sighs,
I'm the slave of your i.s
Ah! restore if you please
By accepting my e.s.

## I am in a Dilemma

'I am in a Dilemma, for want of an Emma,'
'Escaped from the Lips, Of Henry Gipps.'—

## Between Session & Session

'Between Session & Session'*      'And the Villainous Bill'
'The just Prepossession'*         'May be forced to lie Still'
'May rouse up the Nation,'        'Against Wicked Men's will.'*

## When stretch'd on one's bed

When stretch'd on one's bed
With a fierce-throbbing head
Which precludes alike Thought or Repose,
How little one cares
For the grandest affairs
That may busy the world as it goes!—

How little one feels
For the Waltzes & reels*
Of our dance-loving friends at a Ball!
How slight one's concern
To conjecture or learn
What their flounces or hearts may befall.

How little one minds
If a company dines
On the best that the Season affords!
How short is one's muse
O'er the Sauces & Stews,
Or the Guests, be they Beggars or Lords!—


How little the Bells,
Ring they Peels, toll they Knells,
Can attract our attention or Ears!—
The Bride may be married,
The Corse* may be carried,
And touch nor our hopes nor our fears.


Our own bodily pains
Ev'ry faculty chains;
We can feel on no subject beside.
Tis in health & in Ease
We the Power must seize
For our friends & our Souls to provide.

Oct:r 27. 1811
J.A.


## Camilla, good-humoured, & merry, & small

Camilla, good-humoured, & merry, & small
For a Husband was at her last stake;*
And having in vain danced at many a Ball,
Is now happy to jump at a Wake.


## When Winchester races first took their beginning

When Winchester races* first took their beginning
It is said the good people forgot their old Saint*
Not applying at all for the leave of St. Swithin
And that William of Wykham's* approval was faint.

The races however were fix'd and determin'd
The company met & the weather was charming
The Lords & the Ladies were sattin'd & ermin'd
And nobody saw any future alarming.

But when the old Saint was informed of these doings
He made but one spring from his shrine*** to the roof
Of the Palace which now lies so sadly in ruins*
And thus he address'd them all standing aloof.

Oh, subjects rebellious, Oh Venta* depraved
When once we are buried you think we are dead
But behold me Immortal.—By vice you're enslaved
You have sinn'd & must suffer.—Then further he said

These races & revels & dissolute measures
With which you're debasing a neighbouring Plain*
Let them stand—you shall meet with your curse in your pleasures
Set off for your course, I'll pursue with my rain.

Ye cannot but know my command o'er July.
Henceforward I'll triumph in shewing my powers,
Shift your race as you will it shall never be dry
The curse upon Venta is July in showers.

J. A.

## Charades

1

When my 1<sup>st</sup> is a task to a young girl of spirit
And my second confines her to finish the piece
How hard is her fate! but how great is her merit
If by taking my whole she effect her release!

Jane

2

Divided, I'm a Gentleman
In public Deeds and Powers
United, I'm a Man who oft
That Gentleman devours.

Jane

3

You may lie on my first, by the side of a stream,
And my second compose to the Nymph you adore
But if when you've none of my whole, her esteem
And affection diminish, think of her no more.

Jane

# APPENDIX

## A POEM, PRAYERS, AND SERMON SCRAP

Several of the poems, the charades, and the spoof *Plan of a Novel*, included in this volume and securely identified as by JA, contributed to long-standing traditions of family composition. Home-directed pieces, they grew out of and fed into a domestic circle encouraging one another's performance. Lines between individual and collaborative authorship, blurred elsewhere in the published writings of Romantic-period authors, are often difficult to identify in coterie compositions; nor should we wish to unpick the interwoven strands that make up much of their appeal. By contrast, the three items included in this appendix are all puzzles: a poem written in an unknown hand into the copy of a book once owned by JA; prayers, said to be composed by JA, though not in her hand; and a sermon scrap, copied out by JA but declared firmly to be by her brother James—they represent the challenge of assigning authorship to items rooted in family or coterie writing.

The prayers, said to be by JA, contain nothing that we can associate with the content or manner of her known compositions, while James Austen's sermon scrap shares date and subject material with his sister's published novel, *MP*. The poem, 'Sigh Lady sigh', might be in JA's hand, but there is no certainty of that. Though entered across the paste-down and title page of a book that bears an inked inscription from JA, gifting it to her niece, the verses are not anchored directly to that inscription. Written in pencil, the book having been flipped upside down, they form a separate entry that may or may not be JA's. And even if in her hand, are they her composition? JA liked to make copies of poems by others (lines by Byron and Charlotte Smith are preserved in her hand); in the past, family verses by her uncle James Leigh Perrot and a riddle by Catherine Maria Fanshawe ('Charade by a Lady'), both in JA's hand, have been wrongly attributed to her.[1] One detail is worth considering: three words printed here in italics (in manuscript, they are underlined)—*now, not, thee*—suggest that whoever copied the verses into the volume was applying them to a specific person and occasion. Might Aunt Jane have gifted the volume to her niece at a poignant moment for them both, one she wished to commemorate in verse? Nothing connects 'Sigh Lady sigh' with certainty to JA, though

---

[1] Described in Gilson, 'JA's Verses', 56–60; for the identification of Smith's verses, see Deirdre Le Faye, 'Jane Austen and the "Kalendar of Flora": Verses Identified', *Notes and Queries*, 46/4 (1999), 450–1.

given the quality of her general performance as a poet, Southam's verdict that 'the verse is so abysmal and tritely conventional that it is not possible to attribute these lines to JA' is not sufficient reason to exclude them altogether.[2]

### Sigh Lady sigh

[A poem written in pencil across the pasted flyleaf and half-title page of Ann Murry, *Mentoria; or, A Young Lady's Instructor* (2nd edn, 1780), a sententious, pedagogical work for girls. The lines seem to be original. The book was owned by JA and given to her niece Anna Austen (later Lefroy) in 1801, when she was 8 years old. The date is significant: in May 1801, JA, her sister, and parents left Steventon to live in Bath, Anna's father, James Austen, and his family taking over the rectory. JA's father sold his library at this time[3] and JA passed on to Anna her own childhood books, *Mentoria* and *Elegant Extracts...Selected for the Improvement of Scholars* (no date, but much reprinted from the 1780s). Both volumes are now in the collection of Jane Austen's House, Chawton, Hampshire.]

I

Sigh Lady sigh, hide not the tear thats stealing
Down thy young face *now* so pale & cheerless
Let not thy heart ~~weary with~~ ^Abe blighted^ by the feeling
That presses on thy soul, of utter loneliness.

2

In sighs supprest & grief that's ever(?) weeping
Beats slow & mournfully a Mourning(?) heart
A heart oer which decay & death are creeping
In which no sunshine can a gleam impart.

3

Thou art *not* desolate, tho' left forsaken
By one in whom thy very soul was bound
Let Natures voice thy dreary heart awaken
Oh listen to the melodies around.

4

For Summer her pure golden ^tress^ is flinging
On woods & glades & silent gliding streams

[2] Southam, *Jane Austen: A Students' Guide*, 219; Deirdre Le Faye, 'New Marginalia in Jane Austen's Books', *Book Collector*, 49 (2000), 222–6, sets out a case for JA's possible authorship of the verses.
[3] *Letters*, 77.

With joy the very air around is ringing
Oh rouse thee from those mournful ^melancholy mournful dreams.

5

Go forth let not that voice in vain be calling
Join thy hearts voice to that which fills the air
I̶n̶ ̶h̶i̶ ̶u̶l̶u̶i̶ ̶c̶a̶i̶ ̶i̶i̶ ̶q̶u̶i̶c̶i̶u̶u̶ ̶u̶u̶i̶ ̶a̶ ̶f̶i̶i̶u̶u̶ ̶f̶a̶l̶l̶i̶n̶g̶
Makes *thee* an object of peculiar care.

## Prayers

[No manuscript is known to survive in JA's hand; all three prayers are contained in two four-page fair copies apparently made by Austen family members (possibly JA's brother James and sister Cassandra) soon after JA's death in 1817. The first set of pages contains one prayer only, its fourth page annotated: 'Prayers Composed by my ever dear Sister Jane', beneath which the inscription in pencil 'Charles Austen' (JA's youngest brother). The second set of four pages contains two further prayers with no authorial attribution. Advising Charles Austen's granddaughters on the sale of various items, R. W. Chapman listed the two prayer manuscripts by their opening words (as items 18a and 18b) among 'manuscripts by or relating to Jane Austen...recently...dispersed'.[4] Sold at auction in 1927, they were acquired by William Matson Roth who in 1957 presented them to the F. W. Olin Library, Mills College, Oakland, California, where they remain.

Though Chapman had been careful in 1926 not to claim JA's authorship as certain, he nevertheless printed all three prayers in *Minor Works*, 453–7, not from manuscript but from the reformatted presentation version *Three Evening Prayers, written by Jane Austen, now published for the first time*, with an introduction by William Matson Roth (San Francisco: The Colt Press, 1940), issued in a limited edition of 300 copies, inserted at the end of which is a folding facsimile of part of the manuscript of Prayer 3, assumed at that date to be 'partly in JA's hand' (*Minor Works*, 453). *Catharine and Other Writings*, 247–50 and textual notes at 283–4, endorses Chapman's editorial decision and reproduces the prayers as by JA.

A careful examination of the manuscripts and the evidence for and against attribution to JA is offered in *Later Manuscripts*, pp. cxviii–cxxvi, the editors concluding: 'In terms of attribution, these are the works that most trouble us...there is nothing in their content (either in terms of Jane Austen's own writings, or the habits of the Austens and their immediate contemporaries in the exercise of their religious duty) to suggest her authorship; if it had not been for the scribbled annotation probably by her brother Charles...we would not be considering any of these prayers as even

[4] 'A Jane Austen Collection', *Times Literary Supplement*, 14 January 1926, 27.

possibly by Jane Austen' (*Later Manuscripts*, p. cxxv). Without supporting evidence of composition, they place all three prayers, transcribed from the manuscripts, in an appendix (*Later Manuscripts*, 573–6). Despite long association with JA, the attribution has only recently been tested. There now seems sufficient reason to doubt that the prayers are certainly her work: no corroborating evidence suggests why or when JA might have composed prayers.[5]]

I

*Evening Prayer*

Give us Grace Almighty Father, so to pray, as to deserve to be heard, to address thee with our Hearts, as with our Lips.* Thou art every where present, from Thee no secret can be hid.* May the knowledge of this, teach us to fix our Thoughts on Thee, with Reverence & Devotion that we pray not in vain.

Look with Mercy on the Sins we have this day committed, & in Mercy make us feel them deeply, that our Repentance may be sincere, and our Resolutions stedfast of endeavouring against the commission of such in future.—Teach us to understand the sinfulness of our own Hearts, and bring to our knowledge every fault of Temper and every evil Habit in which we have indulged to the dis-comfort of our fellow-creatures, and the danger of our own Souls.—May we now, and on each return of night, consider how the past day has been spent by us, what have been our prevailing Thoughts, words and Actions during it, and how far we can acquit ourselves of Evil. Have we thought irreverently of Thee, have we dis-obeyed thy Commandments, have we neglected any known Duty, or willingly given pain to any human Being? Incline us to ask our Hearts these questions Oh! God, and save us from deceiving ourselves by Pride or Vanity.

Give us a thankful sense of the Blessings in which we live, of the many comforts of our Lot; that we may not deserve to lose them by Discontent or Indifference.

Be Gracious to our Necessities, and guard us, and all we love, from Evil this night.* May the sick and afflicted, be now, & ever thy care; and heartily do we pray for the safety of all that travel by Land or by Sea, for the comfort & protection of the Orphan & Widow, & that thy pity may be shewn, upon all Captives & Prisoners.*

Above all other blessings Oh! God, for ourselves, & our fellow-creatures, we implore Thee to quicken our sense of thy Mercy in the redemption of the World, of the Value of that Holy Religion in which we have been brought up, that we may not, by our own neglect, throw away the Salvation

---

[5]  Southam, *A Students' Guide*, 83–7, speculates on why JA might have written prayers.

Thou hast given us, nor be Christians only in name.—Hear us Almighty
God, for His sake who has redeemed us, & taught us thus to pray.—
Our Father which art in Heaven &c.*

2

Almighty God! Look down with Mercy on thy Servants here assembled &
accept the petitions now offer'd up unto thee.

Pardon Oh God! The offences of the past day. We are conscious of
many frailties; we remember with shame & contrition, many evil
Thoughts & neglected duties, & we have perhaps sinned against Thee &
against our fellow-creatures in many instances of which we have no
remembrance. Pardon Oh God! whatever thou hast seen amiss in us, &
give us a stronger desire of resisting every evil inclination & weakening
every habit of sin. Thou knowest the infirmity of our Nature, & the
temptations which surround us. Be thou merciful, Oh Heavenly Father!
to Creatures so formed & situated.

We bless thee for every comfort of our past and present existence, for
our health of Body & Mind & for every other source of happiness which
Thou hast bountifully bestowed on us & with which we close this day,
imploring their continuance from Thy Fatherly Goodness, with a more
grateful sense of them, than they have hitherto excited. May the comforts
of every day, be thankfully felt by us, may they prompt a willing obedience
of thy commandments & a benevolent spirit towards every fellow-creature.

Have mercy Oh gracious Father! upon all that are now suffering from
whatsoever cause, that are in any circumstance of danger or distress.—Give
them patience under every affliction,* strengthen, comfort and relieve
them.

To Thy Goodness we commend ourselves this night beseeching thy
protection of us through its darkness & dangers. We are helpless &
dependant; Graciously preserve us.—For all whom we love & value, for
every Friend & Connection, we equally pray; However divided & far
asunder, we know that we are alike before Thee, & under thine Eye. May we
be equally united in Thy Faith & Fear, in fervent devotion towards Thee, &
in Thy merciful Protection this night. Pardon Oh Lord! the imperfections
of these our Prayers, & accept them through the mediation of our Blessed
Saviour, in whose Holy Words, we farther address thee; our Father

3

Father of Heaven! whose goodness has brought us in safety to the close of
this day,* dispose our Hearts in fervent prayer.

Another day is now gone, & added to those, for which we were before
accountable. Teach us Almighty Father, to consider this solemn Truth, as

we should do, that we may feel the importance of every day, & every hour as it passes, & earnestly strive to make a better use of what Thy Goodness may yet bestow on us, than we have done of the Time past.

Give us Grace to endeavour after a truly christian Spirit to seek to attain that temper of Forbearance & Patience, of which our Blessed Saviour has set us the highest Example, and which, while it prepares us for the spiritual Happiness of the Life to come, will secure to us the best enjoyment of what this World can give. Incline us Oh God! to think humbly of ourselves, to be severe only in the examination of our own conduct, to consider our fellow-creatures with kindness, & to judge of all they say & do with that Charity which we would desire from men ourselves.

We thank thee with all our hearts for every gracious dispensation, for all the Blessings that have attended our Lives, for every hour of safety, health & peace, of domestic comfort & innocent enjoyment. We feel that we have been blessed far beyond any thing that we have deserved; and though we cannot but pray for a continuance of all these Mercies, we acknowledge our unworthiness of them & implore Thee to pardon the presumption of our desires.

Keep us Oh! Heavenly Father from Evil this night.*—Bring us in safety to the beginning of another day & grant that we may rise again with every serious & religious feeling which now directs us.

May thy mercy be extended over all Mankind, bringing the Ignorant to the knowledge of thy Truth,* awakening the Impenitent, touching the Hardened. Look with compassion upon the afflicted of every condition, assuage the pangs of disease, comfort the broken in spirit.

More particularly do we pray for the safety and welfare of our own family & friends wheresoever dispersed, beseeching Thee to avert from them all material & lasting Evil of Body or Mind; & may we by the assistance of thy Holy Spirit so conduct ourselves on Earth as to secure an Eternity of Happiness with each other in thy Heavenly Kingdom. Grant this most merciful Father, for the sake of our Blessed Saviour in whose Holy Name & Words we further address Thee.

Our Father &c.


## Sermon Scrap

[According to family tradition, this scrap is part of a sermon by James Austen, a clergyman and JA's eldest brother. Previously pasted into a copy of *Memoir* (1870), it came into the collection at Jane Austen's House, Chawton, by purchase in 2013.

The scrap and Austen-Leigh's accompanying letter to an early fan, tell us how famous his aunt had become by 1870. They remind us, too, of JA's religious convictions and environment. Her father, her brother James, and his son, the biographer Austen-Leigh, were all Anglican clergyman. In the attached letter, Austen-Leigh points out that the scrap, copied out in his aunt's hand, is from one of his father's sermons, and he dates it to 1814. He also explains why he is sending it to a fan: as a genuine 'specimen' of JA's handwriting. To that end, he adds a certificate of authentication: 'This is the handwriting, not the composition, of my Aunt Jane Austen, Authoress of Pride & Prejudice' and he signs it 'J. Edwd Austen Leigh'.

The scrap echoes a discussion in *MP*, ch. 34, on the 'art of reading' and its importance to the modern clergyman. *MP*, an intensely serious novel in which religion serves a public/political interest, was published in May 1814. The scrap demonstrates the cross-fertilization between JA's creative writing and the wider life of her family, raising the possibility that her novel inspired James's sermon. Certainly, topics of such high seriousness were under discussion among the Austens in 1814, as witnessed by JA's letter of 2 September, where she writes to Martha Lloyd that 'I place my hope of better things on a claim to the protection of Heaven, as a Religious Nation, a Nation inspite of much Evil improving in Religion'.]

Men may get into a habit of repeating the words of our Prayers by rote, perhaps without thoroughly understanding,—certainly without thoroughly feeling their full force & meaning.

# ABBREVIATIONS

| | |
|---|---|
| JA | Jane Austen |
| E | *Emma* |
| LS | *Lady Susan* |
| MP | *Mansfield Park* |
| NA | *Northanger Abbey* |
| P | *Persuasion* |
| P&P | *Pride and Prejudice* |
| S | *Sanditon* |
| S&S | *Sense and Sensibility* |
| W | *The Watsons* |

| | |
|---|---|
| *Catharine and Other Writings* | Jane Austen, *Catharine and Other Writings*, ed. Margaret Anne Doody and Douglas Murray (Oxford World's Classics; Oxford: Oxford University Press, 1993; repr. 2009) |
| *Chronology* | Deirdre Le Faye, *A Chronology of Jane Austen and Her Family* (Cambridge: Cambridge University Press, 2006) |
| *Collected Poems* | Jane Austen, *Collected Poems and Verse of the Austen Family*, ed. David Selwyn (Manchester: Carcanet Press, 1996) |
| *Family Record* | Deirdre le Faye, *Jane Austen: A Family Record* (2nd edn, Cambridge: Cambridge University Press, 2004) |
| Gilson, 'JA's Verses' | David Gilson, 'Jane Austen's Verses', in *Collected Articles and Introductions* (privately printed, 1998), 42–60; a revised version of two articles appearing in the *Book Collector*, 33 (1984), 23–7; and 34 (1985), 384–5 |
| *Later Manuscripts* | *Later Manuscripts*, ed. Janet Todd and Linda Bree, *The Cambridge Edition of the Works of Jane Austen* (Cambridge: Cambridge University Press, 2008) |
| *Letters* | *Jane Austen's Letters*, ed. Deirdre Le Faye (4th edn, Oxford: Oxford University Press, 2011) |
| *Letters*, ed. Brabourne | *Letters of Jane Austen*, ed. Edward, Lord Brabourne, 2 vols (London: Richard Bentley & Son, 1884) |

| | |
|---|---|
| *Life & Letters* | William Austen-Leigh and Richard Arthur Austen-Leigh, *Jane Austen, Her Life and Letters: A Family Record* (London: Smith, Elder, & Co., 1913) |
| *Memoir* (1870) | James Edward Austen-Leigh, *A Memoir of Jane Austen* (London: Richard Bentley, 1870) |
| *Memoir*, ed. Sutherland | *A Memoir of Jane Austen and Other Family Recollections*, ed. Kathryn Sutherland (Oxford World's Classics; Oxford: Oxford University Press, 2002) |
| *Minor Works* | Jane Austen, *Minor Works*, vol. vi of *The Works of Jane Austen*, ed. R. W. Chapman (1954); rev. B. C. Southam (Oxford: Oxford University Press, 1969) |
| *OED* | *The Oxford English Dictionary* (2nd edn), 20 vols (Oxford: Oxford University Press, 1989), along with revisions in the online edition up to 2019 |
| *Teenage Writings* | Jane Austen, *Teenage Writings*, ed. Kathryn Sutherland and Freya Johnston (Oxford World's Classics; Oxford: Oxford University Press, 2017) |

# TEXTUAL NOTES

In correcting and revising her text, Jane Austen worked in much the same way as anyone writing by hand, that is ... she deleted words by striking through and by erasure (scrubbing out); she wrote alongside, above, and across old material, and, on occasion, she refashioned one word into another without the added clarity of either deletion or erasure; she inserted new text between the lines of old and, where corrections or revisions occurred immediately to her during the process of first writing down, new text emerged directly out of revised material. For extensive reworking, of the kind found in *The Watsons*, Austen shaped patches of paper, cut carefully to size, pinning them in place to hide and substitute for a heavily deleted section or to provide a substantial expansion of text already written.

Those wishing to examine Austen's manuscript revisions in more detail than can be offered here should consult either the digital or print editions *Jane Austen's Fictional Manuscripts*, ed. Kathryn Sutherland (2010 <http://www.janeausten.ac.uk>), 5 vols (Oxford: Oxford University Press, 2018)

To capture the range of textual change within the manuscripts, different symbols, brackets, and type styles are used, as shown in the following examples, where all forms of strikethrough and erasure are represented by a single strikeout line:

25.5    He has ^been^ teizing me

[*addition made above or between the lines of text*]

71.13-14  ^& encreased her sense of the awkwardness^ of  [*addition made below the lines of text*]

74.35   but the first, ~~tuning~~ Scrape of one violin        [*running deletion*]

89.6-7  Emma had ~~taken no~~ ^not caught^ cold at the Ball

[*deletion and substitution above or between the lines of text of one or more whole words*]

98.39   a family ~~party~~ ^~~circle~~^ ^party^

[*deletion and multiple substitutions above the line of text, before choice is settled*]

89.18   I wonder every Lady does not ^.^ ~~ride.~~

[*full stop added as an inline insertion following the deletion of '~~ride.~~'*]

10.32   C^ath^ Vernon        [*inline insertion of part of a word*]

126.38-9  a sweet^ly^ modest~~y~~ . . . Graceful~~ness of~~ Address

['*ly*' *added as an inline insertion accompanied by partial word deletions*]

113.32    as far [as] the future    [*square brackets to indicate missing material editorially supplied*]

4.4      ~~Harriet~~ > Alicia      [*one word erased and overwritten by another*]

21.30    ~~conduct~~ (?) > regard      [*uncertain word erased and overwritten*]

99.25    She & I are ~~gre~~<at> sworn friends

      [*'gre' erased and replaced by 'sworn'; angled brackets around 'at' indicate a conjectural completion of the first version, supplied editorially*]

100.16    a Man who>se ~~meant~~ heart ~~was~~ > had

      [*running deletions and partial refashioning as the sentence develops: 'who meant' > 'whose heart was' > 'whose heart had'*]

*All editorial comments within the Textual Notes appear in italics.*


## LADY SUSAN

4.4      ~~Harriet~~ > Alicia

4.37    ~~his~~ > her Marriage

7.20    that I ^may form

7.26    equally ~~heavy~~ ^dull & proud

10.21   was ~~not~~ ^far from unexceptionable

10.24   ~~what~~ > that

10.32   C^ath^ Vernon

11.14   <…> > my

12.3     into ^a marriage

13.7     ~~this~~ ^a degree

13.18   as low ^as of any Woman

13.24   so ~~pleasing~~ ^attractive

14.13   I > &

18.18   it ^is out of my power

21.30   ~~conduct~~ (?) > regard

25.5     He has ^been teizing me

25.26   as soon [as] we

26.32   ~~who~~ > that

29.30   wit of ^the Conversation

33.19   for I can not ^bear him.

35.16   He then told ^me, mixing in his speech

39.38  only ~~to~~ ^of Good to

40.7-8  moment ^?'^ ~~in your own room?²~~ We went ~~thither directly.~~ ^into my room.

40.30  occurred [to] me

41.21  I would wish to to forget    *repetition of 'to', in error, across the page division in the manuscript, the second instance is omitted in this edition.*

43.1  sensibly ^Ann me

43.9  now be ~~at peace.~~ ^easy.

44.15  ~~To~~ ^It would have been

44.30  the feelings ^of either to remain

46.3  ~~Weakness~~ ^ Flexibility of Mind

49.22  he bears ^pain with such patience

50.33  the present ^posture state of our affairs

52.2  whose ~~feelings~~ ^Sensibilities are not

56.17  formed (?) > founded

## THE WATSONS

65.1  assembly of the Town > assembly in the Town    *undeleted 'of' replaced by 'in'*

65.1  ~~L—~~ > D    *JA appears to have named the town 'L—', subsequently deleting 'L', and reinserting 'L', before finally altering the second 'L' to 'D'. (See Explanatory Notes, pp. 254–5.)*

65.1  Sussex > Surry

65.2  & ~~was~~ ^it was

65.10  to ^dress dine & sleep

65.10-14  On the present occasion, ~~one only of the Family f in Stanton Parsonage could profit by~~ ^as only two of Mr W's children were at home, & one was always necessary ~~to him~~ as companion to himself, for he was sickly & had lost his wife one only could profit by

65.14-20  Miss Emma Watson ~~was to make her first public appearance in the Neighbourhood; & Miss Watson drove her & all her finery in the old Chair to D. on the important morning of the Ball; without being able to stay & share the pleasure herself, because her Father who was an Invalid could not be left to spend the Eveng alone~~ ^who was very recently returned to her family from the care of an Aunt who had brought her up was to make her first public appearance in the neighbourhood—~~& her eldest Sister who had kindly undertaken~~ her eldest Sister, whose delight in a Ball was not lessened by a ten years Enjoyment, had some merit in chearfully undertaking to drive her & all her finery in the old Chair to D. on the important morng.—

65.22-3 I dare say ~~you~~ ^it^ will ~~have~~ ^be^ a very good Ball

65.23-4 you will ~~not~~ ^hardly^ want partners

65.24-5 ~~but~~ ^and^ I would ~~recommend~~ ^advise^

65.27 wish for, > ; ~~& hav~~ if he does

65.31 ~~Charles~~ ^Tom^ Musgrave

65.33 ~~any~~ ^every^ new girl

66.8-9 he is always ~~philandering with~~ ^behaving in a particular way to^ one or ^an^other

66.15-20 I was very much attached to a young Man—~~a neighbour~~^of the name^ of Purvis a particular freind of Robert's, who used to be with us a great deal. ~~& he to me. Perhaps you may see him tonight. His name is Purvis & he has the Living of Alford—about 14 miles off.—We were very much attached to each other~~ ^Every body thought it would have been a Match.' A sigh accompanied^ these words, which Emma ~~would have~~ respected ^in silence—^ ~~too much to urge~~ ^continue^ ~~the subject; farther;~~ but her Sister ~~had pleasure in the communication~~ ^after a short pause, went on—^

66.24-5 with a veiw of ~~getting~~ ^gaining^ him herself

66.25-6 & ^soon after^ marrying somebody else

66.33-5 ~~She wd. Not deny it herself, she makes no secret of wishing to marry~~ ^There is nothing she wd. not do to be>get married— she would as good^ as tell you so herself

66.38-9 ~~I wish she were well married with all my heart; when once she is, she will be a very worthy character—but till then,~~ ^I wish with all my heart she was well married. I declare I had rather have her well married than myself.'—^

67.6-7 ~~Penelope is now~~ ^I have lost^ Purvis, ^it is true^

67.12-13 he ~~meant nothing~~ ^never means anything^

67.14 he began to ~~take notice of~~ ^slight her for^ Margaret

67.16 some match at ~~Southampton~~ ^Chichester^

67.18 she has ~~had a monstrous~~ ^taken a vast^ deal of trouble ^about him^

67.19 When she went away ^the other day,^

67.20 the last time ^.^ ~~of trial.~~

67.21-2 her ^particular^ Business was at ~~Southampton~~ ^Chichester^ ~~you did not suspect~~ ^nor what cou<ld>> guess at the^ object ~~that could~~ ^but t<hat>> that could^ take her away, ~~from home~~ ^from Stanton^

67.23-4 I ~~should never have~~ ^had not the^ smallest suspicion

67.26 ~~I wished to~~ ^to be able to^ make a > an ^immediate^ friend of each

67.27 ~~Gout~~ ^Asthma^

68.12 I must ~~endeavour to~~ correct them

68.16 ^especially in company

68.17-18 ~~has a good deal of spirit~~ ^is a little fretful & perverse

68.18 Poor ~~Margaret~~ ^Creature!–she is possessed

68.19 ^more seriously in love

68.21 the second time ^within this twelvemonth

68.24 to Croydon ^now

68.28 You are afraid of him, ~~& well you may.~~ ^I do not wonder at you.

68.35 Mr Tom Musgrave ^& I find each other

68.39 till late. > ; ^& If

69.1 in the ~~Tea room~~ ^Passage

69.7 ~~was silenced~~ ^made no answer–

69.14-15 I ~~shall~~ ^shd. most readily . . . & should ^not be at all afraid

69.15 quiet old Creature ^home.

69.19-20 ~~What a sweet temper~~-y > You must have!>a ^sweet temper indeed!

69.20 any thing ~~so kind!~~ ^like it

69.22 ~~I shall never forget the kindness of the proposal.   But~~ I am not so selfish as ~~to accept it.~~ ^that comes to.

69.30-1 I will remember ~~their names~~ ^her partners if I can

69.31 but ~~do you wish me particularly to observe them~~ ^know they will be all strangers to me.'

69.32 Capt. ~~Carr~~ ^Hunter

69.32-3 I ~~am rather afraid of~~ ^have my fears in that quarter

69.34 ~~all the worse for~~ ^it is all over with poor Sam

69.36 Did ^not you know

69.37 in ~~Devonshire~~ ^Shropshire

69.38 passing ~~in Sussex?~~ ^of that nature in Surry?

69.38 of ~~so delicate a nature~~ ^such delicacy

70.1 scanty ~~Correspondence~~ ^communication which passed between ~~us for a dozen~~ ^you & me for the last 14 years

70.8 ~~Dorking~~ ^Guilford

70.18 & ~~four~~ ^six thousand pounds

70.23 foolis>shly

70.25 ^& the ~~Town Hall~~ ^White Hart is close by

70.30 trotted ~~stupidly~~ ^heavily

70.34 the best in the ~~town, if~~ ^place, if Mr Tomlinson

70.35-6  his ~~new House~~ ^newly erected one House at the end of the Town ^with a shrubbery & sweep in the Country, ~~which however was not often granted.~~

70.36-9  Mr E's House ~~was of a dull brick colour, & an high Elevation — a flight of stone steps to the Door, & two windows~~ ~~flight of stone steps with white posts, & a chain, divided~~ ^was higher than most of its neighbours with ~~two~~ windows on each side the door, ~~& five~~ the windows guarded by ~~a chain & green~~ posts & chain the door approached by a flight of stone steps.

71.4  Is not it a ~~prett~~ ^nice Town?

71.5  in stile. ~~I assure you.~~

71.5  in Livery & ^with a powder'd head

71.10  in the ~~idea~~ ^thought of all that was ~~fo~~ ^to precede them

71.10-15  Her conversation with Eliz. ^too ~~had given~~ > ing her ~~many~~ ^some very unpleasi-<ing>> ant feelings, ^with respect to her own family; ~~to add to the awkwardness of so slight an acquaintance to the consciousness of~~ ^& > had made her more open to ~~any other~~ disagreable im: pressions, ^ from any other cause, & in particular to the ~~awkwardness~~ ^& encreased her sense of the awkwardness of ^rushing into Intimacy on so slight an acquaintance ^.^ ~~seemed a serious Evil.~~

71.16  immediate ~~dissipation~~ ^change to these Ideas

71.16-18  the Mother ~~was~~ ^tho' a very friendly woman, ~~but of rather formal aspect, &~~ ^had a reserved air, & a great deal of formal Civility

71.18-19  the daughter, ~~the~~ ^a genteel looking girl, ^of 22 with her hair in papers, seemed ~~as was~~ ^very naturally

71.20  ~~She~~ ^Emma was soon

71.25  much easier, ^& more communicative air

71.26  he ~~entered~~ ^came ready

71.31  ~~at 8~~ ^by 9

71.32  credit to ~~the Ball~~ ^our Assemblies

71.34  It is ~~not very reasonable,~~ ^more than they deserve

71.36  g > Great People ~~must always be the vogue,~~ ^have always their charm.' & ~~Little ones love to be infatuated by~~ ^are very fond of looking at them.

72.5  Emma found in Miss E.— ~~the appearance of~~ ^the shew of good sense

72.7-8  was sitting ~~safely~~ ^respectably

72.12  to approve ^of every modern extravagance

72.17  Miss Edwardes ~~obs~~<erved> ^ gently asked

72.23-4  but ~~to compare a young Lady to a Man whose~~ ^his complexion ~~is pretty~~ ^has been rather too much exposed to all weathers

72.25-6 She ~~did~~ ^had not ~~think~~ ^thought a strong ~~degree of~~ Likeness at all incompatible

72.29-30 since he was ~~ten~~ ^7 years old— ~~& if you do not tell me that he is plain therefore~~ ^but let him be ever so plain, I have you know, I have no right to refuse ~~being like him~~

72.32 ~~his~~ ^yr brother's eyes

72.3~~ 3~~ ~~ of every feature is different. The~~ ~~ ~~ ~~ ~~ ~~ ~~ ~~

72.3⁸-73.1 ~~it is very strong~~ — ^a strong one ˃ very strongly— but ~~for the life of me I cannot any of the others that you fancy: No, I am sure there is no likeness between her, &~~ ^I am not sensible of any ˃ the others. ~~I cannot see any other—~~ I do not much think she is like any of the Family **but** Miss Watson

73.3 The ˃ This matter

73.5 he ~~poured~~ helped her to wine

73.5-6 ~~set in for their~~ ^drawn round the fire to enjoy their Desert

73.6 drink ^to his better health

73.9 better than he ~~is;~~ ^does;—& ^very few people that play a ~~better~~ fairer rubber

73.10 ^Now ˃ For now We have a quiet little Whist club

73.12 ~~I think he~~ ^how much he wd. enjoy it ^.'^ ~~very much.~~

73.20-2 retorted the Lady ~~gravely~~ ^calmly. ^The Osbornes are to be no rule for us. You had ^better meet every night, & break up ~~your party at ten, than~~ ^two hours sooner.'

73.23 were ^so wise ~~enough~~ ^as never to pass

73.23-4 Mr Edwards ^now turned to something else.—the ˃ He had lived ~~long sufficiently~~ long ^enough

73.25 & ~~he had~~ ^having some curiosity

73.26-7 the ~~marriage of that Aunt with whom~~ ^the Circumstances of his young Guest ~~had been used to reside,~~ than had yet reached him, he ~~observed to her~~ ^began with

73.28-9 your Aunt ^very well about 30 years ago; ~~one of the~~ ^I am pretty sure I danced with her ~~at Wiltshire's~~ ^in the old rooms at Bath

73.34-5 ~~Mr 'Her name was Turner— I forget what it is now~~ ^ 'Mr Turner had not been dead a great while I think? 'About 2 years Sir.' 'I forget what her name is now?'

74.3 repeated Mrs E, ~~drawing up~~

74.6 said Mrs E. ^gravely, with a quick glance

74.7-8 Emma ^had just recovered . . . ~~just~~ in time

74.8 & ~~to~~ ^in remember˃ ing

74.11 a second ~~match~~ ^choice

74.12-14  ~~The Caution~~ ^Carefulness—Discretion— should not be confined . . . or to a second ~~connection~~ ^marriage choice . . . to young Ladies in their first ^.^ ~~choice.~~

74.15  Rather more so, my dear ^replied he _

74.26  they were ~~to~~ go >ing to sit up late

74.27  ~~to~~ almost to the ~~desirable~~ ^wished for moment

74.29  Mrs Edwards ^to order~~ing~~ hers

74.30  the quiet ~~&~~ warmth of a snug parlour

74.32-3  guarding her own dress, ~~& watching over the~~ ^while she attended with yet greater Solicitude

74.35  but the first, ~~tuning~~ Scrape of one violin

74.37-8  many people ^yet come ^yet, was ~~only~~ told, ^as she knew she should by the Waiter ^as she knew she should, that

74.39  brilliant ^in Candle-lights before them ~~with Candles~~

75.1  a young Man in ^a morning dress & Boots

75.2  ~~seemingly~~ ^apparently on purpose

75.4  easy ~~familiarity~~ air

75.5-7  ~~We shall have an a famous Ball.—~~ ^The Candles are but this moment lit—^^ ~~& I am waiting~~ ~~The Osbornes are certainly coming, I can answer for~~ ^assure you of ~~that; I was with Ld Osborne this morng.~~ —^ 'I like to get a good seat by the fire you know, Mr Musgrave.' replied Mrs E.

75.11-14  along the clean ba<ll>>floor of the Ball-room, ~~where~~ ^to the fire place at the upper end, where one party only . . . ~~& a~~ ^while three or four Officers ^were lounging ~~about, &~~ ^together, passing in & out ^backwards & forwards from the adjoining card-room.

75.16  all du~~lly~~ > duely ~~seated~~ ^placed

75.16-17  in the ~~quiet~~ ^low whisper . . . ~~said~~ ^observed said

75.18  Mr Musgrave, ~~was it?~~— ^then.

75.24-6  The cold & empty ~~air~~ ^appearance of the Room ~~&~~ ^the ~~solemn~~ demure air ~~began soon to~~ of the small cluster of Females ^at one end of it, began ~~now~~ ^soon to give ~~away~~

75.28-31  smartly-dressed ^giggling girls . . . a fresh, ~~straggling Man,~~ ^gentleman straggler who if not enough in Love ~~with any fair She,~~ ^creature to station himself near ~~her,~~ ^any fair Creature seemed glad to escape into the Card-room.

75.34  but watch ~~him~~ > her at such a moment

75.35  looking ~~rather shy than~~ ^rather distressed, but ~~but not~~ > by no means displeased

75.37 think ~~ill of~~ ^poorly her Brothers ~~chances.~~ ^Sam's a hopeless___case.___

76.1 whispered from one ^party to another

76.2-4 the signal been given ~~for beginning~~ . . . ~~& the young to put all the young people in motion,~~ ^which seemed to call the young Men to their duty, & people [to] the centre of the room, than she found herself engaged   *the sense is a little incompleted and after correction, regarding the additional 'to' which I have supplied*

76.6 of the middle>ing height

76.7-10 smooth and ~~brightened with a fine colour~~ ^glowing—; & she had which with ^a lively Eye, a sweet smile, & an open Countenance, ~~she had~~ ^gave beauty to attract, & expression to ~~engage~~ make ~~it seem greater~~ ^that beauty improve on acquaintance

76.11 the ~~Ball~~ ^Eveng began very pleasantly

76.13 were ~~nearly~~ ^not quite

76.23 Mrs Blake, ~~his~~ ^a widow-sister

76.24 Mr Tom Musgrave; who ~~had~~ probably ^imprisoned within his own room, had been listening

76.29 Ly Osborne observe that they ~~were come~~ ^had made a point of coming

76.31 but ~~her eyes~~ ^cheifly & with most interest

76.33-5 Ly Osborne ~~was the~~ ^had by much the finest person . . . & had ~~quite~~ ^all the ~~air of a woman~~ ^Dignity of Rank.

76.36 an air of, ^Coldness, of Carelessness

76.38-9 expedient ^for him to please the ~~Town~~ ^Borough

76.39 & ^he never danced

77.1-2 a^n^ ~~very~~ agreable-looking Man, ^a little more than Thirty

77.7 will not ~~wonder~~ ^be surprised at

77.9 standing near ^her,

77.14-15 a party of young Men were standing ^engaged in very ~~fluent~~ ^lively consultation—& ~~after a short time~~ ^soon afterwards

77.18 engagement, ~~to you,~~

77.21 ^she turned again to Miss Carr

77.22 to ~~the top of the room.~~ ^begin the Set.

77.23 had ^in it's happiness been interesting ~~in it's happiness~~ to Emma

77.24 ~~in~~ ^under this sudden reverse

77.26 her own ~~angry feelings~~ ^mortification

77.27 Miss Osborne's second~~ary~~ promise

77.32  said she, ^holding out her hand^ with the most unaffected good humour

77.33-6  The Boy ~~was again all made of~~ ^in one moment restored to^ all his first delight— ~~wanted no farther solicitation~~ ^looked joyfully at his Mother^; ~~& with a Thank you, as honest as his Smiles, held out his hand in a hurry to~~ ^ ~~but~~ > and ~~instantly~~ stepping forward with an honest & simple 'Thank you Maam' was instantly ready^ to attend his new acquaintance.

77.36  The ~~gratitude~~ ^Thankfulness^ of Mrs Blake

77.37-8  with a ~~truly gratified look~~ ^look, most expressive^ of ~~Astonishment~~ unexpected pleasure, ~~she of~~<fered> ^&^ lively ~~Thankfulness~~ ^Gratitude^, she turned to

77.39  ~~for~~ ^of^ so great

78.1  with ~~great~~ perfect truth ~~assured Mrs B.~~ ^could assure her^ that

78.4  with ^nearly^ equal complacency

78.9  to which ^the happy^ Charles answered

78.10-13  Miss Carr, gave her, ~~she perceived,~~ many ^inquisitive^ glances; & ^after a time^ Ld Osborne himself came & ~~spoke to her partner for the sake of looking at her.~~ ^under pretence of talking to Charles, stood ^to looking at ~~her~~ > his partner.^

78.13  such ~~observance~~ > observation

78.15-16  the latter of whom was ~~continually taking every~~ ^continually making^ opportunit~~y~~ > opportunities of ~~more than civilly, of warmly~~ addressing her with the warmest civility.

78.20  they ^& their Mama^ all lived

78.22-3  ^&^ that he had been out once ^already^ with Ld Osborne's Hounds

78.26  to have them both ~~within a yard of her~~ ^ ~~veiw~~; ^close to her^

78.28  to gain ~~the~~ ^her^ proper station

78.28  It was ^always^ the pleasure of the company ~~always~~

78.29-31  adjourned for ~~what nine out of ten had no inclination~~ ^refreshment;^—The Tea room was a small room within the Card room, & in passing thro' the ~~Card room where~~ latter, where the passage was straightened

78.32-7  for a few moments ~~unable to proceed. Emma saw herself~~ ^hemmed in. It happened^ close by Lady Osborne's Cassino Table; ~~& saw at the same time~~ ^Mr Howard who belonged to it^ Spoke to his Nephew; & Emma on perceiving ~~that both Lady & Gentleman were~~ ^herself the object of attention to both to Ly O. & him,^ had just turned away her eyes in time, ~~when she heard~~ ^to avoid seeming to hear^ her young ~~partner~~ ^companion^ delightedly whisper ~~in a very audible voice~~ ^aloud^ to his Uncle ^Mr H.^ —

78.38-9  As ^To her great relief^ They were immediately in motion again ^however^ & Charles ~~left his Uncle~~ ^was hurried off from^

79.2   were ~~set out~~ ^prepared

79.2-4  was to be seen ~~seated~~ ^quite alone at the end of one, ~~away from every-body else, as if to enjoy his own Thoughts.~~ ^as if retreating as far as he could from the Ball, to enjoy his own thoughts *revision leading into new primary text—she is developing and revising together*

Т'9 ¶   'Thow'n I ood Ooboumt   hi wiiul   ,

79.6   ^But to this ~~Emma could not quite agree to this, & Charles at any rate very happy,~~ ^easily over-ruled— ~~was contented to sit where she chose;~~ ^ 'No, no, ^said Emma laughing^ you must sit with my ~~party~~ friends.' ~~& she~~ ^& when she soon afterwards saw ~~Ld Osborne so soon afterwards driven away by the approach of others that~~ ^a party, she did not ~~she cd not imagine~~ ^fail to remark— that^ to his how very unwelcome^ they should probably have ~~the Companionableness of either Charles or herself would have given his Ldship much~~ ^been very little welcome themselves been at all to his taste.

79.8   ~~almost~~ 'Eleven.'

79.11-12  tho' ~~Emma~~ ^she felt that she had ~~nothing to guide her beleif, but~~ ^no better reason to give than that Miss Osborne's having broken ^had not kept it before.   *'s of Osborne's, left in error after revision; editorially omitted from the text*

79.18   from ~~the~~ Tea ~~Tables,~~ there ~~were~~ > was

79.19-21  ~~& it was~~ ^which happened to be increased by ~~some~~ ^one or two of the card partics having ^just broken up & ~~their members~~ ^the players being disposed to ~~come~~ ^move exactly the different way.

79.22 3  no sooner had ~~they met, than~~ ^were they within reach of Emma

79.24-5  ^my dear Miss Watson, brings all his family upon ~~me~~ > you

79.29   impelled ~~different ways.~~ ^in opposite directions.

79.31   which ~~she liked greatly approved~~ ^suited her—

79.31-5  the value of her Engagement ~~rose~~ ^increased, when as she was sitting ^in the Card room somewhat screened . . . lounging ~~with Tom Musgrave~~ . . . ~~say~~ call ^Tom Musgrave towards him & say, '~~Musgrave, when~~ ^Why do not you dance with ^that beautiful Emma Watson?

79.36   with ~~that girl~~ ^her

79.36-8  ~~She is a beautiful Creature.'~~ 'I was ~~thinking of being~~ ^determining on it this very moment ~~to be introduced, to her~~ my Lord; ~~& t<o>~~ ^I'll be introduced & dance with her directly.'

79.39   much Talking ^to,

80.2   shall find ^her in the Tea room.

80.4-5  hurrying from her corner, ~~into the~~ ^directly exactly the other way

80.13  ~~in~~ > by the coldness

80.19-20  led him to ~~suppose~~ ^beleive her not overpowered ~~by~~ ^with

80.23  Mrs E.; ~~who~~ ^She

80.26  The Gentleman ~~quite~~ ^a little disconcerted

80.29-30  as Emma ~~saw~~ with some amusement ^perceived, he ~~soon~~ soon began to ^make civil enquire >ies after her family.   *'began to enquire' > began to make civil enquiries*

80.33  how to take ~~their absence.~~ ^this neglect.

80.34-5  ~~said Emma with civil~~ ^'Miss Watson the only one at home!   *removing the speech direction to tighten the conversation and make it more dramatic*

80.38  wherever I go.>, ^& I confess It is a shameful length

80.39  But ~~I feel that~~ I shall ~~soon~~ ^now endeavour to make myself

81.1-3  in reply ~~to all this gallantry~~ must have . . . unlike the ~~gratitude of her Sisters~~ encouraging warmth he had been used to receive from her Sisters

81.5  more attention than she ~~gave~~ ^bestowed.

81.6  Miss Car ~~was~~ ^being impatient to <u>call</u>

81.8-9  ~~by seeing~~ ^on seeing Mr Howard ~~come to claim his partner.~~ ^come forward & claim Emma's hand.

81.10  ~~when answering his friend's communication~~ ^when his friend carried him the news

81.11  during the ^two dances

81.12  the only unpleasant part of her engagement, ~~to Emma,~~ the only . . .

81.15  on the commonest ~~matt~~ <ers> ^topics ~~his~~ > he had ~~an easy,~~ ^sensible unaffected, ~~& unpretending manner which~~ ^way of expressing himself, which

81.19-20  the Osborne[s] & ~~Party~~ ^their Train were all on the move   *'s' an editorial insertion*

81.21  to Tom ~~Musgrave~~

81.22-6  I have had ^quite enough of it; ^I assure you— I shall not ^out ~~stay your party~~ ^shew myself here again when I have had the honour of attending ~~Miss~~ ^Ly Osborne to ~~the~~ ^her Carriage. I shall ~~retire~~ > retreat in as much secrecy as possible to ~~my own room, where I have ordered~~ ^the most remote ~~room in~~ ^corner of^ the ~~Inn~~ > House, where I shall order a Barrel of Oysters

81.27  bring me word ~~if you can,~~ how ~~Emma Watson~~ ^she looks

81.29  ^at least a dozen times

81.31-2  something ~~of~~ ^like a jerking curtsey . . . ^even Ly Osborne . . . his Lordship ^actually came back

81.34–5 ~~his~~ > the gloves . . . compressed ~~at the same moment~~ in his hand

81.38 her ~~little parlour~~ ^Bar

81.39 for the ~~D~~ happy Dancers

82.1–2 tho' in ~~such various ways, so much~~ ^some respects unpleasantly, distinguished

82.6–7 as she walked into the ~~Edwards's~~ Dining room, ~~where the Cloth~~^neat ~~was ready for the Table & a preparing, the supper, & the maid~~ Upper maid   *the deletion and reuse of 'neat' appears to show JA applying the adjective first to the supper table and then to the maid*

82.8 soon it is ~~over~~ ^at an end

82.9 ~~They all~~ ^A great deal of kind pleasure was expressed ~~their pleasure~~ in her having enjoyed

82.10–11 Mr Edwards was ~~particularly earnest in praising the excellence of the Meeting~~ ^as warm as herself, in praise of the fullness, brilliancy & Spirit of the Meeting

82.12–14 at ~~one~~ ^the same Table . . . a matter ~~of little concern~~ ^scarcely perceived. ~~known to him.~~

82.14 had won ~~5~~ ^4 rubbers out of 5

82.18–19 ^'I was always engaged when they asked me.' 'I thought you were . . .'

82.21 & ~~you~~ ^I had ~~told me~~ ^heard you say two minutes before

82.23–4 I did not know I was engaged, ~~till Capt Hunter assured me~~ ^—I thought it had been for the 2 Dances after

82.27–8 'Capt Hunter.' ^was repeated, in a very humble tone— 'Hum!—That is being constant however.

82.30–1 'Mr Norton is ~~freind~~ ^a Cousin of Capt Hunter's^.'^ & ^ 'And who is Mr Styles?<'> ~~is~~ o>'One of his particular friends.' *originally all Mary's speech, revision reapportions the passage between Mary and her father*

82.37 no occasion for ~~Engagements~~ ^their engaging themselves so many Dances before hand

83.4–8 It was the ^way of the place always to call on Mrs E. ^on the morng after a Ball, & this neighbourly inclination was ^now increased ^in the present instance by a general spirit of curiosity ~~to see the girl who~~ ^on Emma's account, as Everybody wanted to look again at the girl who

83.11–12 was the annihilation of every ~~thing good looking~~ ^grace, & others could never be persuaded

83.14–15 all the > this succession of Company

83.15–17 astonished ~~to find~~ ^by finding it Two o'clock, ~~and no Chair come for~~ ^& considering that she had heard nothing of her Father's Chair. *an example of new composition growing out of mid-sentence revision*

83.17-18  ~~Twice had she walked~~ ^After this discovery she had walked twice^ to the window to
~~look for it, & she~~ ^examine the Street, &^ was on the point of

83.21-2  instead of the convenient ~~tho'~~ > but very un-smart ~~conveyance~~
^Family equipage^ ~~she~~ ~~too long~~ ~~expected~~ ^perceived^ a neat Curricle

83.22-3  ~~In two minutes~~ Mr Musgrave ~~entered the room~~ ^was shortly afterwards^
announced;

83.24  Mrs Edwards put on ~~a stiffer look than usual~~ ^her very stiffest look^ at the
sound

83.25-6  Not at all dismayed ^however^ by her chilling air, ~~however,~~ he ~~made~~ >
paid his Compts

83.27-8  which he had 'the honour of bringing from her Sister;' But ^to^
which he must ^observe add, that a verbal postscript^ ~~added, will not comment~~
from himself wd be requisite.—' *closing speech marks are erased
after 'Sister' as Musgrave continues his speech.*

83.30  entreated her ~~not to stand on any~~ ^to use no^ ceremony

83.33-4  as ~~he had therefore tak~~ <en> ~~different way~~ ^his Road lay quite wide from R.^
<eigate?>, it was impossible for her to ~~be fetched~~ ^come^ home  *'R. This
may be a survival of an original intention to place the Watsons' village
near Reigate' (Minor Works, 463).*

84.2-3  she was ^at that moment^ in quest of a person to employ on the ~~Embassy~~
^Errand^

84.8  I ~~have~~ ^bring^ your Sister's orders

84.10  on ~~any degree~~ ^terms^ of intimacy

84.10-11  & yet ~~without assistance from the~~ ^fearful of encroaching on the^ Edwardes',
~~she could not avoid going home~~ ^as well as wishing to go home^ herself

84.18  She was rather ~~fearful~~ afraid

84.22  but ^if^ you can not conveniently do ~~it~~ ^so^

84.24-6  what Emma had ~~wished~~ ^longed^ for, ~~but without at all expecting~~ ^& she^
accepted the offer ~~very~~ ^most^ thankfully; ~~Eliz: being quite alone~~ ^acknowledging that as Eliz: was
entirely alone^, it was her wish

84.31  They have ~~no~~ ^none of them the smallest^ scruple

85.6  There seemed no ~~room for any body more~~ ^vacancy anywhere—^

85.7  ~~said Emma~~ ^Emma said this—^—tho' ^against^ her conscience.

85.13  And ~~Miss~~ ^Fanny^ Carr

85.14  —> & What

85.15-16  ^That^ He would be handsome ~~if~~ ^even, tho'^ he were <u>not</u> a Lord

85.26  Miss Ed~~mun~~ > wards

85.26-7  but as ~~Eliz: was just sitting down to dinner~~ ^it was Dinner hour at Stanton

85.28   said ~~Eliz:~~ ^Miss W.

85.35-7  within a mile of Guilford ~~on~~ > the ~~friday or Saturday~~ ^next day.—'
Nanny brought in the dinner; ~~& was not detained to wait.~~ ^soon sent
away. —'We will wait upon ourselves, ^continued Eliz: & then we shall lose
|||| |||||.

86.1   which ~~his bringing me home~~ ^the use of his Carriage must have created.

86.1-2  I should not ^even have liked

86.6-7  it was a ~~nice~~ ^clever way of getting you home; ~~&~~ ^Besides— it won't do, to
be too nice.

86.12  any interest with ~~her.~~ ^Mary.

86.16  but that was ~~most likely~~ ^Perhaps ~~only~~ > solely merely oweing

86.17  have ~~reached~~ ^come to her ^knowledge.'

86.18  ^Yes she has heard enough

86.18  ~~Yes, she knows well~~ ^Poor Sam!—~~It very~~ He is out of luck

86.24  ^Why—~~He is~~ quite one of the great & Grand ones; ~~is not he?~~

86.28  the Osborne's ^set,'

86.33-4  ^On the contrary, he seems ~~He is~~ very vain . . . & ^absolutely contemptible

86.36-7  but ~~he~~ > his ^company gives me no ~~other pleasure.~~ ^Emotion ~~than~~ > other agreable
Emotion.'

86.38-87.1  ~~Do not let Margaret hear such words; she would never forgive
you~~ ^It is well Margaret ~~wi~~ is not by.—You ~~that's all~~ do not offend ~~me~~ tho' I hardly know how to
beleive you. But Margt wd never forgive ~~you.'~~ such words.'

87.11  & looking ~~very~~ proud

87.12-13  to find you ~~are not infatuated by~~ ^can speak as you do, of Tom Musgrave;
~~for~~ my heart ~~misgave~~ ^did misgive me

87.15-16  it will last—. >; ~~But if he should come~~ ^& that he will not come on to pay
you much attention

87.22-3  I wish ~~poor Margt loved~~ ^everybody were as easily satisfied as you—but
poor Margt

87.25  & Penelope ~~say~~<s> owns

87.33  more to my mind ^continued Mr W.—or one better

87.34-7  with great propriety ^& in an ^very impressive manner; & at the same time . . .
I ~~have an abhorrence of~~ ^own, I do not like much action in the pulpit—~~&
of the~~ ^I cannot ~~endure~~ I do not like the studied air & ^artificial inflexions
of voice

88.5-6  ~~as an Invalid~~ ^& seemed to feel for me as an Invalid

88.10-13  There ~~are~~ is a pretty steep . . . which do not ^quite^ agree with . . . & Mr Howard ~~would~~ ^walked by me from the bottom to the top, & would^ make me take his arm.

88.14-15  for ~~except~~ ^I never^ saw him before

88.18-24  as Nanny ^at^ five minutes before three, ~~the dinner hour at Stanton,~~ was beginning to . . . ~~two gentlemen on Horseback~~ ^she was suddenly called^ ^to^ the front door . . . & ~~after a short exercise of wonder & Curiosity~~ ^pause of curiosity on the part^ ~~of the Miss Watsons, they were~~ ^tho' charged by Miss W. to let nobody in, re:^ :turned in half a minute, with a look of ^awkward^ dismay, to hold the ^parlour^ door open for Ld Osborne & Tom Musgrave.

88.25-6  at such ^a^ moment; but such visitors ~~were~~ ^as these—^

88.28  as, ~~after~~ ^on^ being introduced

88.33-4  ^& having^ In her Aunt's family ~~she had~~ been used to many of the Elegancies of Life, ~~& she had not quite philosophy enough to be consider~~ ^she could not without some mortification^ ^was^ fully sensible

88.36  ~~From~~ ^Of^ the pain of such feelings, Eliz: ~~was free~~ ^knew very^ little

88.38-89.1  ~~& she wished them away, more from a Sense of Convenience than of Shame.~~ ^& tho' shrinking under a general sense of Inferiority,^ ^she^ felt no ~~peculiar~~ particular Shame.

89.1-3  as ~~they~~ ^the Gentlemen^ had already heard . . . ~~the gentlemen~~, With much concern ^they^ took their seats.

89.6-7  Emma had ~~taken no~~ ^not caught^ cold at the Ball . . . nothing more to say for some ~~minutes~~ ^time^

89.8  at his ^fair^ neighbour

89.10-11  produced the ~~question~~ ^remark^

89.14-15  nankin galoshed with black ~~have a~~ ^looks^ very ~~good air~~ ^well^

89.16-17  as to ~~loo~~ injure their beauty, they ~~have not advantage in the deep dirt of~~ ^are not fit for^ Country walking

89.18  I wonder every Lady does not ^.^ ~~ride.~~

89.23-39  ~~'You mean~~ ^I am to suppose^ ~~a compliment of course my Lord, said Emma bowing, tho' I do~~ ^can^ ~~not exactly understand~~ ^define^ ~~it.' Lord Osborne laughed rather awkwardly—& then said 'Upon my Soul, I am a bad one for Compliments. Nobody can be a worse hand at it than myself.'~~ ^I wish I knew more of the such things matters^ ~~and after some minutes silence—added, 'Can~~ ^not^ ~~you give me a lesson Miss Watson on the art of paying Compts.—I should be very glad to learn.' I want very much to know how to please the Ladies.—one Lady at least^ ^A cold monosyllable & grave look from Emma repressed the growing~~ ~~freedom of his manner. He had too much sense, not to take the hint—& when he spoke again,~~

it was ~~with a degree of courteous propriety which he had never~~
~~used before~~ ^was not often at the trouble of using. ^employing. ~~He was~~
~~rewarded~~

*all struck through and replaced by a patch with a revised text as follows:*
'Your Lordship thinks . . . Female Economy ~~may~~ ^will do a great deal
ᴬmy Lord ~~l̶u̶t̶ i̶t̶ ̶c̶a̶r̶r̶i̶c̶d̶ . . . t̶l̶u̶s̶u̶ ̶m̶u̶c̶h̶ ̶m̶o̶n̶u̶a̶l̶m̶g̶ ̶m̶ ̶u̶l̶m̶ ̶t̶h̶ ̶v̶a̶l̶d̶~~ ᴵᵗʰ ⁿᴵᴵ
seriousness, as well as in the words themselves which made his Lordship think . . . it was
with ~~courteous~~ ^a degree of considerate propriety . . . '~~You have not been long~~
~~in this Country I understand.~~ ~~I hope you are pleased with its~~ ^It was
a new thing with him to wish to please a woman; it was the first time that he had ever felt ~~the delicate~~ what
was due to a woman, ~~his equal in Education,~~ ^in Emma's situation. . . . not feel
it without ~~resolving on the necessary effort.~~ ^effect. . . . I understand,
said he ^in the tone of a Gentle[ma]n. . . . he was rewarded by a gracious answer

89.39    a more liberal ^full veiw

90.1    had yet bestowed ^.^ ~~on him.~~

90.2–3    he ^then sat in silence for ~~about five~~ ^some minutes longer

90.4–5    who ~~putting~~ ^half opening the door & putting

90.6    why he ben't to have his dinner    *rare use by JA of Hampshire dialect*
*form of the verb 'to be'*

90.6    who had ^hitherto disregarded

90.8    Elizth ~~was calling~~ ^called ~~loudly~~ briskly after Nanny

90.10–11    turning ^goodhumouredly towards Musgrave—but ^you know

90.14–15    Ld Osborne's ^parting Compts took some time, ~~to pay his parting~~
~~Compts to Emma; the~~ ^his rea: ~~:diness at words~~ ^his inclination for speech seeming to increase    *revision and first drafting are interwoven here*

90.17–18    ~~wanted her to~~ ^begged that his Sister might be allow^'d^ ~~his sister~~ to send ~~her~~
^Emma the name

90.19–23    '~~I shall~~ ^My Hounds will . . . on Wednesday—^at 9 o'clock.— ~~I hope you~~
~~will be~~ ^I mention this, in hopes of yr being drawn out to see what's going
on.— ~~Nobody can be indifferent to the glorious sounds~~ ^Everybody allows
that there is not so fine a sight in the world ~~as a pack of~~ ^a pack of Fox Hounds in full cry.
~~I am sure you will be pleased~~ ^delighted ~~to hear the first Burst—if we can~~
^but ~~find there as I dare say we shall.~~— If the morning's tolerable, ~~do~~
~~not be kept at home~~ ^pray do us the honour of giving us your good wishes^    *super-*
in person.'
*linear revision continues below the main, deleted line of text*

90.26–8    Who would have thought of Ld Osborne's coming to Stanton.—~~I~~
~~wish he would give my poor Father a Living, as he makes such~~
~~a point of coming to see him. But~~ ^to be sure ~~Mr Howard will have~~
~~everything he has to give.~~ ^of that kind. sort. ~~—He has a~~ ^Ld O. is very He is very

handsome^;^ ~~young man~~—but Tom Musgrave . . . the ^smartest &^ most fashionable ~~man~~ ^man^ of the two.

90.29-30    I ~~should~~ ^wd^ not have ~~liked~~ ^had^ to ~~to have had to speak to him.~~ ^talk to such a great man for the world.^

90.31    ^But^ Did you hear ~~leave her~~ ^him ask^ where Miss Penelope

90.32    ~~He~~ ^It^ put me out of patience

90.34    ~~just~~ ^just^ the Tray

90.36-8    was ~~was~~ by no means unalloyed; ~~for the~~ ^His coming at was a^ sort of notice ~~tho' agreable to her vanity, was not soothing to her pride to~~ ^which ~~welcome~~ might please her vanity, but ~~cd not be welcome~~ did not ~~soothe~~ suit^ her pride

91.1-2    other unsatisfactory ~~reflections~~ ^feelings^ it ~~had~~ once occurred . . . ~~that~~ ^why^ Mr Howard

91.4-6    or ~~that~~ he > had declined . . . a measure which ~~had~~ ^carried^ quite as much Impertinence ^in it's form^ as Goodbreeding ^.^ ~~in it.~~

91.6-10    ~~When Mr Watson~~ ^Mr W. was very far from being delighted, when he^ heard . . . ~~he expressed no~~ ^—a little^ peevish under immediate pain, & in > illdisposed . . . he only ~~said~~ ^replied^ . . . there be for ~~it.~~^Ld O.'s coming.^

91.10    lived here ~~twelve~~ ^14^ years

91.11    ~~This~~ ^It^ is some foolery

91.14    the too ~~reasonable~~ ^-sufficient^ plea . . . ~~infirmit~~ <y> > infirm

91.16-17    quietly away ~~after this visit, at Stanton Parsonage~~ ^after this visit, before any new bustle^

91.18-19    whose ^mutual^ regard ~~for each other~~ was increasing with the intimate knowledge ^of each other^ which

91.20    to break ^in^ on

91.23-4    bring her home ^& wished to see their Sister Emma.^

91.25    Sisters at ~~hom~~<e> Stanton, & to ~~employ~~ ^busy^ the ~~Corporeal powers~~ ^time hours^ of one of them at least

91.28    ^she^ could make no change

91.29-30    ~~Emma had not heard anything of Margaret to make~~ ^An absence of 14 years had made all her Brothers & Sisters^ Strangers to Emma

91.32    she had ^heard^ things

91.34    conclusion of ^almost^ all that had been comfortable

91.35    & very well satisfied

91.37    of the ~~Man~~ ^Attorney^ to whom he had been Clerk

92.5-6    the ^but the sharp & anxious^ expression of her face, ~~sharp & anxious~~ ^made her beauty^ in general ~~be~~ little felt.

92.7-10  her ^long-absent Sister . . . her ~~smiles were very~~ ^manner was all affection . . . slow articulation ~~were her constant were what she~~ ^had ~~always recoursed to,~~ ^Distinguished her ^being her constant resource

92.11-12  that ~~the words seemed likely never to end.~~ ^she could hardly speak a word in a minute.

92.14-15  ~~such an observation / 'No admittance' &~~

92.17-21  was uppermost in her mind, ~~& in her husband's on meeting her.~~ ^at the moment of meeting; — ~~they had not been ten minutes together before the latter shewed that it was~~ ^& she cd not but feel how much better it was to be the daughter of a gentleman of ~~easy~~ property in Croydon, than the neice of an old woman who ~~gave all her money to~~ ^threw herself away on an Irish ~~officer.~~ ^Captain.

92.22  settling with the ~~Postboy Driver~~ ^Post-Boy

92.23  Exorbitant ~~rise~~ ^advance in Posting

92.28  ~~Overseer~~ ^Surveyor

92.28-32  a little ~~nephew~~ ^neice at Croydon . . . ~~his~~ ^her not being . . . replied ~~his~~ ^her Mother . . . went ^very hard with ~~John~~ ^Augusta to have us . . . without ~~him~~ ^her

92.32-4  forced to ~~send him out~~ a walking, & promise not ^say we were only going to Church & promise to come back for ~~him~~ ^her directly

92.34-5  to bring ~~him~~ ^her without ~~his~~ ^her maid, & I am ~~very~~ ^as particular ^as ever in having ~~him~~ ^her properly attended to

92.37  to leave ~~him~~ ^her.' '^'Then Why was you . . . away from ~~him~~ ^her?

92.39  Such ~~as~~ a visit as this

93.1-2  any of o<ur> > you with us ^—if it be for months together

93.2-3  ^& I am sorry, ~~she added~~ (with a witty smile) ^we ^have not been able to make ~~you have found~~ Croydon ~~so~~ disagreable

93.5-6  to bring me home. ^Spare me, I entreat you— ~~but.~~ I am no match

93.12  I had ~~nine~~ ^seven Tables last week in my ~~two~~ Drawingroom

93.16-17  was ^indeed wondering what sort of a ~~place she~~ ^home Emma cd ^possibly have been used to

93.21-3  & she did not like it better ~~on overhearing Margt saying~~ ^5 minutes afterwards when she heard Margt 5 minutes afterwards say to Eliz: in a sharp quick ~~tone~~ ^accent

93.23-4  from Pen. ~~lately~~ since she went ~~away?~~ ^to Chich<est>er?

93.36  & ^now I do hope

93.38  said Margt ^rather quickly to Emma

94.5-6  ^on entering it she found her brother ~~there~~ alone

94.9-10  I always ~~thought~~ ^said she ought to have settled something on you, ~~when she took you away.'~~ ^as soon as her Husband died.'

94.11    replied Emma ~~smiling~~

94.12    have been secured ^placed to your ~~after~~ future use, ~~in Trust,~~   *example of a revision ('placed') considered and rejected before the first choice ('secured') is confirmed*

94.14    instead of ~~being~~ ^probable Heiress

94.16-17  '~~I beg you~~ ^Do not ~~to~~ speak disrespectfully of ~~my Aunt, Brother.~~ ^her—

94.20-95.3  I thought Turner had been reckoned an extraordinary sensible, clever man . . . & after a short silence, by way of changing the subject, he added   *a section of text written onto a paper patch and added to extend the original text after 'but you know every body must think her an old fool.' And before 'I am just come from my Father's room'*

94.21    to ~~leave~~ make such a will

94.25-6  has been unfortunate ~~for me,~~ but my Uncle's memory is ^if possible endeared

94.28-9  without leaving ~~it all~~ ^every thing that he had to dispose of, or any part of it at her mercy

94.31    he left to her ^self the power

94.33    to your Father, ^& without the power

94.35    for ~~14 years~~ ^such a length of time

94.36    all natural affection ^among us

95.8     a young ^man who wd have

95.10    than listen to ~~her brother~~ ——. ^Robert, who had equally ~~mortified,~~ irritated & greived her.—

95.18-22  visitting, ~~if~~ ^tho' you do not . . . other gentlemen ~~too~~ do . . . pu<t> wear it

95.24-5  ~~his~~ > her Sister in law, Emma, ^(tho' in no Spirits to make such nonsense easy) began

95.27    It has been ~~very much~~ ^excessively admired

95.32-4  profusion ~~of~~ ^on the Table . . . against ~~having~~ ^the entrance of the roast Turkey

95.34-5  'You see your dinner', ~~brought in~~ —'I do beg . . .'

95.38-9  come in, & ^as stay in the Kitchen. ^Besides If it is cut, I am ^in hopes

96.9     to ~~help~~ break a formal circle

96.17-18  ~~but you must~~ ^why do not you get him to play ^at Cribbage

96.18    have ~~always~~ played at Cribbage

96.20-1  at this moment ~~heard;~~ ^caught; every body listened; & it ~~grew m<ore>>~~ became more decided

96.22 no ^very public road

96.24 ^in two minutes the general expectation

96.27-8 was the only ~~person~~ ^creature to be thought of^.^ ~~as tolerably likely~~ ^She might perhaps . . . some ~~sudden~~ ^unexpected opportunity

96.29-31 ~~Foot Steps were heard on along the paved~~ ^distinguished, first along ^upon the ~~ʳ ᵗʰ ᵗ footway which lead~~ . . . ~~from the gate to the front door~~, & then ~~in~~ ^within the passage

96.32-3 & ~~shewed~~ ^displayed Tom Musgrave

96.37 in the present instance ~~he~~ had had the

97.1 As it happened ^however, he did not ~~create~~ ^give

97.2-7 the usual ^little sitting room . . . of the best parlour ^a foot larger each way than the other was thrown open, & ^he beheld . . . ~~sittin<g>~~ arranged . . . the best Pembroke Table, ~~making~~ ^with the best Tea things

97.7 He ~~stopt, for~~ ^stood a few seconds

97.9 to find ~~himself~~ ^such a circle

97.13-15 Emma ~~discerned no more than she had expected, tho'~~ ^who close[ly] observed him, perceived nothing that did not justify Eliz.'s opinions tho' Margaret's modest smiles *JA wrote 'closed' in error for 'closely', here editorially emended*

97.17 ^'For Whether he dined at 8 or 9, ^as he observed

97.18-20 ~~He did not seem to avoid the seat by~~ ^and ~~took~~ without seeming to seek, he did not ~~avoid~~ ^turn away from^ the chair ~~near~~ > close to Margaret . . . She had ^thus secured him

97.23-6 only 4. hours ~~back,~~ ^ago, . . . must be ~~enquired into,~~ ^understood, before Robert could ~~yeild~~ ^let his attention be yeilded to the less national, ~~more domestic enquiries~~ ^& or important demands of the Women

97.27-8 as she ~~feared he must have~~ ^spoke her fears of his having had a most terrible

97.30 at the Bedford ^Horse guards, by a friend^.^ ~~of Lord Osbornes~~

97.32 'He We came only this ~~very~~ mornng.

98.1 ~~how great my enjoyment~~ ^what are my Sensations in finding myself once more at Stanton, ~~in the bosom of my Family.~~

98.6-7 It was lucky that he added that finish.—~~'Oh! You Creature!' was Margaret's reply.~~ 'Were you speaking to me?—' said Emma

98.9 probably doing ~~likewise~~ ^at this moment

98.16 Miss Osborne & Miss Carr [were] likewise fair *JA wrote 'was' in error for 'were', here editorially emended*

98.17-18 as fine as ~~the hue of her ski<n>~~ ^a dark complexion can be

98.19-20 ~~very fair.—Miss Osborne~~ ^my model for a truly feminine complexion

98.20-3 ~~'She is about as fair as I am, I think.'~~ ^Is she fairer than me?'^— ~~Instead of making any reply, Tom~~ ^Tom made no reply.^—'Upon my Honour Ladies . . . I am ~~most fervently ashamed~~ ^highly endebted to your^ Condescension . . . in such ~~a state,~~ ^Dishabille^

98.24 consider how ~~unfit~~ ^unsuitably^ ^unfit^ I was ~~to for your presence~~ ^to be here^,

98.27-8 Robert Watson ~~took~~ ^stealing^ a ~~slight~~ veiw . . . in an opposite glass,—~~and he~~ ^said^ with equal civility, ~~said,~~

98.30 a little ^fresh^ powder

98.32 feelings ~~must be on this occasion.~~ ^at that moment.^

98.34-6 the ^old^ Card Table ~~was placed~~ ^being set out, &^ The fish & counters, ~~&~~ ^with^ a tolerably clean pack brought forward ^from the beaufet^ by Miss Watson

98.37 he ~~would~~ ^agreed to^ allow himself . . . of an hour^.^ ~~in their <company>~~

98.39 a family ~~party~~ ^circle^ ^party^

98.39 ^&^ the others were delighted

99.7-8 pleasant hours ~~enough~~ at Speculation . . . I have not ~~played at~~ been in the way of it

99.12-15 enjoys it ~~amazingly~~ ^famously^ . . . the best Dealer ~~in the world~~ ^without exception that I ever saw>beheld^— . . . he lets nobody dream over ~~it.~~ ^their cards.^

99.15 see him ~~deal himself~~ ^overdraw himself^ on both ^his own^ cards

99.17 it is ^a^ much better game

99.19 Mrs Robert ~~withdrew~~ ^said^ ^offered^ not another word

99.20-1 ~~Osborne Castle carried it, even in her estimation~~ ^She was quite vanquished,^ & the ~~Croydon~~ fashions of Osborne- Castle carried it over ~~those~~ ^the fashions^ of Croydon.

99, after 21 ~~T. Musgrave was a very~~ ^most^ ~~useful addition; without him, it would have been a~~

99.22-37 'Do you see much of the Parsonage-family at the Castle, Mr Musgrave?—' . . . without him, it wd have been a *a section of text written onto a paper patch and added to extend the original text after the deleted lines* 'T. Musgrave was a very ^most^ useful addition; without him, it would have been a' *and before* 'party of such very near relations'

99.23-4 said Emma, ~~while~~ ^as^ they were taking . . . 'Oh! yes—^they are^ almost always there

99.25 She & I are ~~gre<at>~~ sworn friends

99.27 by any of the~~m~~ party

99.28    now & then ^Miss Emma.

99.30    Says ~~Ld Osborne~~ ^Howard to ~~Howard.~~ ^Ld Osborne—'

99.31    he was ~~interrupted~~ ^called on by

99.33-4    in the business ^& afterwards by the course of the game as never to revert

99.34-5    & Emma ~~could not remind him,~~ tho' suffering a good deal from Curiosity, ~~could~~ ˄ ˄ not remind him.

99.36    addition ~~to~~ at their Table

99.37-8    as ~~ed~~ ^must ^could have ~~deadened the~~ ^felt little Interest, & perhaps ~~even impaired the~~ ^maintained little complaisance, ~~of the players~~ but his presence

99.39    He was ^in fact excellently qualified

100.1-4    ~~he never~~ ^& seldom few situations made him ~~appeared to greater advantage^ ^ than when assisting at one.~~ & He talked much ^He played with Eagerness— ^He played with Spirit & had a great deal to say, & tho' ~~without wit, sometimes said a lively thing~~ ^without>with no wit himself, cd sometimes make use of the wit of an absent friend

100.4    a lively way of saying retailing a commonplace

100.5    that ~~was abundantly useful~~ ^did had great effect at a Card Table

100.6    his ^ordinary means of Entertainment

100.7-9    of ~~Miss Osborne~~ ^one Lady, detailed the oversights of ~~Miss Carr~~ ^another, & indulged them ^even with a copy of Ld Osborne's m<an- ner>>stile of overdrawing

100.12    ~~as~~ ^while he went home

100.14-15    cd now ~~prevail; If he staid, he knew~~ ^avail,—for he well knew, that if he staid he must sit down to supper in ^less than ten minutes

100.16-17    a Man who>se ~~meant~~ heart ~~was~~ > had ^been long fixed on ~~a very late dinner, was~~ ^calling his next meal a Dinner, ~~must be~~ ^was^ quite insupportable

100.18    determined ^to go, Margt began

100.20-1    not able to resist, ~~& from her~~ ^hints, which her own hospitable, social temper ~~not above half wishing~~ ^more than half seconded, gave the invitation

100.23-6    ^'That is, if I can possibly get ~~home~~ ^here in time . . . & therefore ~~cannot positively answer~~ ^must not engage— ~~& In another moment~~ ^You will not think of me unless you see me

100.27    had ~~placed~~ ^left it

100.35    jumping up, ~~made her escape~~ ^ran away from a subject

100.37    a doubt to be ~~entertained~~ ^repeated of Musgrave's coming

101.1-3    what had been ~~done~~ deemed necessary the day before ^;^ for ~~Mrs Robert~~ —and ~~superseding all Eliz.'s cares usual cares, she~~ ^taking the office of Superintendance entirely from her Sister ~~for the occasion~~, she was half the morning in the Kitchen, ^herself

101.4-5 After a great deal of ~~Cooking, & waiting~~ ^indifferent Cooking, & anxious Suspense however they were obliged

101.7 her vexation~~, or~~ ^under the disappointment, or repress

101.11 & querulous ~~altercations.~~ ^attacks.— Eliz. was the ^usual object of both.

101.12 ~~She~~ ^Margt had just respect enough

101.14-23 & Emma^,^ ~~found the~~ ^whom she seemed no longer to think about, found the ~~affecte~~ ^continuance of the gentle voice ~~more short-lived even than she had expected.~~ ^even shorter lived beyond her calculation ~~breif~~ short. ~~Delighted~~ ^Glad Eager to be as little among them as possible, Emma was ~~eager to~~ ^glad to each eveng propose ~~take Eliz.'s usual place with in their Father's room,~~ ^ delighted with the alternative of & in just sitting with in attending her Father ~~who~~ sitting ~~upstairs~~ ^above, with her father, ~~who~~ ^& warmly entreated ~~was confined both days to his room~~ ^to be his constant Compn each Eveng.——& ^as Eliz. ^who loved company . . . prefer being below,^when at all risks ~~while she cd beleive > be persuaded to beleive it no sacrifice on Emma's part.~~ ^as She had rather talk of Croydon ~~with~~ ^to Jane, with ~~all the~~ ^every interruptions of Margt's perverseness . . . ~~it~~ ^the affair was ~~soon~~ so settled

101.24-7 To Emma, ~~it~~ ^the Exchange was ~~a~~ most acceptable, & delightful, ~~releif. Mr~~ Her father, if ill, required ~~only~~ ^little more than gentleness & silence; ~~if able to converse, as he was a man of Education & Taste, he was a pleasing~~ ^&, being a man of Sense & ~~being~~ Education, was if able to converse, a welcome companion.—

101.28-31 dreadful ~~Evils~~ ^mortifications of unequal Society . . . ~~meanspirited Self-sufficiency,~~ ^low-minded Conceit ~~and a~~ & wrong-headed ~~illdisposed~~ ^folly, engrafted on an untoward Disposition

101.31-4 She ^still suffered from them ~~only in~~ ^in the Contemplation of their existence . . . she ~~had a pause~~ ^ceased to be tortured by their ~~effusions.~~ ^effects.—She ~~could~~ ^was at leisure, she could read & think^,^ ^tho' her ~~Her~~ situation ^perhaps was ~~not~~ ^hardly such as to make

101.35-9 The ~~misfortunes which her Uncle's death had brought on her,~~ ^Evils arising from the loss of her Uncle were ~~every day~~ ^neither trifling, nor likely to lessen . . . ~~when~~ ^in contrasting the past & the present, ~~had been contrasted, the dissipations~~ ^the employment of mind . . . which only ~~reading~~ ^Books reading could produce, made her thankfully turn to ~~them.~~ ^a book.

102.1-2 ~~The sink~~ ^fall in her fortunes, ~~the~~ ^The change in her home society, ^& stile of Life ~~had~~ in consequence of ~~her Aunt's~~ ^Mrs Turner's the death of one freind & the imprudence ^of another^~~, had been great & greivous.~~ ^ ~~had indeed been most unusualy the infatuation~~ of another had indeed been striking

102.6-11 of a ~~whole~~ House . . . the expected ~~Inh~~<eritor> Heiress . . . was ~~reduced to a House~~ ^become of Importance^ to no one, a burden on ~~an already too full House, where she was felt an Intruder, a Stranger among those~~ ^those, whose affection she cd not expect, an addition to an house, already overstocked, ^surrounded by inferior minds with little chance of domestic ~~enjo~~<yment> comfort, & ~~no~~ ^as little^ hope of ~~a~~ future support

102.12-13 ~~as it was a change which~~ ^for the Change had been such as ~~to~~ ^might^ have plunged weak spirits ~~must have into wretchedness~~ ^gloom & ^in Despondence

102.17 ~~to suppose they~~ ^offer^ could appear in a less ~~favourable~~ ^advantageous^ light to anybody else

102.22 going on ^at^ Croydon

102.23 very kind to you—. ~~It is a pity you should not go.~~ –

102.24 no worse ^off^ without you

102.26 more than ^you^ think

102.27 except to greater ~~affection~~ ^esteem^ for Elizth

## SANDITON

105.2-5 ~~were, on quitting~~ ^being induced by Business to quit^ the high road, & ~~toiling up a very long steep hill through a rough Lane,~~ ^toil attempt a very rough Lane, were^ overturned in toiling up its' long ascent ^half rock, half sand.^

105.6-7 ~~the~~ ^a^ House, which their Driver on being ^first^ required to ~~turn~~ ^take^ that ~~way,~~ ^direction,^ had conceived to be

105.8-10 to pass ^by^ ~~two minutes before grumbling~~ ^He had grumbled, & shaken his Shoulders^ so much indeed, ~~& looking so black, & pitying & cutting~~ ^and pitied & cut^ his Horses so ~~much~~ ^sharply;^

105.12 as the Carriage was ~~not~~ ^not his Masters [but]^ the Gentleman's own   *the passage requires some interpretation. JA may have intended but failed to delete 'the Gentleman's' after adding the alternative 'his Masters' in revision, a substitution perhaps made because 'Gentleman' had already been used twice in the opening 8 lines. This is assumed in all previous OUP editions, which give the reading 'as the Carriage was not his Masters own'. There is another interpretation: in the copy she made of the manuscript, Cassandra Austen offered 'as the Carriage was not his Master's but the Gentleman's own', which involves no greater textual correction than the insertion of 'but'. It clarifies that the Parkers, owners of the carriage, have hired the driver and horses, a common practice. Since it has early authority, I have used Cassandra's reading here.*

105.12-13  if the road ^had not indisputably ~~& evidently~~ become ~~much~~ ^consid-erably worse than before

105.14-16  were ~~passed~~ left behind ~~as bad as it had been before the Change seemed to say,~~ ^saying, expressing ~~and seeming~~ with a most intelligent portentous countenance that beyond it no wheels but cart wheels ~~coul<d> ever thought of proceeding.~~ ^could safely proceed.

105.18-19  & the ~~Travellors beleived found themselves at first only shaken & bruised~~ Gentleman having scrambled out . . . they neither of them ^at first felt more than shaken & bruised  *a characteristic revision, in which JA can be seen lengthening her sentence, reordering and extending the information it contains*

105.21-3  & ^soon becoming sensible of it ~~in a few moments~~, was obliged ^in a few moments to cut short . . . his ~~self~~ congratulations ^to his wife & himself— & sit down

105.28-30  a > the neat-looking . . . ~~appearing~~ which was seen ~~peeping out from among wood, and~~ romantically situated ^among wood on a high Eminence

105.32  terrified & anxious, ~~& not~~ ^neither able to do

106.1-2  now coming ~~from~~ to their assistance

106.2  accident ~~having~~ ^had been discerned

106.9-10  very civil salutation ~~& very~~ much concern

106.11  offers of ~~service in any way~~ ^assistance.

106.12  while ^one or two of the Men

106.16  always ~~better to~~ ^best in these cases to

106.17-18  in ~~the best possible~~ ^a favourable state for

106.21  without ~~any.~~ ^him.

106.22  ~~his Partner~~ if he is not in the way, his Partner

106.22  or ^rather better

106.23-4  I would ~~have~~ ^prefer the attendance of his Partner^.^ ~~by preference.~~

106.24-5  people ~~will~~ ^can be ~~there~~ ^with him in three minutes

106.26  ^for Excepting your own

106.33  but ~~either~~ ^though from the extent

106.34  ^Stay— Can I be mistaken

106.37  in the Parish—^whether you may know it or not.

107.1-2  I cut out myself . . .^only yesterday morng in London— I think you will be convinced

107.3-4  dissolution of ^a Partnership

107.8   said Mr Heywood ^with a good humoured smile

107.9   there > that are printed

107.10  you ~~yo~~ wd   *'you' repeated in error*

107.11-13  in ~~this Parish~~ Willingden,— ~~having~~ ^for I have>having lived here ^Sir . . . Man & Boy ~~Sir~~ 57 years, ~~without ever hearing of the existence~~ ^and ~~never knew before I think I know any known at such a person",~~ ^" before. I ~~think~~ I may venture ~~at least~~ ^therefore to say ^at least that he has not <u>much</u> Business;— ~~Though to~~ ^To be sure . . .

107.16  can assure you ^Sir that

107.18  in the Parish.>, ^and that My Shepherd

107.19  the ~~bits~~ ^peices of paper

107.29  the ^last half hour

107.30  ^where > when ~~&~~>everything ^being ~~in~~ was in the hurry & confusion

107.31  ~~nothing~~ ^One is never able to be ~~completed~~ ^anything   *'be' inadvertently remaining after revision of 'nothing able to be completed' > 'One is never able to complete anything', editorially corrected here*

107.32  Business ^you know till

107.33  ~~I satisfied~~ ^and accordingly satisfying myself

107.34  ^I sought no farther

107.36  this ~~awkward Predicament.~~ ^Scrape.

108.3  at hand ^you know.—

108.4  our ^own Bracing Sea Air

108.5  Saline ^air & immersion

108.13  of ~~use to Service~~ ^service to you & this Lady

108.17  I beleive ~~we had~~ ^it will be better ^for us—' ~~accept this kind offer'~~ he turned again

108.18  & ^in order to do away

108.20  given ^rise to

108.22  on our road ^home

108.23  the first of ~~the~~ my Family

108.25  but Sanditon ^itself

108.27-9  certainly ~~the most favourite~~ ^the favourite spot of all . . . along the ~~favourite~~ Coast of Sussex . . . & ~~consequently~~ ^promising to be the most ~~likely to be~~ chosen

108.32  ~~amazing to me!~~ ^the wonder!

108.33  Money ~~&~~ ^or Time

108.33 for ~~any~~ ^a Country;—^—sure to raise

108.34-5 for nothing—^as I dare say you find^,^ ~~it so~~ Sir

108.39 from ~~feeling~~ ^experiencing any of the evils

109.1 the ~~laying out Gardens~~ ^Nursery Grounds

109.3-6 the > those regular, steady, private Families . . . ~~excite not only~~ ^who are a blessing every where, excite the industry of the Poor ~~but~~ ^and . . . of every ~~kind.~~ ^sort.

109.7 to ~~any~~ ~~one~~ place

109.10 may not ^totally disagree

109.14 & ~~I have no doubt will~~ ^must soon find themselves ~~in the end~~ the Dupes

109.20 no slimey rocks *R. W. Chapman transcribed this in 1925 as 'shiney', silently correcting to 'slimey' in Minor Works (1954), 369, having recorded the correction in the Times Literary Supplement, 14 May 1925, 335. All subsequent editors agree.*

109.23 ~~a~~ ^One complete, measured mile

109.24 advantage of ~~that,~~ ^saving a whole Mile, in a long Journey

109.27-8 ~~situated~~^lying, as it does between . . .^a bleak Moor & the constant effluvia

109.34 ~~grow~~ ^pro <duce> yeild

110.3-4 ~~I fancy Sir~~ ^Why, in truth Sir, I fancy we may apply . . . ~~those~~> that lines

110.8 she ^is quite ~~agrees with me in thinking~~ ^of my opinion & thinks— it a pity

110.10-11 ~~(turning round towards~~ (two or three . . . young women, ~~attended~~ ^who followed by . . . were ^now seen issueing

110.15-16 & said ~~& did what~~ ^every thing that was proper to ~~enforce~~ ^recommend

110.20-1 as ~~it was now ascertained that the Carriage was so much injured~~ ^the Carriage being now set up, was discovered to have received such Injury on the fallen side

110.22 was ^therefore carried

110.25-6 ~~The Parkers were the Guests of the Heywoods a fortnight.~~ ^For a whole fortnight the Travellors were fixed at Willingden; ~~The~~ ^Mr P's sprain ~~was~~ ^being proving too serious for ~~Mr Parker to be sooner able~~ ^him to move sooner.

110.30-1 with ~~equal good will~~ unremitting kindness . . . every ~~act &~~ office of Hospitality

110.34 manners ~~in~~ ^on either

111.1 soon ~~made known.~~ ^unfolded.

111.1-2 he readily told, ~~was he was~~ ^being for he was very openhearted

111.3 he > his ^conversation was . . . information ~~unconsciously~~

111.4-5 ~~in~~ on the subject of

111.8   a ^simple quiet Village ~~interesting only~~ of no ~~consideration inhabited by one Family of consequence, his own, of secondary~~ pretensions

111.10   & ~~some~~ ^some . . . principal ~~Proprietor of the Land~~ ^Land Holder

111.11   its' ~~being~~ ^becoming a profitable Speculation, he > they

111.13   of ~~note~~ young ~~notoriety~~ ^Renown—

111.16   was ~~no Profession~~ ^of a respectable Family

111.20   & ^2 Sisters

111.20-1   the two Brothers ^former ~~in fact~~ ^indeed

111.24   ~~an~~ ^his ancle

111.31-2   a great ^prodigious influx

111.33   deterred ^last year from trying Sanditon

112.7   she ~~was~~ ^remained equally useless

112.10-11   ^not only those of Birth place . . . ^and Home,— it was ~~also~~ his Mine

112.12   ^his Occupation his Hope

112.14   ^and his endeavours

112.16   as his ^own house

112.19   by the Sea^.^ ~~Air.~~

112.24   were ~~almost~~ ^nearly infallible, ~~in every disorder~~

112.25-7   Disorder.>, ~~In cases~~ of the Stomach . . . ~~they were equally sovereign; They were~~ ^They were . . .anti-sceptic, ^anti-bilious & anti-rheumatic

112.28-9   ~~nor cd the most obstinate Cougher retain a cough there 4 & 20 hours.~~ ^Nobody wanted Spirits. Nobody wanted Strength.

112.30   ^seemingly just as

112.33   was ~~palpably~~ ^evidently

112.35   been ~~very long~~ ^long limited

112.39   ~~conveyed~~ ^could carry him

113.2   their ^Eldest Son's

113.6-7   a ~~Summer occasionally~~ ^an occasional month at Tunbridge Wells, & ~~a~~ symptoms . . . ~~to make~~ ^and a Winter

113.9   & ~~forbidding~~ obliged them

113.16-18   could ~~lead them into respectable Company.~~ ^give useful connections or
^ respectable acquaintance to Sons or Daughters. *the line has three levels of development, with a line of sublinear revision following on from the superlinear revision of the original line, which, apart from the first word 'could', has been completely deleted*

113.19   one ~~young Lady~~ ^Daughter

113.23  who ~~in acting for her Mother,~~ ^under her Mother's directions

113.24  ~~&~~ who had attended

113.27  by the ~~grateful feelings~~ ^gratitude

113.28-9  ~~& every thing else that~~ ^for her Sisters & herself at the Library^,^ ~~there,~~ which

113.31  he would ~~recommend~~ ^send everyone to ^go try Sanditon   *there are three revisions: 'go' > 'try' (possibly 'go to' > 'try'); all deleted; 'recommend' > 'send'*

113.32  as far [as] the future   *JA omitted second 'as', here supplied editorially*

113.33  even ~~one night~~ ^5 Shillings

114.7  were ^facts already well known

114.8-9  of ~~names & places~~ ^her history, & ~~some hints of~~ ^her Character ~~(though given with a>~~the light touch of a very friendly hand) ~~were~~ served to lighten . . . a long ~~Pull~~ ^Hill

114.11  the Person ~~wh<o>~~ with whom

114.16  ~~quite~~ an elderly Man

114.19  P<roperty>(?) > Estates

114.31-2  give ~~it~~ ^her conduct that natural explanation

114.34  carried ~~much~~ ^greatly too far

114.36  friendly Neighbour^;^ ~~to us~~ ^a chearful, independent, valuable character.

114.37  faults ~~are to~~ ^may be ~~cheifly~~ ^entirely imputed to ~~the~~ ^her want of Education

115.1  a spirit ~~which one admires~~ ^truly admirable—

115.5  we ~~see~~ ^now & then, see things *differently* ~~now & then~~

115.6  own Story ^you know must be

115.9  common ~~Social order,~~ ^wants of Society—

115.13-14  than ~~they cd~~ ^he had allowed them to be to *his*, and the > those Members

115.18  Mr Hollis' ~~Cous<ins>~~ Kindred

115.24  always ~~able by their vicinity, to~~ ^at hand to preserve their interest

115.27  who ~~always~~ lived with him . . . ~~very~~ principally remembered

115.31  ~~if he~~ had ^he the Power

115.34  ~~he holds under Lady D——~~ , ^Lady D. has granted him,

115.34  no doubt ~~will~~ ^we shall have

115.37  as ~~being~~ having ~~a very fair~~ ^the fairest chance

116.2-4  ~~a>~~After having always . . . ~~deprecating the idea of a Companion, defying & & enjoying~~ ^and long & often enjoyed the repeated defeats . . . of her relations ~~on that head, she had been~~ to introduce . . .

116.5.  at Sanditon ~~Hall~~ House

116.7  to ~~restore~~ secure for herself

116.11  such a ~~young Woman.~~ ^Character.

116.12  heard her ~~delineated~~ described ~~(and not with~~ to be lovely

116.17  very ^promptly & compassionately

116.21-4  avoided ~~being~~ in London . . . ^officially on account . . . ~~the >~~ these ^very Cousins ~~there resident there~~ . . . she had ^& whom she was determined to keep at an distance, she had been obliged to go ~~there~~ ^there

116.27  the ~~proverbial~~ ^reputed expensiveness

116.28  ~~called~~ ^calling for her Bill

116.30  staying ^not another hour

116.30  1  in ~~great~~ ^all the anger . . . which a belief  *'which' is left hanging as the sentence takes a different direction and the clause remains unfinished*

116.34  to have ^a spy on her

116.35-7  ~~induced~~ ^persuaded her . . . such a home ^for the rest of her Stay as their humbler house in ^a very inferior part of London, cd offer^.^ ~~for the rest of her stay.~~

116.39  ~~were~~ ^beyond her expectation worthy people

117.11  for ^a situation

117.12  & ~~unpretending manners~~ ^sweetness merit had now

117.16  of her ~~good Judgement~~ ^steady conduct & mild, ~~unassuming,~~ gentle Temper

117.21-2  & since ~~she had~~ ^having had . . . ~~she was become~~ that Loveliness was complete

117.24-5  they passed ~~in front of~~ ^close by a moderate-sized house

117.25-7  Garden, ~~Ground~~ ^Orchard & ~~Orchards~~ ^Meadows which are . . . of ~~such any~~ ^such a Dwelling

117.28  my ^old House

117.34  given it up ^you know to the Man

118.1-2  one other ~~ascent~~ ^Hill brings us to ~~the heart of~~ Sanditon ^—modern Sanditon—~~we shall soon catch the roof of my new house; my real home,—~~ a beautiful Spot

118.3  in a > this little contracted Nook

118.5  ^& without the smallest advantage

118.9-10  for ~~the~~ ^a little Crescent . . . (as I trust we shall) ~~& a Crescent is a building that always takes —)~~

118.11-13  & the ~~very~~ name ~~will give us choice of Lodgers.~~ ^joined to the form of the Building, which always takes, will give us the command of Lodgers

118.13 ^In a good Season We shd have

118.15 looking ^at it through the back window with ~~a great deal of~~ something like

118.19 we want. We > we want; & We have ^in fact all

118.20-1 without ~~having~~ ^the constant Eyesore of its formalit~~y~~>ies^;^ ~~as an Eyesore, or its occasional~~ ^or the yearly nuisance of its decaying vegetation

118.22-3 ^and We are quite as well off ~~now~~ for Gardenstuff as ~~we used to be~~ ^ever we were—

118.27-8 shade enough ^on the Hill & more than enough ~~about us~~ in the course

118.28-9 ~~my Plantations astonish everybody by their Growth~~ ^The Growth of my Plantations is a general astonishment

118.35-6 will make ~~her so proud!~~ ^her as proud as can be. ~~It will be delightful to see her walking~~ ^How Grave she will walk about with it, ~~so gravely.   — She will~~ ^and fancy herself

118.38-9 want to bathe, ~~now,~~ we

119.2-3 last Winter ~~as we did~~ ^at all

119.3-4 one of ~~our~~ ^those dreadful Nights

119.7 meeting ^with nothing

119.9 in ~~this Pit,~~ this Gutter

119.11-13 ~~if one~~ ^By any one of those dreadful Currents ~~should pour through the~~ ^which do more mischeif in a Valley, ~~which do more mischeif~~ ^when they do arise than an open Country ever ~~knows~~ experiences

119.16-17 ~~deal with old ma<n>~~ ^get go else where . . . & that old ~~Salmon~~ ^Stringer & his son

119.19 do very well ^beyond a doubt —but at first

119.20 what ~~encouragement~~ ^Help we can

119.22 to have them ~~forgotten,~~ ^often wanted, to have something or other forgotten

119.25 our consumption of ~~old Str<inger>~~ >the Stringers

119.25-6 that can ^be easily done

119.26 will be satisfied ~~I hope~~

119.27 ^& says he never brings

119.28 quite ~~out of~~ left behind

119.30-9 ^He pretends to advise me to make a Hospital of it. He pretends to laugh at my Improvements. Sidney says any thing you know. He has always said what he chose ~~of his eldest Br & to his Eldest Br &~~ of & to us, all. ~~A young Man of Abilities & Address, & general ease of manner Miss H.   — who says anything~~

∧Most Families have such a member among them I beleive Miss Heywood.—There is a someone in most families ~~who is privileged~~ ∧privileged by superior abilities or spirits to say anything.— ~~Sidney is~~ ∧In ours, it is Sidney; who is a very clever young Man,— ~~very lively, very pleasant~~ ∧and with great powers of pleasing.— ~~living very~~ ∧He lives too much in the World—~~& liked by every body.~~ ∧to be settled; that is his only fault. ~~I should~~ ∧—I wish we may ∧

~~here & there & what why I I wish we may~~ get him to Sanditon, *74's remarking of* ∧He is *this passage is discussed in the Introduction, p. xxviii*

120.1   it would be a ~~credit to~~ ∧fine thing for the Place!

120.6   & ∧real village of ~~original~~ Sanditon   *R. W. Chapman transcribed this in 1925 as 'neat village'. B. C. Southam, 'The Text of "Sanditon"', Notes and Queries, 8 (1961), 23–4, first made the correction to 'real village', adopted by all subsequent editors.*

120.7   at the foot of the ~~Down~~ ∧Hill

120.9-10   ~~but~~ ∧and whose ~~Top was~~ ∧Height ended in an open Down ~~overlooking the Sea.~~ ∧where the new Buildgs might soon be looked for.

120.10-12   ~~wound~~ ∧winding more obliquely towards the Sea, ~~giving~~ ∧gave a passage . . . & ~~forming~~ ∧formed at its mouth

120.13   Fishermen's > Fisherman's Houses

120.15   with ~~great pleasure~~ ∧delight

120.17-18   ~~were actually~~ two Females . . . were actually

120.20   ~~from~~ through the ~~open~~ ∧upper Casement

120.21   highly ~~exhilarating~~ ∧Blissful

120.25   the Hill ~~must~~ ∧might be

120.28   remember any ∧during the whole ~~Season~~ ∧Summer

120.30   ~~but~~ ∧and whose Mother ~~cd not bear to have them~~ ∧would not let them be nearer ∧the shore, for fear of

120.32-6   ~~old~~ ∧William Heeley's windows . . . such a sight ∧at a Shoemaker's in old Sanditon—∧This is new within the month. There was no blue Shoe when we passed this way a month ∧ago.— Glorious indeed!

120.39   last Building of ~~old erection~~ ∧former Days

121.3-4   to be looked at by Charlotte . . . & ~~by Mr Parker their~~ ∧to be watched by Mr P. with the eager eye

121.6-7   had ~~reckoned~~ ∧calculated on;— ~~fewer~~ and a smaller shew . . . Fewer . . .

121.8-10   ~~but there were the Sands~~ —∧But the Sands ∧& the Terrace always attracted some—. ∧and the Tide must be flowing—about half ~~in~~ ∧-Tide now.

121.11   ∧at his own House . . . out of his House ∧at once.

121.12   & ∧he cd almost feel

121.14-16  elevated Spot ~~of any, was an~~ ^on the Down was a light elegant Building, ~~separated from the Down only by a~~ ^standing in a small Lawn with ^a very young plantations ~~over~~ ^around it, ~~not~~ ^about an hundred yards from the brow of ~~the Cliff, which was~~ a steep, but not ^very lofty Cliff

121.17  excepting one ^short row

121.20  ~~a small space~~ ^a little detached from it

121.21  & ^to the Bathing Machines

121.27  at her ^ample, venetian window

121.29  sparkling ~~under a Sunshiny Breeze~~ ^in sun shine & Freshness

121.33-4  ^But Perhaps it implies . . . ~~Not unlikely.~~ ^I trust it may.

122.3  what wd Sidney ~~guess~~ ^say

122.5  my ^two Sisters' complaints

122.7-8  heard us ^frequently say, & are ~~at times martyrs to very dreadful~~ ^subject to a variety of very serious Disorders

122.11  force themselves    *JA wrote 'themselfes' in error; modern editors supply the correction*

122.16  not ^much above 22 > 20

122.17-18  engage in no Profession, ~~which is most unfortunate~~

122.21  or Arthur ~~had~~ ^wd appear by this Letter to have been at the point of death

122.23  & ~~observed~~ ^began

122.29  the means of ~~bringing about~~ ^accomplishing between you

122.31  her Letters ~~describe~~ ^shew her

122.33  much greived ~~by~~ ^at your accident

122.36-8  found me ~~hardly able to crawl from the~~ ^my Bed to the Sofa ^suffering under a more severe attack . . . Spasmodic Bile ^& hardly able to crawl from my Bed to the Sofa.

123.6.  the immediate ~~application~~ ^use of Friction alone, ~~well~~ ^steadily persevered in

123.7  for ~~4~~ ^six Hours

123.16  for any releif^.^ ~~to be obtained.~~

123.19  I ~~know where to apply~~ could soon put the necessary Irons in the fire

123.26-7  from Headaches. Six Leaches a day > from the Headache, and Six Leaches a day for ~~the last week have~~ ^10 days together releived her ~~a~~ ^so little that I > we thought it right

123.29  She has ^accordingly had 3 Teeth drawn ~~accordingly~~

123.32  on poor Arthur's ~~sneezing~~ ^coughing trying to suppress a cough

124.1   ~~that of~~ ^one a rich West Indian

124.2   respectable ^Girls Boarding School

124.4   ^But Success more than repays

124.5-9   'Well—said Mr P.— ~~having finished & refolded his Letter~~ ^as he concluded finished ~~it.~~— ~~I suppose if~~ ^Though I dare say Sidney ~~wd~~ might find ~~something very amusing~~ ^Though it ~~....~~rily ~~....~~rtaining In this Letter, ^& make us laugh for half an hour together I declare I ~~can see nothing in~~ ^by myself, can see nothing ~~either in~~ it but what is ^either very pitiable or very creditable

124.10   occupied ~~for~~ ^in ~~advancing~~ promoting the Good of others

124.13   & ^extra Beds

124.15-17   I am ~~quite~~ astonished . . . ~~It is really~~ frightful!

124.19   ~~most~~ ^more distressing ~~to one's imagination~~ than all the rest

124.26   to ~~say~~ ^own the truth

124.29   p<oor> Arthur   *JA began to write 'poor', the epithet regularly associated with Arthur Parker*

124.34-5   sit down at 1 & 20, ~~idle & indolent,~~ on the interest . . . or ~~any~~ prospect ^the slightest plan of engaging in

125.3   as much, ^& as quickly as possible

125.5   important ^Business of Dinner

125.7   a solitary ^Elderly Man

125.10   the Cliffs, ^& the Sands

125.12   within ^the House & without

125.12-13   sitting in ~~the little~~ ^her inner ~~parlour~~ ^room . . . for want of ~~something better to do~~ ^Employment

125.17-22   nothing better than ~~such as these.~~—Mrs Mathews...Dr & Mrs ~~Henderson~~ ^Brown . . . Mr P. could not but feel that ~~it~~ ^the List was not only ~~a List~~ without Distinction

125.25   the promised large Families . . . ~~was~~ ^were an ever-~~present source of Joy~~ ^-ready consolation

125.26   came forward ~~immediately~~ ^without delay

125.30-1   to the List ~~with all becoming alacrity~~ as the first offering . . . was ~~proceeding to~~ ^busy in some immediate purchases for the ^further good of Everybody

125.33   glossy Curls & ~~ornamented Combs~~ ^smart Trinkets,

126.1   or rather ~~began to feel~~ ^she reflected that

126.2-4  it wd not do ^for her to be spending . . . the ^very first Evening^.^ ~~of her arrival.   A~~ ^She took up a Book; it happened to be a vol. of <u>Camilla</u>. ~~happened to lie on the Counter.~~

126.5-6  of having her Distress.>, ^so, she turned from the ~~The Gla~~ Drawers of rings & Broches ~~must be resisted~~ repressed farther solicitation

126.11  ~~whence they were~~ ^& had been directed ^thence to the Library

126.11-12  though ~~her having walked a good mile was~~ Lady D. was a great deal too active

126.20-1  just to see ~~our good Neighbours, & be~~ ^you & make sure of ~~their~~ ^your being really come

126.23  ~~without any other species of opposition~~ ^very quietly— without seeming to

126.27-9  ^She observed them well. Lady D. was of middle height . . . a shrewd eye, ~~a~~ ^& self-satisfied air

126.31-4  on ~~free-speaking~~ ^being free-spoken . . . cordiality ~~in it~~ ^about her . . . a heartiness ~~and interest~~ ^of welcome towards her old friends, which ~~was~~ was inspiring

126.38-127.2  a sweet^ly^ modest~~y~~ ^& yet natural^ly^ Graceful~~ness of~~ Address . . . see ^in her only ~~as~~ > the most perfect representation of ~~all the most beautiful & bewitching Heroines~~ ^whatever Heroine might be most beautiful

127.3  ~~in~~ ^on Mrs Whitby's shelves

127.3  it ~~was from~~ might be partly

127.8  ^Such Poverty & Dependance joined to ^such Beauty & Merit

127.13-15  ~~in~~ the ^first 5 minutes . . . which <u>ought</u> to ~~await~~ ^be the Lot of the interesting Clara

127.18  nothing worse in Lady Denham'~~s~~ <behaviour?> than

127.28  ~~too~~> two large Families

127.28  Very ~~very~~ good, very good, said her Ladyship

127.30  No people ~~are said~~ ^spend more freely

127.32  ~~think~~ ^fancy themselves equal

127.33  ~~And~~ ^But then, they who scatter ~~about~~ their Money so freely

128.7-8  smiles ~~at me~~ I see;—^I dare say she thinks me a[n] odd sort of a Creature, ~~may be~~ *editors silently emend to 'an odd'*

128.11-13  such a Servants Hall ~~full~~ to feed . . . that ow<n>> have fewest Servants

128.13  of Parade, ^as all the World knows

128.22  got no more ~~thanks~~ credit from Lady D.

128.31-3 enquiries for a Chamber-House . . . poor Mr Hollis's Chamber Hou>rse   *JA wrote 'Chamber-House' in the first instance and can be seen correcting the second instance, overwriting 'u' with 'r'. Editors correct to 'chamber-horse', as did Cassandra Austen in the copy she made of her sister's manuscript.*

128.36 if ^my poor dear Sir Harry

129.4 Miss Clara ^& I must stay

129.6 amongst ~~others~~ ^them, Sir Edwd Denham

129.9 was ~~in~~ ^settled with Mrs P.—in the Drawing room ~~when they came~~ in time to see

129.21 his ~~pleasing~~ ^very good address

129.24 a ~~very~~ fine Countenance

129.25-8 ~~Charlotte~~ ^she liked him . . . thought him ~~very~~ agreable . . . with the ~~notion~~ ^suspicion of . . . which ~~might be implied~~ ^would arise from his

129.31 more ~~Dull of Mind~~ ^simple dull of Fancy & more ~~ind<ifferent?>~~ careless of pleasing

130.3-4 not ~~only~~ ^merely for moving . . . which ^altogether gave

130.8 his Title did ~~not hurt him~~ ^him no harm

130.31 & ~~devoting himself entirely,~~ ^by addressing his attentions entirely

130.32-4 ^Stationing himself Close by her ~~side~~, he seemed to mean . . . & ^to give

131.1 da<rk>(?) > deep fathoms

131.24 "Oh! ^there is Pathos ~~that~~ ^to ~~maddens~~ one!

131.35 seems to irradiate ~~Scott~~ ^him

132.1 his Spirit ^truly breathed

132.14-16 The Coro>uscations of Talent, ~~of~~ elicited . . . the proa>saic Decencies   *JA too appears to struggle with some of Sir Edward's 'hard words'*

132.25-6 she ~~could comprehend.~~ ^had learnt to understand.

132.27 She ~~could~~ ^had read it . . . glance ~~of two of Sir Edwards~~ ^or two on his side—

132.33 a proposition ~~of~~ for going

132.36 with ~~some~~ looks

132.37 they ~~were to~~ unite^d^

132.39-133.1 ~~deriving considerable amusement from~~ ^amused in considering the contrast ~~of~~ between her two companions

133.2-3 no ^strain of doubtful Sentiment . . . in Lady D.'s ~~manner of talking~~ ^discourse

133.3-6  of Charlotte's arm ~~immediately~~ with the ease of one who ~~had been long used to consider her~~ ^ felt herself doing ~~honour by any Notice she bestowed~~ ^ that any notice from her was an Honour, & communicative...& a ^or a natural love of talking

133.10  get round me ^every way, with her praise

133.15  I had them ^with me last Summer

133.27  we must not ~~rip up the faults of~~ ^find fault with the Dead. ~~We lived perfectly happy together~~ — ^Nobody could live happier together than us—

133.32  in ~~her~~ ^Charlotte's countenance

133.33-5  no ~~legal~~ bequest . . . He ~~had~~ only told me . . . ~~that~~ ^it need not

133.39  he needs it ^bad enough

134.6-7  He is ^a very fine young Man . . . Elegant ^in his Address

134.8  but Charlotte ~~imagined~~ ^directly saw that it was laying her open

134.18  seemed ^quite to to  *'to' repeated in error and removed here*

134.19-39  cried Lady D— . . . She spoke this so seriously, that Charlotte  *this represents 31 manuscript lines first written in pencil, to be traced over subsequently in ink, with a few superlinear insertions—'real', 'Landed or Funded', 'And'—all written in ink only and presumably added at that subsequent stage*

134.24  have any ^real Property.>, ^Landed or Funded.

134.26  ~~Now~~ ^And what good

134.29  but get > get ~~get~~ a young Heiress  *in pencil the manuscript read 'but get'; subsequently 'get' was inked over 'but', leaving the pencilled 'get' redundant, and so it was deleted*

134.30  to take > drink asses milk  *'take' in pencil with 'drink' written over in ink*

135.1  & ~~was~~ prepared for

135.4  in dusting ~~the~~ ^out Bed rooms

135.15  but ~~3 or 4~~ either of the two others

135.24-6  & ^but without attempting . . . ~~while Lady D. still talked~~ ^& only conscious that Lady D. was still talking on in the same way

135.27-30  She is ~~much worse than I expected — meaner — a great deal meaner. She is very mean.~~ ^thoroughly mean. I had not expected anything so bad. —Mr P. spoke too mildly of her.— ~~His own kind Disposition makes him judge too well of others~~ His Judgement is evidently not ^always to be trusted^.^ ~~in his opinion of others.~~ —His own Goodnature misleads him. ^in^ ~~judging of others.~~ He is too kind hearted to see clearly.

135.32  in that ~~respect~~ ^Line

135.36  I can ^not tell

136.1  walking together ~~by~~ ^till rejoined by

136.5  what ~~we have been doing.~~ ^has been our occupation.

136.9  the > those

136.14-16  ^But If you will . . . ^I dare say it will ~~probably~~ give me a clearer idea

136.20  first Germ of ^incipient Susceptibility

136.24  ~~encounter~~ ^atcheive all

136.25-37  peruse with ~~ardour~~ ^delight . . . ~~unconquerable~~ ^indomptible Decision . . . the ^high-toned Machinations of the prime Character . . . of ~~his Rival~~ ^any opposing Character . . . is ^but Eleemosynary . . . the most ~~sagacious~~ ^anti-puerile Man

137.4-5  Sir Edw ^whom Circumstances had confined very much to one spot had read more sentimental Novels

137.7  as have ^since appeared

137.9  of every ~~thing~~ ^opposition of feeling & convenience is concerned

137.13-14  the Ingenuity, & the Perseverance, ~~of the which were the usual~~ ^of the Villain of the Story    'Ingenuity': based on Chapman's 1925 transcription, many modern editions read this as 'Sagacity'. For the amendment, see Arthur M. Axelrad, 'Sir Edward's "Ingenuity": a corrected reading in the Sanditon manuscript', Persuasions, 17 (1995), 47–8.

137.16-17  he ^was always ~~wished it better~~ ^more anxious for its Success ~~than it cd ever have~~ & mourned

137.20  he ~~owed his~~ read nothing else . . . his Language ~~was~~ ^were not formed

137.25-6  the style of ~~our~~ ^the our most approved Writers

137.30-2  ^He felt that He was formed . . . ^The very name of Sir Edward, he thought, carried some degree of fascination with it.— To be generally

137.35-6  with ~~some~~ ^any pretensions . . . to his own ~~mistaken~~ veiws of Society

137.38  it was Clara ^alone on whom he had serious designs

138.15  and he ~~wd have~~ felt ^a^ ~~some~~ ^strong curiosity to ~~know~~ ^ascertain whether . . . some ~~desola~~<te> solitary House

138.27-8  after ~~being~~ ^having been contending

138.31-3  that it ~~was~~ ^could be no acquaintance . . . into the House ^if possible before her^.^ ~~if possible~~ . . . pace ~~was too brisk~~ for ^did not allow this to be accomplished

138.34-5  ~~as~~ ^when the other crossed

139.3  were ~~beginning to astonish Charlotte~~ ^a moment's astonishment

139.5-8  There was ~~great astonis~~<hment> ^much general^ a great deal of surprise & ~~great~~ ^But no still more^ pleasure in seeing her.——^Nothing cd be kinder than her reception from both Husband and Wife.^ How ~~had~~ > did she come?

139.9  And ^that^ she was to

139.11-13  ~~but rather delicate~~ ^delicate looking rather^ than ~~absolutely~~ sickly; ~~in her~~ with an agreable face . . . ~~and~~ her manners ~~resembled~~ ^resembling^ her Brother's . . . though ~~there was~~ ^with^ more decision

139.14  an account of herself ~~as soon as they were in the Drawing-room~~ ^without delay^

139.18  This was ~~a great increase of the Happiness~~ ^better & better^

139.18  We are actually all ~~here~~ come

139.19  ~~A case of Necessity~~ ^Nothing else to be done^

139.24-5  last night ~~which we spent~~ at Chichester, ~~but~~ ^and as^ this is so > not ^so^ common with her ~~that~~ as with me

139.26  kept up ~~charmingly~~ ^wonderfully^

139.26-8  ~~She and~~ ^had^ no Hysterics . . . came ~~to~~ ^within sight of^ poor old Sanditon——and ~~they were quite subsided~~ ^the attack was not very violent—~~quite over~~ nearly over^ by the time we reached

139.30-1  with only ~~young~~ ^Mr^ Woodcock's ~~help~~ ^assistance^ . . . directing ~~where all~~ ^the Disposal of^ the Luggage ~~shd be carried~~; & helping old ~~Hannah~~ ^Sam^ ~~unp~~<ack> uncord the Trunks

139.34  wd not have been ~~afraid for~~ ^unwilling^ himself

139.36-7  hanging ~~over~~ ^about^ him——and ~~therefore~~ ^so^ I helped him . . . to ^the Terrace, to^ take us Lodgings

139.38  at the Hotel^.^ ~~I am sure.~~

139.39  before me ~~in~~ ^on^ the ~~field~~ Down

140.3  a _very_ little ~~stiffened~~ ^affected^

140.10  Best of ~~two Excellent~~ ^the Good^

140.11-12  I ~~have only heard of them~~ ^know them only^ through others.——~~My friend Fanny Noyce I dare say you~~ ^You must^ have heard me mention Miss Capper

140.15  ~~But~~ ^Only^ a _short_ chain

140.18  as to the ~~Spot~~ ^where^

140.20  was consulted ~~as to~~ ^on^ the question

140.24  ~~The~~ ^There^ was but _one_ thing

140.26  large enough ~~for~~ ^to receive^ such a Family

140.29  by the same ~~connecting~~ ^simple^ link ^of connection^

140.31 state of the ~~question~~ ^case^ when I wrote

141.1 on arriving ^there^

141.3 her own account ~~than~~ or her Daughters

141.5 by ^all^ this

141.7 are apt to make ~~the English~~ ^us^

141.9-10 ~~By~~ Whether to offer . . . to ~~you,~~—^or^ to Mrs Whitby?—~~But~~ ^to^ secure them a House?

141.11 when I ~~ought~~ ^am equal^ to act myself

141.12 called for ~~my Exertions~~ ^me^

141.16 ^left Chichester^ at the same hour

141.18 in serving your friends~~.~~ ^& doing Good to all the World.^

141.27 such ~~hasty~~ ^quick^ measures

141.27-9 ~~The part of the story which was really~~ ^most^ ~~astonishing~~ ^to^ ~~Charlotte most, she could not~~ ^bu<t>^ ~~noticed, she had just given it to herself~~ The words ~~of~~ 'Unaccountable Officiousness!—Activity run mad!'—~~but she could only give one explanation of the Amazement which she cd easily beleive to be painted in her face~~ ^had just passed through Charlotte's ~~brain~~ mind ~~and collecting her Thoughts, she replied 'I dare say I look surprised, for I feel so.~~—but ~~that~~ a civil answer was easy

141.29-31 I ^do^ look surprised . . . I know ~~that~~ ^what Invalides^ both you & your Sister are^.'^ ~~sad suffers as to Health~~ ^Invalides'^

141.33 that ~~name~~ ^appellation^

141.36 or ~~which will~~ incline us

141.36-7 ~~Hum<anity>~~ The World is pretty much divided

141.38-9 those who can act & those who can ~~act~~ ^not^ . . . to let ~~none of their faculties be wasted.~~ ^no opportunity of ~~doing Good~~ being useful, escape them.^

142.3 of use [to] *JA wrote 'of use of' in error*

142.11-12 Mr P. ~~particularly urged for~~ ^warmly offered his assistance^ in taking the house for Mrs G.

142.15 on any business ^of mine^

142.19 seeing me again ~~this Eveng~~ ^to day^

142.24 to get into ~~them~~ ^some other^ Lodgings or other & be settled

142.26 to like ~~to undertake it~~ ^the commission^

142.28-30 'Oh!—~~as to your Sisters Dinner~~ ^'No, indeed you should not—^ cried his wife, ~~that's never anything more than a~~ ^for Dinner is such a mere^ name with you all

142.33 Susan never eats ^I grant you^

142.35-6 as for Arthur, he ~~is much more likely to eat too much than too little we~~ ^eats enormously. We is only too much disposed for Food. We are often obliged to check him

143.7-8 settled at Clapham, ~~& attends some of the girls of the Seminary, to give them lessons in Botany &~~ ^who actually attends the Seminary and gives lessons on Eloquence and Belles Lettres

143.10 Without <u>my</u> appearing ^however.

143.12 not a week, ~~ago~~ since Miss Diana Parker

143.22-4 ~~in~~ as a Projector . . . odd complaints^.^ ~~for themselves.~~

143.25 ~~the love of~~ ^a Zeal for being useful

143.26 for the Good [of] others   *JA wrote 'Good or others', corrected here*

143.29 ~~a~~ ^an early tendency ~~to~~ ^at various times, to various Disorders

143.30 the rest ^of^ ^their Sufferings was from Fancy

143.31-4 They had ~~benevolent~~ ^Charitable hearts . . . but ~~the disease~~ ^a spirit of ^restless activity . . . in every exertion of ~~Health, as well as in every inaction of Sickness~~ ^Benevolence—

144.1 Mr & Mr[s] P. spent   *JA wrote 'Mr & Mr P.', corrected here*

144.4 & ~~whose~~ had never employed her

144.8 & ^she found them arranged for the Eveng

144.10 though ^it had been a very fair English Summer-day

144.11 & ^the Table

144.14 with ~~the sort~~ ^a peculiar degree of respectful Compassion

144.18 & except^ing^ that she sat

144.19-20 out of ~~many~~ ^the several Phials already ~~domesticated~~ ^at home on the Mantlepeice

144.21 could perceive no ~~signs~~ ^symptoms of illness

144.24 & ^the Salts

144.25-6 had had ~~great~~ ^considerable curiosity to see . . . having fancied ^him a very puny . . . Man

144.29 and ~~excepting~~ with no other look

144.36 boasted ~~most~~ ^much of sitting by the fire

144.39 not once sat down ~~for~~ during the space

145.4 she had ^also opened so many Treaties

145.9 had ^been hitherto kept up

145.10-11 in the delight of ~~what she had done~~ opening the first Trenches of an acquaintance

145.15–16  had also ~~distinguished~~ ^seen something; ~~of the matter; from their window;~~ —they could distinguish ^from their window that there <u>was</u> an arrival . . . but not ~~the~~ ^its amount^.^ ~~of it.~~

145.21–2  after ~~looking~~ ^some removals to look at the Sea

145.23  sitting ~~close~~ ^next to the Fire

145.24  He pᴇᴇᴇ_____wᴀ₍____ wanting not the own _____ wanting not to take the CHAIᴙ

145.26  with ~~great~~ ^much satisfaction

145.27  of ~~him for~~ ^his Person as a screen

145.28–30  ~~He had in every respect a heavy Look.~~ ^Arthur was heavy in Eye as well as figure, ~~Yet was not~~ ^but by no means indisposed to talk

145.30–1  the other 4 were ~~very much~~ ^cheifly engaged together, ^he evidently felt it no penance to have a^n^ ^agreable ~~good looking~~ ^ ~~well grown~~ ~~Girl~~ ^a fine young Woman next to him

145.32–4  as his Br^,^ ~~observed with much~~ ^gre<at> ~~pleasure~~ who felt the ~~great~~ ^decided want of some motive for action, ~~of something source~~ ^Powerful object of animation for ~~Arthur~~ ^him, observed with ~~no~~ inconsiderable pleasure.  *a characteristic example of JA teasing out a longer construction in the course of drafting*

145.35  that he made ^began even to make a sort of apology

146.1  is wholesome ~~for~~ ^& invigorating to me

146.2  as ~~much~~ ^well as anybody

146.7–8  ~~In my own opinion,~~ ^To say the truth— Nerves are the worst . . . of my Complaints ^in <u>my</u> own opinion.

146.13–14  you wd have ~~thought~~ ^found thought me a very poor creature

146.20  mean to ~~take~~ ^walk a great deal

146.23–4  Not, ~~in~~ ^as to mere distance, but ~~there is such a steep Hill to get up to it!~~ ^the Hill is so steep!

146.27  to Perspiration, ~~which~~ and there cannot

146.31  his own Cocoa ~~Pot~~ from the Tray

146.36  Slices of Bread, ^brought up ready-prepared

146.37–8  but ~~in a faint murmur, &~~ ^the murmuring of a few broken sentences of ^self- approbation ~~of his own Doings & prosperity~~ ^& success

146.39  ~~with quite as much Gallantry as before~~ ^into as gallant a Line as ever, & proved

147.7  of ^rather weak Cocoa

147.9  in a ^very fine, dark coloured Stream

147.14  was ~~not~~ ^by no means so fond

147.15–16  He was ~~evidently~~ ^certainly very happy . . . no more ~~from~~ ^of his Sisters

147.22 said he ~~very much obliged~~ ^exceedingly pleased

147.22-3 quite alike ~~upon that subject~~ ^there

147.23-4 I think it ~~is~~ ^a very bad ^thing for the Stomach

147.29-31 ~~It was rather amusing to see~~ He could not get the command of the Butter ^Glass however . . . His Sisters ~~accused~~ ^accusing him . . . & declar~~ed~~>ing he was . . . ^and he maintain~~ed~~>ing that

147.35-8 when ~~that~~ ^her Toast was done, & he took his own ~~Toast~~ in hand . . . cd hardly contain ~~himself~~ ^herself . . . scraped off ^almost as much

148.2-4 A good deal of Earth^y^ ^Dross hung about him. ~~He seemed to have > of having chosen~~ ^Charlotte could not but suspect him of adopting . . . ~~cheifly~~ ^principally for the indulgence

148.14 it ^acts on me like Poison and wd entirely take away

148.16-17 It ~~is a sort of thing hardly to be beleived~~ ^sounds almost incredible— . . . happened to me ~~three times~~ ^several so often that I cannot doubt it

148.22 ~~Very~~ Soon after Tea

148.29-30 ~~brought~~ ^and the colour ^rushed into her Cheeks, & with ~~a good deal of~~ ^much Perturbation

149.6-7 ~~totally seperate & distinct,~~ such a totally distinct set of people . . . in the reports of ~~them~~ ^each, made that matter quite certain

149.12 an immediate ~~Good~~ ^advantage to counterbalance

149.16 Parker ~~family~~ ^race

149.17-19 than ^that the Family from Surry . . . ~~being~~ ^were one & the same

149.23 at the same ~~time~~ ^period (under ^another representation~~s~~)

149.26 or the ~~mistakes of some~~ ^blunders of the many

149.29-30 enough to ~~throw~~ ^make everything ~~into confusion~~ ^appear what it was not

149.33 a^n^ ^expensive House

149.35-150.1 ~~a~~ > the sort of sensation . . . than she had ~~supposed.~~ beleived herself.

150.4-6 Mrs C. Dupuis & ~~her~~ ^Mrs C. D.'s Neighbour . . . a ~~very~~ ^mere trifle ^of reproach remaining for herself

150.6 was seen ^all the ~~next~~ ^following morng

150.9-10 supported herself by ~~giving a home to~~ ^receiving such great girls & young Ladies, ~~who~~ ^as wanted

150.23 between ~~the~~ ^such pursuit^s^ ~~of what~~ as might attract ~~general~~ admiration

150.30-2 anything to ^Smallness & Retirement, ^yet having ^in the course of the Spring been involved in ~~some~~ the inevitable expence of six new Dresses ^each

150.36-7 ^ very ~~retired~~ ^secluded^ . . . celebrity ~~with~~ ^from^ all

151.5-7 in which they moved ^in Sanditon^ . . . ^to^ the prevalence of which rototary motion *JA's distinct spelling 'rototary' is corrected in Cassandra Austen's fair copy of the manuscript to 'rotatory'*

151.11 she had ~~wanted~~ ^been asking for^

ᵢⱼᵢ ᵢᵢ ᵢᵢᵢᵢ ──── ᵢᵢᵢᵢᵢᵢ

151.15 wd ~~fail her~~ ^be^ vain

151.16 or ~~to have~~ any complaint

151.18 ~~& if Mrs G. ever~~ ^could therefore^ ~~rest~~(?) and his Prescriptions

151.26-31 And ~~indeed~~ ^accordingly^ . . . or ^with^ Drawing paper . . . or > to arrange . . . many ^an^ eye

151.34 without ~~being~~ noticed

151.35-7 little disposed ~~by habit~~ for . . . always ~~went out at this end of~~ ^quitted^ the Terrace, in his ~~walk~~ ^way^ to ~~Trafalgar H——~~ ^his Brothers^ by this corner House

151.38 a qr of a mile ^round—~~about~~

152.7 you had ^better^ mention

152.12 a subscription on foot ~~for them~~

152.17-18 impossible you can ^be^ really ~~be~~ at ~~any~~ ^a^ loss . . . can be ^more^ simple

152.19 their ^earnest^ application to me

152.23 in less time [than] *JA wrote 'that' for 'than', corrected here*

152.27 poor Woman in Worcestershire *JA wrote Worcesteshire, corrected here*

152.31-2 to be ^the^ sort of Person . . . she ~~can be~~ ^is^ prevailed on

152.36 And ~~as to~~ then

153.1 putting them ^all^ out

153.8-9 as that is ~~all~~ over . . . Leaches ~~today~~ ^at one oclock^

153.11 besides that (~~besides~~ between ourselves)

153.14-15 I am sorry ~~for this~~ ^to hear it,^ indeed; but ^if this is the case^ I hope Arthur

153.23-4 all the^ir^ impropriety ~~of them~~

153.28 they could ^not^ for some time

153.29 coming up. ~~it.~~ It appeared

153.36-8 ~~& in the~~ ^it was^ a very friendly meeting . . . who was ^most kindly^ taking it for granted

154.7-8 ~~with a~~ ^with a decided air^ ~~& very much the Man of fashion in his air~~ ^of Ease & Fashion, and a^ lively countenance

154.11-29　The ~~approach~~ ^road to Sanditon H. was ~~at first only~~ ^by a broad, handsome, planted ~~road~~ ^approach, between fields, ~~but ending in about a qr of a mile~~ ^of about a qr of a mile's length, & conducting at the end of a qr of a mile through second Gates into the Grounds, which though ^not extensive ~~were~~ had all the Beauty . . . could give.—~~They were so narrow at the Entrance~~ ^These Entrance Gates were so much in a corner of the Grounds or Paddock, so near one of its Boundaries, that ~~one~~ ^an outside fence was at first almost pressing on the road—till an angle ~~in one~~ ^here, & a curve ~~in the other~~ ^there, ~~gave~~ ^threw them ^to a better distance. The Fence was a proper, Park paling in excellent condition; with ~~vigorous~~ ^rows clusters of fine Elms, or ^rows of old Thorns ~~& Hollies~~ following its ~~course~~ ^line almost every where . . . there were ~~intervals~~ vacant spaces—& through one of them>se, Charlotte . . . caught a glimpse ^over the pales of something White & Womanish ~~over the pales~~ . . . & very ~~distinctly, though at some distance before her~~ ^decidedly inspite of the Mist; Miss B—seated, not far before her, ~~on~~>at the foot of the ~~sloping~~ bank which sloped down from the outside of the Paling & ~~at~~ which a narrow ~~track~~ ^Path seemed to skirt along

154.32　instantly felt ~~that~~ she had nothing to do

154.33-5　but strike ^her rather unfavourably . . . which ~~ought~~ ^must not ~~to~~ be judged

154.36-8　nothing ~~of it~~ had been ~~seen~~ ^discerned &> by Mrs Parker. ^If Charlotte ~~she was~~>had ^not been considerably the tallest . . . ~~or~~ Miss B.'s white ribbons

155.4　thought themselves so ^perfectly secure from observation

155.5-6　by the foot [of] Man ~~behind them~~ ^at their back　*JA wrote 'by the foot by Man', corrected here*

155.7　really ill-used. ~~by her.~~

155.10-11　in the ^order and the Importance of her style of living　*The reading of the insertion 'order and the' is unclear; it could read 'outward'*

155.15　of a ~~portly~~ ^stately Gentleman

155.17　and that ~~a~~>one among many

155.19　~~was~~ ^represented Mr Hollis

155.20　in his ~~room~~ ^own House

## OPINIONS OF MANSFIELD PARK

157.9　Not liked it ^near so well as P.&P.

157.24　^Thought Henry Crawford's going off

158.36　with the greatest ~~pleasure~~ ^interest

158.39 makes it a ~~very~~ ^most desirable

159.14 conducti<ng>

159.16-17 more ^striking & interesting

159.30 ~~Mrs Maling    (Lady Mulgrave's mother) delighted with it; read it through in a day & a half.~~    *comment struck through between those of Charles and Mrs Dickson*

159.33 liked it, ~~&~~ but thought it a mere Novel

160.2 an Incident ~~or~~ > a conversation


## OPINIONS OF EMMA

161.16 did not like it , , , the 3 others. ^Language different from the others, not so easily read.—

161.20 Language superior ^to the others.—

161.21 PP > MP

161.34 Miss Lloyd—^thought it as <u>clever</u>


## PLAN OF A NOVEL

165.1  Heroine the ~~only child~~ ^Daughter

165.5  ~~doing infinite good in his Parish, a Blessing to everybody connected with him, &~~ without the smallest drawback

165.13 on the Piano Forte ^& Harp—

165.15 ^who are to converse in

165.20 to her Mother & a > their Marriage

165.25 buried his ^own Mother

166.6  <u>he</u> being ^driven from his Curacy

166.6  the vile arts of  'the vile acts of' (*Later Manuscripts*, 227), *a possible reading*

166.12 variety of Characters—^But there will be no mixture; the scene will be for ever shifting

166.13-14 ^but All the Good . . . ^and there will be no foibles

166.16 resemblance of ~~Mortal~~ ^Humanity left in them

166.19 ^& only prevented from paying

166.29 ~~after~~ > finding

166.33 Invectives again[st] Holder[s] of tythes  *JA wrote 'again Holder's, here editorially corrected*

## VERSES

### THIS LITTLE BAG

Composed January 1792; manuscript in JA's hand; in family possession.
The poem was first published in *Memoir* (1870), 124; *Minor Works*, 444–5,
reproduces the 1870 text.

A photograph of the manuscript was reproduced by its then owner,
Joan Mason Hurley (Joan Austen-Leigh), in an article, 'Jane Austen's
Housewife', *Country Life*, 172 (28 October 1982), 1323, where it is
described as written on a scrap of paper 2 × 3 inches (51 × 77 mm) and
folded into 'accordian pleats' to form 'a miniscule packet no bigger than
a baby's finger' and placed in a tiny pocket inside the small housewife or
sewing outfit, which was itself inside a bag.

| | |
|---|---|
| l. 3 For, if you thread & needle want: | For should you thread and needles want (1870); For, if you should a needle want (*Catharine and Other Writings*, 234) |
| l. 7 the Bag: | this bag (1870) |
| l. 8 your freind: | your friend (1870) |

*Memoir* (1870) also repunctuates the poem.

### MISS LLOYD HAS NOW SENT TO MISS GREEN

Probably composed April 1805, following the death of Martha Lloyd's
mother (*Letters*, 103–7); no known manuscript in JA's hand.

It was copied, probably after 1855, into the Lefroy Manuscript, a family
history compiled by JA's niece Anna Lefroy; in family possession.

The poem was first published from this source by Deirdre Le Faye, 'Jane
Austen Verses', *Times Literary Supplement*, 20 February 1987, 185. JA's
mother, Mrs Cassandra Austen, penned a reply to this poem, also copied
into the Lefroy Manuscript, in the voice of Miss Green, the dressmaker
(*Collected Poems*, 20–1).

### OH! MR BEST, YOU'RE VERY BAD

Composed July(?) 1806; manuscript in JA's hand; in family possession.

The first three stanzas of this humorous poem were printed in *Life &
Letters*, 70; reprinted in *Minor Works*, 445, as 'Lines to Martha Lloyd'. The
poem was printed in full from the manuscript, by Donald Greene, 'New
Verses by Jane Austen', *Nineteenth-Century Fiction*, 30/3 (1975), 257–60.
According to Greene, the verso of the manuscript reads: 'To Martha'; since
his examination it has been placed in a frame.

l. 23 ~~the friend~~ (?) as Escort
l. 37 ~~Decide to go to Harrowgate~~ ^Convey her safe to Morton's wife
l. 42 ~~Oh! wicked Mr Best~~ I'll never let you rest

### SEE THEY COME, POST HASTE FROM THANET

Composed July 1806; no known manuscript in JA's hand.

~~It was copied, probably after 1855, into the Lefroy Manuscript, where~~
Anna gives it the title 'Lines written by Jane Austen for the amusement of
a Niece (afterwards Lady Katchbull) on the arrival of Captn & Mrs Austen
at Godmersham Park soon after their marriage July 1806'.

The poem was first published from this source by Deirdre Le Faye, 'Jane
Austen Verses', *Times Literary Supplement*, 20 February, 1987, 185; subsequently in *Letters*, 118.

### ON SIR HOME POPHAM'S SENTENCE — APRIL 1807

Composed as dated and surviving in a fair-copy manuscript in JA's hand;
Fondation Martin Bodmer, Geneva (see next entry).

The text was first published in *Letters*, ed. Brabourne, ii. 344; reproduced in *Minor Works*, 446.

### HAPPY THE LAB'RER

Composed August–September 1807(?) and surviving in a fair-copy manuscript in JA's hand; Fondation Martin Bodmer, Geneva.

Written across four pages, the Bodmer Manuscript contains four sets of
'Verses to rhyme with "Rose"'; the other three sets were the composition
of JA's mother, Mrs Cassandra Austen, JA's sister Cassandra, and her
sister-in-law Elizabeth (wife of her brother Edward). The verses by JA and
her sister also exist, with variants, in the hand of F. C. Lefroy (JA's great-
niece), Hampshire Record Office, 23M93/85/1/1,2. All four sets were first
published in *Letters*, ed. Brabourne, ii. 341–3; *Minor Works*, 445–6, uses
Brabourne's text, printing JA's verses only. The manuscript contains
fair-copy texts of further poems by JA: ' On Sir Home Popham's sentence—
April 1807' and sets of verses 'To Miss Bigg previous to her marriage, with
some Pocket handfs. I had hemmed for her' (see below).

### CAMBRICK! WITH GRATEFUL BLESSINGS WOULD I PAY

Composed 26 August 1808; manuscript in JA's hand; Jane Austen's House,
Chawton, Hampshire.

A poem-letter, signed 'JA' and dated 'Aug:st 26—1808' in JA's hand, on
the verso is written 'Miss Bigg'.

A fair copy of the same, also in JA's hand, survives in the Bodmer
Manuscript, where it is given the title 'To Miss Bigg previous to her
marriage, with some Pocket handfs. I had hemmed for her'.

ON THE SAME OCCASION — BUT NOT SENT. —
CAMBRICK! THOU'ST BEEN TO ME A GOOD

Fair-copy manuscript in JA's hand; Fondation Martin Bodmer, Geneva.

One of the poems by JA in this four-page manuscript, it is apparently an unsent fair-copy variant set of verses on the occasion of the previous poem. Both sets of verses were published in *Letters*, ed. Brabourne, ii. 344.

TO THE MEMORY OF MRS LEFROY

Composed after 16 December 1808; manuscript in JA's hand; Winchester Cathedral Library.

Four manuscripts are known: another, currently untraced (two stanzas of which, transcribed in the Sotheby sale catalogue for 3 May 1948, provide variants), may pre-date the Winchester autograph; two later transcripts survive in other hands (see Gilson, 'JA's Verses', 42–5).

The poem was first published in John Henry Lefroy, *Notes and Documents relating to the Family of Loffroy* (Woolwich, privately printed, 1868), 117–18. A version, lacking stanzas 4 and 5, was published in *Memoir* (1870), 76–8; reprinted in *Minor Works*, 440–2, with a transcription below it of the two missing stanzas.

ALAS! POOR BRAG, THOU BOASTFUL GAME!

Dated 17 January 1809; manuscript in JA's hand, in a letter to Cassandra Austen; Morgan Library, New York.

First published in *Letters*, ed. Brabourne, i. 63-4; subsequently, in *Letters*, 174. The manuscript is also reproduced in *Jane Austen's Manuscript Letters in Facsimile*, ed. Jo Modert (Carbondale, IL: Southern Illinois University Press, 1990), F—187.

Layout reproduces that of JA's holograph.

MY DEAREST FRANK, I WISH YOU JOY

Dated 26 July 1809; draft manuscript in JA's hand; Jane Austen's House, Chawton, Hampshire.

Two autograph manuscripts of this poem-letter are known: the draft manuscript, inscribed by JA 'Copy of a letter to Frank, July 26. 1809'; the posted fair-copy, British Library (BL), London.

First published in *Jane Austen's Letters*, ed. R. W. Chapman, 2 vols (Oxford: Oxford University Press, 1932), ii. 264–6; subsequently, in *Letters*, 183–6; *Letters in Facsimile*, ed. Modert, F-199–202.

There are slight differences of punctuation and presentation between the two manuscripts and one difference of substance:

l. 24 neigbouring:                                neighbouring (BL)

l. 41 Cassandra's pen will give our state:   Cassandra's pen will paint our
                                             state (BL)

### IN MEASURED VERSE I'LL NOW REHEARSE

Composed after 1810; no manuscript is known to survive.

First printed in *Memoir* (1870), 117–18; all other printings, including
lh ii, ih i Im Aiiim ihli  h. ipioilii.luig uiu .iiiliiuiiiip tuki, niiliiuii iiiumi), 448  3,
supplied the title 'Mock Panegyric on a Young Friend', taken from Austen-
Leigh's introduction to the verses: 'Once, too, she took it into her head to
write the following mock panegyric on a young friend, who really was
clever and handsome' (*Memoir* (1870), 116–17). Caroline Austen suggested
in a letter of 1 April [1869?] that her brother include the poem in *Memoir*
by way of 'stuffing', as a harmless piece unlikely to embarrass the family or
compromise their aunt's mature reputation (*Memoir*, ed. Sutherland, 185).
It was regarded in the family as written for Anna Austen (later Lefroy) and
to reflect the 'mercurial and excitable' aspects of her character in youth
(*Life & Letters*, 241). As such, the dating within the family is closer to 1810
than the 15 July 1817 date (three days before JA died) inexplicably
attached to it in *Catharine and Other Writings*, 233. In 1810 Anna was 17,
staying in Chawton with her grandmother and aunts Jane and Cassandra
following the breaking off of an unsuitable engagement (*Family Record*,
182). A year later, JA reports of 'an Anna with variations—but she cannot
have reached her last, for that is always the most flourishing &
shewey—she is at about her 3$^{d}$ or 4$^{th}$' (*Letters*, 192). JA continued
to worry over Anna's 'unsteadiness' of temper (to Frank Austen,
25 September 1813, *Letters*, 241). No single circumstance points to a precise date for the poem.

### I'VE A PAIN IN MY HEAD

Dated at the end 'Feby 1811'; manuscript in JA's hand; Winchester City
Museum.

Two autograph manuscripts are known as well as a later family copy in
the Lefroy Manuscript (Gilson, 'JA's Verses', 51–3 and 58–9; and *Collected
Poems*, 67). The second autograph, reproduced as illustration in the *Times
Literary Supplement*, 17 June 1939, 356, and now in the private collection
of Dr Sandy Lerner, includes on the reverse side verses thought to be in
the hand of JA's mother, Cassandra Austen.

The poem was first published in *Minor Works*, 448–9, under the title
'Lines on Maria Beckford', attributed by Chapman.

There are slight differences of punctuation and presentation between
the two autograph manuscripts but no difference of substance.

Feby 1811 (Winchester MS, subscribed): Jane Austen (Lerner MS,
subscribed).

*Minor Works*, 449, and *Catharine and Other Writings*, 242, incorrectly read JA's 'Feb^y' as 'Feb 7'.

### ON THE MARRIAGE OF MR GELL OF EAST BOURN
### TO MISS GILL.——

Composed after 25 February 1811 (the date of the newspaper announcement of the marriage). Two manuscript copies in JA's hand are known to survive: one in a private collection (image reproduced in Sotheby's sale catalogue, 14 March 1979, lot 296); the other in the Roman Baths Museum, Bath and North East Somerset Council.

The copy in private collection is written on the verso of a frontispiece to a Minerva Press novel, *Love, Mystery, and Misery* (1810) by Anthony Frederick Holstein [pseud.]; the Bath manuscript is a bifolium containing two poems (see 'When stretch'd on one's bed' below). The Bath manuscript was first published with slight alterations in *Memoir* (1870), 115, where it is accompanied by a lithographic reproduction (facing p. 122) that differs from both the printed text and the manuscript it appears to represent. Variants between the facsimile and printed text of 1870 (among which its two four-line stanzas collapsed into four lines only) suggest Austen-Leigh 'improved' his aunt's manuscript. He also repunctuated the poem. *Minor Works*, 444, takes its text from the lithographic reproduction in *Memoir* (1870) rather than Austen-Leigh's printed text, thus losing the punning and playfulness of 'i.s' and 'e.s'.

*Title:* On the Marriage of Mr Gell of East Bourn to Miss Gill: On reading in the Newspaper, the Marriage of 'Mr Gell of Eastbourne to Miss Gill' (lithograph);

On Reading in the Newspapers the Marriage of Mr Gell to Miss Gill, of Eastbourne (1870)

l. 1 Of Eastbourn, Mr Gell:      At Eastbourne Mr Gell (1870)
l. 4 For the Love of Miss Gill:  For love of Miss Gill (1870)
l. 6 I'm the Slave of your i.s:   I'm the slave of your *eyes*. (lithograph); I'm the slave of your *iis*; (1870)
l. 7 Ah! restore if you please:  Oh! restore if you please (lithograph and 1870)
l. 8 By accepting my e.s:        By accepting my *ease*. (lithograph); By accepting my *ees*. (1870)

### I AM IN A DILEMMA

Dated 30 April 1811; manuscript in JA's hand; Morgan Library, New York. The verses were sent inside a letter to Cassandra Austen.

First published in *Letters*, ed. Brabourne, ii. 98; subsequently, *Letters*, 194; *Letters in Facsimile*, ed. Modert, F-214.

## BETWEEN SESSION & SESSION

Dated 30 April 1811; manuscript in JA's hand; Morgan Library, New York.

The verses were sent inside the same letter to Cassandra Austen as above.

First published in *Letters*, ed. Brabourne, ii. 99; subsequently, in *Letters*, and *Letters in Facsimile*, ed. Modert, F313

Layout here reproduces that of JA's holograph.

## WHEN STRETCH'D ON ONE'S BED

Dated 27 October 1811; manuscript with revisions in JA's hand; Roman Baths Museum, Bath and North East Somerset Council.

The poem, dated in JA's hand, is included in the same small bifolium as the Bath version of 'On the Marriage of Mr Gell'. It was first published in *Minor Works*, 447–8.

Stanzas 2 and 4 contain extensive revisions, while stanza 5 is deleted and replaced:

l. 10 ~~How little one thinks~~ How slight one's concern
l. 11 ~~Of the Smells~~[?] ~~or the Stinks~~ To conjecture or learn
l. 12 ~~Which pervade~~ the Assembly all What their flounces or hearts may befall
l. 21 Can ~~catch~~^ attract our attention or Ears!
ll. 25–30 ~~For ourselves & our pains~~ [?] | ~~Ev'ry faculty chains.~~ | ~~We can feel on no subject beside.~~ | ~~'Tis for Health & for Ease~~ | ~~The Time present to seize~~ [?] | ~~For their Friends & their Souls to Provide~~

## CAMILLA, GOOD HUMOURED, & MERRY, & SMALL

November 1812; no known manuscript in JA's hand; the Lefroy Manuscript provides a late copy; in family possession.

A further copy (with only slight differences) survives in the diary of Stephen Terry, father-in-law to Anna Lefroy's fourth daughter Georgiana (reproduced in *Letters*, 418 n. 7).

On 29 November 1812, JA jokingly referred to her brother James's 'great improvement' to her lines, suggesting that at least one other version was in circulation (*Letters*, 205). This may be the basis of the markedly variant text with ponderous title ('On the Marriage of a Middle-Aged Flirt with a Mr Wake, whom, it was supposed, she would scarcely have accepted in her youth') and much altered opening line, masking the identity of the victim of JA's wit, first printed by James's son in *Memoir* (1870), 116; subsequently reprinted as authoritative in *Minor Works*, 444.

Lefroy's text is followed here, though without its title ('On the marriage of Miss Camilla Wallop & the Revd Wake'), which appears a later explanatory addition.

Camilla, good humoured, & merry, & small:    Maria, good-humoured, and
                                              handsome, and tall (1870)

WHEN WINCHESTER RACES FIRST TOOK THEIR BEGINNING

Composed Winchester 15 July 1817; no known manuscript in JA's hand; two non-authorial manuscripts: one, in an unknown hand, Berg Collection, New York Public Library; the other, a clean fair copy, with the title 'Written at Winchester on Tuesday the 15th July 1817', in the hand of Cassandra Austen, Jane Austen's House, Chawton, Hampshire, the version reproduced here.

From paper and other evidence, both versions appear to have been written close to the date of composition. JA died barely three days later and it is possible that only dictated copies were made.

First printed in a late family memoir, J. H. and E. C. Hubback, *Jane Austen's Sailor Brothers* (London: John Lane, 1906), 272–3, from Cassandra's copy; in *Minor Works*, 450–2, again from Cassandra's copy, under the attributed title 'Venta' (the Roman name for Winchester); *Catharine and Other Writings*, 246 (and notes at 282–3) reprints from the Berg manuscript.

l. 6 The company met:                The company came (Berg MS)
l. 12 And thus he:                   And then he (Berg MS)
l. 13 Oh Venta depraved:             Oh Ventar depraved (Berg MS)
l. 14 you think we are dead:         ~~you think we are gone~~ (Berg MS)
l. 20 Set off for your course:       set off for your ~~curse~~ course (Berg
                                     MS)

l. 21 my command o'er July:          my command in July (*Minor Works*)
l. 24 The curse upon Venta:          The curse upon Ventar (Berg MS)
Subscribed in Cassandra's hand 'J.A.':   subscribed in a different unknown
                                     hand 'written July 15th 1817: by
                                     Jane Austen who died early in the
                                     morning (1/2 past 4) of July 18th
                                     1817 aged 41 yrs' (Berg MS)

CHARADES

Three verses attributed to JA; date unknown. No manuscript survives in JA's hand.

An undated small early Victorian album, at one time in the Austen-Leigh family, contains late transcriptions in an unknown hand of these and other Austen family charades. Copies of riddles 2 and 3 are also in the Lefroy Manuscript.

First published in [Mary Augusta Austen-Leigh] *Charades &c. Written a hundred years ago by Jane Austen and her family* (London: Spottiswoode & Co., undated, preface, June 1895), nos. 18–20; reprinted from this collection in *Minor Works*, 450. The twenty-two charades printed in 1895 comprise offerings from three generations: James Leigh Perrot (uncle, 4), George Austen (father, 1), Cassandra Austen (mother, 3), James Austen (brother, 6), Henry Austen (brother, 1), Cassandra Austen (sister, 1), Francis Austen (brother, 1), Jane Austen (3), James Edward Austen (nephew, 2).

Texts here are taken from the family manuscript album

Charade 2, l. 3 ~~Man who oft~~ ^Monster who [above the line in pencil]: monster, who (1895)

## APPENDIX

### SIGH LADY SIGH

l. 16 'melancholy', inserted above the line, appears to be offered as an alternative reading.

# EXPLANATORY NOTES

I am indebted to the work of previous editors; in particular, to the explanatory annotations for Austen's unfinished fictions and poetry compiled by R. W. Chapman, Brian Southam, David Selwyn, Margaret Anne Doody, Janet Todd, and Linda Bree. Texts are cited in the notes by volume and chapter, letter, or page number (for novels), by act and scene number (for plays), and by canto, epistle, or book, and line number (for poems), as the most stable form of reference for readers consulting a variety of scholarly, standard, and non-standard editions. References to Austen's novels follow the practice of modern editions and cite continuous chapter numbers, not volume and chapter number.

## LADY SUSAN

3 *My dear Brother*: in this instance, brother-in-law is intended, as is sister-in-law a few lines later. 'Sister' and 'brother' were commonly used to denote the relationship by marriage. See *W*, p. 99.

*in Town*: in London's fashionable West End rather than the business district of the City.

*S. Vernon*: it was not unusual to sign a letter to friends and close relatives with a formal signature. JA frequently signed her letters 'J.A.' or 'J. Austen' when writing to her beloved sister Cassandra.

4 *only four months a widow*: it was expected that a widow would follow strict rules of mourning, with full mourning lasting a year, during which time she was expected to lead a quiet life and certainly not be entertaining lovers or flirting with married men. At Letter 30 Lady Susan refers again to mourning protocol. In *P*, ch. 17, Lady Russell, bent on making a match between Anne Elliot and the widower Mr Elliot, 'was beginning to calculate the number of weeks which would free him from all the remaining restraints of widowhood'.

*romantic*: 'fanciful', even 'impractical' (*OED*, sense 3a) rather than suggesting physical or sexual feeling.

5 *Wigmore St.*: in Marylebone, London, just north of Oxford Street, in the early nineteenth century part of a mixed development of smart housing and multiple-occupancy female businesses, among which were milliners and drapers' shops.

6 *Staffordshire*: the location for fictional Vernon Castle, a county in the English Midlands and therefore a considerable distance from Churchill, which is described in Letter 17 as 'a Thirty mile Journey' from London. 'Staffordshire is a good way off', JA wrote from her Hampshire village in 1799 (*Letters*, 38).

*in agitation*: meaning 'under discussion', now rare (*OED*, sense 3a).

7 *Coquette*: a flirt, a term carrying a serious note of disapproval.

*Stupidity*: dullness (*OED*, sense 2a). At Letter 7 Lady Susan describes her daughter as 'a stupid girl'; dull is again the meaning.

9 *Banking House*: as a gentleman and younger son not standing to inherit, Charles has joined a profession, banking, at this time largely run as private partnerships. JA's brother Henry and partners founded the bank of Austen, Maude, and Tilson, Covent Garden, London, in 1804.

*sensibility*: a key term in eighteenth-century philosophy and literature, referring broadly to one's susceptibility to feeling and often satirized by JA in its misuse or excesses, as in her early story 'Love and Friendship': 'A sensibility too tremblingly alive to every affliction of my Freinds, my Acquaintance and particularly to every affliction of my own, was my only fault, if a fault it could be called' (*Teenage Writings*, 70).

*under cover*: the letter to Manwaring will be folded inside one addressed to Mrs Johnson.

*Symmetry, Brilliancy & Grace*: 'Symmetry... Grace' relates to regularity and beauty of form, as in Hannah More, 'Hers every charm of symmetry and grace' (*The Bleeding Rock* (1778), 224, cited in *OED*, sense 2a). Miss Bingley finds fault with Elizabeth Bennet's complexion as having 'no brilliancy' (*P&P*, ch. 45).

*address*: manner or style of speaking (*OED*, sense 5).

10 *Springs... in Town*: the main social season in London for the fashionable and the elite, coinciding with the sitting of Parliament and ending with the King's official birthday, 4 June, and the summer recess.

*left... to the care of servants... Governess... little better*: the danger of leaving children in the care of uneducated servants forms a common topic in tracts on education and female duties in the period. Mary Wollstonecraft argued that mothers make the best teachers for their children, followed by schools, and with servants coming a very poor third: 'for people who do not manage their children well, and have not large fortunes, must leave them often with servants, where they are in danger of still greater corruptions' (*Thoughts on the Education of Daughters* (1787), 60).

11 *Edward St.*: at the time, an extension of Wigmore Street, and so not far from Frederica's school. In *P&P*, ch. 52, Edward Street is the location of the lodging house of Mrs Younge, at one time governess to Georgiana Darcy.

*grand affair of Education*: though a topic of fierce debate in the period, even the most progressive reformers of female education, writers like Catharine Macaulay (*Letters on Education* (1790)) and Mary Wollstonecraft (*Thoughts on the Education of Daughters*), did not advocate the perfect command of 'all the Languages Arts & Sciences' implied in Lady Susan's exaggerated description. With no possibility of access to university or the professions, daughters of the gentry were at best educated to manage a home and be rational wives and mothers, as in Hester Chapone's popular work (*Letters on the Improvement of the Mind, Addressed to a Young Lady* (1773)); at worst, they were offered mere 'accomplishments' to attract a husband, as in JA's critical assessment of the Miss Beauforts, who are 'very accomplished & very Ignorant' (*S*, p. 150).

*I want her to play . . . my hand & arm*: viewed cynically, as here, for a young woman on the marriage market her performance at the piano or harp were as much to display her physical assets as her musical abilities.

12 *open weather*: dry and frost-free, the conditions preferred for hounds following a fox's scent. The fox hunting season extended roughly from October to the end of March.

*Sussex*: the location of fictional Churchill, a county south of London and, at this time, rural.

*Kent*: the location of fictional Parklands, a county adjoining Sussex to the east.

14 *entailed*: the effect of an entail was to settle legally the line of inheritance. Unlike Vernon Castle, which was presumably unentailed and sold out of the family, Mr de Courcy's estate is bound by law to be inherited by his eldest son.

16 *less insinuating*: makes less effort to please.

17 *interesting to*: of concern to (*OED*, sense 1), with a stronger meaning than now. See, too, *S*, p. 126, where Charlotte Heywood's description of Clara Brereton as an 'Interesting young Woman' implies that she engages the attention particularly keenly.

*absolute engagement*: a firm engagement could not be broken without loss of reputation. This explains Elinor Dashwood's comment in *S&S*, ch. 37 ('I am so sure of his always doing his duty') on Edward Ferrars's refusal to break his secret and now regretted engagement to Lucy Steele.

18 *out of my power . . . Estate*: because the estate is entailed (see note to p. 14). In *P&P* Mrs Bennet's anxiety for the future provision of her five daughters is explained by the entail of the family estate of Longbourn 'in default of male heirs' (ch. 7), meaning that, without a son, it passes by strict settlement to the next male heir, Mr Collins.

*intelligence*: information.

21 *traduced*: spoken ill of.

*on the catch for*: on the lookout for; intending to secure (as a husband), now archaic, though we still use the term 'he/she is a catch'.

*common candour*: fairness, disinterested judgement (*OED*, sense 3).

23 *Shrubbery*: country estates of the time would have a shrubbery near to the house, planted with ornamental trees and bushes, and intersected with gravel paths, designed for walking in most weathers. In *W*, p. 70, the banker Mr Tomlinson's pretensions to a house in the country are justified by having 'a shrubbery' attached.

23 *vastly well*: extremely well. *OED*, sense 3, points to its fashionable use in the eighteenth century.

24 *Milkiness*: meekness, gentleness (*OED*, sense 3, now rare).

*elope*: run away (*OED*, sense 2), without the implication of fleeing with a lover or to marry.

*impertinent*: interfering, but not necessarily rude.

*& look*: the phrasing mirrors that of the previous part of the sentence: 'I infinitely prefer...and [I] look...'.

25 *teizing*: JA's preferred spelling for 'teasing', meaning here that he has been pestering her.

*incog.*: slangy and common abbreviation of 'incognito', meaning his identity is hidden.

*at Tea*: tea was drunk after the main meal of the day, which was dinner, usually eaten in the country around four or five in the afternoon, or later. In *W*, p. 74, in anticipation of the ball and a late night, the Edwardses have tea 'at 7 o'clock'.

*pathetic*: moving, affecting (used ironically here).

26 *untractable*: stubborn, unmanageable (now rare).

28 *stage*: stagecoach, a form of public transport, and not normally used by respectable ladies travelling alone.

29 *prognostics*: symptoms, omens.

*nicety*: scrupulousness, delicacy.

*Lenity*: mildness, lenience.

31 *Pelisses*: a pelisse was a lady's loose-fitting outdoor cloak.

*Rattle*: a foolish chatterbox (*OED*, sense 6b).

*Establishment*: material situation on marriage (*OED*, sense 5a).

33 *unspeakable great kindness*: an acceptable grammatical construction (unspeakable, *OED*, sense 4).

*I would rather work for my bread than marry him*: given the virtual non-existence of respectable employment for gentry women, declarations of this kind in fiction of the time carry a strong element of protest. Compare Emma Watson's 'I would rather be Teacher at a school (and I can think of nothing worse) than marry a Man I did not like' (*W*, p. 67).

34 *no Solomon*: in the Old Testament of the Bible, King Solomon was proverbial for his wisdom.

35 *posture of affairs*: condition of affairs (*OED*, sense 3).

*Chit*: a contemptuous term for a girl (*OED*, sense 2b), brat.

36 *keen*: extremely sharp, willing to cause pain (*OED*, sense 3a).

37 *Hunters*: horses used for hunting.

41 *under par*: below the standard to be expected (*OED*, sense 3b).

*Genius*: natural ability.

42 *warm*: ardent, excitable.

43 *retribution*: recompense (*OED*, sense 1a), with no sense of punishment. This meaning was becoming obsolete in the nineteenth century.

44 *condescension*: submissiveness.

■ ⌐ ⌐⌐⌐⌐⌐⌐⌐⌐⌐⌐ ⌐⌐ ⌐⌐⌐⌐ ⌐⌐ ⌐⌐⌐⌐ ⌐⌐⌐ ⌐⌐⌐⌐⌐⌐⌐⌐⌐ ⌐⌐⌐ ⌐⌐ ⌐⌐⌐⌐⌐⌐ ⌐⌐⌐ ⌐⌐⌐⌐ meeting might result in a duel. If so, she is indulging in a little sensation of her own. Though duelling (illegal in JA's time) was not unknown, it was more frequent in fiction. Colonel Brandon duels with Willoughby after the seduction and abandonment of his ward Eliza (*S&S*, ch. 31).

*Bath*: a well-known resort and spa town in the west of England. Its mineral waters were considered especially beneficial in the treatment of gout, a painful inflammation of the joints. JA lived in Bath from May 1801 to July 1806 and may have made a fair copy of the manuscript of *LS* while there (see Introduction, pp. x–xi).

*Drawing room-apartment in Upper Seymour St.*: a set of furnished rooms, including a formal reception room for visitors, in a town house. Upper Seymour Street runs west from Portman Square, in the same district north of Oxford Street as Edward Street. The area was known to JA: in February 1801 her sister Cassandra stayed with brother Henry at nearby 24 Upper Berkeley Street, Portman Square (*Letters*, 84). Margaret Lesley writes to Charlotte Lutterell from Portman Square in 'Lesley-Castle' (*Teenage Writings*, 116), and the area is again used in *S&S*, ch. 25, as the location of Mrs Jennings's London house.

*Title ... Baronets*: the lowest hereditary title and, unlike dukes, earls, and viscounts, not regarded as aristocracy.

48 *Masters*: professional teachers, especially of drawing and music.

49 *the Lakes*: the Lake District in the north-west of England, a popular tourist destination by the late eighteenth century, and the subject of many travel guides, most famously William Gilpin's *Observations, Relative Chiefly to Picturesque Beauty...particularly the Mountains, and Lakes of Cumberland and Westmoreland*, 2 vols (1786). In *P&P*, ch. 42, the original plan of the Gardiners and Elizabeth Bennet is to visit the Lakes.

50 *scarcely ten months a Widow*: see note to p. 4.

*Lady Susan to Mr De Courcy*: the writing of the letter confirms the information it contains: that they have become engaged. By convention, a man and woman otherwise unrelated might only write to each other once they were formally engaged. In *S&S*, ch. 22, it provides unwelcome confirmation for Elinor Dashwood: 'a correspondence between them by letter, could subsist only under a positive engagement, could be authorised by nothing else'.

51 *imperiously*: by absolute necessity.

52 *abroad*: in company.

54 *Eclaircissement*: a clearing-up or revelation, an explanation (*OED*, sense 1); originally a term from French theatre describing a dramatic discovery. It was by this time in wide literary use in English: for example, Walter Scott, *Guy Mannering* (1815), ch. 20. JA uses the term in *Plan of a Novel* (p. 167).

*manœuvres*: another French loan-word, coming into English around the middle of the eighteenth century. The term retained its original meaning of tactical military movement but also expanded in colloquial use to suggest a scheme of action or ploy (*OED*, sense 2a).

56 *dismissed*: sent.

57 *the Manwarings are to part*: at the time, the separation of husband and wife represented an enormous stigma from which the wife, even when innocent of wrong-doing, as here, would be unlikely to recover either socially or economically. Divorce could only be obtained by Act of Parliament and was restricted to the very wealthy.

60 *Post office Revenue*: a local post for London had begun as a penny post in 1680, rising to twopence in 1801, with letters picked up and delivered as many as eight times daily. Outside London, postage, based on weight and distance travelled, was paid by the recipient of a letter. Though the service was operated by private enterprise, fees went to the state.

62 *an Influenza*: considered then, as now, a highly infectious disease that could kill. There were major epidemics in England in 1782, 1785, and 1794.

*finessed*: from 'finesse', to manipulate someone subtly or delicately into a specified state (*OED*, sense 2a, citing *LS*).

THE WATSONS

65 *winter assembly*: provincial towns had a formal social season in the autumn and winter with select public assemblies for dancing, playing cards, and meeting neighbours. Assemblies, paid for by subscription among the local gentry families who attended, were held in dedicated assembly rooms or large rooms in inns. In her youth, JA attended such assemblies at the Angel Inn, Basingstoke, 8 miles from her home in Steventon, Hampshire.

*D.—— in Surry*: possibly Dorking, a market town approximately 25 miles south of London, in Surrey (which JA spells 'Surry'), and in the early nineteenth century on a main coaching road to the south coast. Box Hill, the scene of an outing in *E*, ch. 43, is just outside Dorking. JA regularly intersperses real place names through her fictions to intensify the air of reality of her imaginary locations. Changes in the manuscript show that she earlier planned the town to be 'L—— in Sussex'. Other alterations show her carefully mapping her story mentally as well as geographically: Southampton is changed to Chichester (p. 67), and at p. 83 'D' is inadvertently referred to as 'R' (Reigate?); Guildford (which JA spells 'Guilford'), 13 miles west of Dorking, is the home of Emma Watson's brother Sam. JA describes travelling from Dorking to Guildford in a letter to her sister on 26 June 1808 (*Letters*, 141).

*Tuesday October the 13th*: like real place names, dating shows JA striving in the story's opening after an air of verisimilitude. Though 13 October fell on a Tuesday in 1795, 1801, and 1807, this need not imply, as has been suggested (by Edith and Francis Brown, *The Watsons* (London: Elkin Mathews and Marrot Ltd, 1928), 7), that she was working with a particular year in mind.

*Country Families*: local gentry families, living on their estates.

*Coach ... close carriage*: JA uses descriptions and kinds of transport as clues to economic circumstances and sometimes to character. The private closed coach, protecting occupants from weather, with the horses to pull it and coachman to drive it, is a marker of the Edwardses' substantial wealth. In a letter to Cassandra, 17 November 1798, JA mentions the reason for missing the next ball at Basingstoke. that their father has 'laid down [given up]' the carriage' (*Letters*, 20).

*the former ... the Latter*: the Watson daughters, unmarried and motherless, would depend for propriety's sake on Mrs Edwards as a chaperone at the public assembly. On 1 November 1800 JA wrote to Cassandra of the ball she attended a few evenings before, where without her mother's company, she had the choice of three chaperones. Mrs Harwood, Mrs Bramston, and Mrs Lefroy, commenting: 'with three methods of going, I must have been more at the Ball than anybody else'. On this occasion, like Emma Watson, she dines and sleeps away from home, at the Harwoods (*Letters*, 55).

*monthly return*: assemblies were planned to coincide with the lunar calendar, a full moon making journeys at night easier.

*Chair*: a modest two-wheel mode of transport, without springs (and there fore uncomfortable), open to the weather, drawn by a single horse, and requiring no coachman.

*Miss Watson*: as the eldest daughter, only Elizabeth is thus designated; Emma is 'Miss Emma' or 'Miss Emma Watson'.

*Tom Musgrave*: in the manuscript, he is first called 'Charles'. JA often tinkers with proper names before settling on a firm choice. Later in the story, she gives 'Charles' to the young boy Charles Blake.

66  *quite independant*: with an income sufficient to support himself. Always attentive to the economic circumstances of her characters, JA is especially so in *W*.

*came into this Country*: arrived in the neighbourhood.

*of the name of Purvis*: the Textual Notes (p. 196) show JA originally giving more particulars about Purvis—a clergyman with a nearby parish—before striking out these extra details. JA is a great recycler of names and all kinds of small detail: in *P&P*, ch. 50, Purvis Lodge is one of the houses considered by Mrs Bennet as a future home for her daughter Lydia once she is married to Wickham.

67  *Asthma*: JA's original choice of ailment for the doctor was gout, perhaps
    altered because too regularly resorted to in fiction as an ailment for elderly
    males.

    *Teacher at a school*: one of the few occupations open at the time to
    educated gentlewomen but nonetheless regarded as degrading. See
    Wollstonecraft, *Thoughts on the Education of Daughters*, 71: 'A teacher at
    a school is only a kind of upper servant, who has more work than the
    menial ones.'

    *I have been at school*: in the eighteenth century, boarding schools were an
    increasingly popular choice for daughters of the gentry. JA and her sister
    Cassandra were sent away to school: briefly to Southampton in 1783 and
    to the Abbey House, Reading, at the time a private school for the daugh-
    ters of the clergy and minor gentry, in 1785–6.

68  *fretful & perverse*: JA's original words were less pointed, describing
    Penelope as having 'a good deal of spirit'.

    *Croydon*: approximately 10 miles south of London and 20 miles north-east
    of Dorking, further strengthening the Surrey–Sussex location of the
    story. Croydon is the home of Emma's married brother Robert and his
    socially ambitious wife.

69  *like officers*: for most of JA's adult life Britain was at war with France and,
    in the south of England especially, a visible military presence was the
    norm. Regiments of militia and regular soldiers were garrisoned in many
    towns, their reputation for drinking and womanizing not conducive to
    local peace and morality. In *P&P*, ch. 41, silly teenage Lydia Bennet fol-
    lows the militia to their new camp at Brighton where she imagines herself
    'tenderly flirting with at least six officers at once'. She eventually elopes
    with the soldier George Wickham.

    *Shropshire*: the manuscript shows that JA's first plan was to place Emma in
    'Devonshire', a county in the south-west of England. To the north and
    west, Shropshire is on the border with Wales, and therefore even more
    distant from Stanton.

70  *our great wash*: probably the kind of thorough cleaning hinted at by JA on
    21 April 1816 (*Letters*, 328) as likely to disrupt the whole household. We
    learn later that Elizabeth 'had at all times more good will than method in
    her guidance of the house' (p. 91).

    *at least ten thousand pounds*: whether a dowry to be given to her husband on
    marriage or an inheritance in prospect at her father's death, this is a sub-
    stantial fortune. A few lines later we learn that Emma's brother Robert is
    'lucky' with a wife who brings him 'six thousand pounds' (originally 'four')
    (Textual Notes, p. 197). JA is careful with sums of money, using them instruct-
    ively to imply degrees of affluence or real hardship or to capture aspects of
    character, like meanness or superiority. In 1805, around the time she was
    writing *W*, her father's death left his widow and two daughters in reduced
    circumstances, with just £450 a year between them, much of this contributed

by JA's brothers. This is roughly half the yearly amount she gives later to Tom Musgrave as a comfortable income for a single man (p. 75).

*a Surgeon*: also styled 'surgeon apothecary', a general practitioner who dispensed medicines and treated a range of surgical and physical conditions. As yet, the general country practitioner was a relatively low-status profession, though gaining greater esteem and requiring more formal qualification in JA's lifetime, for example, the 1815 Apothecaries Act introduced compulsory apprenticeship. Advising her niece Anna writing her own novel in August 1814, JA commented: 'I have also scratched out the Introduction between Lord P. & his Brother, & Mr Griffin. A Country Surgeon...would not be introduced to Men of their rank' (*Letters*, 280).

*Turnpike*: a road and the gate on it where a toll or fee was collected to maintain it in good repair. The turnpike in Dorking was constructed in 1750.

*pitching*. the road's stone surface (*OED*, sense 8a).

*shrubbery & sweep*: both features suggestive of the pretensions of the owner to call his house a country estate. For shrubbery, see note to p. 23. A sweep was a curved drive allowing turning for carriages and leading up to the house.

*Mr E's House...stone steps*: the Textual Notes show JA writing and rewriting this small section with considerable attention to the details of the house façade: its elevation and brickwork, the street-facing windows (at first, two, and then unnumbered), the chained posts (first white, then green, and finally just posts) preventing parking directly outside, the stone steps up to the door.

71 *Man in Livery... powder'd head*: the uniformed servant, his hair lightened and stiffened with powder (made from flour or starch) is a further sign that the Edwardses are 'people of fortune'. Both ladies and gentlemen powdered their hair in the eighteenth century, but with a sales tax on powder, introduced in 1786 and raised in 1795, to gain revenue from the fashion, it was dying out by 1800. By the early nineteenth century and the composition of *W*, the fashion is for more natural hairstyles, with powdered hair relegated to provincial males like Robert Watson (see p. 95) and to servants.

*hair in papers*: hair twisted around slips of paper to produce fashionable curls.

*his morning's lounge*: his morning stroll (*OED*, sense 1a).

72 *new Cap*: as a mature woman, Mrs Edwards would wear a cap. JA's nephew and early biographer James Edward Austen-Leigh records how both JA and Cassandra adopted this middle-aged garb quite early: 'she never was seen, either morning or evening, without a cap' (*Memoir*, ed. Sutherland, 70).

*since he was 7 years old*: JA originally wrote 'ten years old'. The change is consistent with her lengthening earlier (see Textual Notes, p. 197, for 70.1) Emma's absence from her birth family.

73 *rubber*: a set of three or five games at whist and other card games. Mr Edwards later states he won 'four rubbers out of five' (p. 82). The men's whist club at the White Hart has its equivalent at the Crown Inn, Highbury, in *E*, ch. 24.

*dinner at midnight*: an exaggeration but also an indicator of status and fashion. At p. 88, Elizabeth and Emma Watson sit down to an unfashionably early dinner at 3 p.m. while Tom Musgrave is eager to be known to dine as late as possible (p. 96). Writing from Southampton in December 1808, JA informs Cassandra, 'we never dine now till five'. Staying with her wealthy, leisured brother at Godmersham in Kent, October 1813, dinner is delayed until 6.30 p.m. (*Letters*, 164 and 254).

*old rooms at Bath*: the old or Lower Assembly Rooms were built in 1708. The larger, new, and more fashionable or Upper Assembly Rooms were opened in 1771. JA describes a rather dull evening in the Upper Rooms on 11 May 1801 (*Letters*, 88). In *NA*, ch. 3, Catherine Morland is introduced to Henry Tilney in the Lower Rooms.

*Ireland…that Country*: the Irish fortune hunter was a stock character in plays and novels of the time. In *Camilla; or, A Picture of Youth* (1796), the second novel of Frances Burney (1752–1840), Mr Macdersey is accused of being 'another Irish fortune-hunter' all the more dangerous for 'being a real Irishman' (bk 5, ch. 8). As a widow with substantial wealth under her own control, Mrs Turner would be a very attractive target; once remarried, her property would become her second husband's, unless some prior legal arrangement protected it. Around 1800 and in light of recent political unrest, many English considered Ireland a wild and ungovernable place.

74 *Cockade*: the knot of ribbons or rosette worn by a soldier, often in the cap, as a badge of office.

*Tea things*: see note to p. 25.

*extraordinary*: additional.

*Shoulders & Throats*: describing to Cassandra in December 1808 the recent ball at the Dolphin Inn, Southampton, JA writes somewhat cruelly, 'the melancholy part was to see so many dozen young Women standing by without partners, & each of them with two ugly naked shoulders!' (*Letters*, 163).

75 *accosted*: waylaid, without the suggestion of hostility.

*morning dress*: his outdoor and daytime clothing since he is not yet changed into formal evening wear.

*8 or 900£ a year*: see note to p. 70.

*Chaperons*: see note to p. 65. JA described her own transition from dancer to chaperone, writing to Cassandra in November 1813 'as I must leave off being young, I find many Douceurs in being a sort of Chaperon for I am put on the Sofa near the Fire & can drink as much wine as I like' (*Letters*, 261).

*Empressément*: effusiveness, and, perhaps, self-importance.

*two first dances*: dancing in polite society was governed by strict rules of etiquette, designed to involve all who wished to dance and to discourage anyone monopolizing a partner, although this did not prevent advance arrangements being made. By convention, dances were arranged in pairs; so in choosing a partner you were committing to two dances. Mrs Bennet's ⁓⁓⁓⁓⁓⁓⁓⁓⁓⁓⁓⁓⁓⁓⁓⁓⁓⁓⁓⁓⁓⁓⁓⁓⁓⁓⁓⁓⁓⁓⁓⁓⁓⁓⁓⁓⁓⁓⁓⁓⁓⁓⁓ is helpful here (*P&P*, ch. 3). Rules for the evening might be posted outside assembly rooms. There were also general books of dance etiquette: for example, Thomas Wilson, *A Companion to the Ball-room* (1816).

76 *well made & plump . . . very brown*: Emma's figure is rounded and, like Marianne Dashwood's in *S&S*, ch. 10, her skin is 'very brown', rather than conventionally fair.

*the Borough*: JA refers here to those men who constitute the voting members of the community, thus able to influence the choice of a candidate for Parliament. As a peer, Lord Osborne automatically sits in the House of Lords, but he may still wish to promote his own or another's political interest at the local level, however ill-equipped he appears for public relations exercises.

77 *dance down every couple*: the majority of the dances at balls at this time were country dances in which each couple worked their way from top to bottom of a 'set'. A large set could mean a lot of waiting one's turn to reach the head and so would offer opportunities for conversation with a partner or even with non-dancers standing nearby.

*order the dance*: as the highest placed socially of the dancers, Miss Osborne stands at the head of the line and by convention 'calls' the tune the musicians will play. The other dancers fall in line beneath her, at some assemblies according to numbers they draw on entering the ballroom. At the conclusion of the first dance, the call falls to the next lady in line, and so on.

*little expecting Partner*: as in the description of Mary Crawford as 'a talking pretty young woman' (*MP*, ch. 5), neither JA nor her early printers found a need to clarify a phrasal structure that to us sounds odd in its mixing of adjective ('little') and verbal form used adjectivally ('expecting'). See *S*, p. 114, 'the visiting young Lady'.

*not keeping my engagement*: Miss Osborne may consider that Charles Blake's age excuses what is an unforgivable breach of the rules of the assembly. In *NA*, ch. 8, Catherine Morland, to her 'severe mortification', may not accept Henry Tilney as a partner even though her own, Mr Thorpe, is late in arriving.

*interesting*: engaging emotional attention, affecting.

*condescending*: Emma is generously adapting her behaviour to the little boy; the word carries a benign sense, with no suggestion that she acts in a superior manner. In Johnson's *Dictionary* (1755), 'condescension' is defined as 'voluntary submission to equality with inferiors'. But JA's lifetime spans the period in which the negative sense is beginning to predominate: in *P&P*, ch. 28, Lady Catherine de Bourgh's 'condescension', as fawningly praised by Mr Collins, comes closer to the modern understanding of the word.

78 *gloves*: male ball attire included white gloves, to be worn throughout the dancing.

*complacency*: delight; enjoyment (*OED*, sense 3). As with 'condescension', the modern critical shading of the term (in this case, smug self-satisfaction) is not here implied. But see p. 95, where Mrs Robert Watson's 'complacency' is undoubtedly self-satisfied.

*straightened*: JA presumably means 'straitened'; that is, the space was contracted or narrowed by the tables.

*Cassino*: a card game in which the ten of diamonds (great cass) counts two points and the two of spades (little cass) one point. The aim of the game is to achieve eleven points. It is played in *S&S*, ch. 23.

79 *suffrage*: opinion, verdict (*OED*, sense II 4a).

*gape*: yawn (*OED*, sense 6a) and the regular meaning of stare are probably both implied.

80 *rules of the Assembly*: established Assembly Rooms in fashionable resorts (at Bath or Brighton, for example) would have published 'Rules' and a Master of Ceremonies to enforce them. Tom Musgrave is making facetious comment on Charles Blake monopolizing his partner, which would of course be against the rules.

*very sad neighbour*: 'sad' was slang of the period, meaning 'deplorable' (*OED*, sense 6).

81 *impatient to call*: see note to p. 77, on ordering the dance. Miss Osborne called the previous dance; so the honour now falls to Miss Carr as next in rank.

*Negus*: a drink made from mixing port or sherry with hot water, sugar, and spices.

82 *Upper maid*: a housemaid in senior position (see *P*, ch. 6).

83 *Equipage... Curricle*: 'Equipage' is here simply a general term for carriage, but see *S*, p. 120 and note, for the extended meaning of equipage. A curricle was a light, fashionable, and fast two-wheeled carriage drawn by two horses abreast—a period equivalent of a sports car.

*visitation*: a formal gathering of clergy to examine the state of a parish or diocese.

*from R.*: presumably this should be 'D' (Dorking). See note to p. 65.

85 *not critically handsome*: not strictly handsome.

*naive or piquante*: unaffected and fascinating. The reader is meant to notice Musgrave's affected choice of French words. Compare Mary

Wollstonecraft, *A Vindication of the Rights of Woman* (1792), ch. 4: 'may I be allowed to use a significant French word, *piquant* society'.

*pelisse*: see note to p. 31.

86 *his address*: style of speaking (as at *LS*, p. 9). Emma's self-correction is significant: by distinguishing 'address' from 'manners' (behaviour or conduct), Emma implies that Musgrave is superficially pleasing.

87 *out of the Country*: away from the neighbourhood (see p. 66)

*I do not like much action in the pulpit*: the preacher's skill in holding the attention and winning the hearts of his congregation was a topical issue. In *MP*, ch. 34, Edmund Bertram debates with Henry Crawford the 'art of reading' from the pulpit, noting approvingly the recent 'spirit of improvement'. But where the sophisticated Crawford is drawn to a degree of theatricality in preaching, Edmund, newly ordained a clergyman, insists on the 'solid truths' that must underlie any performance.

88 *partridges…pretty high*: game birds are hung at least for a few days, to intensify their tenderness and high, gamey flavour, before being eaten.

89 *half-boots…nankin galoshed with black*: half-boots reach halfway to the knee, or considerably above the ankle (*OED*). In *E*, ch. 10, Emma Woodhouse wears half-boots for walking in the country in December. Nankin or nankeen is 'a kind of pale yellowish cloth, originally made at Nanking' in China (*OED*); the material was hard-wearing and so not impractical for the uppers of ladies' boots; subsequently, the term also meant the colour of nankin, 'pale yellow, or buff' (*OED*, sense 1a and 1c). Galoshing refers to the protective trim around the lower part of the boot.

*Your Lordship thinks*: the opening words of a revised passage replacing a heavily deleted earlier section (ending 'he was rewarded') in which Lord Osborne spoke far more impertinently (see Textual Notes, pp. 208–9).

*Female Economy*: domestic management. Throughout the eighteenth century, it was one of the few branches of education taught to women. In Hester Chapone's hugely influential *Letters on the Improvement of the Mind*, 'Economy' is described as both '*art*' and '*virtue*', which 'ought to have the precedence of all other accomplishments' (Letter 7).

90 *why he ben't to have*: servants are rarely seen or heard in JA's adult fiction. Nanny is the Watsons' old nurse, who has stayed on as a general servant. Her words suggest Hampshire dialect: 'why isn't he to have'. In her 1809 poem-letter to brother Frank, JA reminds him of his childish dialect phrase, 'my be not come to bide' ('I haven't come to stay') (see p. 176).

*throw off*: be released.

*what's going on*: in an earlier draft, this was followed by a section on 'the glorious sounds [of] a pack of Fox Hounds in full cry' altered to 'there is not so fine a sight in the world' before it is all struck through (see Textual Notes, p. 209).

*coming to Stanton*: originally followed by the sharp remark from Elizabeth: 'I wish he would give my poor Father a Living, as he makes such a point of

262 *Explanatory Notes*

coming to see him. But to be sure Mr Howard will have everything he has to give of that kind' (see Textual Notes, p. 209).

91 *Attorney at Croydon . . . six thousand pounds*: in *P&P*, ch. 7, Mrs Bennet is the daughter of an attorney in Meryton who left her a fortune of £4,000, while her sister, like Mrs Robert Watson, married their father's clerk. For a contemporary estimate of Mrs Robert Watson's fortune, see p. 70. In terms of social hierarchy, this makes her 'only moderately genteel', the description offered of the Coles in *E*, ch. 25.

92 *wanted Countenance*: her general appearance or demeanour fails to appeal.

*Post-Boy . . . Posting*: Robert Watson and his wife have travelled 'post'; that is, by postchaise or hired carriage, the horses changed at intervals (at 'posts' or 'post inns'). The post-boy or postilion would ride the leading horse.

*doubtful halfcrown*: a half-crown was worth two shillings and sixpence, with eight to a pound. With a shortage during the war years (1793–1815) of silver, counterfeited and counter-stamped coins were a problem.

*endite*: indict, bring a charge against.

*Surveyor*: local roads were a local responsibility of the parish through which they ran. The surveyor of highways would be elected from propertied men in the neighbourhood to oversee repairs. One reason the road through Willingden is in such poor state is that Mr Heywood's large family absorbs much of his income (*S*, p. 113).

*Augusta*: in a revision to the manuscript that required several small textual adjustments, JA changed the Watson child from a son, John, to a daughter, perhaps because she had already introduced one boy, Charles Blake, into her story (see Textual Notes, p. 211).

*sad shabby*: contemporary slang, meaning 'deplorable' (see p. 80) and 'ungenerous' (though offered as playful rather than serious criticism).

93 *rather too mixed*: in view of Mrs Robert Watson's aggressive regard for social position, an ironic comment. In *E*, ch. 25, snobbish Emma Woodhouse has reservations about mixing socially with the Coles, who would be on a par with the small-town status of Mrs Watson; while in *P&P*, ch. 8, the Bingley sisters dismiss the Bennet girls, whose uncle, like Robert Watson, is a country attorney, as having 'low connections'. Mrs Robert Watson is set up for a fall: see p. 99, when 'the fashions of Osborne-Castle carried it over the fashions of Croydon'.

*seven Tables*: before revision, there were 'nine' tables and 'two' drawing rooms. A table would ordinarily seat four people for a game of whist.

95 *fresh powder in your hair*: see note to p. 71; a further sign that the aggressively aspiring Mrs Robert Watson would cut an inferior figure in really fashionable society.

*putting up*: packing to bring.

96 *a round game*: a game of cards for any number of individual players rather than fixed numbers playing in pairs.

*Speculation*: a round card game involving the buying and selling of trump cards with 'fish' or counters in place of money, the holder of the highest trump card in a round winning the pool. With speculative bidding for unturned cards, it could be a noisy game and one well suited to a family party It is played in *MP*, ch. 25, and we know that JA enjoyed it herself (*Letters*, 170–1).

*Cribbage*: a quieter card game, requiring more skill, for two, three, or four players.

*postchaise*: a light, covered carriage in this case, since it contains only one passenger, probably hired with horses from a posting stage or inn. Its sound would suggest travel from a considerable distance.

*wrap*: 'an additional outer garment used or intended to be worn as a defence against wind or weather when driving, travelling' (*OED*, sense 2b, where this sentence is cited as the first example of this usage).

*8 o'clock dinner*: see note to p. 73.

97 *Pembroke Table*: a small table with a hinged drop-leaf on each side, a useful design where space is limited.

*the Bedford*: Bedford Coffee House in Covent Garden, London, famous in the mid-eighteenth century among poets, playwrights, and artistic types. In *NA*, ch 12, John Thorpe boasted of having met General Tilney there. In a revision in the manuscript, JA replaced the Bedford by 'Horse guards', a coffee house near Horse Guards Parade, favoured by military men. Its reputation as a haunt of prostitutes was possibly too unsavoury for the character she proposed to develop in Tom Musgrave and, on further thought, she struck through 'Horse guards' and restored the Bedford.

98 *open weather*: as in *LS*, p. 12, dry and frost-free weather, the conditions preferred for hounds following a fox's scent.

*Dishabille*: negligently informal dress for an evening visit. A manuscript revision: JA originally wrote 'a state'.

*fish . . . clean pack*: small, flat pieces of bone or ivory, used for keeping count in games, not always in the shape of fish (*OED*, sense 3). In *P&P*, ch. 16, Lydia Bennet 'talked incessantly . . . of the fish she had lost and the fish she had won'. The pack is of cards.

*beaufet*: a sideboard or side-table, buffet.

99 *Vingt-un*: a round game of cards in which the object is to make the number twenty-one or as near as possible without exceeding it. To exceed is to 'overdraw'.

*complaisance*: desire to please, obligingness.

100 *Bason of Gruel*: JA's older style spelling of 'basin'; gruel is a thin porridge, associated with invalids. In *E*, ch. 12, Mr Woodhouse, a habitual invalid, discourses 'in praise of gruel' as the perfect light supper dish.

100 *give Robert the meeting*: 'have a meeting with' now rare (*OED*, sense I 1b). For form's sake, the invitation would be issued to Tom Musgrave as from Robert Watson, the male visitor.

101 *of their existence; in memory & in prospect*: part of the heavily revised final section of the manuscript and the attempt to match Emma's emotional and mental state to the reversal in her circumstances. As Margaret Drabble notes, the semicolon 'might more logically come after "prospect"' (*Lady Susan, The Watsons, Sanditon*, ed. Drabble, 218).

## SANDITON

105 *Tunbridge...Hastings...E. Bourne*: in the opening pages JA takes great care to locate her imaginary characters, Mr and Mrs Parker, and later the rival fictional seaside resorts of Sanditon and Brinshore, within precise and real geographic coordinates. Tunbridge is JA's spelling for Tonbridge in Kent, 29 miles south-east of London. Willingden, where the Parkers' coach overturns, is a real place (Willingdon) about 2 miles inland from Eastbourne on the Sussex coast. Great Willingden and Willingden Abbots are fictional. Seaside resorts were springing up all along England's extensive southern coastline from the later eighteenth century. Brighton (originally Brighthelmston(e)) was the first, developed in the 1750s and 1760s. As one early nineteenth-century guidebook observed: 'In process of time, should the present taste continue, it is not improbable but that every paltry village on the Sussex coast which has a convenient beach for bathing will rise to a considerable town' (*A Guide to all the Watering and Sea-Bathing Places* (1803), 202). Other locations mentioned are Battel (JA's spelling for Battle), 8 miles from Hastings, and Hailsham, 10 miles north of Eastbourne, both inland towns in East Sussex. Worthing is a seaside resort 10 miles west of Brighton (Eastbourne is about 20 miles east of Brighton), and the Weald stretches between the chalk uplands of the North and South Downs. Sanditon is placed at the foot of the South Downs in East Sussex.

*as the Carriage was not his Masters but the Gentleman's own*: Cassandra Austen's resolution of an uncertain reading in the manuscript (see Textual Notes, p. 217). The meaning shifts in revision: before correction, the driver is the Parkers' employee and the carriage is hired; after revision, both the driver and horses have been hired and the vehicle belongs to the Parkers. In *P&P*, ch. 7, the Hursts have their own carriage at Netherfield but no horses.

106 *Surgeon*: also styled 'surgeon apothecary'. See note to p. 70. At p. 123, Diana Parker uses 'Apothecary' to cover the same profession.

107 *Morning Post...Kentish Gazette*: actual newspapers of the time. The *Morning Post*, a London daily newspaper, began publication in 1772; the *Kentish Gazette* was a twice-weekly local paper published in Canterbury from 1768 and covering the area of East Sussex in which the imaginary town of Sanditon is located.

*Postchaises*: the most luxurious form of transport, usually four-wheeled closed carriages whose horses were changed at regular 'posts'. See note to p. 92.

108  *Turnpike road*: see note to p. 70.

*Saline air & immersion*: the growth in English seaside resorts fuelled a spate of books and pamphlets extolling the health benefits of sea air, sea bathing, and sea-water baths (buildings to which sea water was pumped): Dr Richard Russell, *A Dissertation on the Use of Sea-Water in the Diseases of the Glands* (in Latin, 1750; English version 1752); A. P. Buchan, *Practical Observations concerning Sea Bathing* (1804); William Nisbet, *A Medical Guide for the Invalid to the Principal Watering Places of Great Britain; containing a view for the medicinal effects of water, etc.* (1804); John Gibney, *Practical Observations on the Use and Abuse of Cold and Warm Sea-Bathing, in various diseases* (1813). Hot and cold sea baths were constructed at Brighton in 1759; a sea-bathing infirmary opened at Margate in 1796 and a sea-water bath at Worthing in 1798.

*large, overgrown Places, like Brighton, or Worthing, or East Bourne*: Brighton doubled its permanent population between 1801 and 1817 (from approximately 7,500 to 16,000), doubling that again during the summer season. John Evans described Worthing after a summer visit of 1804 as transformed in a few years, thanks to royal patronage, from 'an obscure fishing town, consisting of a few miserable huts' to a fashionable resort with its 'Montague Place and Bedford Row . . . appropriate habitations for persons of fortune and respectability' (*Picture of Worthing* (1805), 10 and 13). JA spent several months there with her mother and sister in late 1805.

109  *Nursery Grounds*: 'an area of land used for raising young plants' (*OED*).

*diffuse comfort . . . of every sort*: the conversation between Mr Parker and Mr Heywood on the size and number of established and new seaside resorts along the south coast introduces what will be a thread of socio-economic thinking running through *S* to do with pricing, industry, and the effects more generally of supply and demand upon the whole of society. JA's source may have been a recent publication, Jane Marcet's *Conversations on Political Economy* (1816), a work that successfully explained the influential doctrines of Adam Smith, the great eighteenth-century economist, for a popular audience.

*distance from London*: contemporary guidebooks noted distances from and the accessibility of London as major selling points for the resorts they promoted. Evans, for example, describes Worthing as 56 miles from London and gives a suggested route (*Picture of Worthing*, 118).

*two or three speculating People*: people gambling on quick or high returns for their investments. As here, an economic term, 'speculation' was morally loaded at the time, carrying a suggestion of irresponsibility. Adam Smith described the 'speculative merchant' as one who 'exercises no one regular, established, or well-known branch of business . . . He enters into every trade when he foresees that it is likely to be more than commonly profitable, and he quits it when he foresees that its profits are likely to return to the level of other trades...A bold adventurer may sometimes acquire a considerable fortune by two or three successful speculations; but is just as likely to lose one by two or three unsuccessful ones' (*An Inquiry into the Nature and Causes of the Wealth of Nations*, 2 vols (1776), i. 140 (bk 1, ch. 10)). Speculation of various kinds is set to be a major theme in the novel (see Introduction, pp. xxi–xxii). The association with gaming was reinforced by the contemporary card game of Speculation, for which, see *W*, p. 96 and note.

109 *effluvia*: disgusting smells (here of seaweed) thought to transmit infection and so be harmful to health. ('According to the kind of effluvia and its degree, different diseases are produced...When putrid ones are diffused in the air, scurvies, plagues, gangrenes, etc. are the consequence', George Motherby, *A New Medical Dictionary* (3rd edn, 1791), 271.)

110 *that line of the Poet Cowper*: William Cowper (1731–1800). The quotation is from 'Truth', l. 334, in *Poems* (1782), 89–90, and contrasts a happy peasant, content with her faith, with the famous philosopher Voltaire (pseudonym of François-Marie Arouet, 1694–1782), imagined as unhappy because of his scepticism:

> Just knows, and knows no more, her Bible true—
> A truth the brilliant Frenchman never knew;
>
> .    .    .    .    .    .
>
> O happy peasant! O unhappy Bard!
> His the mere tinsel, hers the rich reward;
> He prais'd perhaps for ages yet to come;
> She never heard of half a mile from home.

Its application here, where Brinshore is likened to the happy peasant, wrenches the passage a considerable way from its original meaning.

111 *Enthusiast*: applied (from the seventeenth century) to religious zealots, the term carried both positive and negative connotations. In his *Dictionary* (1755), Samuel Johnson offers the primary definition as 'One who vainly imagines a private revelation'. Mr Parker is clearly a passionate advocate for Sanditon, with an early hint that he may also be obsessively self-deluded.

*of no pretensions*: a deleted phrase describes the village as 'of no consideration inhabited by one Family of consequence, his own' (see Textual Notes, p. 221).

*puffed*: promoted, advertised extravagantly (*OED*, sense 6a). Mr Parker seems to have learned the art of puffing direct from Mr Puff himself, who, in Richard Brinsley Sheridan's play *The Critic* (1771), speaks of how he has taught others 'to enlay their phraseology with variegated chips of exotic metaphor' (Act 1, scene 2).

*collateral Inheritance*: an inheritance from a childless relative.

112 *his Mine... Lottery... Speculation... Hobby Horse*: all examples to show Mr Parker as a fantasist willing to risk his 'easy though not large fortune' (p. 111) in unlikely money-making ventures or speculations. As Adam Smith noted: 'That the chance of gain is naturally overvalued, we may learn from the universal success of lotteries... There is not... a more certain proposition in mathematicks than that the more tickets you adventure upon, the more likely you are to be a loser' (*The Wealth of Nations*, i 137 (bk 1, ch. 10)). State lotteries had flourished since 1694 and ran almost uninterrupted to 1826. They were viewed as a legitimate method of raising funds for ventures in the public interest—in London, the building of the British Museum and construction of Westminster Bridge. But from the 1770s, when cash prizes could be as high as £20,000, their use was more widespread and open to abuse. Several private lotteries were authorized by Parliament at this time. In JA's teenage story 'Edgar & Emma', Mr Willmot owns a share in a lead mine and has bought a ticket in the state lottery (*Teenage Writings*, 25). A hobby horse (originally a child's toy consisting of a long stick with a horse's head at one end) is something pursued out of all proportion.

*his Futurity*: the word is carefully chosen. *S* shows JA, a writer regularly commended for her understatement, experimenting with figurative language and the creative potential of words. 'Futurity', meaning 'what will exist or happen in the future' (*OED*, sense 3), conventionally carries solemn religious or philosophical overtones. But in Mr Parker's case, those 'highest claims' on human attention are transferred to his Sanditon obsession: Sanditon, not heaven, is his hereafter.

*anti-spasmodic... anti-rheumatic*: JA makes fun of the medical jargon of the time with its obscure coinages. Motherby, *New Medical Dictionary*, 89 ff., includes many terms with the prefix '*anti*' (against): '*antiarthritica*, medicines against the gout'; '*antifebrile*, remedies against a fever'; '*antispasmodicum*, a remedy against convulsions'. Later, in chapters 7 and 8, Sir Edward Denham's absurd literary jargon satirizes his critical pretensions. Here and elsewhere in *S*, JA is not beyond coining a few bizarre words of her own, like 'anti-sceptic' (presumably for 'antiseptic').

*Nobody wanted Spirits. Nobody wanted Strength*: replacing in the manuscript 'nor cd the most obstinate Cougher retain a cough there 4 & 20 hours' (see Textual Notes, p. 221).

*softing*: 'that makes something soft or softer, or less intense or severe' (*OED*, describing the word as rare and citing this usage).

*Dividends*: meaning that some of Mr Heywood's income derives from investments, the profits on which he collects periodically on visits to London.

113 *occasional month at Tunbridge Wells... Winter at Bath*: in their heyday, leading spa towns attracting gentry visitors for health and holidays. Overtaken by the newer seaside resorts, neither was as fashionable by 1800 as they had been earlier in the eighteenth century. Visits to spa towns would be

luxuries within the reach of a socially conservative couple of modest fortune, if only their family were less numerous. Instead, the Heywoods stay at home and make do with the 'old Coach', reupholstered (not replaced) only once in over thirty years.

113 *Library*: an important social venue in every spa and seaside resort. As well as loaning books, the library would be expected to stock trinkets to tempt holidaymakers, to sell tickets for local entertainments, and perhaps to hire out musical instruments. At Bognor Regis on the Sussex coast, still a modest resort in 1815, 'the proprietor has diversified his library with an assortment of fancy articles, jewelry, music, prints ... so that this may be justly said, to be the only place of resort for those who seek to vary the tranquil pleasures of retirement, by the recreation of a library' (*A Guide to all the Watering and Sea-Bathing Places* (1815), 147). Lydia Bennet saw in the library at Brighton 'such beautiful ornaments as made her quite wild' (*P&P*, ch. 42).

*5 Shillings*: in JA's manuscript, it was originally 'one night' rather than '5 Shillings' (roughly equivalent to £25 today) that Mr Heywood promised not to spend at Brinshore.

*Lady Denham*: as the widow of Sir Harry Denham, a mere baronet (the lowest hereditary British title), she is scarcely on a par with the fashionable great people attracted by royal patronage to Brighton and Worthing. Hannah More's *Coelebs in Search of a Wife* (1808), a pious novel recommended to JA by Cassandra (*Letters*, 177), contains a mean-spirited and self-important Lady Denham. More describes her as 'a dowager of fashion, who had grown old in the trammels of the world' and an 'uncharitable gossip' whose granddaughter, Miss Denham, lives with her, is set to have 'a handsome fortune', and is being trained up to follow in her steps (ch. 10).

114 *visiting young Lady*: for this phrasal construction, see note to p. 77.

*all at her Disposal*: an unusual situation at the time, as JA is keen to emphasize, and not dissimilar from that of Mrs Turner in *W*, to whom her husband has left 'every thing that he had to dispose of ... at her mercy' (p. 94). In Lady Denham's case it appears especially unusual as it involves 'all his Estates', land and control over the village (normally entailed on to male heirs), not just portable property.

115 *Original Thirty Thousand Pounds*: the precise sum that 'rich' Emma Woodhouse will inherit (*E*, ch. 16).

*Coadjutor*: helper in a project or task.

*Cottage Ornèe*: (JA uses 'è' rather than the expected 'é'); a mock-rustic retreat for wealthy holidaymakers wishing to play at simple country living. The cottage orné, fashionable from the later eighteenth century, was designed for both picturesque effect and modern convenience. See John Plaw, *Ferme Ornée; or, rural improvements ... calculated for landscape and picturesque effects* (1800); and *Rural Residences, consisting of a series of designs for cottages, decorated cottages, small villas, and other ornamental buildings* (1818).

116 *a Companion*: among the few positions available to impoverished gentlewomen at this time, hired to entertain and accompany a wealthy woman in exchange for room, board, and clothes. The situation was rich in opportunities to humiliate the female dependant, described in stark terms by Mary Wollstonecraft, herself at one time companion to a widow in Bath: 'It is impossible to enumerate the many hours of anguish such a person must spend. Above the servants, yet considered by them as a spy, and ever reminded of her inferiority when in conversation with the superiors. If she cannot condescend to mean flattery, she has not a chance of being a favorite; and should any of the visitors take notice of her, and she for a moment forget her subordinate state, she is sure to be reminded of it' (*Thoughts on the Education of Daughters*, 70). Not surprisingly, the victimized companion was a familiar figure in fiction of the period, Charlotte's response, a mix of 'solicitude & Enjoyment', suggesting a readiness to appreciate this. Mary Wynne endures a position as companion to Lady Halifax in JA's early story 'Kitty, or the Bower' (*Teenage Writings*, 177–9).

*Michaelmas*: 29 September, the feast day of St Michael and one of the four 'quarter days' of the year, when regular legal and financial transactions took place.

118 *South foreland & the Land's end*: the full length of England's south coast, from Dover in the east to the far tip of Cornwall in the west.

*Trafalgar House ... Waterloo Crescent*: the enthusiasm for naming buildings after national wartime victories was nothing new. *S* is set in the immediate aftermath of Britain's long wars against Revolutionary and Napoleonic France. The Battle of Trafalgar, 21 October 1805, saw Admiral Nelson's victory over the French fleet; the Battle of Waterloo, 18 June 1815, marked Napoleon's final defeat. The Strand Bridge, in London, begun in 1811, was renamed Waterloo Bridge in 1816. Terraces of houses constructed in the shape of a crescent were relatively recent. The name was first used for the Royal Crescent at Bath, built 1767–75 (*OED*). Brighton's Royal Crescent, 1798–1807, was the first to be built facing the sea. Crescents were associated with luxurious accommodation. These topical points of reference all show Mr Parker's determination to be up to date. For him, national events of little more than ten years earlier already lie in the distant past.

*Parasol*: *OED*, sense 2, describes the parasol or sunshade as becoming fashionable in Western countries from the early nineteenth century.

119 *Grandeur of the Storm*: as in the reference to 'the state of the Air', a few lines later, Mr Parker's phrases take on the flavour of sublime aesthetics mixed with pseudo-science exploited in the language and niche marketing of the contemporary guidebook; for example, in this description of the sea air at Brighton: 'when we consider the means by which the purity and healthy state of the atmosphere is constantly renovated ... It is on a grand

scale that this process is performed by the ocean, more especially when its waves are agitated by a storm: the air, after such an occurrence, is invariably found to be more salubrious' (*A Guide to all the Watering and Sea-Bathing Places* (1815), 130). See, too, Sir Edward Denham's apostrophe to the sea in ch. 7.

119 *a Hospital*: potentially profitable investments in sea-water cures (and this may be implied in Sidney's humorous suggestion), hospitals were also funded by charitable subscription. In Thomas Skinner Scurr's satirical contemporary novel *The Magic of Wealth*, 3 vols (1815), the developers of the new seaside resort of Flimflamton hold a 'Grand Subscription Public Breakfast' at the New Assembly Rooms and Gardens, the profits to go to the 'establishment of a Marine Infirmary' (ii. 197–9).

*my Improvements*: according to the social historian J. H. Plumb, '"Improvement" was the most overused word of eighteenth-century England—landscapes, gardens, agriculture, science, manufacture, music, art, literature, instruction both secular and religious, were constantly described as improved' ('The Acceptance of Modernity', in Neil McKendrick, John Brewer, and J. H. Plumb, *The Birth of a Consumer Society: The Commercialization of Eighteenth-Century England* (London: Europa Publications, 1982), 332). Improvement is a word to be approached cautiously in reading JA: the merely fashionable, or cynical instances of 'improvement' (favoured by the Crawfords in *MP*) are criticized as disrespectful self-gratification; on the other hand, a morally charged understanding of self-improvement (associated with Fanny Price in the same novel) is a personal and social duty. In this instance, Mr Parker's improvements are tinged with irresponsibility.

120 *equipage*: this might refer simply to Sidney Parker's generally fashionable appearance or 'get up', or more widely to his carriage, horses, and attendant servants. Either way, an equipage was a clear indication of social status.

*a Harp*: an indirect reference to the harp-playing heroine who figured in contemporary novels (Germaine de Staël's *Corinne* (1807), Walter Scott's *Waverley* (1814)). A fashionable instrument, the harp was designed to show off the form of its female player. JA's Mary Crawford exploits her harp with great artistry: 'a young woman . . . with a harp as elegant as herself; and both placed near a window, cut down to the ground . . . was enough to catch any man's heart' (*MP*, ch. 7), and see *LS*, p. 11 and note.

*hooping Cough*: whooping-cough, a contagious disease mainly affecting children and characterized by short, violent, and convulsive coughs followed by whooping sounds.

*Blue Shoes, & nankin Boots*: blue shoes were fashionable for women from the 1790s; but the reference may be more specific—to the bright blue known as 'Waterloo blue': 'The most fashionable colours are—cinnamon, brown, Waterloo-blue, and different shades of green' (*British Lady's Magazine*, 1815) (quoted in *OED*). For a qualification, see Elizabeth Smith (Grant), *Memoirs of a Highland Lady*, ed. Andrew Tod, 2 vols

(Edinburgh: Canongate Classics, 1988), ii. 35, describing events in 1815–16: 'We were inundated this whole winter with a deluge of a dull ugly colour called Waterloo bleu, copied from the dye used in Flanders for the calico of which the peasantry make their smock frocks or blouses. Everything new was Waterloo, not unreasonably, it has been such a victory, such an event, after so many years of exhausting suffering. And as a sur-nam̃e to hats, caps, ribbands, hr̃aceletẽ, buttons, it was very well—a very fair way of trying to perpetuate the return of tranquillity; but to deluge us with that vile indigo, so unbecoming even to the fairest! It was really a punishment…that Waterloo [blue] was really an affliction, none of us were sufficiently patriotick to deform ourselves by trying it.' For 'nankin' or 'nankeen' boots, see note to p. 89.

121 *the Terrace…Mall of the Place*: the terrace was a style of building associated with spa towns and seaside resorts, being a row of linked houses. With a raised public walkway in front, it approximated to the most fashionable promenade, the Mall, in St James's Park, London. At Worthing in 1804, a new development, 'A little row of houses on the edge of the beach, pleasantly situated, is denominated the Terrace; though the number of the houses is scarcely sufficient to merit that appellation' (*Picture of Worthing*, 13–14). At Exmouth, Devon, 'a delightful terrace…not many years since, was made at the expence of Lord Rolle, to whom the manor of Exmouth belongs'. Among the most fashionable residences in Regency Weymouth are 'Royal Terrace', 'Augusta Place', and 'Belle Vue', all being 'in the vicinity of the rooms, the libraries, and the theatre, and commanding extensive views, both by sea and land' (*A Guide to all the Watering…Places* (1815), 284, 491).

*Bathing Machines*: huts on wheels with a door at either end, they were drawn by horse into the sea. The bather stripped inside the hut and entered the water with the assistance of a helper of their own sex. Different fashions were observed in different resorts. At Bognor, on the Sussex coast, there were in 1815 'ten or twelve machines…which are drawn to any depth required: at low water the bathers may go even as far out as the rocks. The ladies will find a female guide, but there is no awning to the machines, as is customary on the Kentish, and some other coast' (*A Guide to all the Watering and Sea-Bathing Places* (1815), 149). Since nude bathing was recommended as most beneficial, the Bognor machines clearly offered less protection for female modesty.

*venetian window*: a window with three separate openings, the two side ones being narrow. A recent innovation, the design let in more light and air than traditional smaller, leaded panes. The *OED* notes a first use in English in 1775.

122 *very serious Disorders*: toned down from Mr Parker's first description of his sisters as 'at times martyrs to very dreadful Disorders' (see Textual Notes, p. 226).

*such excellent useful Women*: a sentiment Mr Parker is at pains to repeat (see p. 124). The phrase was borrowed by the Austen enthusiast Barbara

Pym for the title of her 1952 comedy of manners, *Excellent Women*, about another set of post-war spinsters sating their frustrated energies in good works and busyness.

122 *Spasmodic Bile*: bile is the bitter fluid produced by the liver. Excessive production by or obstruction of the bile ducts would cause bouts of nausea and pain. In her final illness, JA suffered bilious attacks and became 'more & more convinced that <u>Bile</u> is at the bottom of all I have suffered' (*Letters*, 341).

123 *Friction*: vigorous rubbing. Like others of Diana Parker's medications, this is extreme. Advice of the period favoured the application of ointments and compresses (Sir John Elliot, *The Medical Pocket-Book* (1791), 146), in some cases accompanied by gentle rubbing with a warm hand (*The Family Guide to Health…from the writings and practice of the most eminent physicians* (1767), 265). In the manuscript JA can be seen revising upwards the number of hours Diana Parker applies friction alone: from four to six.

*Leaches*: bloodsucking worms, leeches were specifically bred for and widely used in a variety of medical purposes. 'Though one *leech* may be allowed only to draw one ounce of blood…ten or twelve *leeches* applied about the temples have relieved a violent cephalalgia [headache] almost immediately' (Motherby, *New Medical Dictionary*, 417–18).

*3 Teeth drawn*: another extreme measure at a time before effective pain relief for extractions. See *Letters*, 232–3, where JA describes 'the two sharp hasty Screams' of her niece as two teeth were extracted on a visit to the dentist in London.

*I. of Wight*: a small island off the south coast of England and already a popular tourist destination in the eighteenth century.

*Beau Monde*: already a rather clichéd term for fashionable society.

124 *West Indian*: not natives of the West Indies but a European family made wealthy by investment or trade there. In *MP*, ch. 3, Sir Thomas Bertram has an 'estate', presumably a sugar plantation, in the West Indies. As the responses of the Sanditon gentry indicate, West Indian families were envied and courted for their riches but they might also be considered inferior to the best society and tainted by association with slavery.

*Camberwell*: in 1817, a country village in Surrey, a few miles south of London. At one time noted for its mineral waters, it was popular as a retreat from the city pollution and therefore a good place to establish a school for young ladies.

125 *Library Subscription book*: the hub of the seaside resort at this time, the library, a private institution, would be subscribed to by all genteel visitors whether or not they were keen readers. Its register of book lenders would therefore act as a social directory. In Surr's satirical portrait of the seaside resort, the library, to be successful, should be 'a staring-room for fashionables', its subscription book filled with 'High-flyers', not 'cits' and 'cockneys' (*The Magic of Wealth*, ii. 239, 244). The entries so far (banal names

and lowly occupations) suggest that, like Flimflamton, Sanditon is not yet attracting a distinguished set.

126 *Camilla*: Frances Burney's novel of that name, whose heroine, Camilla Tyrold, just 17, has many misadventures, including overspending on keepsakes and clothing on her visit to the fashionable spa town of Tunbridge Wells (*Camilla*, bk 6, ch. 2). JA greatly admired Burney, one of the most esteemed writers of the day, acknowledging her in a famous passage in *NA*, ch. 5, on the importance of the novel genre. JA's copy of *Camilla* is now in the Bodleian Library, Oxford.

*Interesting young Woman*: for 'interesting' as used here, see note to p. 17.

*Address*: manner or style of speaking (*OED*, sense 5), as at *LS*, p. 9.

128 *more Good than harm*: in the immediate post-war years of 1815–17, the time JA is writing, Britain was thrust into economic depression. Among national remedies under consideration was increasing the money supply to stimulate circulation, prices, and production. The exchange between Lady Denham and Mr Parker on the relationship between spending, price, and profits of 'consumeable Articles' (economic jargon for articles intended to be used up) scales national debate down to the local level. More generally, the 'natural' working of the market with regard to price finds its best authority in the classic theory of Adam Smith, recently reinterpreted for a wider readership in Marcet's *Conversations on Political Economy*. Especially relevant here is Conversation 15: 'On Value and Price'.

*French Boarding School*: run by a French woman or a woman purporting to be French, like Mrs La Tournelle (actually Sarah Hackitt) who ran the Abbey House School in Reading attended by JA and her sister Cassandra in the mid-1780s. From the late eighteenth century, boarding schools were an increasingly popular choice for the education of girls of wealthy families.

*Asses milk*: easily digested, it was recommended for those suffering from a variety of ailments, including asthma and consumption (tuberculosis). Motherby recommends it as an 'antispasmodicum' (against convulsions) (*New Medical Dictionary*, 94).

*Chamber Horse*: 'a piece of exercise equipment which simulates the motion of horse riding, typically consisting of a sprung chair on which the user sits and bounces up and down' (*OED*), and see Textual Notes (p. 229).

129 *Gig*: a light, two-wheeled open carriage drawn by a single horse.

130 *Sublimity . . . Sensibility*: key terms and concepts in eighteenth-century literature and aesthetics. Edmund Burke's influential treatise *A Philosophical Enquiry into the Origin of our Ideas of the Sublime and Beautiful* (1757) defines the sublime over against the beautiful: the former provoked by objects that overwhelm the senses and arouse terror (the meaning of 'terrific' as used here by Sir Edward). Sensibility encompasses a broad code of feeling from refined susceptibility to extravagant excesses of emotion. By

the close of the eighteenth century, sensibility, once fashionable in novels (Laurence Sterne's *A Sentimental Journey through France and Italy* (1768), Goethe's *The Sorrows of Young Werther* (1774)), is regularly satirized: heavily so in JA's teenage story 'Love and Friendship' (1790); with more complexity in the character of Marianne Dashwood in *S&S* (1811), her first published novel. In Sir Edward Denham's case, heightened sensibility, real or feigned, the product of ill-digested and undisciplined reading, has undermined any good sense.

131 *a Man of Feeling*: possibly a specific allusion to the novel by Henry Mackenzie (1745–1831), *The Man of Feeling* (1771), with its hypersensitive hero, incapacitated for normal living by his exquisite feelings. If so, Sir Edward Denham, with his clichéd responses, is a ludicrous caricature of the literary type.

*either of Scott's Poems*: by 1817, Walter Scott (1771–1832), the best-selling poet of the age, had published many more than two poems. *OED*, sense 4c, records 'either' meaning 'any one (of more than two)'; but JA and Charlotte Heywood probably refer here to those two of Scott's poems scantily quoted from by Sir Edward Denham a few lines later: *Marmion* (1808), canto 6, verse 30 ('O, Woman! In our Hours of Ease') and *The Lady of the Lake* (1810), canto 2, verse 22 ('Some feelings are to Mortals given').

*Burns Lines to his Mary*: Robert Burns (1759–96), whose love poems to Mary Campbell ('Highland Mary') are probably referred to here: 'The Highland Lassie O', 'Will ye go to the Indies, my Mary', and, after her early death, 'To Mary in Heaven' ('Thou ling'ring star with less'ning ray'). By the early nineteenth century, the 'Irregularities' of Burns's character (sex and drink), referred to by Charlotte Heywood a few lines later, had been much biographized and conflated with the sentiments expressed in his poetry.

*Montgomery ... Wordsworth ... Campbell*: contemporary poets James Montgomery (1771–1854); William Wordsworth (1770–1850); Thomas Campbell (1777–1844), whose *The Pleasures of Hope* (1799), pt 2, l. 224, is quoted here. Given Sir Edward's inability to recall more than a line from poems he claims to adore, this begins to read like no more than a checklist, as likely gleaned from the ample reviews in the journals of the day as from reading specific works. Curious by its omission from the list is any reference to the hugely popular and much discussed poetry of Lord Byron (1788–1824), as flawed and glamorous a figure as Burns. Later writers, attempting to continue JA's novel (for example, Alice Cobbett's *Somehow Lengthened* (1932)), bring out Sir Edward's obvious Byronic features— notably his 'danger' to women.

134 *Dowager ... Heir*: as the widow of the baronet, Lady Denham would expect to be dependent on a lifetime provision from her deceased husband's estate, the bulk of which would go to his heir. In this case, however, it is she who is independently wealthy and Sir Edward, though titled, impoverished and in need of her assistance.

*a Co-*: a co-heiress, sharing her inheritance with at least one other person.

*real Property, Landed or Funded*: Lady Denham is distinguishing the real gentry, whose status derives from land and its income or from money invested in government stocks, from those who, engaged in one of the professions (generally socially inferior), rely on salaries.

*Half pay officers*: officers in the navy and army not currently on active service.

*Jointure*: property settled on a woman at marriage, to be used when her husband has died. Although Lady Denham, in possession of unusual independent wealth, seems to scorn such provision, it could be a source of great enjoyment, as Mrs Jennings proves in *S&S*.

136 *Alembic*: an apparatus used for distilling chemicals, the term also had a recognized figurative use. In this case, the suggestion of a scientific test for extracting literary nuggets from trashy novels contributes nothing meaningful to Sir Edward's nonsensical use of language.

*indomptible . . . anti-puerile Man*: more examples of Sir Edward's addiction, as Charlotte Heywood expresses it, 'to all the newest-fashioned hard words' (p. 132). Here he peppers his vocabulary with yet more 'anti-' and 'pseudo-' words. 'Indomptible' is JA's spelling for 'indomptable', listed in the *OED* as a rare or obsolete form of 'indomitable' (meaning 'unyielding', 'resolute'). The surviving manuscript shows that, like 'anti-puerile' later in his speech, the word was a revision, as JA deliberately heightened Sir Edward's language to make it more bizarre ('indomptible' replacing the tamer 'unconquerable', 'anti-puerile' replacing 'sagacious'). 'Eleemosynary' is a hard word for 'charitable'. The repetition of 'high-toned' (in 'high-toned Machinations'), when earlier he claimed for Burns 'the soul of high toned Genius' (p. 132), may hint at the narrow range of Sir Edward's hard words. His bizarre vocabulary may be another sign that JA has Burney's *Camilla* (a volume of which Charlotte picks up at p. 126) in her mind. In that novel, Sir Sedley Clarendel's 'quaint remarks' make him 'the least comprehensible person [Camilla] had ever known' (bk 4, ch. 8).

137 *most exceptionable parts of Richardsons . . . the Lovelaces*: the reader already knows that Sir Edward has read too many improbable romances and fancies his sex appeal is irresistible. Here JA ties down his character more firmly: he models himself on Robert Lovelace, the seducer and eventual rapist of Clarissa Harlowe, virtuous heroine of Samuel Richardson's extremely long novel-in-letters, *Clarissa, or, The History of a Young Lady* (1747–8). Richardson (1689–1761) was a favourite with JA, but she was not above making fun of his morally complex (even ambiguous) work and the crudely melodramatic fictions replete with rakish anti-heroes that it spawned.

138 *Tombuctoo*: Timbuktu, in present-day Mali, on the edge of the Sahara Desert, but meaning here simply a sufficiently remote place. In the spoof 'Plan of a Novel, according to hints from various quarters', probably written in spring 1816, JA imagines a heroine who, fleeing from the alarming

advances of an 'anti-hero' is 'compelled to retreat into Kamschatka' (modern Kamchatka, a peninsula in the Russian Far East) (see p. 166). She was ridiculing the improbable settings of some contemporary novels, like Sophie Cottin's *Elizabeth; or, The Exiles of Siberia* (1806) and Mary Brunton's *Self-Control* (1810). In Brunton's novel, the heroine is kidnapped from London by her would-be seducer and confined among Indians in the wilds of Canada before she eventually escapes by canoe. Brian Southam suggested that Timbuktu was in the British papers and reviews 'at the very time JA was working on *S*, following the account that appeared in *The Narrative of Robert Adams* (1816)' (*Jane Austen: A Students' Guide to the Later Manuscript Works* (London: Concord Books, 2007), 167).

138 *Post Horses*: see note to p. 92.

139 *Chichester*: a cathedral city 5 miles from the English south coast and west of fictitious Sanditon.

140 *Seminary*: 'In the earlier half of the 19$^{th}$ cent. "Seminary for Young Ladies" was very common as the designation of a private school for girls' (*OED*, sense 4). In *E*, ch. 3, 'Mrs Goddard was the mistress of a School—not of a seminary, or an establishment, or any thing which professed, in long sentences of refined nonsense, to combine liberal acquirements with elegant morality upon new principles and new systems—and where young ladies for enormous pay might be screwed out of health and into vanity—but a real, honest, old-fashioned Boarding-school, where a reasonable quantity of accomplishments were sold at a reasonable price.'

142 *Bitters...decocting*: either quinine or bitter native herbs (wormwood, tansy, for example), boiled down to a concentrate and mixed with other prescribed ingredients. 'In weakness of the stomach, loss of appetite, indigestion, and the like disorders...medicines of this tribe do singular service.' Bitters were considered especially beneficial for Diana Parker's 'old greivance, Spasmodic Bile' (p. 122): 'in disorders where the bile is defective, they are administered with considerable advantage' (Motherby, *New Medical Dictionary*, 57).

*too much disposed for Food*: a wonderfully evocative revision. JA originally wrote: 'as for Arthur, he is much more likely to eat too much than too little' (see Textual Notes, p. 234).

143 *Eloquence...Belles Lettres*: branches of Rhetoric designed to develop elegant spoken and written discourse according to the taste of the day. Eloquence or public speaking placed an emphasis on articulation, modulation, expression as well as deportment, while belles-lettres taught the foundations of fine writing and literary appreciation using chosen examples from ancient and modern works. JA originally wrote 'Botany & Belles Lettres'. The revision, suggestive of a redundancy in the range of topics offered, is perhaps a swipe at the fashionable (rather than useful) nature of the curriculum.

*Projector*: Johnson, *Dictionary*, sense 1: 'One who forms schemes or designs'; sense 2: 'One who forms wild impracticable schemes'.

*spirit of restless activity*: JA originally wrote 'the disease of activity', with its more open criticism of the meddling Parker sisters.

144 *posting*: hurrying (*OED*, sense 2a), with an allusion to the speed of a post-chaise, but not suggesting Diana Parker is in a carriage. See, for example, JA's description of walking fast: 'we posted away under a fine hot sun' (*Letters*, 91).

Stouter Lusty both words imply Arthur Parker is thick set and solid, with a possible meaning of 'fat' ('Lusty' (*OED*, sense 10, with a first reference to such usage, 1777)).

*sodden*: heavy, dull (*OED*, sense 2).

145 *Bathing Women*: employed to help female bathers get in and out of the water from the bathing machines (see p. 121). 'The machines are about forty, which may give some idea of the number that require them. They are well attended and drawn into any depth the bathers chuse. A boy generally drives the horse, and men and women guides attend, if required, in the machines' (*A Guide to all the Watering and Sea-Bathing Places* (1815), 432, describing bathing at Scarborough).

*Hack-Chaises*: hired carriages, like taxis.

146 *Physics*: natural sciences in general; the science of medicine (*OED*, sense 2, now obsolete).

147 *Coats of the Stomach*: a medical term, referring to the four protective membrane layers lining the stomach.

149 *catastrophé*: 'the change or revolution that produces the conclusion or final event of a dramatic piece' (Johnson, *Dictionary*).

150 *half-mulatto*: mulatto is 'a person having one white and one black parent...of mixed race' (*OED*). Miss Lambe presumably therefore has one black grandparent and is perhaps the child of a plantation owner and a freed slave, an heiress within a wealthy slave-owning family. The term 'mulatto', though now offensive, appears elsewhere in the literature of the period. JA's use of 'half-mulatto' is, however, unusual.

151 *rototary motion*: JA's spelling, describing the fashionable aspirations of the Miss Beauforts to move in the right circles. The social climber Mrs Elton advises Jane Fairfax of the importance of 'moving in a certain circle', *E*, ch. 35. The narrator's satiric comment points up the advantage for the new seaside resort in attracting the right sort of people.

*Tonic Pills*: a patent medicine with financial investors, like Mrs Griffiths's cousin, in the business of their manufacture and sale.

152 *Worcestershire*: a district of west central England and therefore a long way from either fictional Sanditon or Hampshire (the home of the Parker sisters). Charity was usually organized on a local basis.

*Charitable Repository*: a kind of charity shop from which donated goods were sold for the benefit of the poor. The end of European war in 1815 saw economic depression with chronic unemployment and food shortages.

With no welfare state and little instituted poor relief of any kind, private charitable giving was a necessity. The signatures or subscriptions of prominent figures, like Lady Denham, would encourage others to pledge their support to funds for individual cases of need or wider worthy causes.

152 *Burton on Trent... York*: Burton, a manufacturing town in the middle of England, around 200 miles north of fictional Sanditon, and York, around 300 miles to the north. Both are examples of Diana Parker's long-distance charitable enthusiasms rather than of effective locally directed relief.

153 *putting them all out*: setting them up in apprenticeships or other ways of earning a living (*OED*, sense 10a).

*Gig... Pheaton... Tandem*: a gig was a light, two-wheeled open carriage drawn by a single horse; a phaeton (usual spelling) had four wheels, was drawn by a pair of horses, and had one or two seats facing forwards; a tandem was two-wheeled with two horses harnessed one behind the other.

154 *paling*: a fence made from wooden pales or stakes.

## OPINIONS OF MANSFIELD PARK AND EMMA

*MP* was published in May 1814. JA was collecting opinions of the novel, from correspondence and remarks passed on by friends and family, by November 1814, perhaps in the absence of printed reviews. Since their dating coincides with plans for a second edition of the novel, it is possible that *Opinions of MP* were marshalled to put pressure on her then publisher, Thomas Egerton, and to boost an early approach to a potential new publisher, John Murray. On 24 November 1814, JA wrote to her niece, Anna Lefroy: 'Mrs Creed's opinion is gone down on my list; but fortunately I may excuse myself from entering Mr [*cut out*] as my paper only relates to Mansfield Park.' A week later, on 30 November, from London, she informed another niece, Fanny Knight: 'it is not settled yet whether I *do* hazard a 2ᵈ Edition. We are to see Egerton today' (*Letters*, 295, 299). (For an 1814 approach to Murray, see Kathryn Sutherland, 'Jane Austen's Dealings with John Murray and His Firm', *Review of English Studies*, NS 64 (2012), 122.) *Opinions of E*, collected after December 1815 when the novel was published, may share a common paper stock with *Plan of a Novel*, suggesting they were both transcribed around the same time, in early 1816. The layout in manuscript of *Opinions of E*, with its indentation of entries alongside each name, is closer, though not exactly similar, to that of *Plan of a Novel* than to *Opinions of MP*. It seems likely that she was adding to the list over time: writing to Fanny Knight on 20–1 February 1817, she thanks her for sending Mrs C. Cage's 'praise of Emma' (*Letters*, 344), set down towards the end of her list. Names are shared across the three manuscripts and all three contain names that appear only once.

   I provide here information about the various opinion holders in the order in which they occur, including where relevant reference to JA's association and correspondence with them. Where names feature in both lists of *Opinions* and in *Plan of a Novel*, I attach annotation to the most significant appearance.

*Opinions of MP* lists the names and views of the following individuals:

157 *F. W. A.*: JA's brother Frank (Francis William) Austen (1774–1865).

*Mr K.*: JA's brother Edward (1767–1852), who took the name Knight in 1812.

*Edward & George*: JA's nephews, the two eldest of Edward Knight's sons, ⟨illegible⟩

*Fanny Knight*: JA's niece (Fanny Catherine, 1793–1882) and Edward Knight's eldest child; see note to p. 165.

*Anna*: JA's niece and namesake (Jane Anna Elizabeth Austen, 1793–1872) and James Austen's eldest child. She married Ben Lefroy in November 1814.

*Mrs James Austen*: James Austen's second wife (1771–1843), born Mary Lloyd, sister of Martha (see note to 'Miss Lloyd' below).

*Miss Clewes*: governess to Edward Knight's children from 1813 to 1820.

*Miss Lloyd*: Martha Lloyd (1765–1843), sister of Mrs James Austen (see note above). She lived with JA, Cassandra, and Mrs Austen from 1807. In 1828 she became Frank Austen's second wife.

*My Mother*: Cassandra Austen (1739–1827), born Leigh.

*Cassandra*: Cassandra Elizabeth Austen (1773–1845), JA's sister.

*My Eldest Brother*: Revd James Austen (1765–1819).

158 *Edward*: James Edward Austen (1798–1874), usually named Edward in the family, JA's future biographer and, in his teens, a keen fiction writer.

*Mr B. L.*: Benjamin Lefroy (1791–1829), son of JA's old friend Mrs Anne Lefroy, in whose memory JA wrote a poem (see p. 173). Ben married JA's niece Anna (see note above) in November 1814.

*Miss Burdett*: possibly Frances, sister of Sir Francis Burdett, a Radical MP, mentioned in a letter of August 1814 as among JA's brother Henry Austen's London social circle (*Letters*, 282).

*Mrs James Tilson*: Frances Sanford (1777–1823), wife of Henry Austen's partner James Tilson in the London bank of Austen, Maunde, and Tilson. First mentioned in a letter of October 1808, subsequent correspondence confirms she continued to be among JA's social circle in London; she was perhaps also the recipient of JA's last known letter of 28–9 May 1817 (*Letters*, 146, 194, 358–9).

*Fanny Cage*: cousin, contemporary (1793–1874), and friend of Fanny Knight. Brought up by her grandmother Lady Bridges, Edward Knight's mother-in-law, she spent much of her childhood with the Knight children.

*Mr and Mrs Cooke*: see note to 'Mary Cooke', their daughter, p. 165. JA also recorded their enjoyment of *MP* in a letter to Cassandra in June 1814 (*Letters*, 275).

*Mary Cooke*: see note to p. 165.

158 *Miss Burrel*: she may have been a connection through Henry Austen's wife, Eliza, whose friend Lady Burrell died in 1802. Lady Burrell's father had been a friend of Warren Hastings, officially godfather to Eliza (Deirdre Le Faye, *Jane Austen's 'Outlandish Cousin': The Life and Letters of Eliza de Feuillide* (London: British Library, 20002), 73).

*Mrs Bramstone*: Mary Chute (1763–1822), a neighbour from Steventon days, who had known JA since childhood. JA is not complimentary about her in a letter of January 1813, writing, 'Mrs Bramstone is the sort of Woman I detest' (*Letters*, 209).

*Mrs Augusta Bramstone*: Augusta Bramston (1747–1819), sister-in-law of the above, 'Mrs' being a courtesy title.

*The families at Deane*: the Harwoods, who lived at Deane House, near Steventon, where JA spent her early life. Mrs Anna Harwood is Betty Anna Maria Harwood (1751–1838), 'Mrs' being a courtesy title.

*The Kintbury Family*: Kintbury, in Berkshire, the home of JA's great friends the Fowles. Four of the Fowles had been pupils of the Revd George Austen at Steventon. Of these, Tom Fowle (1765–97) was engaged to be married to Cassandra; Fulwar (referred to here) (1764–1840) was vicar of Kintbury and married to Eliza, sister of Mary and Martha Lloyd (see notes to 'Mrs James Austen' and 'Miss Lloyd', p. 157).

*Mr Egerton the Publisher*: Thomas Egerton (1750–1830), who published *S&S*, *P&P*, and *MP*.

*Lady Robert Kerr*: Mary Gilbert (1780–1861) married Lord Robert Kerr in 1806. Henry Austen revealed the authorship of *P&P* to her on hearing her praise the novel (*Letters*, 227 and 241).

159 *Miss Sharpe*: Anne Sharp or Sharpe, governess to Edward Knight's children at Godmersham from 1804 to 1806. She stayed in touch with both Cassandra and JA, who described her as 'an excellent kind friend'. She stayed at Chawton in June 1815 and was the recipient of one of JA's last letters (*Chronology*, 509 (entry under 26 June 1815); *Letters*, 260 and 355–7).

*Mrs Carrick*: mentioned in the same November 1813 letter in which JA lists what seem to be admiring responses to *P&P* from Anne Sharp and other readers unknown to her: 'I am read & admired in Ireland too.—There is a Mrs Fletcher, the wife of a Judge...This comes through Mrs Carrick, not through Mrs Gore'. Le Faye speculates that Mrs Carrick could be an Irish acquaintance of Henry Austen's (*Letters*, 260 and 504). Henry had spent some months in 1799 in Ireland with the Oxford Militia.

*Mr J. Plumptre*: John Plumptre (1791–1864), a neighbour of the Knights in Kent and an admirer of Fanny's, who for a time in 1814 considered marrying him. JA's letters to Fanny from November 1814 survive in which she writes of 'Poor dear Mr J. P.!' but advises her niece not to marry without love (*Letters*, 290–4 and 297–300).

*Sir James Langham & Mr H. Sanford*: the two men were cousins, and Henry Sanford was Henry Austen's business associate; see note to p. 167.

*Alethea Bigg*: Alethea (1777–1847) and her sisters Elizabeth and Catherine were long-standing friends of JA and Cassandra Austen. Their friendship survived their brother Harris Bigg-Wither's proposal to JA in December 1802 and her own swift change of mind after accepting him. By 1814 Alethea and Elizabeth (now Heathcote) were living together in Winchester where they would provide support during JA's final illness of 1817.

*Charles*: JA's youngest brother Charles John Austen (1779–1852). At this point the name *Mrs Maling* (subsequently deleted) appeared; probably Mrs Maling of Hans Place, Chelsea, a neighbour of Henry Austen (*Letters*, 311 and 316).

*Mrs Dickson*: Le Faye speculates that this may be the wife of a naval officer and associate of Frank Austen who is mentioned in two letters of 1807 (*Letters*, 120 and 125).

*Mrs Lefroy*: Sophia, wife of John Henry George Lefroy, eldest son of JA's old friend Madam Lefroy, and brother of Ben; see note to 'Mr B. L.', p. 158.

*Mrs Portal*: wife of William Portal (1755–1846), neighbours from Steventon days. The Portals owned paper mills at Laverstoke, Hampshire, which made paper for Bank of England notes.

*Lady Gordon*: Harriet Finch (d. 1821), wife of Sir Jenison Gordon of Lincolnshire. Her brother was George Finch-Hatton of Ashford, Kent, neighbour of Edward Knight. JA met them at Godmersham in August 1805 (*Letters*, 111).

160 *Mrs Pole*: possibly a connection of Henry Austen's (see *Later Manuscripts*, 701, where it is suggested that the reference may be to Felizarda Buller, wife of Charles Pole, a director of the Bank of England (1796–1818)).

*Admiral Foote*: Edward James Foote (1767–1833), naval officer and friend of Frank Austen's from Southampton days (*Letters*, 120).

*Mrs Creed*: possibly Catherine Herries who married Henry Knowles Creed. Henry probably knew Mrs Creed through his Chelsea neighbours, the Herries family. Her father, Charles Herries (d. 1819), was colonel of the Light Horse Volunteers of London and Westminster. In a letter conjecturally dated to 24 November 1814, JA wrote, 'Mrs Creed's opinion is gone down on my list' (*Letters*, 295; and see 303–5).

*Opinions of E* lists the names and views of the following individuals:

161 *Captain Austen*: JA's brother Frank; see note to p. 157.

*Mrs F. A.*: Frank Austen's wife Mary Gibson (1785–1823).

*Mrs J. Bridges*: Charlotte Hawley, wife of Revd Brook John Bridges, brother of Edward Knight's wife Elizabeth. She was at Godmersham with Fanny when Cassandra Austen wrote with news of JA's death in July 1817 (*Letters*, 361).

*Miss Sharp*: Anne Sharp or Sharpe; see note to p. 159.

161 *Cassandra*: JA's sister; see note to p. 157.

*Fanny K.*: Fanny Knight; see note to p. 165.

*Mr & Mrs J. A.*: JA's eldest brother James and his wife Mary; see notes to 'my eldest brother' and 'Mrs James Austen', p. 157.

*Edward*: probably James Edward Austen, son of the above; see note to p. 158.

*Miss Bigg*: Alethea Bigg; see note to p. 159.

*My Mother*: see note to p. 157.

*Miss Lloyd*: Martha Lloyd; see note to p. 157.

*Mrs & Miss Craven*: Catherine Craven, widow of Revd John Craven, uncle to Martha and Mary Lloyd, and their daughter Charlotte; see note to 'Mrs Craven', p. 167.

*Fanny Cage*: see note to p. 158.

*Mr Sherer*: Revd Joseph Sherer; see note to p. 165.

162 *The family at Upton Gray... Mrs Beaufoy*: the inhabitants of the Manor House at Upton Grey, a village in Hampshire near Chawton.

*Mr & Mrs Leigh Perrot*: JA's maternal uncle James Leigh (1735–1817), who added Perrot to his name in 1751 in order to inherit a family estate. His wife Jane Cholmeley (1744–1836) was one of JA's more colourful relations; see *Memoir*, ed. Sutherland, 59 and n.

*Countess Craven*: the former Shakespearean actress Louise Brunton (?1785–1860), married William, Lord Craven in 1807. Lord Craven was a distant cousin of Mary and Martha Lloyd's mother.

*Mrs Guiton*: possibly a connection from Southampton days (1806–9). *Later Manuscripts*, 703, offers the conjectural suggestion that this may be the wife of J. Guiton of Fareham, Hampshire, and perhaps known to the Austens' Southampton cousins the Harrisons.

*Mrs Digweed*: Jane Terry (1776–1860), wife of Harry Digweed, whose father was tenant of Steventon manor house when JA was a girl. In the 1810s Jane and Harry Digweed were neighbours of the Austens in Alton near Chawton.

*Miss Terry*: probably Mary Terry, Jane Digweed's sister.

*Henry Sanford*: see note to 'Mr H. Sanford', p. 167; and see *Opinions of MP*.

*Mr Haden*: Charles Haden (1768–1824), surgeon, and doctor attending Henry Austen during his illness in the autumn and winter of 1815. JA and her niece Fanny Knight were staying with Henry at the time, and several references to Mr Haden in JA's letters suggest how entertaining she found his company: 'he is a Haden...something between a Man & an Angel' (*Letters*, 304, 311, 313, and 315–16).

*Miss Isabella Herries*: a neighbour of Henry Austen's in Chelsea. JA records dining with 'the Herrieses—a large family party—clever &

accomplished' in a letter of 17 October 1815 (*Letters*, 303). Isabella's sister, Catherine (Mrs Creed), offered an opinion on *MP*.

*Miss Harriet Moore*: Le Faye conjectures that Harriet and Eliza Moore were connected to one of Henry Austen's London business associates (*Letters*, 257 and 555–6). In a letter to Cassandra of August 1814, JA speculated that Harriet, the 'Hanwell favourite', might be a possible wife for the recently widowed Henry, but by November she finds both sisters rather dull (*Letters*, 283 and 299).

*Countess Morley*: Frances Talbot (1782–1857), second wife of John Parker, created in 1815 1st Earl of Morley. A witty woman with literary interests, she was for a time thought to be the author of *S&S* and *P&P*. It is not known how JA became acquainted with her, but the likeliest explanation is that it was through Henry Austen's London society connections. JA sent Countess Morley one of the twelve presentation copies of *Emma*, which resulted in the brief surviving correspondence between them. The Countess expressed a less favourable opinion of *E* to her sister-in-law (*Letters*, 321–2; *Family Record*, 231).

*Mr Cockerell*: possibly the architect Samuel Pepys Cockerell (1753–1827), but it may simply have been a young acquaintance of Fanny Knight's (*Later Manuscripts*, 704–5).

*Mrs Dickson*: see note to p. 159.

*Mrs Brandreth*: so far unidentified.

*Mr B. Lefroy*: Ben Lefroy; see note to p. 158.

163 *Mrs B. Lefroy*: Anna, JA's niece, who married Ben Lefroy in November 1814, and now earns this formal reference, quite different from the listing of '*Anna*' in *Opinions of MP*.

*Mrs Lefroy*: Sophia Lefroy; see note to p. 159.

*Mr Fowle*: see note to 'The Kintbury Family', p. 158.

*Mrs Lutley Sclater*: Penelope Lutley-Sclater (?1752–1843), who lived at Tangier Park, near Manydown, not far from Steventon, in Hampshire. She was unmarried, 'Mrs' being a courtesy title. She is mentioned in letters of February 1813 and July 1816 (*Letters*, 215 and 330).

*Mrs C. Cage*: a family connection through Edward Knight's wife. Mrs Cage was married to Revd Charles Cage, whose brother Lewis married Edward's wife's sister (the mother of 'Fanny Cage' in *Opinions of MP*). In February 1817 JA wrote to Fanny Knight that 'I am very fond of Mrs C. Cage, for reasons good. Thank you for mentioning her praise of Emma &c.' (*Letters*, 344).

*Mrs Wroughton*: so far unidentified.

*Sir J. Langham*: see note to p. 159.

*Mr Jeffrey*: the name of Francis Jeffrey (1773–1850), editor of the *Edinburgh Review* (1802–29) and one of the most influential critics of the age, injects a different note of public esteem into the list. JA may have heard of Jeffrey's opinion through her publisher John Murray or through William Gifford, editor of the *Quarterly Review*.

163 *Miss Murden*: Jane Murden, daughter of Christiana Fowle, and thus a relative of JA's friends the Fowles of Kintbury. She turns up in Southampton in 1808– 9 and is mentioned in several of JA's letters as a rather forlorn creature (*Letters*, 180 and 206).

*Captain C. Austen*: JA's brother Charles; see *Opinions of MP*. He had been sent a copy of *E* while serving in the Eastern Mediterranean.

*Mrs D. Dundas*: Janet Whitley Dundas, a neighbour of the Fowles of Kintbury. On her marriage to James Deans, a naval captain, the couple took the married name of Deans-Dundas (*Letters*, 518).

## PLAN OF A NOVEL

Ostensibly drafted 'according to hints from various quarters', the *Plan* was probably written in response to the well-meaning but pompous interference of the Revd James Stanier Clarke, librarian to the Prince Regent, with whom JA negotiated in late 1815 over the royal dedication of *E*, published in December of that year (with an 1816 date on the title page). Clarke far exceeded his original commission, offering themes, topics, and characters (among which, a highly romanticized self-portrait) to the novelist, with the additional suggestion: 'Pray continue to write, & make all your friends send Sketches to help you' (*Letters*, 320). The *Plan* makes reference to several sources of comment and advice, ranging from Austen's niece Fanny Knight to William Gifford, editor of John Murray's *Quarterly Review*, who read *E* for the press. Setting in ludicrous light many of the devices of contemporary commercial fiction, it rounds off its critique with the words 'name of the work *not* to be *Emma*'. Written at a stage in her career as published author when she can express with some confidence her views on the novel, the *Plan* contains, by implication, JA's 'art of fiction'. It may share a composition and transcription date, as it appears to share paper stock and features of layout, with *Opinions of E*. The *Plan* includes fifteen marginal notes by JA (printed here at the foot of the text page), naming eight individuals and 'Many Critics', to whom the 'hints from various quarters' are attributed.

165 *Mr Gifford*: William Gifford (1756–1826), reader and adviser to the publisher John Murray II (1778–1843). Gifford admired *P&P* and *MP* and in September 1815 recommended that Murray publish *E*.

*Fanny Knight*: eldest daughter of JA's brother Edward, whose family took the name Knight in 1812. Fanny stayed with JA's brother Henry in London in late 1815 around the time of JA's visit to Carlton House, the Prince Regent's London residence, and the beginning of her correspondence with Clarke.

*Mary Cooke*: (1781–post-1818), daughter of JA's godfather Revd Samuel Cooke and his wife Cassandra, first cousin to JA's mother. The Cookes were acquainted with the novelist Frances Burney and Cassandra Cooke published a novel of her own, *Battleridge, An Historical Tale Founded on Facts* (1799). JA stayed with the Cookes at their home in Great Bookham, Surrey, in summer 1814; the views of the Cookes, including Mary, are listed in *Opinions of MP*.

*dark eyes & plump cheeks*: possibly a humorous description of JA herself, recognizable from Cassandra's famous watercolour sketch of her sister (*c.*1810) now in the National Portrait Gallery, London.

*Father... his Life*: the idealized cleric is a regular figure in eighteenth-century literature from Rousseau's Savoyard Vicar in *Émile* (1762) and Charles Primrose, the vicar of Oliver Goldsmith's hugely popular novel *The Vicar of Wakefield* (1766) to the unworldly father in Ann Radcliffe's *The Romance of the Forest* (1791). The narrative sketched out by JA also draws word for word on elements and phrases suggested by the egotistical Clarke himself (*Letters*, 308–9 and 320–1).

*Mr Clarke*: Revd James Stanier Clarke (1767–1834), domestic chaplain and librarian to the Prince Regent. He met JA in November 1815 when he showed her the library at Carlton House and intimated that she might dedicate *E* to the Prince. His correspondence with JA continued until April 1816, and we have it on the authority of Caroline Austen that Clarke's acquaintance 'afforded some amusement' (*Memoir*, ed. Sutherland, 177). For a life, see Chris Viveash, *James Stanier Clarke: A Biography* (Winchester: privately printed, 2006).

*Tythes*: tithes, 'The tenth part of the annual produce of agriculture, etc., being a due or payment (orig. in kind) for the support of the priesthood, religious establishments, etc.' (*OED*). Landowners were meant to make such payments to the rector of a parish; the amounts of money involved varied considerably, led to much inequality among the clergy, and were the subject of public debate. This is one of the topics recommended by Clarke for fictional treatment (*Letters*, 320). JA's fictional clergyman, Mr Collins, anticipates some of Clarke's pomposity and self-conceit as well as his concern over tithes (*P&P*, ch. 18).

*nobody's Enemy but his own*: another direct quotation from Clarke (*Letters*, 309), who filched it from Henry Fielding, *The History of Tom Jones, a Foundling* (1749), bk 4, ch. 5, where it is a description of the hero.

*Mr Sherer*: Revd Joseph Sherer (1770–1824), vicar of Godmersham, Kent, the parish in which the Knights had their main residence. In *Opinions of E*, Mr Sherer is described by JA as 'Displeased with my pictures of Clergymen'. This reference to an 'exemplary Parish Priest' may be her revenge.

166 *Story... adventures*: JA conflates the more extravagant elements of a number of contemporary novels, including Charlotte Smith's *Emmeline: The Orphan of the Castle* (1788), Regina Maria Roche's *The Children of the Abbey* (1796), Mary Brunton's *Self-Control* (1811), and Frances Burney's *The Wanderer* (1814).

166 *Mrs Pearse of Chilton-Lodge*: Anne, wife of John Pearse, Director and then Governor of the Bank of England. Chilton Lodge was just a few miles from Kintbury, Berkshire, where JA's old friends the Fowles lived.

*the anti-hero*: the first usage of the term given in the *OED* is by the essayist Richard Steele, *The Lover* (1715), 13, where the spelling is 'anti-heroe'; in the 1789 edition 'anti-hero' (22).

*work for her Bread*: in Brunton's *Self-Control*, the heroine Laura Montreville determines to 'labour night and day, deprive herself of recreation, of rest, even of daily food' in working to maintain her father and herself by selling drawings (ch. 15). For Ellis-Juliet, in Burney's *The Wanderer*, trying unsuccessfully to earn a living by needlework, 'the unvarying repetition of stitch after stitch, nearly closed in sleep her faculties, as well as her eyes' (ch. 48). If in the *Plan*, JA mocks some of the more improbable devices of contemporary fiction, she had, in the plight of Jane Fairfax in *E*, confronted the meanness of opportunity and sheer vulnerability of the economically distressed female.

*Kamschatka*: Kamchatka, a volcanic peninsula, even now almost entirely wilderness, in the Russian Far East; in other words, an extremely remote (and unlikely) location, comparable to the setting of Sophie Ristaud Cottin's *Elizabeth; Or, The Exiles of Siberia* (1807).

167 *Eclaircissement*: see note to p. 54.

*Mrs Craven*: Catherine Craven lived near Kintbury, Berkshire. She and her daughter Charlotte are recorded as enjoying *E*; see *Opinions of E*.

*Mr H. Sanford*: Henry Sanford, friend and business associate of Henry Austen. JA wrote to Fanny Knight in November 1814 that 'Mr Sanford is to join us at dinner...he shall tell me comical things & I will laugh at them, which will be a pleasure to both' (*Letters*, 299). His comments on *E* are also recorded; see *Opinions of E*.

## VERSES

### THIS LITTLE BAG

Written to accompany a small bag containing a 'housewife' or cloth sewing case for needles, pins, and thread, a common homemade gift between women friends. JA made the gift for Mary Lloyd (for whom, see *Opinions of MP*, 'Mrs James Austen'), dating the poem January 1792, when the Lloyd family moved from nearby Deane Parsonage to Ibthorp, 15 miles away. Mary would become JA's sister-in-law in 1797. Publishing the poem in 1870, Austen-Leigh wrote: 'Her needlework both plain and ornamental was excellent, and might almost have put a sewing machine to shame...There still remains a curious specimen of her needlework made for a sister-in-law, my mother. In a very small bag is deposited a little rolled up housewife, furnished with minikin needles and fine thread. In the housewife is a tiny pocket, and in the pocket is enclosed a slip of paper, on which, written as with a crow quill, are these lines' (*Memoir*, ed. Sutherland, 77–9).

## MISS LLOYD HAS NOW SENT TO MISS GREEN

Martha Lloyd (for whom, see *Opinions of MP*), eldest daughter of the Revd Nowes Lloyd and his wife. The Lloyds were long-standing friends of the Austens (see headnote to 'This little bag', p. 170), Martha joining their household soon after her mother's death, which occurred 16 April 1805, and around this time of the poem's composition JA wrote on an April of 'our household Partnership with Martha' (*Letters*, 109). Anna Lefroy's title for the verses as she copied them after 1855—'Lines supposed to have been sent to an uncivil Dressmaker'—suggests what might have occasioned their composition (the delay in making Martha's mourning clothes) and also the unlikelihood that they were ever actually sent. This is confirmed by 'Miss Green's Reply', written by Mrs Austen, JA's mother (*Collected Poems*, 20–1).

170 *Miss Green*: a professional dressmaker, employed to make up the necessary garment from fabric provided by her customer. Strict social rules dictated that a mourning outfit would be required for immediate wear.

*Black Ploughman's Gauze*: black for mourning. 'Ploughman's gauze' is harder to define: *Later Manuscripts*, 708, suggests 'a coarse kind of crape', citing Penelope Byrde, *Jane Austen Fashion: Fashion and Needlework in the Works of Jane Austen* (Ludlow: Excellent Press, 1999), 79.

## OH! MR BEST, YOU'RE VERY BAD

Martha Lloyd had been living with the Austen women since April 1805. In July 1806, when this poem was composed, they were holidaying in Clifton, a spa village, now a suburb of Bristol. Martha left them for Harrogate, hoping to be escorted there by an acquaintance, Mr Best, who for some reason was reluctant to make his usual summer visit; hence the occasion of these humorous verses (see *Family Record*, 154). Other than his name, nothing is known of Mr Best, though Le Faye speculates that he may be Revd Thomas Best of Newbury (*Later Manuscripts*, 710).

170 *Harrowgate*: Harrogate, a spa town in North Yorkshire and the northern rival of Bath. The medicinal properties of its waters were publicized from the seventeenth century.

*Posting*: the cost of getting to Harrogate by hired carriage.

171 *stouter*: stronger, healthier.

*Richard's pills*: presumably a patent medicine, but it is so far unidentified.

*New'bry…Speen Hill*: Newbury, Berkshire, around 20 miles from JA's childhood home in Steventon, Hampshire. Speen is a mile outside Newbury on the Bath road. Martha Lloyd's aunt, Mrs John Craven, lived at Speen Hill.

*Morton's wife*: *Letters*, 205 and 557, identify Martha Lloyd's friends as William Morton and his wife Louisa, living at Masham, about 18 miles north of Harrogate.

SEE THEY COME, POST HASTE FROM THANET

JA's fifth brother, Captain Frank Austen, married Mary Gibson at St Lawrence's church, Ramsgate, on 24 July 1806. The couple then travelled the 25 miles to Godmersham Park, home of their third brother Edward, where they spent their honeymoon. JA must have written the poem within days of 'Oh! Mr Best, you're very bad'. Fanny, Edward's eldest child, at the time aged 13, recorded her receipt of it from JA in her diary for 29 July (Centre for Kentish Studies U951. F24/1–69; *Letters*, 397). The lines are written as if by Fanny.

172  *Thanet*: the historical name of a district of north-east Kent, comprising the seaside towns of Margate, Broadstairs, and Ramsgate.

*Richard Kennet*: possibly a member of the Godmersham staff; *Later Manuscripts*, 712, suggests a groom.

*Canterbury...village*: JA names places on the route through Kent from Ramsgate to Godmersham, including the cathedral city of Canterbury, the village of Chilham, and Shalmsford (not Stamford) Bridge. *Later Manuscripts*, 712, suggests Anna Lefroy, whose copy is the authority for the poem, misread JA's original.

*my Brothers*: in 1806 Fanny had five brothers.

*Pier gate*: a gate hung from brick posts or piers (*OED*, sense 1c).

ON SIR HOME POPHAM'S SENTENCE—APRIL 1807

This poem was written in support of Sir Home Riggs Popham (1762–1820), a celebrated British naval commander who saw active service during the Revolutionary and Napoleonic Wars. Popham was charged in March 1807 with leaving his station at the Cape of Good Hope undefended in order to take forces to capture Buenos Aires from the Spanish. The attack was unsuccessful. His subsequent trial for desertion caused a stir nationally, to which this poem responds. He was severely reprimanded but not disgraced and soon resumed naval duties, his career unaffected. Popham was appointed Captain of the Fleet only months later, in July 1807, on an expedition against the Dano-Norwegian fleet; was made rear admiral in 1814; and Knight Commander of the Order of the Bath in 1815. A likely connection through Frank Austen's naval connections and postings explains JA's unusual foray into topical polit-ical satire. At the time of Popham's trial, JA, her mother, and sister were sharing lodgings in Southampton with Frank and his wife (see Brian Southam, *Jane Austen and the Navy* (London: National Maritime Museum, 2005), 155–63).

*Ministry...mean*: William Wyndham, Lord Greville, presided over the misnamed and generally ineffectual 'Ministry of all the Talents', a coali-tion government formed in February 1806 after the death of the previous prime minister William Pitt the Younger. It fell on 25 March 1807.

*stand*: the word does double duty, suggesting that Popham 'stands for' 'promptitude, vigour, success' and 'stands condemned' by his trial.

HAPPY THE LAB'RER

One from a collection of four sets of comic 'Verses to rhyme with "Rose"', the other three sets being by JA's mother, her sister Cassandra, and her sister-in-law Elizabeth (wife of Edward). The verses, a fair copy in JA's hand, are undated but were perhaps composed as family entertainment during a visit to Edward and his family, staying in Chawton in August–September 1807. Elizabeth Austen died October 1808.

172 *light-drab*: a thick, closely woven woollen cloth, of a yellowish, grey, or brown colour.

173 *Cabbage rose*: a large, highly scented, double rose. Its Latin name is *Rosa centifolia*, the rose of a hundred petals.

*among the rows*: the ordinary seating in church, as opposed to the enclosed box pews often reserved for prominent local families.

CAMBRICK! WITH GRATEFUL BLESSINGS WOULD I PAY

A poem-letter, signed 'JA' and dated 'Aug:st 26—1808', it is addressed to Catherine Bigg (1775–1848), a close friend of the Austens and sister of Harris Bigg-Wither, to whom JA was briefly (one night only, 2–3 December 1802) engaged to be married. The poem was sent with a gift of handkerchiefs. In October 1808 Catherine married the Revd Herbert Hill, uncle of the poet Robert Southey. JA expressed reservations about the marriage to Cassandra (*Letters*, 156): Catherine was in her early thirties (JA's own age) and Hill almost 60.

*Cambrick*: a fine white linen cloth also used for making shirts. It was originally made in Cambrai, France.

ON THE SAME OCCASION—BUT NOT SENT.—

CAMBRICK! THOU'ST BEEN TO ME A GOOD

JA wrote two different sets of verses to accompany the handkerchiefs, deciding not to send this version. She kept it, however, copying both versions, along with 'On Sir Home Popham's sentence' and all four sets of 'Verses to rhyme with "Rose"' into a manuscript now in the Fondation Martin Bodmer, Geneva (see Textual Notes, pp. 241–2).

*bear her name*: suggesting that JA had embroidered Catherine's name or initials onto the handkerchiefs.

TO THE MEMORY OF MRS LEFROY, WHO DIED DEC:R 16.—MY BIRTHDAY.—WRITTEN 1808

Mrs Anne Lefroy (born Anne Brydges) (1749–1804) was the wife of George Lefroy, rector of Ashe, 2 miles north-west of Steventon, JA's childhood home. Known locally as 'Madam Lefroy', she was a great friend to and intellectual inspiration for the young JA, mentioned often in her early letters, and named in the spoof teenage 'History of England' (*Teenage Writings*, 130) as a fellow advocate for Mary Queen of Scots. She played a part in ending the early flirtation between her nephew Tom Lefroy and JA. A distant cousin of JA's mother, Mrs Lefroy, by her brother's account 'had an exquisite taste for poetry... and she composed verses herself with great facility' (Egerton Brydges, *The Autobiography, Times, Opinions, and Contemporaries of Sir Egerton Brydges*, 2 vols (1834), i. 5). On 16 December 1804, JA's twenty-ninth birthday, Mrs Lefroy died in a riding accident and was buried at Ashe on 21 December, JA's brother James officiating (*Family Record*, 145).

174 *At Johnson's death*: Samuel Johnson, dictionary-maker, essayist, poet, and critic, also died during December: 13 December 1784. In his 'Biographical Notice of the Author', coincidentally dated 13 December 1817, JA's brother Henry described Johnson as his sister's 'favourite moral writer... in prose' (*Memoir*, ed. Sutherland, 141).

*by Hamilton... the Man*: William Gerard Hamilton (1729–96), the 'eminent friend' quoted in James Boswell's *Life of Samuel Johnson*, 2 vols (1791), ii. 580–1. Gilson records that in the second autograph manuscript of this poem (sold in 1948 at Sotheby's and now untraced) the line reads 'At Johnson's death by Burke 'twas finely said', with 'Burke 'twas finely' struck through and replaced by 'Hamilton 'twas said' (Gilson, 'JA's Verses', 44). This is a correction JA might have made after consulting the expanded third edition of Boswell's *Life* (1799), where the 'eminent friend' is first identified as Hamilton.

### ALAS! POOR BRAG, THOU BOASTFUL GAME!

This poem is included in a letter to JA's sister Cassandra, 17 January 1809, then staying with their brother Edward at Godmersham Park, Kent. Its occasion is a dispute over the rival card games of Speculation and Brag played at Christmas in the Kent family. JA writes: 'I have just received some verses in an unknown hand, & am desired to forward them to my nephew Edwd at Godmersham.—' (*Letters*, 174). There is no reason to think the lines are not by JA, who is clearly continuing a humorous defence of Speculation ('When one comes to reason upon it, it cannot stand its' ground against Speculation... I hope Edward is now convinced') begun in her previous letter to Cassandra (*Letters*, 171). Edward (for whom, see *Opinions of MP*, 'Edward & George') is the eldest son of her brother, also Edward. In her next letter (24 January), JA wrote: 'I am sorry my verses did not bring any return from Edward, I was in hopes they might—but I suppose he does not rate them highly enough.—It might be partiality, but they seemed to me purely classical—just like Homer & Virgil, Ovid & Propria que Maribus' (*Letters*, 177), a Latin tag from the widely used Eton Latin Grammar (*Letters*, 409 n. 8). The reader is to imagine Speculation speaking and commiserating in comic-moral tones with Brag, which, after brief popularity, has also fallen victim to a new fashion.

175 *Alas! poor Brag*: a humorous riff on 'Alas! poor Yorick', *Hamlet*, Act 5, scene 1, and the moralizing over mortality it occasions. Brag is a card game 'essentially identical with the modern game of poker' (*OED*, sense 6).

*Speculation*: see note to p. 96.

## MY DEAREST FRANK, I WISH YOU JOY

Dated 26 July 1809, this is a poem-letter (*Letters*, 185–6) to JA's brother Captain Frank Austen, on naval duty in China, announcing the birth of his son, Francis William, on 12 July, and sharing another important item of news: the Austen women at last have a home of their own, the gift of brother Edward on his estate in Chawton, Hampshire (*Letters*, 160). JA had previously written verses to celebrate Frank's wedding (see p. 172). With her mother, sister, and their friend Martha Lloyd, she shared a home with Frank and his wife Mary Gibson in Southampton from October 1806. The poem rapidly shifts from news of the birth to reminiscence about Frank's own childhood naughtiness ('His saucy words and fiery ways'), offering rare insight into the Austens' early family life. Passages in *Memoir*, ed. Sutherland (17 and 36) reinforce JA's brief portraits of Frank as a fearless, precocious child and disciplined sailor. The verse letter is written in rhymed tetrameter couplets, the same metrical form as Walter Scott's best-selling romance *Marmion* (1808), a copy of which JA had sent to Frank a few months earlier to pass on to their brother Charles (reported in *Letters*, 171).

175 *Mary Jane*: Frank Austen and Mary Gibson's first child, born in April 1807, while sharing lodgings in Southampton with the Austen women.

176 *'Bet...to hide'*: JA is reminding Frank of his own Hampshire dialect baby talk ('Bet, I haven't come to stay'). After their first few months, all the Austen children were handed over to a village woman for the next year or longer, until able to walk. A couple called John and Elizabeth Littleworth may have been regular foster-parents to the Austen children, their daughter Bet their nursemaid and playfellow (Deirdre Le Faye, 'The Austens and the Littleworths', *Jane Austen Society Report* (1987), 64–70).

*Our Chawton home*: the Austen women, with Martha Lloyd, had arrived at Chawton less than three weeks earlier on 7 July; building work was probably still going on. Austen-Leigh described the house in some detail, drawing on his sister Caroline's detailed recollections (*Memoir*, ed. Sutherland, 67–9 and 166–8).

177 *Charles & Fanny*: JA's youngest brother Charles and his wife Frances Palmer, whom he married in Bermuda in May 1807. JA did not meet her until they returned to England in summer 1811.

*over-right us*: Hampshire dialect meaning 'directly opposite us'. They would stay only half a mile away at Chawton House, brother Edward's manor house on his Hampshire estate, which became a temporary home to the Austen brothers when they visited.

## IN MEASURED VERSE I'LL NOW REHEARSE

Austen-Leigh suggested that the geography of the poem was simply dictated by the rhyme with the name 'Anna': 'I believe that all this nonsense was nearly extempore, and that the fancy of drawing the images from America arose at the moment from the obvious rhyme...in the first stanza' (*Memoir*, ed. Sutherland, 76). But this is to ignore the wide currency of such imagery in literature of the

period, when 'Ontario's lake', 'Niagara's Fall', and 'transatlantic groves' represented popular, even hackneyed, settings for romantic adventure. Commenting
on Mary Brunton's *Self-Control* (1810) in a letter to Cassandra, JA remarked:
'an excellently-meant, elegantly-written Work, without anything of Nature or
Probability in it. I declare I do not know whether Laura's passage down the
American River, is not the most natural, possible, every-day thing she ever
does' (*Letters*, 244). As for the rhyme upon 'Anna' and 'savannah', it appears in
Robert Burns's song 'Yestreen I had a pint of wine', where there are multiple
rhymes on Anna, among which:

> 'Ye Monarchs take the East and West,
> Frae Indus to Savannah!
> Gie me within my straining grasp
> The melting form of Anna.'
>
> (1790; in Robert Burns, *Complete Poems and Songs*, ed.
> James Kinsley (Oxford: Oxford University Press, 1969),
> 442–3)

177 *measured verse*: verse written in metrical lines.

*savannah*: an open plain of grass and trees, in almost any geographic
location at this time.

*Ontario's lake*: with a shoreline of 712 miles and an area of 7,340 square
miles, the smallest of the Great Lakes of North America. It was a much-
used fictional setting (Charlotte Smith, *The Old Manor House* (1793);
Mary Brunton, *Self-Control* (1810)).

*Niagara's Fall*: descending into Lake Ontario. Described in Oliver
Goldsmith's poem *The Traveller, or A Prospect of Society* (1764): 'Niagara
stuns with thund'ring sound' (l. 412).

*transatlantic groves*: groves beyond the Atlantic (that is, North American).
The groves may be 'thick, black, profound', but it is less easy to interpret
how this works as a compliment to Anna's judgement.

### I'VE A PAIN IN MY HEAD

Maria Beckford, daughter of Francis Beckford, of Basing Park, Hampshire
(and a cousin of the novelist William Beckford (1759–1844)), was by 1811 man-
aging the household of her brother-in-law, John Middleton, Edward Austen's
tenant at Chawton House from 1808 to 1813. In February 1811, JA took
Maria into Alton to see Charles Newnham, an apothecary-surgeon (see note to
p. 70). It is recorded that JA overheard their conversation and turned it into
verse (*Collected Poems*, 13; *Family Record*, 199).

178 *calomel*: mercurous chloride, formerly used as a purgative; so an odd
choice to cure a headache. But in the nineteenth century it was widely
prescribed in small doses as a general restorative and for a range of
diseases from gout to sexually transmitted infections and even
cataracts.

ON THE MARRIAGE OF MR GELL OF EAST BOURN
TO MISS GILL.—

It is thought that JA wrote these verses at home in Chawton, Hampshire, after seeing the announcement of the marriage of Mr Gell of Eastbourne to Miss Gill of Well Street Hackney in the *Hampshire Telegraph and Sussex Chronicle*, 25 February 1811. We know nothing of the couple other than the newspaper account and the punning it inspired. Despite the simplicity of the pun, it occasioned some orthographic variation in transmission: two autograph manuscripts, each resolving the pun differently, as well as a first published version in *Memoir* (1870) that 'improves' both the text as it is printed and the lithographic reproduction from manuscript. Austen-Leigh's source was the manuscript now in the possession of Bath and North East Somerset Council, but the more interesting manuscript is that in private ownership. Written on the verso of an octavo frontispiece from a popular Minerva Press romance, *Love, Mystery, and Misery* (1810) by Anthony Frederick Holstein [pseud.], the poem in this version becomes a comment upon the engraved image of 'An interesting Scene from the Novel', in which two dramatically posed, masked figures appear transfixed as they direct their piercing gaze upon each other. Two sources of reading matter converge in this version—an amusing report from the local newspaper and the latest trashy pulp fiction—suggesting a doubly ludicrous origin for the composition.

There was a family precedent for creating a poem of this kind from a newspaper announcement in a verse written by JA's uncle, James Leigh Perrot, 'On Capt. Foote's Marriage with Miss Patton':

> Thro' the rough ways of Life, with a patten your Guard,
>> May you safely and pleasantly jog.
> May the ring never break, nor the knot press too hard,
>> Nor the Foot find the Patten a Clog.

Though already ascribed to Leigh Perrot in the nineteenth century (Aldenham, 'Pattens', *Notes & Queries*, 7–11 (17 December 1898), 494), these verses were included in *Minor Works* (1969), 452, as by JA. They are now firmly reassigned.

I AM IN A DILEMMA

This little poem forms part of a letter from JA, 30 April 1811, staying in London with brother Henry, to Cassandra, at Godmersham with brother Edward and his family. JA introduces the comic lines with the remark: 'Oh! yes, I remember Miss Emma Plumbtree's *Local* consequence perfectly' (*Letters*, 194). A friend of Edward's 18-year-old daughter Fanny, Emma was clearly popular with the 'local' East Kent Militia, based in Canterbury in 1811. Here as in others of her verses, JA shares the Austen family appreciation of the comic and punning potential of proper names. Reporting the arrival of a new governess, Miss Clewes, at Godmersham, JA wrote to Cassandra, 9 February 1813: 'is not it a name for Edward to pun on?—is not a Clew a Nail?' (*Letters*, 214). Henry Gipps and Emma's brother John, in whom Fanny showed a romantic interest, were officers in the local militia.

Emma Plumptre and Henry Gipps became engaged on 18 September 1811 and married in 1812. In a letter of 6–7 November 1813, JA remarked on encountering 'the useful Mr Gipps, whose attentions came in as acceptably to us in handing us to the Carriage, for want of a better Man, as they did to Emma Plumptre' (*Letters*, 263).

### BETWEEN SESSION & SESSION

These verses are included in the same letter of 30 April 1811 as 'I am in a Dilemma' (see above); both poems address topics of interest to the Godmersham family. JA had read the latest newspaper report and wrote: 'I congratulate Edward on the Weald of Kent Canal-Bill being put off till another Session, as I have had the pleasure of reading.—There is always something to be hoped from Delay' (*Letters*, 194). The Bill proposed cutting a canal from north to south through Kent, starting at the English Channel and linking eventually with the Thames estuary, providing a saving on the sea route. The canal, it was mistakenly believed, would cross Edward's Godmersham estate. The Bill had passed its second reading in April 1811 but was then postponed, to be reintroduced and approved in February 1812. The project was never carried out.

179 *Session*: the period during which Parliamentary business was conducted. In this case, the session ended on 24 July 1811 and the next began on 7 January 1812.

*just Prepossession*: correcting the earlier reading of 'first Prepossession', Southam points out that 'first' 'makes no sense in this context', whereas 'just', a word used by JA a few lines earlier in her letter, is 'calligraphically identical' with the strokes here (*Jane Austen: A Students' Guide*, 209). A 'prepossession' is a preconceived opinion.

*Wicked Men's will*: like the phrase 'Villainous Bill', the language here seems unwarrantably extreme. JA implies that the commercial value of the project serves only the interests of those promoting it and not the wider community—scarcely different, then, from her brother's self-interested rejection.

### WHEN STRETCH'D ON ONE'S BED

The poem is dated 'Oct:r 27. 1811' and signed 'J.A.'. Untitled, it was probably written at Chawton where JA was awaiting the publication of her first novel, *S&S*, advertised on 30 October.

*Waltzes & reels*: the waltz was a recent introduction from mainland Europe and still considered rather daring on account of the close bodily contact of the partners, as in Lord Byron, *The Waltz* (published anonymously, 1813), ll. 113–16:

> Waltz—Waltz alone—both legs and arms demands,
> Liberal of feet, and lavish of her hands;
> Hands which may freely range in public sight
> Where ne'er before—but—pray 'put out the light'.

Reels, lively Scottish or Irish dances, performed by couples facing each other and tracing figures of eight, were a more regular feature of assemblies and considered quite proper.

180 *Corse*: poetic form of corpse.

### CAMILLA, GOOD-HUMOURED, & MERRY, & SMALL

On 29 November 1812, JA wrote to her friend Martha Lloyd, 'The 4 lines on Miss W. which I sent you were all my own, but James afterwards suggested what I thought a great improvement & as it stands in the Steventon Edition' (*Letters*, 205).

The verses are another example of composition prompted by JA's relish of the ludicrous: in this case, the names and circumstances of the recently engaged couple: Urania Katharine Camilla Wallop and the Revd Henry Wake. (They married in March 1813.) Camilla Wallop, relative of the 2nd Earl of Portsmouth, was known to JA, who, on 11 April 1805, had commented on the names of two ships, 'the Urania' and 'the Camilla', bound for Nova Scotia, that 'The Wallop Race seem very fond of Nova Scotia' (*Letters*, 106). The improvements made by JA's eldest brother James at Steventon Rectory might have included, for discretion's sake, the changes found in the text eventually published by his son in 1870 and reproduced in *Minor Works*, 444: 'Camilla' replaced by 'Maria'; and the more flattering 'handsome, and tall' (replacing 'merry, & small'). It seems that James's children, James Edward and Anna, kept both versions alive—one for private enjoyment and the other for wider circulation (see Textual Notes, pp. 245–6).

*her last stake*: in November 1812, Camilla Wallop turned 38.

### WHEN WINCHESTER RACES FIRST TOOK THEIR BEGINNING

JA composed this poem on 15 July 1817 at 8 College Street, Winchester. She had been living there with Cassandra since May for medical treatment. The degenerative disease that took her life only three days later (in the early hours of 18 July) had been characterized by occasional periods of rallying that gave hope of recovery. As late as 28 May, she wrote that her doctor, Giles Lyford (*Family Record*, 248), 'talks of making me quite well' (*Letters*, 358); and on 14 July her mother had written to Anna Lefroy: 'I had a very comfortable account of your Aunt Jane this morning, she now sits up a little' (Joan Austen-Leigh, 'Great Novel Readers', *Collected Reports of the Jane Austen Society*, 4 (1986–95), 248).

Of JA's verses, these have been the most discussed. They were mentioned (though unpublished) in Henry Austen's 'Biographical Notice of the Author', attached to the posthumous *NA* and *P* (1818), issued within months of his sister's death: 'The day preceding her death she composed some stanzas replete with fancy and vigour' (*Memoir*, ed. Sutherland, 138). The reference to something so frivolous intruding upon JA's deathbed meditations caused the next generation of the family, Victorians of a pious and conventional turn, much discomfort. It was excised from Henry's revised 'Memoir of Miss Austen' (1833), and in 1870 Austen-Leigh approached the topic of her final thoughts cautiously: 'Her sweetness of temper never failed. She was ever considerate and grateful to those who attended on her. At times, when she felt rather better, her playfulness of spirit revived, and she amused them even in their sadness' (*Memoir*, ed. Sutherland, 130–1). Since, once again, the verses were not published, to mention them at all, however indirectly, was injudicious. As JA's last literary work, the poem was immediately called for. Her niece Caroline Austen, referring to Uncle Henry's unlucky allusion, commented: 'see what it is to have a growing posthumous reputation! we cannot keep any thing to ourselves *now*, it seems' (*Memoir*, ed. Sutherland, 190). They were finally published in 1906, in another family memoir, J. H. and E. C. Hubback, *Jane Austen's Sailor Brothers*, 272–3. See, too, Le Faye, 'Jane Austen's Verses and Lord Stanhope's Disappointment', *Book Collector*, 37/1 (Spring 1988), 86–91.

180 *Winchester races*: steeplechases were held regularly at Worthy Down, 3 miles north of Winchester, from the seventeenth to the end of the nineteenth century. The *Hampshire Chronicle and Courier* (Monday, 14 July) advertised the forthcoming race meeting. JA's family often attended race meetings (*Letters*, 5, 141, 142, 238).

*old Saint*: Swithin was bishop of Winchester from 852 until his death in 862. According to legend, his body was transferred into the Cathedral on 15 July 971, when he was adopted as its patron. Swithin is supposed to have expressed his disapproval of the move by causing forty days of rainfall. JA's poem was written on St Swithin's day, 1817.

*William of Wykham*: William of Wykeham (1324–1404) was bishop of Winchester from 1366 until his death. He became Chancellor of England, founded New College, Oxford, and Winchester College, where several of JA's nephews were educated.

181 *his shrine*: St Swithin's shrine, supposedly a site of miracles in the Middle Ages, had been destroyed as early as 1538 during the Reformation, when King Henry VIII seized control of the Roman Catholic Church in England.

*Palace...in ruins*: the remains of Wolvesey Palace, the former bishops' residence. A new palace was built in the late seventeenth century.

*Venta*: the Roman name for Winchester was Venta Belgarum (capital of the Belgae, a Celtic tribe). JA's eldest brother James, himself too ill to attend his sister's funeral, later wrote a poem, 'Venta! within thy sacred fane', an elegy to the memory of his sister now, too, enshrined in Winchester Cathedral (*Collected Poems*, 46–7).

*neighbouring Plain*: Worthy Down, where the races were held.

## CHARADES

The Austen family enjoyed composing, recording, and sharing charades, 'a kind of riddle in which each syllable of a word, or a complete word or phrase, is enigmatically described, or (now more usually) dramatically represented... a game of presenting and solving such riddles' (*OED*). 'We admire your Charades excessively, but as yet have guessed only the 1ˢᵗ. The others seem very difficult', JA wrote to Cassandra, 29 January 1813 (*Letters*, 210–11). In her teenage spoof 'The History of England', JA included a bold charade joking on King James I's sexual preferences (*Teenage Writings*, 132); in *E*, ch. 9, Emma Woodhouse and Harriet Smith set about collecting riddles and charades, including one from Mr Elton whose clues Emma fails miserably to understand. Like the charades ⟨assembled by Emma and Harriet, those attributed to JA have not proved in⟩ every instance her own; the Austens regularly copied favourite items from other sources. For example, a charade-poem in JA's hand, long considered as 'of doubtful authorship' (Chapman, *Times Literary Supplement*, 14 January 1926, 27) has been decisively reattributed to Catherine Maria Fanshawe (Gilson, 'JA's Verses', 60). However, there seems no reason to question the origins of the three recorded here.

Solutions: 1. Hemlock; 2. Agent; 3. Banknote.

# APPENDIX

## PRAYERS

It is clear from language and style that the prayers are based upon the Book of Common Prayer, used within the Church of England, of which JA was a member. The daughter and sister of clergymen, she was familiar from childhood with its services and forms of worship. The diction, rhythms, and cadences of the three prayers fall easily into the established patterns of the Prayer Book. Though the modern reader does not feel compelled to address JA's novels from an Anglican or even a Christian perspective, it is worth remembering that her brother Henry closed his 'Biographical Notice' of 1818 with reference to her Christian principles: 'On serious subjects she was well-instructed, both by reading and meditation, and her opinions accorded strictly with those of our Established Church' (*Memoir*, ed. Sutherland, 141). That said, we cannot certainly attribute these prayers to JA (see headnote, pp. 185–6).

All references and quotations below are from the Book of Common Prayer (1771).

186  *Hearts... Lips*: echoing the General Thanksgiving 'that we may shew forth thy praise not only with our lips, but in our lives'.

 *secret... hid*: echoing the collect at the opening of the Communion Service: 'Almighty God, unto whom all hearts be open...and from whom no secrets are hid'.

 *guard us... this night*: the Collect for Aid against all Perils, from the service of Evening Prayer, reads 'by thy great mercy, defend us from all perils and dangers of this night'.

 *the sick... Prisoners*: paraphrasing the Great Litany: 'That it may please thee to preserve all that travel by land or by water, all women labouring of child, all sick persons and young children, and to shew thy pity upon all prisoners and captives...That it may please thee to defend and provide for the fatherless children and widows, and all that are desolate and oppressed.'

187  *Our Father...Heaven &c*: the Lord's Prayer, which concludes each of these three Evening Prayers. It is set out in the Bible, Matthew 6: 9–13.

*Give...affliction*: the Collect or Prayer 'for all conditions of men, to be used at such times when the Litany is not appointed to be read' reads, 'giving them patience under their sufferings, and a happy issue out of all their afflictions'.

*brought...close of this day*: compare with the opening of the third Collect, for Grace, in the service of Morning Prayer: 'O...heavenly Father...who hast safely brought us to the beginning of this day.'

188  *Keep...night*: from the Collect for Aid against All Perils (see note to p. 186).

*knowledge...Truth*: see the Prayer of St Chrysostom, at the close of the service of Evening Prayer: 'granting us in this world knowledge of thy truth'.

American Literature

British and Irish Literature

Children's Literature

Classics and Ancient Literature

Colonial Literature

Eastern Literature

European Literature

Gothic Literature

History

Medieval Literature

Oxford English Drama

Philosophy

Poetry

Politics

Religion

The Oxford Shakespeare

---

A complete list of Oxford World's Classics, including Authors in Context, Oxford English Drama, and the Oxford Shakespeare, is available in the UK from the Marketing Services Department, Oxford University Press, Great Clarendon Street, Oxford OX2 6DP, or visit the website at www.oup.com/uk/worldsclassics.

In the USA, visit www.oup.com/us/owc for a complete title list.

Oxford World's Classics are available from all good bookshops. In case of difficulty, customers in the UK should contact Oxford University Press Bookshop, 116 High Street, Oxford OX1 4BR.

| | |
|---|---|
| | Travel Writing 1700–1830 |
| | Women's Writing 1778–1838 |
| WILLIAM BECKFORD | **Vathek** |
| JAMES BOSWELL | **Life of Johnson** |
| FRANCES BURNEY | **Camilla** |
| | **Cecilia** |
| | **Evelina** |
| ROBERT BURNS | **Selected Poems and Songs** |
| LORD CHESTERFIELD | **Lord Chesterfield's Letters** |
| JOHN CLELAND | **Memoirs of a Woman of Pleasure** |
| DANIEL DEFOE | **A Journal of the Plague Year** |
| | **Moll Flanders** |
| | **Robinson Crusoe** |
| | **Roxana** |
| HENRY FIELDING | **Jonathan Wild** |
| | **Joseph Andrews and Shamela** |
| | **Tom Jones** |
| JOHN GAY | **The Beggar's Opera and Polly** |
| WILLIAM GODWIN | **Caleb Williams** |
| OLIVER GOLDSMITH | **The Vicar of Wakefield** |
| MARY HAYS | **Memoirs of Emma Courtney** |
| ELIZABETH INCHBALD | **A Simple Story** |
| SAMUEL JOHNSON | **The History of Rasselas** |
| | **Lives of the Poets** |
| | **The Major Works** |
| CHARLOTTE LENNOX | **The Female Quixote** |
| MATTHEW LEWIS | **The Monk** |